Chronicles of Rimírnon Auroras, Volume I

Dreamforgers

Séamus Muir

Chronicles of Rimírnon Auroras, Volume I
Dreamforgers
Séamus Muir

Author's Note: this is a work of fiction/fantasy, derived solely from the
imagination of the author; as such, any resemblance to persons, places,
or events is entirely coincidental.

ISBN: 9781076143020

Table of Contents

Book One: A Tale of Lost Souls

Dark forebodings,
The world of the jyuga-trees
Imperiled;
Long singing sufferers awaken
Chaos unbound;
Harmony intertwining,
A balance forsaken,
but the pendulum swings again.

Holding at her breast love
The Star Queen,
Her eyes bright,
Passion bursts within her--
Seasons turn;
Years bring together
The Lost Ones,
the Lost Souls will unite.

Master of Song, come
And give the world your vision:
Together they fly
Free from constraining chains
Yet restraining themselves;
And the world of the jyuga-trees
Waits in silence
as the Lost Souls carry on.

Sing now and remember long
The darkness
As we tell to you a tale.
A tale long in the making,
a tale of Lost Souls.

Prologue: A Dream of Stars and Light

Lost, lost, that is all I will ever be... the young girl thought to herself as she wandered through the vast forest; she was dreaming, the same dream she had always had since she was three summers of age, since that fateful night when her family had been taken from her. Her violet eyes gazed out at the starry scene of night from the bottom of a dell in the dream-wood, and she reached up one of her hands to smooth the dark hair out of her face, revealing pointed ears. She was an elf, her lithe form belying the strength of her people within her. A wind blew through the dream-wood, blowing her hair back into her face and billowing out the skirts of her night-robe. The wind did not move her from her gazing, nor did it concern her; all she could think about in these moments was her family, torn from her in a midnight raid by the demonic forces of the Sorcerer King. From the deep depths of the Fire Lake they had come, and they had ravaged the plains of the world for a year, a month, a week, and a day before returning to the haunts of their master in the Halls of the Damned across the Sea of a Thousand Souls. She could hear the screams of her mother, the rage of her father, and the death-cry of her brother as the wind rippled across her; with a longing sigh she shook her head, wishing as she always did for an escape, or some way to undo the past, to bring back the dead and restore the Forests of Alastria. Her home had not escaped ravaging; the great and legendary forest was all but burnt to the ground, a sad memory of all surviving Elves who had escaped the Great Destruction of the wide world. Now, she and a few others lived in an isolated colony in one of the few surviving pockets of wood that remained from the ancient wood, proudly tending and defending this bastion of Elvendom from any that sought to take it from them by force. *Will I ever be found again?* She wondered to herself as a tear escaped her eye. Without warning, a different noise entered her dream, the sound of a high-pitched flute, being played by a master of its intricacies in a song that was both mournful and uplifting at once. She listened eagerly to it, reveling in the beautiful sound; *who could play such a thing but a god?* She asked herself with a smile, turning towards the sound; before her was not a spirit or a deity, but a mortal man. A man. Handsome, with hair as dark as her own; his eyes were closed, and all his being was bent into playing the instrument upon his lips. She let out a gasp at his appearance, her violet eyes widening at the sight of him. As he continued to play, the moons and the stars seemed to shine all the brighter, and she felt an urge to dance. Dance she did, and then the tune sprang into a livelier melody, as if chasing her with its own wild movements as she capered about in the graceful steps of her people. All the dream-wood seemed to be dancing with her, and as she danced about she caught a sight of the man opening his eyes; they were grey-blue, and they gazed upon her with rapturous awe. Slowly he stood up, still playing, and danced with her as he continued doing so. She felt a laughter well up inside her, and she let it loose, finally carefree for once in her dreams that had so often taken her back to a grave solemnity. A smile lit up on his own face as well, and the two of them continued capering about to the sound of his music. Who knows how long they danced the night away in the realm of dreams, where time is irrelevant, and each moment is a lifetime of wonder and imagination? And who cared? She was happy, happier than she had ever been for quite some time in her life. And so they danced the night away, heedless of other things, until at last the tune came to a halt, and he replaced the instrument into its pouch slowly as they gazed at each other. *Who are you...* she felt herself thinking, and she knew he was thinking the same thing. He had to be. Above them, the stars seemed to be humming the tune that had just been played, adding in their own mystical crescendos of light and radiance to the otherworldly song that they had just danced to; the two of them drew closer, and she saw an Amulet of Cassandra about his neck. Cassandra, the High Priestess of Murana Day, the last bastion of faith untouched by the unholy ones from the Sorcerer King. Was he one of their number? A cleric, or a temple-attendant of some sort? What was he? *Who are you?* She felt the words again as they drew closer still; his arms wrapped around her, as if they knew each other, yet both of them still bore expressions that conveyed puzzlement. Despite this, she put her own arms around his neck, and felt the sensation of his lips upon her own. In that kiss was peace, a peace that banished all thoughts but the thought of him as they stood there. *Tell me, please tell me who you are...* the words came to her mind as she kissed him, hoping it would never end. A mortal man, kissing the immortal lips of an Elven-maiden; would wonders never cease? The kiss came to an end, and she looked deeply into his eyes one last time. Did she know him? Did he know her? Would they ever really know each other? What was happening in this moment, and why had she never experienced this before? Why... when... who...?

A noise started the young Elven-maiden awake; her eyes sprang open, and she caught sight of the grey cat trotting out of the room, its tail swishing back and forth as it headed off for its food in the kitchens. She cast a baleful look after it, and then rolled over with a sigh as she looked up at the ceiling of her room. Outside, the stars were in their foredawn positions, preparing to give way for the sun as the moons and their entourage made their descent below the eastern hills. Curling up for one last bout of sleep, she made a wish upon them, that she should find her dream again, and revel forever in the land of dreams, if such a thing were indeed possible. For never in twenty years had the dream of solitude been intruded upon--and certainly never by a mortal man. But was he real, or did he belong only to that realm wherein the thoughts of mortal and immortal alike are all flights of fancy?

Chapter One: Evelyn

"Evelyn! Breakfast shalt not be warm forever!" the keeper of the house announced from downstairs to wake her up. With a sudden jerk she sprang out of bed, putting a robe on over her night-shift as she headed down to eat; going back to sleep after the dream had made her more tired in the long run than she had realized. Everyone else had already finished and gone out into the village, save for Mala, the matriarch of their settlement and the keeper of the communal house Evelyn dwelt in. As Evelyn had come from a house of minor nobility, Mala kept her close, for who knew if some other noble would come along, seeking a bride to reestablish the broken and scattered dynasty of Elven monarchy? And where should they find her? In a worker's house? Never! Let them find her in the house of a respectable Elf, where she was looked after and treated with the dignity that had become them who were of noble bearing. Mala smiled at the young Elven-maiden as she heartily ate the nye-bread and goat's cheese; the nye wheat was a wheat indigenous to their own lands, and made a bread that surpassed even the best of mortal breads, though mortals indeed had a great skill in culinary arts--for people of short lives, they were prolific indeed. There was something in the young girl's eyes that seemed different this morning as well; she was almost... cheerful. Yes, that was the word. Evelyn had been melancholy all these long years, barely hiding it as time went on; but today she seemed to be returning to a vitality that reminded the golden-haired matriarch of the young girl who would dance on any whim or fancy, never caring who saw. She let be the question in her mind until breakfast had mostly been eaten, and as Evelyn set down a cup of mulled mead a smile came to Mala's lips.

"Of what didst thou dream last night, dear girl?" she asked gently, and Evelyn closed her eyes, sighing. It was not to be hidden. Oh well. Better Mala than someone else.

"I dreamed of a music-maker, one who set my feet and my heart alight with a passion and a fire, and who made me forget that I had ever known sorrow or loss." she confessed, and Mala nodded slowly.

"Was he of noble birth? Didst thou seest any distinguishing thing upon him?" the older Elven-lady asked her, and Evelyn sighed again; this time, her voice dropped to a quieter tone, and as she spoke Mala understood why.

"I saw upon him an Amulet of Cassandra." Evelyn told her protector, whose eyes went wide as she mentioned the thing, a thing that only one race in the wide world would wear.

"A mortal man..." Mala breathed softly, leaning back into her chair with a slow nod. Evelyn's melancholic demeanor returned, seeing what she thought was disapproval in Mala's eyes. "Nay, child, I do not disprove; dream as thou wouldst wish! But thinketh not that yon match-makers wouldst approve of such a thing in the waking world. Thou must be wed to one of our own people one day; it is not for thee to decide to whom thou shouldst betroth thyself."

"And why not?" Evelyn returned, suddenly emboldened. "I may be the last noble of our people--is it not mine to decide to whom I should give myself, if anyone?" she persisted, and Mala raised her eyebrows.

"Thou wouldst create quite a stir, defying our peoples for a whim that hast never had its bearing in our world ever before." the matriarch returned.

"Oh, Mala, 'thees' and 'thous' are hardly something I have time for... the world as you knew it is changed; what purpose lies in preserving the antique speech of our forerunners?" Evelyn prodded her with a cheeky grin.

Mala returned the look, but acquiesced.

"You are right, child. If we cannot change when it is required, we may find ourselves at the mercy of oblivion. But come now, surely you know the laws of our people." she resumed as Evelyn began pacing about with frustration. "There has never been a union between the races: *any* of them. Elves, Men, Dwarves, Gnomes, Valkyries, Giants, or Werecats, none has ever dared to cross the border between our races in all recorded history."

"In all *recorded* history." Evelyn said with a knowing smirk. "Who is to say that, in the times before anything was recorded, that such mixing did not take place?"

"If you think that--" Mala began again, but was cut off by the now quite chipper Evelyn.

"Did you not just admit that unless we allow ourselves to change, oblivion may find us?"

"Evelyn, Evelyn, Evelyn..." Mala said with a weary sigh as the younger Elf crossed her arms over her chest. "If you seek to make such change, it would have to be done far away from our people, many of whom still cling desperately to the old ways--it is all they have, child! Don't you see?" the older Elf said to her in a reproachful way. Evelyn considered this; it was true. The Elves, of all peoples except the Dwarves, clung proudly to their heritage; even moreso after the ravaging hordes of the Sorcerer King had destroyed their world. But to leave it all behind... such a thought was more than she could bear. With a sudden shock of what her dream implied to her, to a life of abandoning everything her people had suffered for, she sat down on the chair again, a tear coming to her eye. Was it only a dream? "Oh, Evelyn..." Mala cooed to her, "Never mind it now; get thee ready for the day, and pay no heed to thoughts of dreams for a time." the matriarch said in an effort to encourage her, and Evelyn slowly nodded, rising up just as slowly some moments later to dress for the day's activity. In the matriarch's own mind, the thought of her young protectorate's yearning for a mortal man was, oddly enough, a confirmation.

Long ago, many long years before Evelyn had been a baby in her mother's arms, there had been an obscure priest who had once prophesied that a great darkness was coming, and that it would not be banished until a world of differences was cast aside for unity of purpose, culminating in the betrothal and marriage of two people from two different races. He had been laughed at, mocked, and his own order had almost declared him a heretic for implying such a thing could happen, for though they lived in tolerance of one another, the races had never truly cooperated with each other--not even when their lands had been ripped apart by the great hordes of the Fiery Lake. But when such a thing had happened, when the ashes of their civilizations were plainly before them, they remembered his words, and wondered what it betokened; if one part was right, would the second not follow it? And how was such a thing to be achieved? Who among any of them would dare to cross the tense borders that had sprung up between the races? The Elves and Dwarves were isolationists; the Gnomes were consumed with a desire for improving technology; Men were passionate about all they did, and found fault with those who would not try to improve their lives or try something new; Werecats were aloof, borderline isolationists who wandered about in troupes as merchants or mercenaries; the Valkyries clung proudly to their halls in the Ice Regions, an all-female warrior caste who disdained all others without hint of subtlety; and as for the Giants who shared their mountains, they feared no one and nothing, believing themselves invincible on account of their hulking size. Ironically, it made them the more amiable of all peoples, but such amiability did not outweigh the inevitable arrogance that sprang up from their towering size. *Nay... the man was mad, truly mad... there will be no harmony between the races, now or ever.* Mala said to herself as she shook her head; she got up to clean the tables, thinking again about what Evelyn had told her. There was a young prince headed for their village, a scout had reported; he would be here in three days. Would the young maiden reject him for an impossible love? Or would she put aside her feelings for the sake of her people?

***

Sometime later, Evelyn was absorbed in a book, one of those barely saved from the burning of the Forest of Alastria some years ago. It was a book of genealogy and heraldry, a book that she often read over now, speculating over which noble house of Elvendom besides hers was still alive. And were there indeed male heirs seeking her? Or were they all females instead? What a laughing-stock all Elvendom would be, if all her surviving royal heirs were female! Or perhaps the matter had already been resolved, unbeknownst to them in Mala's village, and there was no need for her to be married off at all to rebirth an Elven Monarchy. With a smirk, she continued reading, until she came at last to where the pages left off. The High Nobility of the Elves had been wiped out, and only a very few of the Petty Monarchs had remained, so rumors said. As far as Evelyn knew, no one had ever come for her, therefore she had a right to her own choices in marriage. But Mala had been almost insistent this morning; did she know something? Was there someone else, another long-lost noble, on his way to her even now? The blank pages of the old manuscript seemed to almost beg her to aid in filling their spaces; would her own children be listed in this old book by some unknown scribe? Surely there was time for thoughts of children. Was there not? *Now wait... what am I doing, thinking of such things when I don't even... by all the stars!* Evelyn thought to herself as she snapped out of the train of thoughts, shaking her head in disgust at the prospect of being yet another name in a gilded manuscript. She shut the book with a loud clap, and let it fall onto its back as she leaned back in the chair, glowering at it. *I don't want to end up in a book like that! I don't want to be a tool of... of... power and intrigue! I want love, and romance, and... and...and what...?* she suddenly trailed off with a sigh, not knowing what it was she truly wanted. A sound of birdsong grabbed her attention, and she almost ran to the window to gaze out at the happy creatures flitting through the air with a will. It was springtime, and the birds were wide awake. High above, a falcon cried out to the endless skies, and the call seemed to echo in the basin of land that protected their refuge. The great bird soared off into the distance, and Evelyn felt a great desire to join it, to cast off all of herself and fly in the air with the birds. Another sound of music caught her ears, the sound of a harp; she looked down, and there by the pond were two lovers, the young maiden playing her instrument skillfully while her prospective mate laid in her lap. Children were also about the pond, swimming and splashing about; the last few years had seen quite a few of them born, the Elves eager to rebuild their people in the face of the near-annihilation that had almost wiped them out.

With a smile, Evelyn turned from the window and headed out the door to wander the village. At the bottom of the stairs that led up to the great tree-house, an archer sat lazily in the sun that basked over him; a few paces away was a stable, where horses and elk were carefully looked after by gentle masters. Further beyond the stables was a pen where the sheep and the goats were grazed; a colony of rabbits nearby was also tended to, and a goose pond further beyond this. A large series of rice and nye-grain field bordered these, and those who tilled the land were hard at work under the warm sun; orchards and gardens dotted the land about the central village, and as Evelyn made her way through their thriving town, she could not but feel that, perhaps, she was meant to aid in completing their rebuilding by becoming a queen.

There was Janus the Smith, hard at work on a plough-blade; his coal came from a travelling caravan of Dwarves that made a pass by their village about every two weeks. The Dwarves were polite, but they did not stay longer than was necessary for them to complete their trades. Evelyn had managed to grab a tale or two out of them on occasion, and was fascinated by their depictions of their own home, a grand hall carved deep in the mountains, the one place in the wide world that had remained mostly unscathed from the dark times several years ago. Further along the dusty lane were tailors and weavers, plying their craft with a will, as were the bakers across the street from them. Just beyond the bakery was a mill, where the nye-grain was taken so that it could be turned into flour for bread. Beside the mill was a distillery, where some of the rice and grain would be sent to be fermented into alcohol. Red Nye had become a notable beverage of their community, and was one of the things the Dwarves would barter for, as well as the rice-wine. As Evelyn looked to her right, there were the old garden patches, where fruits and vegetables of other sorts would be grown to go along with their meals.

Beyond these, a group of twenty Elves were practicing the martial forms of war, handed down for countless years by their people as the ages went on; armed or unarmed, very few people could match an Elf in battle. And if an Elf chose the path of more mystical arts, such as druidism, there were even fewer that could match them. Only the demonic hordes had overcome the legendary Elven warriors, and that because of their being creatures not of this world.

Everyone knew it: the only reason the Elves had been overcome was because of their enemy's infernal origins. And now their dark master held them back, in the land across the seas, far away from the places they had once terrorized. No one knew why, but they were grateful, and did as much as they could to try and rebuild, preparing for any possible engagements in the future.

As she got further along the lane, where the artisans were hard at work on their own crafts, two of her friends came up to her with great giggling, and Evelyn gave them a funny look as they continued smiling. They knew something. Something of great interest, and they were just *dying* to tell her what. Evelyn crossed her arms over her chest as she stood there, waiting for them to speak. Tashana, the one with red hair winked an eye at her while Nya with the golden hair spoke first.

"Did you hear, Evelyn? Did you hear the news from the scouts?" Nya asked her, and Evelyn frowned, shaking her head. "Oh! Well, then we get to tell you!" she said cheerily.

"Tell me what, Nya?" Evelyn asked with an almost bored tone; the two of them had done this quite often, and it was irritating to her at this age, when they should all be preparing to be respectable and not gossiping idiots. Nya caught the tone at once, and reformed herself to a more serious demeanor all at once as she spoke again.

"There's a report that a convoy is coming our way. A royal convoy. A royal convoy of Elves." Nya said to her, and for once Evelyn's eyes widened in real surprise.

"What!" she exclaimed softly, and the other two nodded.

"Mala didn't tell you?" Tashana asked her in a somewhat concerned tone. "That isn't like her... she should have given you warning! After all, the scouts see her first!" she added, and Evelyn put a hand on her cheek, feeling herself flushing with embarrassment.

"So soon! So soon!" Evelyn said to herself in a soft tone, shaking her head. "I'm not *ready*, not yet... not now!" she said ruefully, and Nya smiled cheekily.

"Then maybe I can talk to the prince." she said dreamily.

"Ha!" Tashana said, poking her in the side.

"Ow!" the other exclaimed, poking her back.

"As if a prince would see us. Look at us, plain-clothes daughters of a shepherd."

"That's not going to stop me from dreaming!"

"As you wish." Tashana said with a shrug before turning back to Evelyn. "Are you sure Mala didn't say anything to you? I mean--" she began, but their conversation was then interrupted by a loud cough. They turned to the sound, and there was Mala herself.

"Get thee hence, foolish gossips, and tendest thou to thine sheep!" the matriarch said in a commanding tone, and they bowed, dashing off at once. Evelyn gazed after them for a moment, and then returned her gaze to Mala, who was gazing at her solemnly.

"You didn't tell me." Evelyn said rhetorically. Mala let out a sigh, shaking her head.

"I should have counseled discretion with my scouts; thee were not ready to hear it."

"How soon?" Evelyn asked her.

"The convoy will be here in three days' time." Mala returned, and Evelyn stamped her foot angrily, fixing her with a glare.

"And I didn't need to hear this sooner?!" she demanded in a louder voice.

"Calm thyself, child; thy voice carriest to the winds; thou wouldst not want yon birds to fly with it, would thee?" Mala said as she raised one eyebrow, chiding her as she would a girl a quarter of Evelyn's age. Evelyn said nothing, but frowned darkly before turning on her heel and walking quickly away to her room in the central house. Mala sighed; there would be no talking to her the rest of the day, and perhaps the night. She had her father's temper, never mind her mother's beauty. By tomorrow she would be turning from her anger and instead fretting about what to wear for the day after to meet their guest; perhaps she should thank those two gossips for saving her the trouble--perhaps.

Tashana and Nya were some of the only children Evelyn's age that had made it out of their old home alive, along with five others; one of these had died of heartbreak some days after, and the others were now courting each other. For right now, however, she would occupy herself with the chastising of her scouts. The prince's journey was intended to be secret, and could not risk being found out; Elven nobility was, after all, in a precarious position.

As for Evelyn herself, she had flung herself into bed with a scream, her stomach tying itself in knots at the thought of being married off so soon. Was that why Mala had been rushing to try and complete her education and lessons in regards to being a noble? Why she had been so adamant in trying to make Evelyn rethink her dream at the breakfast table that morning? Oh, to be an ordinary person, so that she might run off with whomever loved her and not bound to one who only saw the hard lines between commoner and noble. The grey cat then sprang out from some hiding spot in the room, and bounced up to the bed to curl up on top of her. Evelyn gave it a wry smile as the furry creature began kneading her for a bed, and reached over to stroke it behind the ears. "Silly thing." she murmured softly. She then settled in for a light nap, and awoke some time later when it was darkening outside and the village lamps were lit for the evening and thence the night; dinner was well past. Oh well. Right now, she didn't care.

Deciding to head out again, Evelyn walked about more leisurely this time, eventually ending up near the pond and casting off her clothes for a swim. The sounds of the frogs and crickets relaxed her as she lounged by the water's edge, heedless of who might see her. A splash then startled her; this was followed by a second, and then she saw them. Tashana and Nya. The two of them had snuck up on her for a moonlight swim of their own. As the three of them began to splash each other, they let out shrieks of laughter, and after a few moments more had settled by another spot on the edge of the pond, huddling together as they gazed up at the stars.

"So are you still angry?" Nya wondered, and Evelyn shook her head.

"I'm just... confused. Three days isn't very long. Well, soon it'll be two..." she said, and Tashana smiled.

"And what will you say?" she wondered.

"I don't know." the dark haired maiden returned, letting her hair fall into her face.

"You *have* to say yes, Evelyn." Nya retorted at once. "It's who you are; you're a queen-to-be, and if he's here for you, then you *have* to say yes. Our people are counting on it."

"How ironic that a woman in power has no power to marry whom she loves." Evelyn quipped, and Nya gave her a knowing look.

"Perhaps."

"Is there someone else?" Tashana said, catching the note in her voice.

"We'll never know if I don't refuse, will we?" Evelyn said offhandedly, throwing off her immediate suspicions. The conversation halted with that, and they simply sat there, content to listen to the sounds of night as it wore on. When the other two had gone on to their home, Evelyn continued sitting at the pond's edge, until at last she too gathered up her clothes and headed for her home. When she was dried off, she curled up under the covers, and drifted off again to the world of dreams.

***

It was the same sight of stars, the same woods, the same hillocks and dells; it was as it always was in her dreams, but again, as before, the sound of music came again. There he was; the master-musician was atop one of the hills, playing away with a passion that would make an Elf of even the stiffest demeanor melt at the sound of his revelry. Evelyn chased after him, eager to catch up to him and to know his name.

He led her on a mad caper through the dream-world, dancing as they would while the stars shone brightly upon them. She laughed as they made their way through a marshy terrain, and he hopped about while trying to play his instrument and keep from sinking. When their caper was through, he stopped, and looked at her longingly once again; she looked at him, her heart beating faster as he approached.

"Who are you?" she asked, this time aloud.

"Who are you?" he asked in reply, gazing at her violet eyes.

"I'm... Evelyn." she said softly as he reached her, and he smiled at the words.

"Evelyn... I'm Caspar." he returned gently, and she smiled back.

"Caspar..." she repeated softly, the name sending a thrill through her body. He took her hands, and drew them up to his lips. "Where are you from?" she asked, her smile gleaming in the light, he smiled back and was about to answer, but at that moment he faded away, and the dream returned to its normalcy of melancholic imagery; Evelyn felt a pang of loss, and resigned herself to having the old dream back. No good thing lasts forever, after all... perhaps Mala was right. Perhaps it was just a dream.

Chapter Two: Caspar

The young man sprang awake at the sound of his name being called. It was early morning, and his duties as a farmhand required him to be awake. Rushing to put on his clothes, he dashed aside all thoughts of the Elven-maiden in his dreams, and when he was dressed he dashed down the steps and out the door to tend to the chickens. Farmer Jorgan Wells and his wife Mira had five children of their own, but they were all below the age of ten summers, and so had hired the orphan minstrel as a farmhand some eight years ago. They lived on a communal farm settlement some two miles outside of the great city known as Murana Day, where the Order of Cassandra, an order of clerics, bards, and druids, kept their famous headquarters. Caspar was one of these bards, skilled in all manner of musical instruments, chiefly the flute and the lute, along with the harp and a set of fire-side pipes, which lay carefully packed away in his room.

When not working on the farm, he was out and about in the countryside, playing or singing away to amuse the villagers as he rode about on a horse gifted to him by the Order some years ago. It was the least they could do for him, his parents having been part of the Order when they were alive; they had been in one of the border towns that had been ravaged by the Fiery Hordes, and he himself had been saved by an older cousin, who had brought him to Murana Day twenty years ago. Now at twenty-four, he had a fully-fledged reputation as one of the most skilled music-makers of his time, and many a young girl had sought his attentions. But that was before his dreams had shown him the only lady he knew was worth striving for. Now, he vowed to let no one but the Elven-maiden in his dreams take his heart; and if he could not be hers, then he must die for love. A fine end, if ever there was one. So his thoughts ran as he tended the rows of chickens, the birds clucking as he saw to their feed and took up any eggs he found so that they might be sold at market. When he was through with them, he headed over to the cows, where he found Farmer Wells already tending them.

"Never mind here, boy," the kindly man said to him, "get after those damned pigs on the north reaches. And get Dusty to help you, lazy-good-for-nothing hound that he is..." Wells told him, and Caspar smiled, nodding as he headed off to do as bidden. He whistled for Dusty, the farmer's big wolfhound, and the dog came running up to aid him in his quest of rounding up the pigs to lead them to another field. The wolfhound barked happily, and within moments the two of them had teamed up to herd the pigs to the west fields. Across the way, he could see Maggie Hazel shepherding her sheep to the east pens for the day as her brother Jon was chasing after some straying cows. He could hear the frustrated man yelling at the animals as they tried to go where they would, and chuckled to himself as he gazed back towards his own charges. Three of the pigs were trying to break off. He whistled once, and Dusty began charging, guiding the would-be "deserters" back into place as they made their way to the west fields.

"That's right." he said to them, and resumed walking along the way to the fields; when they were secured in the pens for the day, Caspar whistled for Dusty to get into guard mode, and the dog began patrolling the grounds at once while he himself headed up to the north fields to get them presentable for the next rotation. It was a job that took him most of the morning, and Farmer Wells found him finishing up two hours before lunchtime.

"Are you still out here?" Wells asked him with a surprised tone.

"Yes, sir?" Caspar returned, uncertain of why he was surprised.

"Dusty's still circling about the pens. Don't know how you get him to do it." the farmer said with a shake of his head. "Anyway; lunch is almost ready... as soon as you're cleaned up, anyway." he added, and Caspar nodded.

"I'll be down in a few moments." he replied, and resumed scraping the last bit of field as Wells nodded back at him.

"Boy, if I had my way, I'd see to it that the Order treated you properly... this is no way for a young minstrel to be living." he said with another shake of his head, and began plodding off for the house. Caspar let out a sigh as he continued working; he was content, of that there was no doubt--or, at least, he had *been* content. Now, with the vision of a beautiful woman in his mind, he was not so sure he was content. How would he find her? And would she really be waiting for him? Or was it a flight of fancy? *"I'm... Evelyn."* Evelyn. Evelyn. *Very well, Evelyn.. I, Caspar, shall search for you.* He said to himself with a faint smile as he began returning to the farmhouse to wash. After a thorough cleansing, he headed up to the main room to join the family for lunch. The children were at their usual antics of irritating one another and their parents; Jorgan was often quoted as saying "I don't have five children, I have five monkeys," and there was little evidence to the contrary. As the meal went on, they eventually subsided to a tolerable state of being, and the three adults sighed in relief. "You want my advice on having children, boy? Don't!" the farmer said to him, and his wife gave him a mock-pout. One of his boys then flicked a pea into his face, and Jorgan glowered at him until the cheeky brat mumbled an apology. Caspar shrugged, as if he was indifferent to the idea of romance, as he usually would, and resumed eating. Mira, however, saw something in his eyes, something that spoke of longing and desire; she kept it to herself all the same, not wanting to embarrass the poor boy here of all places. Certainly not in front of her five little rascals.

And so lunch went on, until Jorgan and Caspar headed out to tend to the crops; after three hours of this, Caspar was left to his own devices, and he began wandering about, riding in an aimless manner until he reached Murana Day itself. He was let in, being recognized from the old silver amulet that hung about his neck, and he let the horse gently trot along the streets as the two of them continued roaming. He began idly fiddling around with his lute, eventually strumming in to a tune, a tune which he slowly began adding words to as he rode along through the markets, heedless of who heard him.

> *Oh, maiden of starlight and moonlight*
> *Come dance with me evermore*
> *Come dance with me, under forest and tree*
> *And mayhaps down to the white shores*
>
> *Oh, maiden of starlight and moonlight*
> *Your entrancing eyes hold for me*
> *The sight and the sum of the future*
> *And I long, oh my heart longs for thee*
>
> *Entrancing and dancing, laughter and merriment*
> *Singing and ringing the night all away*
> *Forever and ever, let singing go on*
> *For the night, and for all the day*
>
> *Oh maiden of starlight and moonlight*
> *How I long to be by thy side*
> *Where the forest is gleaming in starlight*
> *And where the world indeed seems wide*
>
> *Ah! Maiden of starlight and moonlight*
> *Will you come with me and dance with me,*
> *To the edge of night, to the dawning of day;*

Oh maiden, oh maiden, to the dawning of day!

He sang as he wandered about, and those listening to him noticed his almost trance-like state as he sang, as if he was singing from experience and not a mere repetition of a timeless song that was ever reinvented by those of his craft. He continued fiddling around idly with his lute for some time after this, eventually settling the horse in a paddock near a tavern. Caspar then headed inside the tavern itself, settling in a corner that he frequented on his visits to the city. Here, he could hear quite a bit, and picked up on stories or news from all corners of the wide world. Things were indeed lively this night, and Caspar heard quite a bit of news from those around him. In their mountain halls, the Dwarves were said to be forging armaments for a great war, as if the hordes of death were coming to attack again; the Valkyries had been seen patrolling the ancient trade routes, as if searching for something or someone; a Giant had been spotted by a crew of sailors that had just pulled into port for the night in a place where Giants did not usually go. It was said to have been a place of great meaning to them, though they rarely visited the place anymore; if one was doing so now, something big was brewing.

"Mark me, the Giant is nothing to the Dwarves--or the Valkyries; when did one of those man-hating witches creep out of their mountains last? And for what?" one of them said.

"I'd like to see a Valkyrie myself, and get between her, if you know what I mean." a second said, and those around him started laughing.

"You'd be a eunuch for sure for trying!" another jeered.

"By all the gods, even seeing a Valkyrie would be worth it!"

"And what of the Dwarves? What are they forging weapons and armour for, unless a war's coming? And who are they fighting? Who'll they be attacking? Hm?" a fourth voice called.

"Never mind them forging; they're always forging. What're the Valkyries looking for? That's what I want to know!" the first one said again.

"Their Merfolk cousins for all we know." someone beside him returned.

"Merfolk my eye! What's in that mug of yours? I want some now!" the other retorted, and the others laughed. The conversation then devolved into a discussion of having mermaids versus having a Valkyrie, and Caspar left in disgust, leading his horse through the streets towards the gates. A young noblewoman two years younger than he was stopped him for a moment when he passed by her residence, and kissed him on the cheeks.

"My bard, my bard; have you come to play me like a pipe? Or shall we be entertained in better ways this night? A night of romance and passion, perchance?" she asked him longingly, and he smiled at her, sighing.

"Isabel, Isabel... but I have seen the woman of my dreams, and alas, she is not thee!" he said to her gently, and she pouted at him.

"Would you give up being my consort for a real romance? Do not consorts get paid, and does not romance cost the price of eking a living from the earth?" Isabel asked him again.

"Would you have me betray my heart, and would you betray the man who would have you for the sake of a night's whim, dear Isabel?" he asked her pointedly, and she smiled at him.

"Noble Caspar; commoner you are, but common, no. I would that you were a prince, for then perchance no one would think me silly for trying to love you."

"As much as people have thought me silly for entertaining you these many moons past, dear Isabel."

"Alas, such silly fools as we are, is there any place for us?" she asked him with a sigh, and he gently shrugged.

"In a ballad, perhaps, or a children's story." Caspar returned.

"Then make it a pretty ballad, and sing it on my wedding day." Isabel said in reply, kissing him again.

"If I am indeed here, I shall make certain to do so."

"If you're here?" she asked, suddenly alarmed. "What do you mean 'if'? Are you going away?" Isabel pressed him in a worried tone as she looked up at him.

"I don't know. I don't know." Caspar admitted. "I'd probably be a fool for chasing a girl in a dream, but at least that too would be something to sing about. Would it not?" he said with a faint smile, and she allowed herself a grin.

"Chasing a dream is no bad thing. Perhaps. But at least it's worth singing about, to be sure. Just make sure you're back to sing of that as well." Isabel told him. "I shouldn't keep you... farmers like having their workers up early, and it's a good ride back to Idoma."

"Farewell, Lady Isabel." Caspar said with a bow, and mounted his horse as he headed away. Isabel waved at him longingly, wondering if he was even now preparing to take off. Would he really do such a thing? Or was it one of his fanciful imaginings?

***

The next day passed in a similar fashion to the previous one; Caspar finished his chores in the morning with milking the cows as Farmer Wells tended the pigs. Dusty was barking at the silly animals as they made their way to the south pens, and Maggie's sheep and cows were being herded to the north ones. As the day wore on, Caspar ended up siting on the fence with his lute, idly strumming away again; the dream had not happened again, and he wondered what it meant. Was it merely a dream? Should he have spurned the desires of a noblewoman so readily, when such a thing could elevate his status but even a little? Deciding to shrug off such thoughts, he continued strumming, eventually drifting off into another song.

I sang of the summer, and spring so bright
I sang of the day, I sang of the night
Of winter I sang and of autumn's gold
I sang a song of the seasons ever-bold
A song for the seasons ever-bold

Blossoms blue in the starlight dim
Flowering trees that sing of the breeze
See the merry birds as they caper away
Singing and flying in a brand new day

Nonsense you call it: I call it a song
For as long as you're singing
Your words are never really wrong
It's the heart and the soul
That makes the music roll
And so I keep singing the song
For if I can never be wrong
Then as long as the words come along
I'll go on, and on, and on!

Dance in the starlight, dance with me
Dance in the moonlight, lady come with me!
We'll dance forever by the pearl white shores
And I'll be yours, forever yours, forever yours

Fields of barley, fields of corn
Fields on a bright and sunny morn'
Harvest comes along, and the fields grow bare
And the barns are filled with little room to spare

Sing along, sing with me
Sing a merry melody
Sing with me, and sing along
You're never wrong, you're ne-ver wrong, oh!

Spring is lovely, Summer is lively
Autumn is bright, Winter a fright
Daytime is merry, Nighttime is scary
Sunlight is grand, and Rain is bland
A cloudy day makes the heart sink low
When sunlight comes out, she's all aglow
So dance with me, sing with me
Sing a merry song, a merry me-lo-dy!
Sing with me, and you're never wrong
For it's the soul of the song
And not the words, not the words
That make it right, or wrong!

And so Caspar went on, quite content to keep on with his "merry nonsense", as he called it, but as he was just finishing the previous verses he caught sight of five riders that were riding as fast as they could for the farm. He paused, and then snapped into action, racing to the farmhouse to put his lute away and get out his bow. They might be raiders. He shouted for Jorgan, and warned him of what he had seen. The farmer was ready in moments, and Caspar all but made a jump down the stairs as he raced out just behind him; the five riders got up to the farm and then halted, their horses clearly exhausted, and they themselves no less so. "What in the Iron Hells is this?" Jorgan asked them, and their leader spoke.

"Just attacked... our waggons... all destroyed... the merchants dead..." he gasped out, and then collapsed, along with two of the others; three of the horses also went down, and at once Caspar ran for water, while Jorgan shouted for his wife to get some as well. After a few minutes, all the local farmers of Idoma were on their way to Wells' farm to aid the five strangers, who, it seemed, had been hired guards protecting a caravan that had been on its way to Murana Day when they had been attacked by an unknown force in the night. The caravan had been slaughtered, and two of the merchants had escaped with three of the guards. "We were a caravan of thirty-seven." the man told them, and they all shook their heads, shocked at the story. "Five from thirty-seven, not counting the loss in merchandise and livestock. Our home-village must also be under attack, if it hasn't been already. We weren't that far out from it." the man continued, holding his head in his hands.

"By all the gods! Is the Sorcerer King back again?" Jon Hazel wondered, and the others began murmuring similar sentiments.

"Now see here!" Farmer Wells interrupted. "We've more important things to worry about now: there's raiders of some sort about, and someone needs to ride for Murana Day and tell the Duke! He'll have his knights roaming about in no time at all, and if we get attacked here, we can run for the city in good time." he said, and they began nodding.

"I'll go." Caspar said.

"I'll come with you." the guard told him.

"Not on that poor horse of yours, you don't." Jorgan told him. "Hold up, boy, let's get the waggon out and ride him up." he said to Caspar, who nodded as he ran out with a couple of the others to get the thing hitched up and ready. "Now the rest of you make these people feel at home; seems they're gonna be with us for a time." he added, and went out to help with the waggon.

***

In the next couple of hours, Farmer Wells' waggon was rolling in to Murana Day; some were surprised, for the farmer usually did not come until Market Day, but then they saw it heading up to the Duke's palace, and they knew that something dire was afoot. "I told you! Strange things going on!" a drunk said to his companion.

"Oh, hell!" the other returned, hiccuping. "Damn your c'nspir'cy natterings... let's get a jug!" he said, and they stumbled into the tavern once more.

Meanwhile, the three in the waggon had gained an audience with Duke Melchior, who listened intently to the guard that Wells and Caspar had brought to see him. The man's home, a small forest village called Woodmark, was a tributary of his domain, and the possibility of its being under attack or destroyed was something that he at once gave orders to be looked into. Two knights headed out at once, and a page went to go and summon the rest of them to be on standby if needed. As to the destruction of the caravan that had been coming their way, Duke Melchior gave his solemn word that their remains would be sought out, and anything or anyone that had survived would be escorted with all possible haste to the city. "This is a matter most grave indeed." he said. "Twenty years ago, we barely escaped the ravaging of the Infernal Hordes; if they are back, then who knows what could happen to us? Word must be sent to the crown; I shall send my fastest ship to the city of Auschternople at once." he continued.

"Not that it will do any good, the crown being in the state it's in..." another man said; the duke gave him a dark glance, and snapped his fingers at another page when he had finished composing a brief missive, sending him off to the harbor at once.

"I trust that you and your fellows are being well looked after by mine subjects?" he inquired to the man, who nodded.

"You have generous people, my lord Duke." he said, and the Duke smiled.

"It is our common quality." he said with a nod. "Very well. I shall send my riders to you if I receive any news on those matters pertinent to yourself. I bid you a good night." he said, and the three bowed to him as he rose and departed. They were escorted back out, and when they were aboard the waggon once more they headed for the gates of the city. Just as they did so, the young lady Isabel came running up, shouting for the waggon to halt. Caspar, seeing her insistence, got out at once to see what was the matter; an old man was coming up just behind her. Farmer Wells shouted for Caspar to make it quick, and the young man nodded back.

"Caspar, I'm so glad I caught you. Listen, this is Simeon; he's a seer from the Order of Cassandra, do you know him?" she asked as the old man came up, and Caspar shook his head.

"I'm afraid I'm not as familiar with everyone as I'd like to be."

"Well, you know him now. What he has to say is important; please listen, you'll know why I'm insistent when he tells you." she said to him, and he turned to the older man.

"Sir?" he asked, and Simeon began speaking.

"The wandering bard goes to find love immortal on the day that danger breaks forth; a rushing tide, a vast wilderness through death's valley; forged companions make the journey true." the old man recited, giving him a knowing look before heading back towards the ancient temple. The words did not register in Caspar's mind until Isabel looked at him insistently, and then they hit him: "the wandering bard goes to find love immortal on the day that danger breaks forth"; the wandering bard. She had heard him speak of leaving the night before, and immediately thought of him when the old man spoke those words. He turned to her with a nod, smiling at her.

"Thank you, my lady. My path is clearer now." he said sincerely.

"I know." she said, a tear in her eye. "Will we ever meet again? I do care for you." she asked him lovingly, and he let out a sigh, putting a hand on her cheek.

"I don't know." he said, and headed off to the waggon. She gazed after him, a lump in her throat as he climbed back up, looking back at her with a faint smile. Isabel could not but smile after him as the waggon was let out of the gates, and she turned to head for her own home, letting out a sigh of regret at his parting.

***

When they had returned home, the Wells and their guests sat down to dinner; it was, for once, a silent affair, and the five newcomers ate heartily. Jorgan looked at Caspar with a curious look; the young man had come home changed. What had that old man said to him?

"You all right, boy?" he suddenly asked, and Caspar shrugged.

"It's nothing." he returned.

27

"Uh-huh." Wells remarked, unconvinced. Caspar looked up at him, and gave him a faint smile.

"I'll tell you a bit later, sir. Right now I need to think about it." he said, and the good-natured farmer accepted this.

They finished their evening meal in silence, and then Caspar headed out to sit on the front porch; the farmer followed him out soon after, sitting down beside him with a long sigh as he lit up a pipe. He gave it a few puffs, and then turned to his hireling with a gentle smile.

"You've got a load on your mind." he said, and Caspar nodded.

"I have to leave. That man was a seer. He told me I have to leave." the younger man said in an almost trance-like fashion as he gazed into the distance.

"And go where?" Wells asked him pointedly in his down-to-earth manner. "Life ain't no song, Caspar; and it certainly ain't no ballad. Where do you think you're gonna go?"

"I don't know. But I've got to go; you yourself said this is no life for a minstrel. Even if all I do is wander, I must go." Caspar said, and Wells shrugged.

"If that's your mind made up, I won't change it. We've got some help here for a time, at least; these folks needs some honest work to keep themselves occupied, no mistake." he said, and Caspar nodded.

"I'm sure they'll be happy to do something in return for your hospitality." Caspar said to him with a smile.

"Ain't that about it." the farmer remarked as he puffed away. They spent the next few moments in silence, contemplating the starry scene above them as the moons began rising. Caspar wondered if Evelyn, his dream-girl, was also staring up at the stars. The farmer gave him another curious glance, and then shook his head. When his pipe was through, he emptied it out, and let out a cough. "You've more than that on your mind, but I won't push it. Just get morning chores done, and then you can go off, and all the luck to you; fair deal?" he said, holding out his hand. Caspar smiled, and placed his own hand in the farmer's.

"Fair deal, sir." he said as they shook hands. Wells gave him a pat on the back, and they then turned in for the night. That night, Caspar dreamed of his lady fair once again, and in the morning he awoke with a certainty; she *was* real, and he *had* to find her. That was the only certain thing in his mind. Love immortal. And whom could be more immortal than an Elf?

Chapter Three: The Prince

As Mala had predicted, Evelyn fell to worrying about clothes the day before the prince would arrive. By the noon hour, she had given up and stormed off to go and work in the orchards, and it was here that Mala found her around the late afternoon, gingerly shimmying up one of the taller trees to get a fruit that looked promisingly ripe. Mala gazed up after her, shaking her head; the girl enjoyed hard labor such as this, disdaining her status when she could to help around the village. It was something that had endeared her to many who had since taken refuge in this hideaway, and they often forgot she was of the noble houses. Covered here and there in dirt, and with a few small scratches about her arms and legs, and a very faint one on her cheek, Evelyn slowly but surely got up to where this prize among fruits was situated, and with a satisfied smile she examined it; it was indeed ripe, and she plucked it from the branch and placed it in her sack as she began to slowly head back down. When she had gotten to ground, one of the others came to relieve her of the sack, and it was then she noticed Mala. Evelyn gave her a wry smile, and Mala shook her head, silently shaking with laughter.

"What wouldst yon prince think of thee, so covered in grime that thou canst not be distinguished from thy friends hereabouts?" she suddenly said.

"If that is truly so, then I would not mind; for I could go on with my life and the desire to follow my dreams." she said wittily, and Mala gave her a sigh.

"As thou sayest; but come now, child, we hast the cleaning of thee to see to, and then thou shalt be pleased to hear we hath found at last a dress worthy of the occasion." Mala said as she held out her hand, and Evelyn resigned herself to the situation at last, heading in with the older Elf to the lower basements of the tree-house, where a bath was prepared for her. It was soothing, and she almost fell asleep as Mala tended her there, washing her with a practiced experience. When the bath was over and she was mostly dried off, she was given a robe, and they headed up to her room; here there was a dress, a dress that made

Evelyn gasp in shock; it was a replica of one of her mother's favorite dresses, a sky-blue lace patterned with floral designs and trimmed with a silver edging. She turned to Mala, who nodded.

"I remember well the dresses of thy mother, child; in faithfulness I drew the pattern long ago, knowing this day would come, and so I passed it off to yon tailors, who hath faithfully brought to life that which I gave them to do. And now it is thine." the older Elf said, and Evelyn closed her eyes, bringing to mind the image of her mother in such a dress. She let out a smile, and embraced her guardian, who embraced her back. After it had been tried on, the dress was put away carefully, and they went down to the evening meal; the coming prince was now the talk of the village, but Evelyn refused to make a comment upon the matter. He was, it seemed, expected by the late morning, and planned to take her with him, from the report of the scouts. Evelyn was not the last princess, he had said; but her house was closer to that of the higher nobility, and was thought more suitable on account of such a thing.

With disgust, the young Elf-maiden rose up and bid them good night, heading off to her room with thoughts of how very chauvinistic it all was. "More suitable"--"more suitable"; more *suitable*? Had he said such a thing to the other maiden? If he had, was she broken with weeping at such a slight, an insult to her integrity and honor? Or had it been an unspoken thing, a thing implied, to leave her to her own imaginings of what he might have said? By the stars! Was it a mere matter of heraldry that made Evelyn "more suitable" than this other maiden? What pathetic nonsense! How were the Elves to survive the changes of the world if they could not change their views on such things? Evelyn could not decide, and she laid upon her bed with a sigh of frustration, staring blankly out the window until at last she fell asleep some hours later.

***

"Lost... lost... that is all I will ever be..." Evelyn sighed to herself as she wandered in the dream-wood, softly passing underneath the silver canopies that here and there gave a glimpse to the starry scene above.

"Not as lost as I." another voice said. Evelyn turned; it was her dream-man, Caspar.

"What do you mean?" she asked him with a funny look.

"I'm setting out tomorrow to find you." he said sincerely, and she was taken aback. He was coming to find her? The look in his eyes was a serious one, and she gazed at him in wide wonder.

"We barely know each other." Evelyn returned, feeling somehow that the words were not true.

"And yet we know each other so well." he replied as they advanced

towards each other slowly. "And besides, a seer has spoken of my leaving. It is fate now, and I cannot avoid it."

"But the prince... he won't understand..." Evelyn told him. "How am I to explain this to anyone...?" she said softly, turning her gaze to the ground as she put a hand to her cheek. He took the hand, and she placed her other hand on his, bringing it to her mouth to kiss it and then holding it against her cheek.

"You see? We know each other so well. I never knew a peace like this, not even in the days when I had a family." Caspar said to her, and she looked at him in understanding.

"Is that why we share each other's dream? My dream? Because we're both lost?" she wondered as he enveloped her in an embrace.

"Perhaps. Who knows the mysteries? A simple bard am I, a wandering minstrel, and not a great scholar. But I will find you, I promise." he said.

"Then... I will do the same." she said to him. "We are far from each other; it is only fair for me to--"

"But you are a--"

"A what? A female?" she said as she withdrew, and he held up his hands at the words, the rebuking tone evident. "We are not as you, mortal man; I say it in love now, but do not make me repeat myself. The Elves endure things that would kill your kind. I will travel, and I will come through just as many dangers and hardships as you to find you."

"Forgive me, Evelyn." Caspar said genuinely. "I am not knowledgeable of the Elves save for what songs tell us, and those are inadequate. I would gladly learn and atone for such words as I meant to say, so that I do not repeat their offense and so lose your love." he added, and she smiled back at him.

"Then kiss me." Evelyn said to him, and once again their lips locked in a passionate embrace, a kiss that seemed to last for all the length of eternity, until at last the dreams faded away into nothingness, and morning recalled them to their waking lives.

***

Whatever else it was, it was a beautiful morning in the hidden dell that sheltered their village, and as Evelyn woke to the sound of birdsong she smiled. Putting on her robe, she headed down quickly to partake of the morning meal, where most of the others were still eating. One of the older among them gave her a smile, and she smiled back at him.

"Are you ready to meet a prince, Lady Evelyn?" he asked her.

"Oh, yes." Evelyn replied at once; Mala's attention was caught by the tone in which she said it. She had been very reluctant to go through with this; what was changing her mind now? Or *had* her mind been changed? Their conversation three days ago came back to her, and the older Elf found herself wondering again if Evelyn was about to spurn thousands of years of Elven history and tradition for the sake of a mortal man. She could glean no insight from the young lady before her, poised in cheeriness as she ate her breakfast, and so Mala returned her attention to the mint tea before her. When breakfast had been eaten, Evelyn bathed again, and then prepared herself for the visitation of the prince; her hair was bound back, and a blue flower placed in its locks, and the dress was put upon her gingerly as an attendant saw to her makeup. She eventually looked a queen indeed, and all Mala's thoughts of her running off for a dream were banished. It was not the half of an hour later when a horn sounded; the prince had arrived.

***

"His royal highness, Prince Thadolin of the House Reginus!" the page announced, and the golden haired Elf in his regal attire descended from the carriage to the ground as those around bowed to pay their respects. At the far end of the dusty lane, he saw the matriarch of the village descending the winding stairs of the great house with her protectorate, and nodded to his prince, who nodded back to him. Thadolin then advanced proudly to meet her whom he thought of as his equal, and whom he now swore was the most beautiful of Elven maidens he had ever seen. The page and the guards were told to be at ease, and they began dispersing themselves throughout the village as they would as their leader made his way to Evelyn. Thadolin bowed, and Evelyn gave him a polite curtsy; he held out his arm, and she took it gracefully as they began walking. It was only then that Mala caught the look of mischief in her eye, but she held her peace. Perhaps it was merely a sense of play that tingled Evelyn's fancy this day, and nothing so drastic as her earlier suspicions. The matriarch then retired to her chambers, leaving the two of them to walk as they would.

Evelyn and Thadolin walked about the village in silence for a time, the prince admiring the sights that were so familiar to his companion as they made their way about; the orchard trees were blossoming with a vibrant life today, and the gardens hummed with activity. Further beyond them, a vintner was plucking fruits from the vines that grew about her house, and a small child was helping her. In the distance they could see shepherds tending the flocks, and a scout was riding about the bounds, patrolling the area for signs of danger. A warm breeze began fluttering by the two of them, and Thadolin turned to Evelyn, admiring her beauty; surely she was a prize worth having! He suddenly flushed, realizing he had said such words aloud, and that she was *not* pleased by them.

"Am I a prize sought after, Prince Thadolin? Have I nothing of my

32

own merit to endear me to you other than status and beauty, or was such your goal all along? To have and to keep for your own advancement?" she said to him in a gentle but harsh reproach, and he relaxed himself, his quick mind hurriedly thinking up an apt reply.

"Forgive me, I meant it not in offense. But surely you cannot deny a valiant attempt at a compliment, though it were given in an ungenerous fashion? If we are to spend our lives in union together, we must know one another better--and I must confess that I have not the social graces my family meant to instill within me." Thadolin said in reply, and Evelyn nodded slowly.

"So intent on having me. Did you spare no thought for the other?" she asked him.

"A passing thought. I told her I would return with my choice made, and in that I did not lie."

"And if I should spurn you?"

"Ha!" he scoffed as they resumed walking. "I am the last prince of all Elvendom; you would refuse the honor of being my queen?"

"What honor is there in being a wallflower, a silent trophy for your chambers?" Evelyn said with a crisp wit, and he was taken aback. They passed in silence for a moment more, and then he spoke again.

"I must tell the truth; your house is the nobler one of status, closer to the line of kings. So you see, it is Elven Law that requires me to make advances upon you, not mere desire." he said to her, and in his lack of bluster Evelyn saw he spoke truly. He was the only male noble, and she the closest female heir to the royal lines; Elven Law was strict upon the matter. She could not give refusal without good reason--and her own reason was not good enough for the law.

"No easy choice in such a matter, dear prince." she returned softly.

"Would you have another? Would you give yourself for love, and spurn tradition? Our traditions?" he asked her, searching her features for the answer. "Ah! You *do* love another--and the love is not something we of Elvendom would approve of in any way; nay, deny me not! I was taught by the best to read people by their silence and their expressions, and you, dear lady, are but an open book upon my table."

"Am I so transparent then as to be read by any passing by?" Evelyn asked him with a sigh of veiled exasperation. He smiled gently.

"Not at all. Only the most skilled of seekers could find thy secrets-- and I shall keep it!--but think of our people, Lady Evelyn. What would they think if they knew you were spurning our ways to live as you saw fit? To fly in the face of all our traditions on a whim of fancy?"

"Perhaps then they might see that there is more to life than being stuck in a past that cannot return, no matter how much we want it: that we must accept our losses and try to change for a better tomorrow, so that those who have died will not have died in vain." she said to him, and he looked at her with a new-found respect.

"Perhaps... but we may never know. For now, Elven Law requires me to make public our betrothal, and we must do so at once."

"Betrothal?" Evelyn retorted. "We've barely been talking to each other and you think that--"

"The Law, Evelyn! The Law!" Thadolin hissed to calm her down. She caught a look in his eyes, and stopped to listen at once. "I don't give a damn about the traditions either; I did not lie when I said you were the most beautiful Elf-maid I have seen, but the other fell head over heels for me, and I for her. I would have her for love and for honor, and leave you to your fancies, but the Law forbids it; unless-- unless you were to... 'disappear'... to take such fancies as you have and go in search of them. But alas, I know not where you should go, nor could I glean from our conversation anything that even remotely implied you were dissatisfied with the thought of our being married. All I know is that you seemed perfectly happy, and I was greatly shocked that you should have taken off for who knows where, never dreaming that such a thing as your displeasure in these matters was indeed true." he said to her, and she nodded slowly as they resumed walking once more. They completed their circuit about the village, and then returned to the center of town to find preparations for the evening festivities were being made. Mala gave Evelyn a suspicious look as the two of them reentered the main hub of their village, but the younger Elf gave no hint of anything in her features, and was as calm as a sleeping cat. As the afternoon wore on, songsters came to entertain those who had gathered about, and a dance sprang up as dinner began to be set upon the tables; Evelyn danced with Thadolin in courtesy, her mind on Caspar all the while. Had he indeed taken off in search of her? And how was she to search for him in turn? How indeed were they to find each other? Was it not indeed a wild fancy, and should she not surrender to her people's ways, and make life easier? Nay; easier in action, but not easier upon the heart, which would be forever broken if Caspar was real and she had given in to her people's traditions instead. And after making her own promise to find him, how could she then back down? Nay; there would be no queenly life for her. She would take the long road to find real love, and so prove the stronger in doing so. Thus her mind raced as the dance went on, interrupted at last by the bell tolling for the evening meal.

It was in the midst of the meal that Thadolin announced his intentions to wed her, and there was a great applause throughout the village at the words. Their beloved Evelyn was about to seize upon her destiny; if they had known exactly what destiny she was about to seize, they would have restrained her at once, but for now, they were merry. Let them be merry, and let them then be struck with wonder as to where she had gone. Evelyn had chosen; she would leave that very night, when all were asleep, and take off towards the south, where men were said to live.

***

Mala caught Evelyn on her way to her room later that night, and gave her a look that brooked no refusal; there was something the older Elf wanted to say, and Evelyn stopped to listen. "What is in thy head, child?" the matriarch asked her softly and plainly. The younger Elf blinked, and gave her a look of confusion. "I see thy eyes, I note thy postures, and I knoweth thy mind's workings; tell me thou art not thinking of spurning such a prince after all this?" Mala asked her, and Evelyn affected a smile.

"Dear Mala, your suspicions have driven you to this? After all the games I played upon you? Oh, dear, how silly of me." Evelyn returned with an airy tone, leaving Mala stuck for a reply; had the young maiden been playing tricks, as she had been wont to do in older times?

"This is no time for your games, Evelyn! This is our people's future! I will *not* have thee casting aside responsibilities for any sort of fancy!" Mala said to her adamantly, and Evelyn let out a sigh.

"I cast aside nothing for fancy, Mala. I embrace my destiny with open arms and an open heart, and if you think me capable of doing otherwise you are fooling yourself at long last."

"As may be, child, but I know thee too well to put aside any such doubts as to your full intentions... I did not become matriarch of our people for being too trusting."

"As you say. May I go to bed now? There's such a long ride in the morning, after all." Evelyn said to her, and Mala, still not able to get a read on the girl, acquiesced to the request with a nod. That, at least, was not a lie; Thadolin's home was a long way from their own village. As the young maiden went up the stairs to her room, Mala was still filled with doubts; but she could not find a reasonable excuse for them, and so retired herself to bed as well. Let the girl have her last night here in peace.

***

When Evelyn reached her room, she silently shut the door, getting out of her dress and hurriedly wiping off the makeup from her face. She put the dress in its place, and quickly began pulling out some old clothes and putting them into a haversack as she got into a long tunic, putting a belt on over this and then lacing up her soft leather boots. Taking the flower out of her hair, she set it upon the nightstand, and then listened intently; no one was moving about the house. Evelyn then

35

softly made her way downstairs, and snitched some bread and some water-flasks, and put these in a separate carry-bag before heading out of the house and down into the now quiet village. She took a bow and a quiver of arrows from the fletcher's shop, and was almost past the vineyards when a voice halted her in her tracks.

"So you really are leaving." the prince's voice said, and she stopped, her eyes wide with fear. He smiled, and shook his head. "Nay, I'm not going to call you out. I simply wanted to know if you were adamant about it."

"Does this answer your question?" Evelyn said to him as she drew an arrow to the bow, faster than any human could have done.

"It does indeed." Thadolin told her. "Now go, if you're still adamant. I have an act to prepare for, and I can't do it if you've an arrow in me." he said to her again, and she lowered the bow, gently taking the arrow and putting it back in its quiver.

"Thank you." she softly whispered, and then raced off as fast as she could towards the south. He gazed after her, smiling to himself; they were now both free to do as they wished. Let love forever win over all the rules and boundaries of tradition!

Life had begun in an ordinary way at the homestead of Farmer Jorgan Wells; the chickens were tended to, the cows milked, and the pigs herded from their previous field to the next in their daily rotation, yet all the while Caspar was thinking of his upcoming journey, a journey which he dared not delay a moment longer than he had to. While Farmer Wells showed their newcomers how to tend to this, that, and the other about the farm, he was packing his bags, and Mira Wells was fixing him up both a farewell meal and a wayfarer's bag of food for his journey. She had been right. There had been something about him that had been speaking of leaving for the past couple of days now, and now he was about to do just that.

When Caspar had seen to his bags, he went to check on his horse; Dusty was lounging about nearby, the dog idly gazing over the boy with a sad look, as if he knew his friend was leaving. Satisfied with knowing that Elvar (the horse, that is) would be fine until needed, Caspar then departed the stable, and gave the dog a pat on the head as he left. Lunch was then being served, and it was a merry affair, despite his imminent departure. As they dined on the bounty before them, a knock came at the door. It was one of the Duke's knights, and he was bearing a bundle. They invited him in at once, and he sat down, still gently holding the thing in his arms, whatever it was.

"Good sir knight, what is it you have in your arms?" one of the merchants, a woman, asked him.

"Can it be...?" her companion said with wonder.

"Lady, 'tis a hound-pup I recovered from thy caravan's wreckage, and he is sorely full of fear from the terror of it all. I blame you not at all for fleeing whatever it was that haunted thee that night; I doubt even the most stalwart among us would have stayed to die there." the knight told her, and she nodded. He held out the little animal, and she came over to take it from his arms, cradling the little thing to her bosom.

"Oh, poor thing, poor thing..." she cooed gently, heading over to a corner of the room as the farmer's wife went to find food for it. Dusty barked, sensing one of his distant kin in the room, and Farmer Wells, stroked his ears.

"So that's all you found from that massacre?" he said to the knight.

"All that was living, friend. The rest? Well, some of the goods need a bit of repair; we salvaged some of the more readily accessible things, and sent back to the main companies for aid in recovering more, but I thought it prudent to bring this one back at once." the other replied, and the farmer nodded.

"Was there word or sight of the village?" one of the other survivors asked.

"We saw smoke on the horizon, and so fear the worst; two of our order are riding there now, they will have the truer report of it." he said, and she bit her lip, blinking back tears as the man beside her took her in his arms.

"We will have vengeance in living." he said to her softly, and she nodded.

After that, the conversation went to more pleasant matters, during which Caspar slipped out with his own pack to see to Elvar. When he had saddled the horse for his journey, he began leading him out of the stable, only to see that Lady Isabel was not done with saying farewell just yet. She rode up on her white stallion, dismounting at the sight of him and rushing over. Dusty barked as she came up, and Caspar suddenly felt the sweet sensation of Isabel's lips upon his own, the young girl kissing him for one passionate moment before holding him close to her.

"I couldn't let last night be the last time I saw you, not when we parted so distantly." she said to him, and he rocked her gently in his arms as he held her.

"As you say, dear lady." he said to her in reply.

"And now that you're leaving, where will you truly go?" she asked him, looking up at him as she let go a bit. He smiled, shrugging his shoulders as he let go of her.

"I'll follow my heart; what else can I do?" he returned, and she gave him a sad smile.

"As you say, dear bard." Isabel said to him.

"And now, dear lady, I really must go... I can't have half the town weeping over me as I leave, or I'll feel obligated to stay on, and that will not do." Caspar told her, and she nodded.

"You're right, of course." Isabel said, as if chiding herself. "I'm being selfish. Good luck to you, Caspar, and remember us always." she added with a smile, and he nodded back to her.

"Always." he returned, and Dusty barked again as Farmer Wells came out. The dog yowled pitifully at the young man, and Wells gave the furry animal an amused grin.

"He'll be half-mad if you leave him behind." the farmer told Caspar, and Isabel smiled as Caspar blinked.

"But, sir! He's--"

"He's always been fond of you, boy; and besides, that new pup needs a home. Maybe I'll get it right with the training this time. Go on, varmint! Take care of your boy!" the farmer said to the dog, who barked again as he trotted up to Caspar, who knelt down to pet him as Isabel put a hand on his shoulder.

"Good luck, my friends." she said again, and then headed over to her own horse so that she could ride for home. Wells then tossed Caspar the lead for the wolfhound, and when this had been fastened about the dog's collar, he mounted his own horse, and Jorgan Wells nodded at him.

"Go on, boy. We'll keep the light on for you." he said with a wave as he turned in, and Caspar smiled back.

"Good luck, sir." he returned, and with that he turned the horse towards the road, and set off at a lively pace towards the crossroads. As they made their way along the old stone-paved road, the familiar sights and people of Idoma seemed to be saying farewell to him; the blacksmith looked up, giving him a second look as he took in the young man's travelling gear; the tanner and the chandler waved as he passed them by; the Hazels smiled as he rode past their house, and Old Barns the drunkard blinked several times as he went by.

"Blazes in tarnation is goin' on?" the old drunk blinked again. "Aw, blazes... where's my, my... (hic!)... ah, blazes to darn, I fergit it again... Barns, ye daft (hic!) fool!" he mumbled to himself, falling back into his barrel as he tried to look for something in his pockets. The innkeeper came out to see what the noise was, and doubled over in laughter as he saw two feet sticking out of the barrel.

Caspar shook his head as he looked back and saw Old Barns falling back into the barrel he sat upon; as the innkeeper came out to check, he returned his attention to the road before him, wondering how long and how far it would be until he found a hint of Evelyn. Evelyn... was she too on her way even now, searching and seeking for him as he was seeking for her? How far away *was* her homeland from his? How many leagues and days lay between them? A merchant waggon started out into the road, and he made way for the thing, gently pulling Dusty out of the way as they continued on their own route as the waggon started off towards Murana Day. After another few moments, he found himself at the crossroads, where the road split off into three very different directions; one turned just slightly off from the adjoining road he was coming off of, the second made its winding way towards the hill-country towards the south, and the third was a worn-down route that led north. Wasn't the Forest of Alastria said to be in the north, far away from the realms of men? Deciding that rumor was better than nothing, he set off towards the north at a more eager pace than before, riding for the better part of the day.

The open road was something he had always expected to end up on, for such was his imminent vocation; yet it was altogether strange and removed from the songs he had sung about it, and its lonesome quality hinted at near-sinister doings upon its bounds. What secrets did the old north road hold, its weathered stones looking as if they might cry out at any moment to testify to what they had seen? Only once in two-hundred years had anyone come this way en-masse; during the invasion of the Sorcerer King, many had fled down the weathered path, seeking refuge from the terror of the demonic hordes that had come to ravage their lands. Caspar could only vaguely remember that journey, for all of it had been a blur to him--the screams, the burning fires, the rushing feet, unearthly howls and bellowing--and he cared not to think upon it. His old village lay somewhere off to the west of the worn highway; hopefully, he would not encounter it. As he gave a look back towards Idoma, he could see it just barely upon the horizon, and he could swear he saw the gleam of a spire in Murana Day further beyond. His attention returned to the road, and he pulled out his lute, idly strumming as he slowed his pace. For the rest of his afternoon, he played upon its strings, until at last he became aware of a need to find shelter for the night.

Dismounting from Elvar, he continued leading the horse along as Dusty sniffed about, seeking whatever it was dogs sought as they sniffed the ground for scents and signs invisible to such as their masters. A copse of oak lay before him, their boughs intertwining to form an neat canopy; deciding that this would do for the night, he made for it, tying Elvar to one of the trees and Dusty to another. Caspar then pulled out food for himself and Dusty as Elvar grazed upon the grass, the horse content to rest for a time. When they had eaten, Caspar made a fire, and settled in beside it as Dusty came to sit nearby him. The stars seemed to be shining brighter here; or was it only his imagination? He played around with tunes on his lute for most of the rest of that evening, until at last sleep overtook him, and he lay in a dreamless slumber for the rest of the night.

***

On that next morning, he and the dog had a quick breakfast, and then set off once more upon their journey on the fading north road. Birds were singing in the trees, and woodland animals were scurrying about their daily routine; a hawk flew overhead, and a party of rabbits dashed for cover. A fox led her litter through the trees off to the right, and Caspar could see another animal, possibly a badger, slowly meandering along. On the road itself was an ancient tortoise, which made no sign of being dead or alive as he passed it by; further along the road was a herd of deer, which looked up as his little party traversed the ancient path. What were these strange creatures doing on the old stone path, they seemed to be wondering, and Caspar almost asked himself the same question as he smiled. A wolf could be seen in the distance beyond them, and as they kept on their way they saw a family of bears crossing the road. Caspar wisely decided to wait for them to finish crossing, and then resumed his own journey, much to Dusty's satisfaction. The dog had been very eager to try and greet the bears, but Caspar had held him back with a gentle tug, and the old hound had obeyed faithfully.

For several hours they traversed the ancient road, seeing all sorts of similar sights; here there were chattering squirrels, there a group of fidgeting starlings, and in the distance there was a river being dammed by a beaver family. Honey-bees darted about, seeking flowers for their colony in the warm spring weather, and another bear was seen in the distance. At long last, Caspar could discern a sight of smoke far off to the right in the distance; it was not the smoke of something burning, but the smoke of a chimney, as he knew well from living in Idoma. Was this--of course! It was Cloverdell, one of the old monastic communities. Isolated out of religious necessity, they nevertheless welcomed passersby, as many of the Monastic Orders would do. Cloverdell had not been heard from in a long while; since the invasion, more or less, and it had been assumed that they had either moved on or died out; it seemed, however, that they had simply become more independent and self-sufficient, not needing to rely on the Crown or the Duke for their needs.

The overgrown road and forest about it had most certainly helped in such regards, Caspar could not but note, and as he drew closer his suspicions were confirmed; Cloverdell was alive and well. He reached the gate, and the porter welcomed him in cheerily. Elvar was led to the stables by a novice, and Caspar himself, along with Dusty, was led to a room for the night. He suddenly found it odd that the monastery was but two days' riding away from Idoma, and began to wonder about the monks and their community; was it truly so free of its need for neighbors who supported them that they had not been heard from in over twenty years? It was not until the evening that he received an answer to his bursting questions, and saw that the repast being laid out for supper was fair but sparse. They were not as self-sufficient as he had been thinking. He looked up at the abbot, and nodded his thanks as their prayers concluded. "Father, forgive my ignorance; why have you not journeyed for aid before now?" Caspar asked as they began eating, and the abbot wearily shrugged.

"We were not certain that the danger had passed, and we remain unconvinced; unless you have a tale that says otherwise?" the abbot told him.

"The village of Idoma on the edge of Murana Day is but a two-day journey."

"On the Forsaken Road, yes. We dare not risk it without knowing for certain if there is no danger." the older man told him, and the other monks murmured assent.

"Only the beasts stand between you and friends." Caspar said in reply.

"Then perhaps we may try."

"Twenty years is a long time, Father Abbot."

"Indeed, my son." the man returned. Caspar was about to speak again, but suddenly he felt at a loss for words; he resumed a tactful silence until a few more minutes had passed, and then spoke again.

"Will I owe you anything for a night's lodging, Father?" he asked.

"Nay, child. Be welcome, and when you leave, we will give you a blessing on the way as you journey on." the man smiled, and Caspar nodded. The rest of their meal passed in silence, and Caspar headed up to his room later in the evening, falling asleep to the sounds of night about him.

***

In the morning, Caspar felt a sudden chill, and stirred awake in confusion; he was on the cold hard floor of the monastery... the ruined monastery... it was all in ruins, and Dusty was in a curled up position just next to him. The horse was grazing below them; but how...? How, what, when? What was going on, Caspar wondered to himself as he stood up; Dusty got up as well, the dog whining in confusion as they looked about for a way down. There were the steps, the stone stairs that he had come up somehow or another in the night; they were mostly intact, save for a short jump at the bottom. He nodded to Dusty, and the two of them headed down this.

Feeling an urge to know what happened, Caspar spent most of the morning exploring, finding two old and weathered books, one of them seemingly touched by fire and the other gnawed upon by some tiny animal. He gingerly placed them in one of the saddlebags, and when he was satisfied that there was nothing more he rode on, still wondering what sort of spectres had given him lodging last night. Again he took to his lute, strumming a somewhat melancholy tune as he traversed the old and weathered road.

Cloverdell, Cloverdell; what fate has befallen thee?
Majestic, regal, holy place; a haven for all to be
Cloverdell, Cloverdell; what fate befell thee, Cloverdell?
Did the dark hordes of the Sorcerer King
Come even unto thee?

Oh! Monastery in the woods beyond Murana Day
Wondrous, friendly, ever-kind, a refuge along the way
What fate washed o'er thee, oh, Cloverdell?
Where have you gone and why did you not
Call thy closest friends for aid?

Cloverdell, ah, Cloverdell!
What fate upon thee, Cloverdell?
The dark hordes of the Sorcerer King we see
Within the mischief in thy walls, once proud
The haven lost, the peaceful refuge gone
Alas! Dear old Cloverdell!

And so on and on he sang, composing a lament for the ruined monastery and its long-gone monks; wherever they had gone, he wished them well--and if they had died, well, then, may they be at peace with death. He travelled all through the day and most of the night, and at the end of the day following that night he reached a small hunter's outpost, where he performed for his night's rest among those who were living. Whatever he had encountered in the ruins of Cloverdell, he dared not to try and name it: for they had been, after all, a most benevolent group of spectres, and he told no living soul for quite some time about his encounter at the ancient place. He did, however, glance at the last written pages of one of the books he had recovered; it was an older dialect of his native tongue, but he could still read it. *The dark hordes of Malachon have come. We are preparing to flee, but we may not have time; may grace see us through, so that we may live to begin anew either here or somewhere far-off. The bells ring; I have no time.* Thus read the last few words written within it; Malachon... Malachon... who was Malachon, Caspar wondered as he fell into slumber, and was he related to the Sorcerer King?

Such thoughts were banished from his mind in sleep; he dreamed of a ship, a ship not so grand or majestic as those in the harbor of Murana Day, but a magnificent one nevertheless; he was sailing, sailing on this ship to who knew where. There was someone in the lookout post, and a Werecat at the helm; a Werecat? What did it mean? And where was his usual dream-companion, the one he had become accustomed to seeing in the random thoughts of night? But no: this was not her forest, this was the sea.

Caspar... a voice called. He turned, and there she was: Evelyn.

Chapter Five: Who Mourns for Alastria?

On the morning after Evelyn had ran off from the village, Mala, having grown quite impatient with trying to call for her to join breakfast, headed up the stairs to knock on her door. There was no response. Again she knocked, and then a third time; when a fourth, combined with the calling of Evelyn's name, failed to evoke a response, she opened the door and found the room tidied and its occupant nowhere in sight. Alarmed, Mala at once called for the scouts, and they came running to her, along with the prince and his guards. Prince Thadolin looked at the matriarch's features with concern as he took in her seeming fright, and at once asked what was the matter.

"Our Lady Evelyn has gone, disappeared, vanished! She is not in her room, my lord, and I do not know where she has gone." Mala told him.

"Then I shall not impede thee; but I shall have my guards assist thee in thy search." he said to her in reply, and she nodded.

"Very good, my lord." Mala replied, and she resumed giving orders to her scouts; the prince, knowing which direction Evelyn had taken, told his guards to search towards the north and west, while Mala's scouts headed towards the east. Thus the south would remain unchecked, and Evelyn could flee as she would.

***

It was late evening on that same day when Evelyn at last stopped for rest, having all but exhausted herself on the long run from Mala's village to the outlying trees that remained from the great Forest of Alastria. They were tall, taller than even the tallest of trees that man has ever seen or known, and not a branch protruded from them until their crowning heights far above the ground below; their bark was golden in appearance, and the leaves were similarly shaded and tinged, ever present upon the trees through all seasons and weather. The Forest of Alastria had been named for the first Elven Queen, who had, with her mate, retired from the throne some thousands of years ago to seek the Land of the Ever Young. Thus did all Elves travel when they wearied of life in the mortal planes, seeking to find a land as eternal as they were.

Now, in the present day, only a few examples of all these trees remained, and here in the place where Evelyn took her rest there were but seven.

As Evelyn took in their size, she began thinking again about all the traditions and ritual courtesies and graces that she had been taught to adore and respect; it was not that she did not, but how could one cling to the past, when the past was fading away? Was it not time to try and build a new thing from the ashes of the old? Or would the Elves, like their forest, be content to remain in stagnation until only isolated pockets remained of a once beautiful people, until the last of them were wiped out by a new resurgence of some unknown enemy? These thoughts went through her mind as she pulled out a book to read for the night; it was an old tome of plays, philosophy plays from the golden years of Elvendom. Evelyn randomly flipped through the pages, and settled on one in particular that caught her eyes.

> *Alonzo: And what, pray tell, wouldst thou have me to be?*
> *Canst thou not guarantee but the smallest part of*
> *satisfaction, shouldst I incline mine self to thy whims?*
>
> *Rafael: Alas, cousin! Thinkest thou not of what dreams*
> *might be, if only thou wert not so stubborn in thine*
> * refusals! Yon maiden is of beauty unsurpassed,*
> *and thou wilst not give her one glance!*
>
> *Alonzo: Love, cousin, is not some knowledge*
> *learned and known--nay! That is respect,*
> *trust, and mayhaps adoration;*
> *but love, pure love; thou canst not measure it*
> *but as a sudden happening,*
> *a feeling beyond all feelings.*
> *One doth not learn it,*
> *save perhaps when it is already there,*
> *and thou learnest to grow in it, but never to*
> *learn how to have it, or when to have*
> *it. The best of fealty is but a learned respect;*
> *canst thou reasonably expect me to love,*
> *where no passion for love comes forth?*
>
> *Rafael: I see that I wert mistaken in mine persuasions;*
> *thou lovest a commoner better than one of thine*
> *own noble blood; but thinkest thou of thy duties;*
> *thy weighty responsibilities as*

our king-to-be: nay! Refuse me not mine counsel
in this matter; thou shouldst be the greatest of fools,
shouldst thou not heed my words. And wouldst thou
be in our ancient texts recorded as one
who destroyed all Elvendom for the love of a
common maiden?

Alonzo: Thou damned, damned fiend! Thinkest thou
my love lieth in a state of concupiscence? I shalt not
brook thy insults cousin! Thou thyself shouldst take the
throne, and leave me to my love, my true love!

Rafael: O! What folly we weave, mine cousin; what folly
brooks our hearts! Wouldst thou spurn noble blood for a
seeming noble cause? But what dignity, what integrity,
wilt thou have left to thee in such a thing as thou
proposest to me?

Alonzo: I hath the integrity of knowing that I didst not
betray she whom I love with truth.

Rafael: Indeed!

Alonzo: And the dignity to do so of mine own free will,
laying aside the crown to one more qualified and more
interested in its vestments than ever I could pretend to be!
Thinkest thou not such an idea a fair exchange, or
wouldst thou have me beholden to slavery of ideology?

Rafael: Then love thy maiden! Go, begone with thee! I
shalt take the throne, as thou wishest me to do; but I
banish thee, I banish thee and thy love
from Elvendom forever!

Alonzo: Cruel, damnable Rafael! One moment thou
sayest this, and the next moment thou sayest aught else!
Be damned thy throne; but I shall have love, and thou
shalt see which of us twain shall live the longer in these
wretched mortal plains!

(Exit Alonzo; Rafael looks after him scorningly, pacing
about before resuming a soliloquy-stance)

Rafael: Thou sayest it, then;
let the throne be damned, and so
it shall when its rightful king passes by its charge; thou
condemneth all our history, Alonzo! Spurnest thou all our
heritage, all our tradition--for love! Love--pah! Flights of
fancy for fools who have not one drop of blood accounted
rightful to rule! And when thou seest me in mine
magnificence, and thou art but a squalling insect in some
netherland, remembrest thou that I did warn thee!
Yea, verily, I warned thee
that thou shouldst never be content
with love, when thou wert born to be a king! Fool, fool
Alonzo! Be thou content in thy fantasies, and I shalt be
content with thy heritage! Hail, hail, King Rafael of the
Silver Crown! Ha ha ha! A true king shall reign this day,
and nevermore shalt our crown go to fools who spurn our
ways for whims unbecoming a noble! Fair maiden,
I come now to thee!

(Exit Rafael; scene-change to palace gardens; enter
Alonzo and Mia)

Mia: Thinkest thou thy course wisest? That we shouldst
be wed, outcast among our people for all time?

Alonzo: If we are but the only outcasts of our day,
daring to show our people what could be
if they wouldst but dare,
then I shalt count it not a loss, but a gain, O Mia!
Precious Mia! Darest thou to stay with me, now that
cruel Rafael hast the crown?

Mia: I dare, Alonzo; I dare to face all the dangers of life
with thee, beside thee forever,
until the world spins upon itself
again, and all that folk hold dear
shalt come crashing down
in ruin! Only let our love be complete;
givest thou thy hand to me!

Rafael: I givest thou more;
I gift to thee all of myself! Now
come, let us away; let us away,

and make our abode in some
brighter corner of the world,
far beyond the petty prejudices
of our people, that they might see
how foolish they are,
and so remember us!
Ah, Mia, how I love thee!

Mia: And O, Alonzo! How I love thee! Let us away, away!

(Exit Mia and Alonzo)

As Evelyn read, she could not help but notice that the play was slighted to favor those who opposed the view of the two lovers; the play ended with their lives in tragedy, while Rafael and his queen outlived them, and counted them as both a great loss and a loss insignificant, for having dared to do what none dared to do, but all for the sake of defying tradition. Suddenly aware that the whole of the book was filled with plays and morality tales about adhering to tradition and customs, Evelyn was filled with disgust, and she buried the book under one of the great trees that bordered her shelter for the night. She fell asleep some time after, watching the moons as they made their ever-cyclic trek through the vast field of uncountable stars.

***

In the morning, Evelyn again broke into a run, desiring to put as much distance as she could between herself and her people before another day ended. Her light and lithe form made no imprint on the ground as she ran, and with ease she crossed through open meadows as the woods gave way to a more grassy domain; there were still trees here and there, but nothing so entangling as a forest. Ancient stone buildings also dotted the landscape here and there, and Evelyn caught herself wondering on several occasions as to who had lived in them. She stopped at a rather large one near midday, a building that seemed to have been a castle or a monastery of some sort; a tall tower still proudly stood in one corner, though it was badly ruined and weathered. A carved stone caught her eyes, and she gingerly brushed off a layer of grime and dirt to see what it was; it was an inscription, a dedication stone. *Memorus Exactumono Bateo Nixum Deutoraneum.* "In the grand memory of his Royal Highness the Duke of Aneum." it read; it was an ancient tongue, a tongue that both Elves and Men knew and which had evolved into the common speech now known by all races. But that was not terribly important to Evelyn at the moment; what fascinated her was the discovery of this being, in fact, a castle. She looked around at the ruined citadel-fortress, trying to imagine what it must have looked like before; was it an ancient ruin, or was it something else that had been massacred in the Invasion? But nay; there were no marks of fire or blasting upon the stones. There was, however, a massive graveyard just beyond the castle walls; wondering if the stones there held any clues, she ventured towards it, and examined the inscriptions. It was the fifth that held what she wanted. *Maximonus; Piace Respitus; Gortem Nos Voxumus; Virplagus.* "Here lies Max, at peace forever, slain by that which torments us all: the Plague." A plague. A plague! This was one of the ancient plague villages; suddenly horrified, Evelyn raced out of the place as fast as she could, and when she came at last to a river she at once stripped down to bathe, fearing lest she should have been infected by something left behind.

When she had finished bathing, she lay upon the grass beside her things, waiting to dry off before resuming her trek. Animals were the only thing that came near her, gazing upon her with interest as they passed by. After an hour, she was mostly dry, and she began putting on a fresh tunic; when this was on, and her boots were laced up, she forded across the river to resume her journey. *And where am I going?* She wondered to herself as she continued on at a slower pace than before; where indeed was she going? Men were in the south, but how far south? If any maps of the wide world had existed at all, they had been lost in the Invasion; now, all she had were stories and legends, legends of knights and great castles, monks cloistered in hallowed monastery grounds, wandering bards who would sing or make love at the drop of a hat, and the vagabonds who dwelt in the forests or upon the seas, the outlaws and pirates that earned their reputations by instilling fear.

Such thoughts filled her mind with questions, and she puzzled and puzzled over them again and again as she kept walking, not noticing when she kept walking on in the gloaming dark of night. The stars and moons gave her light for her journey, and when dawn broke forth again she was still travelling; it was at noontide again when she suddenly realized how far and how long she had been walking, and she let out a soft groan at the realization. Evelyn hurried over to a dense patch of underbrush, hiding herself away for a rest as the day wore on. Upon waking, she ate a quick meal to restore herself, and then resumed her trek across the wide world. Mountains of a majestic purple color rose up before her, not so towering as those where the Dwarves came from, but mountains nonetheless; did other kinds of peoples live in such mountains? And where they friendly, or were they hostile? She looked towards the east and the west; the mountains stretched on as far as she could see. There was no circumventing their passes. Evelyn allowed herself a wry smile, and then prepared herself for whomever or whatever lay in their reaches.

***

"It appears, Lady Mala, that the Lady Evelyn is nowhere to be found." the scout said in a regretful tone. The matriarch grimly nodded, then dismissed him and his fellows as Thadolin and his own knights came up.

"Thou hadst better have better news than yon scouts." she said to him.

"Forgeteth thou thy place in mine presence?" Thadolin said to her darkly, and Mala let out a sigh, relenting.

"Forgive me. I am old, and wearied with frivolous flights of fancy such as hath betaken my Evelyn to their bosom."

"Think nothing of it, Lady. But we hath no trace of her either, I regret. If she went in another direction, it is now too late to try and search for her, even if our kind are not so weary as the mortal races." the prince said, and she nodded.

"Thou speakest truly. Sorry I am that thou hast had thy hopes dashed here, prince; I hope that thou will overlook this, and forgive me for it."

"It is already forgiven. But I must away, for now I must prepare to court another; I bid thee farewell." Thadolin said, saluting her in the ancient manner of Elven Royalty, and she made a return gesture as the prince rode off to gather his company.

Wretched girl! Mala thought to herself. *All these years I kept thee safe; now thou hast spurned thy own kin for a foolish man! May the curse of Alonzo and Mia bite thee all the way!* She swore silently, and then shook her head. *Nay... nay, forgive me... do not curse them... bless them, and may the change they wish to make endure, so that it might be learned from.* Mala said to the unseen spirits in repentance of her harsh words, and then sighed, getting up to prepare an evening meal before Thadolin rode for home.

***

The mountains, it seemed, were further away than their appearance had suggested, for it took most of the rest of that day and some of the night to reach their foothills. Upon reaching them, Evelyn found what seemed to be a well-used cart path off to her left; deciding that it was perhaps best to follow this instead of aimlessly trekking across the mountain sides, she made for it at once, following it as it led upwards in a somewhat winding manner towards a gap between the peaks of the nearest mountains.

As she got further up into the heights of the winding path, she began to notice there were signs, signs that pointed in one direction or another alongside the path she now walked; examining one of these,

Evelyn found that the path she was on led towards a small village in the cleft of these two mountains. It was named as Riverdell, and from the language and script she assumed it was a village of men. Was it possible that Caspar was here? Or that he had been? She could not know, but she dared to hope, and she ran at a faster pace along the path; a few hours later, the town of Riverdell lay before her.

It was alive and well, a small community that seemed to be centered around a large structure of wood and stone; who dwelt here, she wondered, and did they know of a young man named Caspar? Evelyn looked back towards whence she had come from; one small pang of regret welled up inside her for a brief moment, and she then tossed it aside, disdaining her ritualistic people one last time before continuing on with her self-appointed odyssey; if the Forest of Alastria and its people were content to stay in the past, then let them. Who would mourn for who, when the years passed at long last, and the forest was but a memory?

Chapter Six: Roaming Gnome

Caspar was once again roaming alone, heading up the faded north road despite the warnings of the hunters he had lodged with the night before. All the "villages" in these regions were small hunter's posts that were connected to some larger village further away to the east or the west; no one dared to traverse the haunted road unless it were the knights of some noble or another, men who feared nothing. Brushing off the superstitious nonsense as just that, Caspar rode along at a merry pace, and Dusty trotted happily along side him, listening to his master play away with one instrument or another as they traversed the road.

Now he sang a shanty; next he sang of an outlaw band that riled the magistrate of a certain town; then he sang of a glorious king in an epoch of legends; he piped a jig, and the dog began to howl along as the instrument let loose its droning hums; turning to his harp, he played a more melancholy tune as he slowed the horse to a walk, and when the tune then turned to a livelier melody, they began to pick up their pace once more. They passed along like this for the day, and then for a second day, heedless of any that might seek to cause him grief. As far as he was concerned, the only other one that was travelling about the wide world was Evelyn, seeking him out as he sought her, and thus his confidence in travelling what some around now called the "haunted road".

> *Says I to the villain, to the villain says I, I says*
> *"Bedraggle thee! Flound'ring wretch" I says, says I;*
> *"And betake thee to a better master!"*
> *Says he to me, he says to me, says he, he says*
> *"I've the sea to see, ye see," he says to me, your man*
> *says he, he says to me*
>
> *Hey-nonny-no! And away we go!*
> *Riddle me this, rime me that*
> *Your man says to me, says he to me, he says, says he*
> *"I've the sea to see, ye see," says he to me, your man*

to me, he says, says he

And the one with the nut-brown hair!
And her sparkling sapphire eyes!
Whereupon, my lady, whereupon
Shall I compare thee to a summer's day?
Nay, nay, not I!

More lovely, more beautiful, and more
Full of warmth and mirth's delight!
Joyously we sing to thee!
Dear lady of the green-gabled hills
Of yestre'eve!

And other such nonsense as Caspar was wont to sing poured forth from his lips as he sang; he could make a spectacle of any of his songs, and make it so delightful to listen to that you soon forgot that most of it was nonsensical. He was just putting his harp away to bring out his lute once more, when upon a sudden he heard a most cantankerous noise, a noise that sounded as if someone had jumbled several instruments into one horrifying blasphemy of an instrument, a near heresy insofar as the musical world was concerned. Bells were jingling, the sound of a drum being beaten could be heard, cymbals were crashing, and several reed-instruments and whistles were going off at random intervals in astounding dissonance with each other.

Then, as if the sound was not enough, the instrument itself loomed into view; the pitiful amalgamation of instruments was cluttered together on a wheeled contraption being pedaled along by--a Gnome!

Caspar blinked twice, and then rubbed his eyes. Yes, it was indeed a Gnome. The pointy red hat was bent in its middle, hanging foppishly to one side as the diminutive creature pedaled his monstrosity with much exertion, stopping as he noticed a fellow traveller upon the road. To Caspar's relief, the noise also stopped, and he dismounted to greet the creature.

"Hello hello helloo!" the Gnome said as it jumped off and ran forward to greet him. "I am Percy Von Daumer, a Gnome of distinct and honorable repute! And who be you, a fellow traveller as bold as I upon a road that none seem to favor?"

"Hello, Percy." Caspar said as he knelt down so that they could look each other in the eyes (more or less). "I'm Caspar, a wandering minstrel." he added as they shook hands.

"By gads! A fellow musicant! Tell me, what think you of my latest and greatest?" the Gnome said, gesturing towards the contraption he was riding.

"Well..." Caspar said in a tone that suggested criticism without outright disdaining the thing.

"Ah, of course, of course. It needs improvement. I see your point. But I've nothing for it, now... all my grants have run out. To tell the truth, I do have a distinct repute, but not the one I so desired; it is the repute of being a fool, and all my imaginative genius that I might try elsewhere now has nowhere to go." the Gnome said again, and Caspar nodded. The poor fellow was an outcast, shunned by his brethren for being too outlandish--even for them. Never mind that; he might have other talents about him. Gnomes were, after all, an imaginative and inventive race, a people widely known for their intellect and ingenuity across the wide world, never mind their oddities. Was this Gnome sent his way by some quirk of fate, that they might find a place where they both belonged? There was, at least, a way to see if he would be of assistance, and it was with this thought that Caspar subtly introduced his next words to the diminutive figure.

"And to tell the truth, I'm on a quest, Sir Percy." Caspar said to grab his attention, and at once the Gnome perked up.

"Eh? What's that? Quest? Dangerous? Marvelous? Damsels and dragons? Mysteries and long travels?" Percy chattered back, and Caspar nodded.

"Oh, yes. Long travels indeed; I am seeking an Elven-maiden, and I know not where to go, save where the heart leads me." he said, and Percy nodded back at once.

"Understandable, understandable." he agreed. "Well... I do also happen to have a fine collection of maps... rare treasures... couldn't part with them though." the Gnome said, and Dusty let out a whine. "Although..." Percy added, giving his contraption a wry glare, "I could be of a mind to leave this poor thing behind and join with you, if you'd care for company upon the road?" he said to the young man, who smiled at him.

"I wouldn't dream of parting you from your maps, Sir Percy. Come with me if it suits your fancy, and let us see what we can see!" the young man said to him, pleased that his subtlety had borne fruit. *Now* he could get somewhere, perhaps, and be that much closer to finding Evelyn.

"A most agreeable pact! Consider me signed on, Lord Caspar!" the Gnome said in a cheery air, and went to grab his more pertinent belongings, including the maps, from his invention. When he was mounted up in front of Caspar, they began riding off at a steady pace, and Caspar gave a look at the odd musical contraption once more.

"Are you sure you can just leave that?" he wondered, hoping the answer was yes but not wanting to offend the Gnome by simply walking by it.

"Ha! Who's going to bother it? A bird? A squirrel?" Percy quipped back. "Nay; only a fellow Gnome would give thought to trying to take it." he added, and Caspar accepted this. At once Percy began looking through his maps, trying to get a bearing on where they were.

"Now... Elves, is it... that's very far north... across the Bay of Paupalousas. I suppose one could hire a ship at Mercy's Haven and sail to Auschternople... or perhaps simply take the scenic route through the western villages... if only I had my grandfather's wing-machine!" Percy chattered on as they rode along the road, and Caspar listened with amusement as he went on and on about all the possible routes one could take to try and reach the Elves.

***

After several hours of chattering on, Percy fell asleep, and Caspar grabbed up one of his maps just in time to save it from falling to earth. He looked it over; as the road went further to the north, it adjoined another that led towards the northwest. This northwest road went around the bay, on the outer edges of the principalities that lay alongside it. Deciding to stick to land for their journey, Caspar thought it prudent to keep to this road, and so perhaps come to Auschternople in about three weeks' time. From there they could perhaps barter for better supplies and transport; a waggon of some sort, perhaps... yes, a waggon might be best.

With that decided, he carefully put the map back in its owner's sack, and when he decided that it was too late at night to continue, he made for a copse of aspen and birch, making a small camp for the four of them to rest in for the remainder of that night. The Gnome was fast asleep, worn out from chattering; Caspar wondered if indeed all his race chattered on so. It was, the stories had said, their most recognizable habit--talking, that is; having now experienced it for himself, the young man was not certain of how long he might be gracious enough to endure it. *Still, I must be polite...* he reasoned to himself; *there's no sense in offending him by telling him to 'shut up' when his own people have cast him out! And what a brute I would seem, a minstrel such as I, berating a Gnome who has done me no true harm!* He continued to himself, shaking his head and resolving to be a good friend to Percy no matter how much he chattered on. And so with this determination, and the determination of his course, he fell asleep at last.

***

In the morning, Caspar awoke to the smell of hot oats, and rubbed the drowsiness from his eyes as he arose; there was Percy, tending a small fire with a pot hanging over it. It was from this pot that the scent of food was wafting from, and Caspar suddenly realized how hungry he was. The Gnome, it seemed, was at the very least a good cook--he hoped. "There you are!" Percy said as Caspar rose up. "This is almost done. I'm not my grandmother, but they always said that I was better at cooking than inventing, and in fact they insisted that I keep at it--so I have! And now here we are, a pot of oats for a morning repast!" he continued on, and Caspar smiled.

"It's a small pot for me." he said good-naturedly as he came over to sit down.

"Ah, never mind that. I'm smaller than you are; this pot is meant to feed eight Gnomes of my own size: there'll be quite enough for you, O giant!" Percy said in reply, and Caspar had to agree. The tallest Gnomes, Percy told him as they ate, were just above knee-height of Men and Elves, and the smallest were shorter than a rose-stem. All of them wore the same little hats, and they came in shades of red, green, blue, white, and orange. Rumors said that they and the Dwarves had a common origin, to which Percy himself commented upon as being "outstanding nonsense".

"Why! All Dwarves seem to think about is greed and gain, forever delving beneath mountains and hills for ores and gems to craft treasures--and for what? All to be stolen by some rival tribe, or taken from them by some dragon twice and thrice as greedy as they themselves are! We Gnomes are of a scientific mindset, eagerly delving into the arts and mechanics and studies that even Men seem to have forgotten. Though you are quite the imaginative race when you want to be! Mostly in the arts, but there we are. A fine specimen of the arts you are yourself, no doubt!" he chattered on, and Caspar smiled, nodding back.

"So dragons are real?" he wondered as they rode along; breakfast had been finished a good while ago, and they were now some miles from their campsite.

"Oh yes! Quite real. My great-great-great-grandfather's mother's third cousin's sister twice removed on my aunt's side of the family even got to see one up close, so her journal says. Of course, this dragon was quite dead, being all bones (thankfully!), but as we all know, bones had to have been something, once upon a time. It was of tremendous size; bigger than some of your ships are said to be! I'm surprised no dragons came with the Demonic Hordes of the Sorcerer King those twenty years ago. Or maybe they're not demons in a true sense of the word, merely one of the many mystical creatures that still haunt the land from primeval times."

"Are there many creatures that still live or exist from those long years ago?" Caspar wondered, genuinely intrigued at learning so much from someone who seemed to know the world better than anyone he had known did.

"Eh? Of course!" Percy remarked, nodding as they rode along. "Why, there's dragons, for starters; there's a tribe of Dwarves still afraid of going back to their mountain homes because of one that drove their ancestors out some fifty years ago. They live quite long lives, you see; some even think that they're immortal as the Elves are. And then of course there's the Centaurs and the Werecats; the Werecats are seen quite often by my people and yours--they're not so *very* much mysterious and mystical. But the Centaurs: now they dwell across the seas to the east, on a different land entirely, roaming among the steppes. Steppes are a semi-mountainous terrain; not really mountains, more among the manner of cliffs and valleys, but there we are. And besides them there's the Valkyries; they're said to have been angels, once upon a time, but they came to earth to live in a place they thought of as suitable for them, and they've lived here ever since. The sea, however, is a place of true mystery; the Merfolk or Sirens and all. Some Gnomes have tried to go and prove they exist on several occasions; not one has come back. The Scientific Coalition Council has since demanded and insisted that no Gnome ever go and try again. And then, of course, there's the Leviathan--the one primordial creature that's said to be the one and only of its kind, dwarfing dragons and whales, making them look as if they were tadpoles!" Percy told him, shaking his head as he said this. "If it makes a dragon a tadpole, then I hope I never see it!" he added.

"If something as big as a ship is so tiny next to such a creature, then I heartily agree with you, friend!" Caspar agreed.

"Quite, quite!" Percy nodded back. "But there's also far more pleasant creatures still said to roam around; Furlings, for instance. They seem to be of a bear's appearance, but they're considerably smaller and much more friendly. They're tribal primitives, for the most part, and they disdain most of the things that you and I take for granted. Something about disrupting the ancient ways of harmony and balance in nature. The Satyrs across the sea are much like them when it comes to such thinking; but they're a more warlike people. Often they battle the Centaurs; neither side really wins. It's mostly territorial disputes, from what I've heard. The Plains People that live near them hide in the woods to keep out of it. And then..." the Gnome broke off, and Caspar gave him an inquiring look when he was silent for several moments.

"Then, what?" the young man asked, and the Gnome gave him a solemn look.

"Then, my friend, we have the creatures of pure darkness. The ones that live around the lands of the Sorcerer King. Summoned back up by his vile magics to a land they repossessed as their own." Percy said softly but gravely, and Caspar blinked.

"Summoned... 'back'? 'Repossessed'? I don't understand..." he said with a nervous laugh as the sun began making its descent. Percy chuckled softly, and coughed to clear his throat.

"No, I don't suppose you would. We Gnomes, being one of the Elder Races, keep very meticulous records, and it is clear from these that those twenty years ago was not the first time the demonic hordes have been upon the face of the world. We can't say for certain how long ago it was; the records are in a very primitive Gnomish dialect-- possibly related to High Fruscasian, but there you are. But it makes it clear that the hordes were, once upon a time, just as much of a scourge then as they were twenty years' past."

"But then they can be driven back to the Fiery Hells, can they not?" Caspar said as his companion related in short what he knew of the matter.

"Oh... possibly. We don't know how it was done, however; there's a vague reference to some king or another, possibly an Elf. Couldn't have been a Gnome. Maybe an early leader of Men, but more likely an Elf. They're the eldest, next to the Giants and the Valkyries. The Giants are too daft to organize hierarchically, and the Valkyries are all female. Don't ask me how that works, I'm not a student of biology." Percy told him, and Caspar took in the words with a nod, wondering if there was something to be done about the Demonic Hordes sitting across the sea, waiting for some unknown signal to terrorize them all again. Their talk turned to more pleasant matters after a time, and when they settled in for the night they were both worn from talking all the day.

***

As the two of them travelled on the next day, they came to a part of the road that was so overgrown that it forced them to seek a way through the less dense foliage off to their left; Percy swore that it had not been so overgrown when last he had passed this way, and Caspar, in spite of his doubts, could not but trust his word--for how else could the Gnome's contraption have gotten to where they had met, if not on a (more or less) clear highway? Suddenly remembering a song he had once sang of a wizard enchanting the flowers and trees and bushes to grow and grow until they concealed his tower, Caspar became very alert, wondering if there was indeed some mischievous magic at work. When he told his suspicions to Percy, the Gnome began excitedly chattering in a soft tone, going on and on about historical wizards and the various enchantments or spells they had cast; wizards were mostly humans, but there were occasional Werecats or Elves that took up the magic arts, as well as the increasingly rare Dwarf acolytes. Some wizards could summon great storms of weather, blanketing an area in snow or rain or hail, along with great and booming thunders and spectacular lightnings; others preferred elemental magics, dealing with fire and wind and water, casting cold blasts of icy air, or drowning an area in water, or summoning up a fiery chasm from the deeps of the earth; still more dealt with animals, enchanting the beasts to do all sorts of things for them (one wizard, Percy said, had even enchanted a school of fish); and there were yet more that dealt in various branches of other wild magics throughout the land. "Now it must be remembered," Percy went on, "that not *all* magic users are strictly wizards--that's a very common misconception to most; why, the Valkyries use magic, and they're certainly not wizards. And then in regards to the other races you have different kinds of magic users: sorcerers, for example--they're a sort of 'black-arts' wizard: whereas a wizard will seek to perhaps improve life around him, sorcerers seek to dominate; they're often found delving into the arts of the warlocks, such as the infamous Sorcerer King, who summoned up demons from the Great Fire. Then you have necromancers, those who deal with the arts of death, summoning up corpses and skeletons, delving into secrets of poisons and such; and then you have witches and hags--all female, of course, just as the songs say, and just as tumultuously unpredictable in what they do and to whom. And then of course you have the druids, in your own Order of Cassandra, those who deal with nature in all its aspects."

"So they say, but I've never met one." Caspar said to Percy as they continued on.

"Never met a druid? Hm! Well, I mean, I suppose that may be expected--they're all a bunch of secretive folk, magic users, that is. Not too keen on forming friendships save inside their own little groups, because most seem to misunderstand or misrepresent them, you see." Percy said in reply, and Caspar considered this thought.

"I suppose that's true." he allowed. "For my own part, I try to give them respect in the songs: unless of course they're the villain, in which case it's expected of me to cast them in either a comic or a distasteful light."

"And thus the disparagement between bards and magic users." the Gnome chuckled.

"How *do* you know so much, anyway? You're very well-versed on nearly anything we bring to mind; are all Gnomes so studious?" Caspar wondered at him.

"Why of course!" Percy said at once. "Some more, some less, but on average we all know quite a good deal about more than one might expect; not to insult the other races by any means, but none of you (save perhaps the Elves, and to an extent, your own kind) seem to have the grasp of or the knack for being a studious people. We Gnomes go through rigorous educations to pass into our trade and vocation schools, never mind universities or other great centers of learning. Not that there isn't dissonance in regards to such policies, but for the most part, the Gnomish folk are proud of their educators and students; it's our niche, you see. And we're driven by the need to know and to study; philosophy, philology, history, biology, psychology, cartography, topography, geology, geography, ecology, economy--well, in short, anything that can be studied, quantified, or observed in one manner or another. And as we get older, we become more specialized in a field of our liking. When one's wants are simply the desire to obtain knowledge, it becomes easier to live life; we're not hindered by greed or grasping for gain, we simply like to know things: and if it leads to a success or an adventure, well, then, that's all a happy byproduct!" he said, and Caspar took in this last sentence thoughtfully.

"So the Gnomes have never really taken sides in any of the great conflicts? Or gotten involved in something they might think of as frivolous or wasteful?" he asked, and Percy raised an eyebrow.

"Say rather that our ambitions, insofar as we have them, are not for the base passions that most others seem to exhibit; desires for control, retribution, wealth, and luxury never had a place in Gnomish culture. We're too concerned with trying to benefit society with knowledge. Not to say that there hasn't been the occasional 'black-sheep', as the saying goes; but by and large those are outnumbered by those of a more polite-mindset." he amended, and Caspar nodded. By this time, they had come to a place where the foliage was lessening, and the old road became mostly visible once more. They got back on to this, and when they looked back, they both gaped in great astonishment; all the wildflowers and plants that had been in their way were now gone, and the road was clear as it could possibly be in its deterioration.

"What! By the stars, friend Gnome, I will not stay here--let us away; hie on, Elvar!" Caspar said at once, and the Gnome nodded his head as they galloped off from the scene, not once halting until it was well past dark and the strange patch of land was far, far behind them. Caspar gave one look back towards whence they had came; it may have been his imagination, spurred on by the words of the Gnome in regards to magic-users, but he would have sworn he could discern a tower far off in the distance. Were not wizards said to dwell in towers? But for now, he let the matter be, content in the knowledge that the enchanted wood was nowhere near them. Looking back at what lay before them, he could discern a small hamlet with one or two chimneys rising up in the distance. Percy was also looking at this, as well as his maps.

"Hm... yes, yes, this is on the charts... of course it is: good Gnomish cartography, yet to fail!" he chattered, more to himself than to Caspar, whom he turned to when he seemed more or less consoled by his map. "This little village is called Black Water Rapids; not *very* much here, it's more of a convenient stop on the way, as it were. An inn, a stable, a small chapel, some fishermen, a small market, and a smithy."

"That's good enough for me, friend Percy." Caspar nodded back to him, and they took to a swifter pace until they were just on the borders of the small hamlet; an archer guarding the small path into the main village eyed them curiously, but did not challenge them. A Gnome and a minstrel. Let them pass, let them pass; there would be stories and songs tonight, if the bard did not have coin!

Caspar and Percy dismounted near the stables, and allowed one of the hired hands to take Elvar in for the night, along with Dusty, whom the young man ordered to stay with the horse. The faithful hound barked once, and trotted after the stable-hand, while the minstrel himself took a brief jog to catch up to his diminutive companion, who was almost at the door of the inn. "Hold up, Percy!" he called as the Gnome reached the door; they entered together, and found a small but lively crowd. The proprietor was a woman not much older than Caspar himself, and he forgot all about Evelyn at the sight of her.

"Room for two?" she asked him as he took in her beauty, enchanted by her. He heard the question, so he thought, but all he could think of was wanting a--

"Yes, thank you, madam." Percy nodded back, looking up at Caspar and nudging him as they followed her up. "Fool human! Snap out of it!" he hissed softly, and the young man shook his head, blinking. He looked from Percy to the woman and then back again as they reached the second floor, and whispered back.

"What!" he asked.

"From our first meeting I was given to know that you seek someone--perhaps, in a romantic pursuit?" the Gnome returned candidly, and Caspar flushed as the innkeeper halted; she gestured to the room on her right with a smile, and the two of them nodded their thanks as they headed in for the night, Percy digging out three gold coins to hand her before he did so. "Much obliged!" he said to her, and she smiled again before bustling off. The Gnome shut the door, and then gave Caspar an inquiring look. For his own part, the young man returned the wry, candid stare, and then let out a sigh.

"You're right, of course. I *am* seeking Evelyn in love, and I should not have forgotten her so quickly at the sight of our hostess."

"Love is a folly more often sought than given." was all Percy said in reply, and Caspar spent the rest of the night thinking about these words.

In the morning, the keeper of the inn tried to make several passes at the young man, but Caspar was still absorbed in Percy's quip from the night before. Giving up, she resigned herself to the usual crowd, and when the Gnome and his minstrel friend left the inn she gave Caspar a very wistful look, sighing to herself as he vanished from sight. Within the next few minutes, they were on the road again, heading north into a small mountain range. Caspar fiddled idly with his lute, while Percy made notations of what he heard on some blank parchments, eager to keep a transcription of music for his musical friend, should he seek to try and return to a melody later on.

"You're right." Caspar said eventually, halting with the lute as they reached the pinnacle of a small hill. "Love should be given more than sought, for in giving it one can find it better." he said, and the Gnome raised an eyebrow, nodding.

"That's it, that's it precisely. Very good. You're not so dull of wit after all, for a mortal man." Percy returned, and Caspar smiled.

"Did you ever love anyone, friend Gnome?"

"Eh? Me? No! Not at all. Was always too busy with work; but I've heard lots and lots of philosophical discussions on the matter; all I did was repeat something that seemed particularly poignant when first I heard it. It's from 'The Matter of Romance Versus Aphrodisia', a work that was written some one-hundred and thirteen years ago by a Gnome called Pallus Rober. Quite a thinker, that one." Percy remarked hastily.

"So it's from a dialogue, a play?"

"Quite. A dialogue. Usually just read, but some will perform it as a morality play." the Gnome remarked, and then cleared his throat.

> *Jonas: But why, why, must you deny me,*
> *fairest of women?*
> *Is not my desire a desire*
> *to encompass thee entirely, beyond*
> *thy wildest dreams?*
>
> *Aquiel: Ah, foolish, foolish Jonas--*
> *thou knowest nothing of the matter at all!*
> *You prove truly the words of my father*
> *to me, that love is a folly more often sought than given;*
> *thou doth not seek to give, but to take!*
> *Thou wouldst take, and leave me*
> *barren and desperate for requited feelings!*
>
> *Jonas: Ah, but the passion, the passion! Seest thou not*

the passion in my body for thee, Aquiel, Aquiel?

Aquiel: Passion thou hast--I deny it not!--but sincerity?
Nay! Thou art a poor excuse of a man, seeking thy own
pleasure and not that of the woman you feign to love!

Percy quoted, and Caspar reflected on the words again, intrigued at hearing them in their context. They rode on in silence for a few moments after that, and Caspar eventually turned to simply plucking the strings of his lute in an idle fashion. "Ah, but what have I to give but love? Is that enough? Is that ever enough?" he wondered softly.

"Perhaps it is." the Gnome returned. "At least, that's what your tales say. Whether or not such a thing is practical, however, is quite beyond me." he added as they continued riding.

"Kings and emperors war for love; I suppose a minstrel wandering to find it is of no greater or lesser difference in the grand scheme of the wide world." Caspar shrugged.

"Now *that* is a thing which we shall have to see for ourselves." Percy returned, and then began scribing on a different parchment as he caught sight of a plant that he had never seen before, the roaming scholar in his element as he travelled with his minstrel friend.

Chapter Seven: Sword of Magus

As Evelyn got closer to the town named by the sign as Riverdell she saw that it was enclosed by a weathered palisade with a small gate that was just now being opened as dawn began to shower the earth below it with sunlight; the large structure in its midst seemed to be a manor-hall of some minor noble, and within the walls about this was a neatly-ordered town. On her right, Evelyn saw that there were some farms outside the walls, built into what seemed to be natural terraces of the hills that had been shored up by its nearby residents for better crop divisions; on her left, she could discern grazing land for various herd animals off in the distance. Two guards brought her attention back to her path as she walked up to the gate; they barred her entrance with two ancient halberds, which, upon close scrutiny, Evelyn knew to be less than a match for her skill. Still, out of courtesy and respect for them, she resigned herself to their show of authority, and held her peace as another one came up.

This one looked older than the other two, or maybe it was his great beard; it was almost grey of color, but maintained in the most part a bold and defiant black, covering his face as if he were a bear. The man crossed his arms over his chest, and spoke in the common tongue. He was clearly surprised, but did not seem over-violent, Evelyn hoped.

"By the Fabled Fountains of Algernon; what in the blazes is this? An Elf? Ha! Hi, boys, keep your eyes ope'! Well, Elf, what's it to be? Who are you that comes so bold to our little town, the domain of our lord the Earl of Riverdell?"

"I am Evelyn, a traveller." she replied to him in the same language. "I mean no harm to the people of your village; I seek only respite from the road for a night, and to trade if I may for supplies that I may need upon my way." she continued, and the man grunted, but waved his two underlings apparent to stand down their halberds. Evelyn let out a small smile, and he nodded to her as she came in the gate.

"Don't mind me asking so, Lady Elf; but there's been naught but ill coming to our gates since the Great Invasion. Safest thing would be to head to the Earl himself. He's not as suspicious or superstitious as most of these people." he said to her softly, and she nodded back at him. With that in mind, she made her way quickly to the large wood and stone manor-hall in the midst of the town. The people indeed eyed her with a suspicious look or a wary eye; some even looked as if they were frightened of her as she made her way through the little village, and she did her best not to give them continuing reasons for their suspicions or their fears. A crowd began to gather in spite of this, and when she was almost to the manor-hall they had all but surrounded her, and then a big man stepped forth; the guards about the town stood up, raising their weapons, but the big man seemed not to mind them.

"Well, well, well... an Elf-witch. Come to finish the job, hm? Come to work your dark magic upon our sovereign? Nay--not you! We'll see to you right now, before you can even try to cause trouble, how's that? Hm?" he said in a decidedly unfriendly tone.

"Hold, civilian!" one of the guards called out.

"Damn your eyes, Jacoby!" he spat back.

"Sir, I mean no one harm." Evelyn said. "Please, just let me be on my way, and--"

"Oh, it's too late for that, witch: what say, boys? Ever see an Elf-witch naked before? Well, we're going to today!" he cackled, and Evelyn readied herself for a fight as he advanced; the angry thug was almost two paces before her when upon a sudden an arrow landed at his feet. He looked up with anger, and then fell to the ground as he saw a man in rich cloth; Evelyn looked, and saw the same man. It had to be the Earl.

"Mattis, begone with you, contemptible blacksmith!" he said in a commanding voice, and the man and his fellows dispersed. The crowd dissipated, and soon all that was left before the manor-hall were Evelyn, the Earl, and some of his guards. For his own part, the Earl smiled, and set down his bow to greet her. Grateful for his intervention, she allowed him to embrace her, and from there to escort her inside. "Believe me, he's the worst of them. Unfortunately, he's also the loudest and most influential." the Earl remarked, and Evelyn smiled.

"There is no harm to me, Lord Earl." she returned.

"Please, my name is Jeremias." the Earl said to her.

"As you wish, Earl Jeremias." Evelyn said again, and he smiled.

"As you like it, Lady Elf."

"Call me Evelyn, Lord Earl."

"Lady Evelyn, then; what a pair we make and naught but a few words are between us!" he said cheerily, and she laughed as two guards opened the door to let them inside. The interior of the manor-hall was resplendent with objects and decorations that seemed to suit the quality of the land about them; here was a tapestry on one wall; across from it was a wall of shields; the antlers of great beasts filled in intermittent spaces, and some had been turned into a great chandelier that hung from the ceiling; torches also lined the walls, and candles sat upon richly carved tables that were surrounded by cushioned chairs or benches; a stained glass window was situated behind the Earl's throne, depicting a scene of knights and a castle, with four coat-of-arms in the four corners; and all of this was but the great hall of the manor. Above, Evelyn could see a walkway that lined the upper area of the manor-hall; the stairs leading up were now behind them, and she wondered what the rooms of this place were like. A third floor could be discerned, and just above this was yet a fourth; had it been this big from the outside? It must have been, else how could it be so on the inside? Evelyn felt herself being seated, and almost blushed when she realized she was being seated at the right hand of the Earl.

"But, sir! Don't you have a--" she began to protest.

"A wife?" he asked her, and Evelyn nodded. "Nay; she is gone, dead these long years. Now all I have is my daughter." he said solemnly, and she bowed her head.

"Forgive me."

"There is naught to forgive; you could not know. I don't imagine even the Elves were immune to the tragedy in that great upheaval." Jeremias remarked softly, and Evelyn shook her head.

"No... we were not." she said, and he smiled as his daughter came to join them.

"There you are! You were right, as usual; and here she is, just as you said." the Earl said to his daughter, and Evelyn blinked. The Earl's daughter smiled back at her, nodding.

"So surprised at us mortals, never dreaming to think we could be more than simply fragile or errant fools; I am a seer, friend Elf, and I saw you coming before you touched the foot of the mountains. My name is Hannah. And you are Evelyn." the blonde girl smiled, and Evelyn let out a smile in return.

"Fools, no; errant, perhaps; fragile? It is no boast to say that most of the other races are more hardy than Men, is it not so?" she said in return.

"You say truly." the Earl nodded.

"Perhaps." Hannah allowed.

"So if you are a seer, then do you know why I am travelling?" Evelyn wondered. The other girl smiled back mischievously.

"I only see that which is relevant to our little corner of the world. Your journey is your own; all I see is that part of it which lies here, in these mountains." Hannah told her.

"Hmm." the Elf remarked.

"Though it *is* rather unusual to see an Elf at all, especially in these days. What *does* bring you south from the Forest of Alastria?" Earl Jeremias wondered, and Evelyn smiled faintly.

"I seek a young man; yes, a mortal man, and one who has desired to win my heart." she told them, and the Earl raised his eyebrows, but his daughter smiled.

"Does he have a name? Or is it a face only?" she asked.

"His name is Caspar." Evelyn returned, and the girl looked at her father, who shook his head.

"Caspar is not a name in these regions; it is a southern one, far to the south of that still great city where the last great king resides: Auschternople." the Earl told her, and Evelyn felt her heart sinking. He then laughed, and she looked at him with a look of confusion as he did so. "Ah! Forgive me. The absurdity of what I am hearing--nay, nay, I know you mean truth; but after all these long years, and all the differences between us--ha ha ha! Oh, do forgive me!" he said as he continued chuckling, and Evelyn gave him a bemused smile.

"I'm not familiar with that much of history; was there blood between our races?" she asked him, and when he had finished laughing, he grew solemn. The Earl nodded towards the old tapestry on the wall, and Evelyn looked at it again.

"You see that, dear lady? Over four-hundred years old it is; it tells the tale of the last person who tried to win the heart of an Elf: it was a lady, a young woman, who fell in love with an Elven prince. Prejudices shot up at once, and there was a great war between the two families involved; the two lovers eventually retreated to a village of men far to the north, near the Dwarven borders, but not within them. There they lived happily for quite some time, until one day a Dwarf betrayed their location to the Elves in exchange for gems and treasures. That village was burned to the ground by the Elves, and the two lovers tied to a stake in its midst so that they and their child not yet born would be killed by it. A greater war broke out soon after, and there was bad blood 'twixt Elf, Man, and Dwarf for many long years, until it brooded down to the solemn but still perceptible rage that exists today." he said, and Evelyn felt her heart sink again; would her love for this man cause more death? "I trust, dear lady, that you are not of noble rank?" he asked, and at once she let her hair fall over her face, obscuring her reaction. Hannah put a hand on her father's arm, and said something to him in their own language; it was rhythmic to Evelyn's ears, and almost guttural, but it retained a near musical quality to it. "Never mind that, then." the Earl then said. "You are my guest, and we have dinner being readied as we speak; now, bards!" Earl Jeremias commanded, and a merry troupe of troubadours sprang out, their lively colored costumes and richly ornamented instruments a sight to behold; at once they launched in to an impromptu series of ballads, reels, and waltzes, continuing on as the night's repast was brought forth. Evelyn could not remember even her own people celebrating in so lively a fashion as these did, and was genuinely happy as they made merry throughout the evening; when she went to rest, she did so with a smile, contented with how her night had been and wondering how far Caspar had gotten in his own travels.

***

In the morning, Evelyn woke to find herself in a room that was as lively decorated as the hall below it; forgetting where she was for a few moments, she blinked in confusion until it came back to her. She was in Riverdell, in the manor-hall. Quickly she jumped out of bed, and went to the prepared bath down the hall; after bathing, Evelyn hurried back to her own room, and put on a fresh long-tunic before heading down the stairs to find the Earl and his daughter at the table. The morning meal was just being served, and the Earl greeted her amicably as she came to sit with them. "I trust the night was spent well?" he inquired after she was seated.

"Yes, Earl Jeremias, very well indeed." she told him, and he nodded back.

"Good, good." he said, and the three of them then turned to the repast laid out before them, focused upon its bounty for some time until the Earl broke the silence yet again. "There is aught we must confess to thee, Lady Elf; as my daughter has said, she knows of your path through these mountains, and it is that passage of your journey that concerns us. Hannah has told me that you are to find an artifact, a precious artifact indeed--one that is meant to be with you until your journey's end." he told her, and Evelyn gave him a bemused smile.

"Lord Earl, my journey's end will be with Caspar in some remote place where we will being harm to no one." she told him. "You speak as if that is not the end of the road for us."

"Who knows the way of such things?" the Earl returned. "But Hannah has never been wrong; though the words themselves often do not find their full meaning as might be expected. It is oft noted that those who try to avoid a fate end up fulfilling it most inadvertently; may it not be such a drastic and unpleasant experience for you as it oft is for those in the songs."

"And exactly what will I find, Lady Hannah?" Evelyn asked the young lady, who took a sip of her drink before answering.

"Farther along this road is a monastery; I am headed there this noon, I can take you to it if you desire. The monastics once guarded an ancient weapon, the Sword of Magus, a powerful mage from long, long ago." she began, and Evelyn recognized the name "Magus"; he was indeed a most powerful wizard--said to be more powerful than even the Sorcerer King. "But, some forty and eight years ago, the sword was stolen by a thief, and the thief, it is reported, was slain by a great and terrible creature which no man truly knows of, save that it is vile, strong beyond belief, wretched beyond compare, and wicked beyond understanding; the sight is said to drive mortals mad, and let even the Elves and other immortals take care in its presence!" she added, and Evelyn gazed at her curiously.

"It is this sword you believe I am to find? The sword of a man more powerful than he who has no known name, the Sorcerer King who lies across the sea, through the dark forests and beyond the dreaded wastelands?" Evelyn asked her, and she nodded as her father chuckled.

"No known name? Verily; I heard he had none indeed--though a rumor told to us by a merchant caravan from the south say he was once a monastic." the Earl remarked.

"What sad irony!" Evelyn exclaimed.

"Indeed."

"The sword awaits you, but so does the monster." Hannah said softly, and Evelyn then frowned. How had the sword come to be here in the first place, in these more northerly regions of the continent called Argorro by the races who dwelt here? Was not Magus a man of the far, far south, where the name "Caspar" was a name? She voiced this thought aloud, and the Earl then answered.

"Magus was a great wizard of the southern lands, but he came north, and, eventually, he turned from his magics and founded the monastery that is now but a day's riding from our little village. There his sword remained, an almost obscure artifact in a remote corner of the world. It is a miracle that these heights were spared the hordes, or else the monster may have inadvertently revealed it to our enemies! But now the sword remains in its grasp, if it lives still, and its hiding place is not known." Jeremias told her, and Evelyn nodded at these words.

"There is much of Man's history I know naught of, it seems." she remarked.

"A short-lived but prolific race." the Earl replied.

"When will you set forth for this monastery, Lady Hannah?" Evelyn then asked.

"As I told you, about the noon hour." the girl replied wittily. "Will you accompany me, then?" she asked with a smile.

"It would be my honor." the other returned with her own smile, and when the finer details of the trip had been discussed, they retired from the breakfast and went to see to their own affairs for the day.

As Evelyn walked through the simple streets of Riverdell that day, awaiting a page to summon her to Hannah's side when the time came, she was calmed by the people's lively routine; it was not that much different from daily life back in Mala's village, and she caught herself smiling as she felt reminded of one Elf or another as she made her way about. It was just before the noon hour when her simple merriment came to an end; Mattis, the blacksmith, came out of the tavern, and he was quite drunk. He laughed for a bit with one of his fellows, and then he caught sight of Evelyn, who tried to hurry away so that there would be no scene--too late! "Hoy! Elf!" he called out in a loud voice, and a crowd began gathering again. "Ha! No Earl today--we've business to finish, you and I!" the smith said as he stormed over to her.

"Is that so?" Evelyn said in a haughty tone of voice, hoping to catch him off guard; her words had the opposite effect, seemingly enticing him.

"Oh, yes, my pretty one: you're mine today! Ha! Let's see if it goes the same way with Elves as it does that shrine-girl down the lane, shall we boys?" he laughed as two of his friends came up, chuckling as he did.

"Let's see them, Elf!" one of them jeered.

"How about this instead?" Evelyn asked, and before they could blink she had knocked the two of them down with two well-placed kicks to the jaw; they staggered back, one falling into a horse-trough and the other into a pile of manure. Those standing around watching burst out with laughter at the sight of the town thugs being made sport of by a stranger, but Mattis darkened with rage.

"Why you--!" he exclaimed, and rushed Evelyn; her first kick was to his groin, but in his drunken stupor he did not collapse, but only staggered back a few paces. Her next kick was to his face, and again he blinked stupidly, tottering about as the sensation of pain slowly reached his intoxicated mind; a murmur of nonsense escaped his lips, and Evelyn's third and final kick was delivered to his chest, knocking him off his feet and back several paces, where he landed in a heap of garbage, just in time for a serving maid of the tavern to accidentally pour out more garbage atop of him from a window above.

As the crowd roared in laughter, the young lady suddenly saw what had happened, and put a hand to her mouth as she began laughing. The guards came up, and they were also laughing as they pulled the three belligerents to their feet to take them to a cell; their captain gave Evelyn a grin, and she shrugged helplessly; if a mortal man was foolish enough to try and take on an Elf, they would invariably end up in some sort of a heap. The sound of a horse then caught her attention; it was the page. Lady Hannah was ready to leave for the monastery.

***

As the day wore on, the worn passage led the two of them and their escort higher into the mountains; even some of the trees seemed taller, or perhaps it was Evelyn's imagination. What was certain and definite was that the beasts were getting larger. There were mountain goats the size of their horses grazing about; birds the size of cats were flying about, or roosting in the trees; a large herbivore the size of a house plodded by as they rode; wolves of equal size to the goats could be discerned; and in the distance they could see a great bear. Hannah told her guest to not be fooled by its appearance from so far away: up close, the bear towered above the lumbering beast that had passed them but moments ago. Large rabbits bounded by in groups of threes and fours, and squirrel-like creatures could be seen darting up the trees at breakneck paces. The trees were predominantly evergreen, and now they were getting shorter as the path led them higher. Some four hours later, they could just make out the monastery in the distance; one spire of its hallowed halls was in their sights, and one of the guards commented that it would be another hour or two before they at last arrived. Evelyn stared towards it in wonder; all the wide world was new to her, it seemed, but for certain she could not recall that the Elves ever made something so as to be seen from far-off. They blended themselves into the wood; these mortals made towering and imposing structures, so as to be seen all around. "Here we are!" the buildings seemed to say; "This is our own land: come and take it!"

It took longer to reach the place than the guard had anticipated; a river flowed across their path, and the bridge, it seemed, had fallen prey to some accident--they hoped; for if it was not an accident, then it was the creature, and they did not want to be around when the plaguing monstrosity was about. After some time they managed to ford the river, but the doing so cost them nearly an hour, and they rode at a brisk pace to try and make up for it. When they at last reached the monastery, the horses were greatly tired from the exercise, and they were let in by a porter at once. The horses were led to the stables, and they themselves to the guest chambers; Evelyn gazed about curiously as they made their way inside. Greyish stones of varying shades made up the old walls, and they were covered with torches or tapestries; and in some places an iron-framed window took their place, mostly of the plain-glass kind, but there were several colorful stained-glass ones that caught her eye as they headed along. Chandeliers of exquisite crafting hung upon the ceilings at intervals, and ornately made candelabras stood about at the doors or were placed in the halls; they held two candles at the least, and the most Evelyn saw one of them holding was five.

By the time she and Hannah had been escorted to their room, she had lost track of where she was, and felt as if she was in a maze indeed.

Hannah smiled as she gazed about in confusion, and then the two of them headed in the room to change for the evening. One of the sisters of the monastery brought them a hot meal that was just out of the kitchens, and they thanked her for her kindness; the older woman smiled, and just before she left the room she turned back.

"Our Abbot Geron will be up to see you after the evening prayers, Lady Hannah." she said to the princess, who nodded back as the other headed out to attend to other duties. Evelyn, when she had finished with her meal, sat upon the bed nearer the window and gazed at its intricate patterns of stained-glass. It seemed to be telling a story of sorts, or perhaps it was a representation of holy text; at its top was a great sun, stretching out from two hands, and descending to the bottom were motifs of nature and created beings, and much more besides.

"Ex Binaga Domum Frashting excelsiso nos vorastoros amenica; amenica nos distilos vosotron vorastorionos meximaculuum." a baritone voice intoned behind her; she turned swiftly, and saw only the figure of a man whom she supposed was the abbot. Hannah's bow confirmed this, and Evelyn rose to curtsey as well. "In the beginning the One made all that we here below now enjoy and exult in; below his eyes we in our own humility worship him." he added as he smiled, translating the ancient words.

"Is that what the window means, Father Abbot?" Evelyn asked of him.

"Indeed, Lady Elf." he returned with a nod. "Dispense with formalities, please," he said again as she opened her mouth. "I am a servant of my faith and of others, and will address thee in no other way, even should you command it."

"As you say, Good Abbot." she returned, and the three of them sat down at the table.

"Lady Hannah, what brings you our way? And with such a guest as has not been seen in these halls for many a passing year?" Geron wondered.

"A vision, Lord Abbot." Hannah told him simply. "Here is one whom I saw reclaim the Sword of Magus, and who will carry it forth from here so that its purpose may live again." the earl's daughter continued, and Abbot Geron eyed the young Elf-woman curiously.

"Surely you don't think that--" he began, cut off by Evelyn herself.

"Surely you of all people, Father Abbot, are not about to patronize me in some way?" she asked him with a keen glance, and the abbot shook his head, smiling.

"Nay, nay; the Elves are a strong race, this I know. What I meant to ask, is that surely the Sword's purpose is long dead, its master buried long ago? What purpose could the Sword of Magus have in this day and age?" Geron asked, turning back to Hannah as he did so.

"You ask that, Lord Abbot, when the hordes of the Sorcerer King lie in wait for some unknown signal to strike again?" she asked him, and with a weary shrug he nodded back.

"I admit that the Sword could be a powerful ally in the days to come. But after all these long years, surely the hordes are just a living nightmare best forgotten?" the abbot returned in a tone that clearly signaled he was weary of such things.

"The Hordes were called away, dear friend." Hannah told him. "If they were called away, they can be called back. Such is their nature, lest someone banish them utterly."

"And the Sword of Magus could do such a thing." Evelyn said in understanding.

"Yes, indeed, Lady Evelyn." her friend smiled back. A moment of silence followed these words, silence in which Evelyn felt she almost understood the reason for her journey, for Caspar, for everything... but it was lost when words at last were spoken again, dragging her out of such thoughts. Still, she did not fully grasp the sounds until moments later, when the abbot had mostly finished his statement.

"... then I suppose I cannot stop you; but at least take rest for the night, and perhaps visit the Chambers of Memory or the Meditation Grove on the morrow." he finished saying, and Hannah nodded at these words. Evelyn blinked, slowly nodding her own head as well. After a cordial farewell for the night, the abbot left their room, and a few moments later, Hannah began telling Evelyn more of the story behind the story in the window. It was, as she had suspected, a holy text that dealt with creation. It was rare for the race of Man to follow a monotheistic faith, as these apparently did, but it was not unheard of; the Monastery of Oaken Grove and its members were renowned in this part of Man's world, it seemed, as Hannah told her.

Had all this been so close to her own home, Evelyn wondered, and if so, how had it been ignored for so long? How could such beauty as this window be the work of an evil hand, as so many Elves might say? She gazed at it long into the night, even after Hannah had fallen asleep from her recitations. Sleep then came for her next, and she drifted into the world of dreams.

***

Noontide the next day saw the sun hidden from Evelyn's sight by clouds and by trees; she wandered again by herself, given only the hint of a direction to go on. Breakfast in the great hall had been followed indeed by morning prayers (for those who prayed after eating, that is), and then Evelyn went out into the grove while Hannah had gone to the chapel. Here, the Elf-lady had found a better respite among the trees of nature than the monastics did in their worn stone halls. She could almost feel as if there was indeed something, *spiritual*, perhaps even *holy* in this place, this grove within the walls of the monastery. There was a peace, a peace not unlike that which had encompassed her with the dreams of Caspar, and it was lovely to her. But when she had made ready to seek the Sword of Magus later that morning, the abbot's sincere, loving, but grim warning to her caused such a feeling to dwindle. He had not given her a confident hope for achieving her goal, despite his faith, and Hannah watched her go off in a somewhat terse mood. The earl's daughter then let out a sigh, shaking her head at the melancholy send-off the abbot had given her guest, and retired to her chambers in the monastery once more.

Now, almost three hours after she had set out, Evelyn was sighing in frustration at the shadows of clouds and the closeness of the trees. How did a great creature move about in such a place as this? She was about to return and demand a guard or two for help when she suddenly stumbled upon a great print in the ground; it almost looked like the print of a bear, but there was something not quite right about it... *what 'is' wrong with it?* Evelyn wondered to herself, staring with scrutiny at the track before her. There was not much she knew of woodlore, but the prints of animals she knew fairly well. She looked up slowly, scanning ahead for more of the tracks; there they were, trailing off into the distance at intervals.

Evelyn looked again and again, not certain what was giving her unease. Then she looked back absentmindedly at her own faint prints, and at seeing them she understood; the creature, whatever it was, roamed on two legs. Quickly she ran through her mind the lore of living creatures.

> *Elves the fairest, and immortal sages;*
> *Valkyries proudest, determined warriors;*
> *Giants the tallest, old as stone;*
> *Dwarves the toughest, short but fiery;*
> *Man the feistiest, short-lived;*
> *Gnomes the wisest, clever-tinkers;*
> *Werecats the sly ones, changing shapes;*
> *Dragons the oldest, proud and haughty;*
> *Centaurs the grandest, majestic beings;*
> *Satyrs the stubbornest, fighting centaurs;*
> *Trolls the dimmest, hiding from sunlight;*
> *Goblins feckless, heedless, foolish;*
> *Ogres the cruelest, hating all;*
> *Sirens and Merfolk, below the sea...*

Wait... *Ogres the cruelest... hating all... Ogres...* Ogres... Ogres... they had lived long ago on the borderlands of Alastria, until driven away by three successive wars led by the Elven King Thristran, who fought against several Ogre Clan Chiefs; could there still be some around? Or at least one? Evelyn looked at the prints again; how could she not have noticed? The track was more to a man-shape than that of an animal. Ogres, the older ones, anyway, could get larger than trolls, according to the ancient lore. And they were more likely to be loners, coming together in large numbers only when a common enemy was found, such as during the infamous Ogre Wars. Evelyn continued on, thinking about these things as she followed the revealed trail. Certainly this explained the loss of the sword; only an ogre or a clever troll would hang on to such a thing. And trolls lived further west and south. *So there's an old, Elf-hating creature living somewhere around these woods with the sword of an old mage...* it seemed odd, Evelyn reflected; wouldn't the Sword of Magus be protected against such--no. If a thief could steal it from a monastery, then certainly an ogre could hang on to it.

It was about an hour later when she saw the trail fading in to a cave... or was it a cave? The entryway had the distinct impression of seeming... constructed, as if... as if... *can this be a castle? Was there a castle here once, long ago, now buried in the mountains?* Evelyn wondered to herself as she approached; examining closer, she found that the entryway was an old window, a window so faded into the landscape that it could only be discerned as a window by those who were very astute--such as herself. The remaining question was, what was the window situated in? An old house? A tall tower? A faded church?

Steeling herself, she headed inside, and let her night-vision take over. Evelyn looked around inside; it was a tower indeed, and an old rotting stairwell lead down into its depths. *If that hulking thing can get down here, so can I!* She thought to herself as she soundlessly descended the steps, not too arrogantly, lest she find the one spot that might crack beneath her feet. As she got lower and lower, she heard a great rumbling, a rumbling that seemed to make the ground shake--or was that her imagination? It would rise and fall in intensity, but by the time she got to the bottom she was paying it no mind, thinking it might be some trick of the wind running through the old chambers of the sunken tower.

Now she was at the bottom, and a large doorway was before her. The door was ripped off of its hinges, lying in pieces upon the floor. *This is the strength of the thing I am trying to steal from...* Evelyn thought to herself. The sound reached her ears again, and it now sounded almost familiar. Steeling herself again, she pressed forward, slipping through the corridors and trying to discern which door or passage might lead to--wait, there! The great hall. An old plaque still hung above the doorway; the castle was yet another ruin of Men from the ancient days. Now the sound grew to its loudest yet, and Evelyn froze as she put a foot forward to enter the room. It fell, and then rose and fell again, and it was at this that Evelyn knew why she recognized it: it was the sound of snoring. The Ogre was asleep. Looking around, she scanned the room intensely for her sleeping adversary, and as she did so she saw that the room around her held many artifacts of the old days when this castle was still above ground.

Wondrous shields and worn furs lined the walls; swords, pikes, spears, and axes of all sorts were placed on stands or hung above shields; tapestries still proudly hung upon the heights of the walls; chandeliers and candelabras, preciously wrought of the most valuable metals, hung from the ceiling or stood about the walls; a grand table sat in the midst of the room, surrounded by matching chairs, and when Evelyn touched them she found them to be of skillfully crafted mahogany; cups, goblets, plates, silverware, and many other precious things lined the room. But it was just above the Ogre himself, who sat snoring upon the ancient throne, that Evelyn's prize was situated. Of all the races in all the wide world, only trolls come nearer to being animals than ogres--save perhaps for the stupidest of goblins--yet ogres were, by far, the more feared for that very reason; they *could* think, they *could* reason, and they *could* understand at the very least the concepts of strategy and tactics in fighting. Niceties escaped them, but what need had they of niceties, whose very roaming about inspired fear? But, for now, this one was asleep, and Evelyn intended to keep it that way. The Sword of Magus, scabbard and all, was placed on a display case just over the throne.

Looking around, Evelyn saw other precious items, most notably coins; quietly, she scavenged these, and softly placed as many as she dared to in a bag, along with a few of the goblets and a small collection of daggers. Setting the bag down, she then slipped up to the throne without so much as a sound, and deftly maneuvered about the snoring ogre. There were empty and spilled jugs lying about his feet. *He's drunk!* Evelyn thought to herself, the realization encouraging her, but not to the point of foolishness. *He's stone drunk; if I can just keep as quiet as I am now, I can get the sword and get out, and be far from here by the time he wakes up!* She said to herself, slowly but confidently stepping up onto the arm of the throne as she calmly took in a deep and silent breath; when she was upon this, she reached out cautiously, gingerly towards the sword, fearing lest she stumble at the last. Evelyn did not stumble, but the sword was heavier than she had first realized, and she reached out her other hand to help her lift it from the display. When it was in her grasp, she cautiously stepped down off of the throne, and without a sound she strode over to her bag, picking this up and heading out. It was then she noticed the book. Books of all kinds are of interest to Elves, who by nature have a keen interest in lore and scholarly pursuits, similar to the Gnomes; but this one had a particular feel to it for Evelyn--as if, as if somehow it was bound up in her journey.

She took it to place in her bag, and looked bag as the ogre hit a particularly violent decibel in his snoring; the giant thing smacked its lips in its sleep, and with a yawn resumed slumbering. Silently releasing a sigh of relief, Evelyn then hastened back out to the tower. Quickly but carefully she ascended the stairs, not daring to run lest they break; but at the very top, one partially gave way, and she could not help but let out a small shriek as it snapped and crumbled. She jumped out of the old window, hoping that the beast below had not been disturbed. The sound of a low rumble reached her ears. It was *not* the sound of a snore.

It was the sound of a growl.

Evelyn looked back in a fright, backing away slowly, riveted by some inexplicable fear and need to know if it would pursue her. She heard the sound of heavy footfalls far below, and she at once went off in a dash back towards the monastery. But she did not hear the sound of steps. The sound that reached her ears was that of a chain winding and creaking. *A chain! So that's how the ogre gets his bulk up and down that tower!* Evelyn realized, and began running at full speed. A thud shook the ground just slightly. She had no need to look back. The Ogre had ascended the tower and jumped out to pursue her. It would know the scent of Elf; Evelyn had heard stories about the Ogre Wars. Even bloodied and hacked beyond recognition, an Ogre was still deadly. They could play dead for days, weeks perhaps, lying in wait for some fool to come along and prod them; this the Elves had found out at terrible cost in the First Ogre War. But it was no dead fiend that chased her now; it was a live one. It was not one who had been wounded nearly to death; it was fresh, strong, hale. And it was gaining on her.

As goblins are a natural enemy of the Dwarves, Ogres are a natural enemy of the Elves, both powerful in their own rights and suited to fighting each other on moderately even terms. But Evelyn had never killed anything in her life. Not like this. Still she ran, and still the creature kept gaining, its hoarse breath and grunting growls looming closer and closer; Evelyn was almost in a state of panic.

"Mine! Mine mine mine! You steal! Elves steal! Always stealing, always taking, always killing!" the Ogre shouted. "I am Ragak! I am the last of the Guruht Tribe you filthy gagakna slaughtered and butchered as if we were animals! Now I will slay you as an animal! I will butcher you for the crows!" it shouted after her, and the fear gave her a second wind with which to keep on running. On and on she ran, and would have kept running, but an old root suddenly tripped her as she ran. Flying through the air as she did, she saw the Ogre's eyes light up in exultation, a wicked grin upon its face.

Anger coursed through her veins. She could not die like this! She could not die at the hands of a maddened beast, whose thoughts of revenge had carried it through the ages. It was unfair! *Caspar!* She thought to herself. The thought of never seeing him again, never knowing the true sensation of his lips upon hers, never knowing the tenderness of his embrace in person sent a second wave of anger through her veins. And the third wave of anger sprang from what she saw around the Ogre's neck: it was a medallion. An Elven medallion. A medallion whose signet she knew well; it was her father's. Somehow, this fiend had stolen from another thief her family heirloom. Who could guess how the Ogre claimed it those two decades ago, when the ravaging hordes burned over the land? Evelyn did not care.

As she went sprawling and tumbling onto the ground, she drew the Sword of Magus by instinct, and raised it with a look of intense anger at the beast. The Ogre blanched, suddenly scraping to try and back away; but it was not Evelyn's face that gave him pause. The Sword of Magus lit up in response to Evelyn's strong emotions, and a bolt of light emanated from it to his the fiend squarely in the chest, burning a hole through him; Ragak stumbled to the ground. Evelyn, shocked at first, quickly regained her senses as the beast fell, and spun about quickly, slicing her enemy's throat with a hefty swing. Ragak's eyes dimmed, and the green blood of his people poured from his wounds. Evelyn caught her breath, and, when she had recovered the things that had fallen out from her tumble, she snatched the medallion from the thing's neck, and then spun on her heel to leave her foe to die in the woods.

"Siyaka ne wanguru fochre fhal--nege fochre diso." she said loudly as she departed, knowing that the Ogre understood the language of the Elves, and this phrase in particular, for it was a common insult in the Ogre Wars. *There is nothing more stupid than a drunk ogre--except a sober one.* Smirking to herself as she headed off, she heard a low moaning sound, the sound of a dying ogre. Only the smallest wave of pity came to her, and like the leaves blown by the wind, this too passed by airily, never to be seen again.

***

When Evelyn returned to the monastery, those who dwelt there welcomed her warmly, and Lady Hannah was overjoyed to see her friend return from her small quest. Abbot Geron at once blessed her, insisting that the sword was hers by right and that their guardianship of it was ended. When she told them the tale of her escapade, he insisted all the more, knowing that the Sword of Magus could only react in such a way to one who was destined to hold it.

"Long ago, the fourth bearer of the sword came to us to return it to our keeping. 'Since Magus used this blade, three others have used it with its full potential, myself being the fourth bearer; there will not be a fifth for many long years, and so again I commend to you this sword as Magus did until such time as they come to claim it: the Sword will speak for itself'. Thus he said, and thus has it happened; the Sword of Magus has bestowed upon you the right to use it. It is yours." Geron told her, and Evelyn looked at the sword again, mystified by its story.

"And as for this book..." Hannah added to her, "it is a rare treasure indeed. This is the Tome of Magus." she said, and the Abbot made the sign against evil.

"A spell-book! In my monastery! Nay, take it with you as well! Magus' it may be, but a relic of his past life, not his monastic one!" he all but shouted.

"Do not fear, abbot." Evelyn told him. "I will leave on the morrow; I cannot be kept from my journey any longer than that." she added, and the abbot nodded. Hannah smiled softly at her, and the Elf-maiden smiled back as the human girl handed her back the tome. They headed up to their chambers, bidding the abbot and other monastics good-night as they did so. Evelyn slept soundly. She had bested an ogre; a besotted one, perhaps, but an ogre nonetheless. Nothing would stand in her way of finding Caspar now.

Chapter Eight: The Bells of Chloe

For Caspar and Percy, the journey north had taken on a drearier tone; it had been unceasingly wet and rainy for two days, and the weather had quite literally dampened their spirits. By the end of a third day, they came to a sprawling city surrounded by palisades, and were admitted in by a porter as grumpy as they were from being out in the weather. Percy indeed almost took him to task when he complained about being out in the rain for ten hours, telling him in a snapped tone that they themselves had been near to drowning for three days now. The porter raised his hands in an acquiescent apology that pacified the Gnome, and they headed on towards an inn. Despite the weather, the cobbled streets of the city were fairly filled with people, horses, carts, and carriages of all sorts. It was a trade-center, Percy told Caspar, and one of the more lively ones, insofar as inland trade-cities were lively.

"Not as polite and sophisticated as Murana Day or Auschternople, but there we are. Even so, Frostvale has its highlights; the local farmers are hops farmers, who grow a particularly lively crop that is used in the brewing of fine ales. There's distilleries of all sorts about the city; spirits are the most popular: liqueurs, whiskeys and scotch-whiskeys all in abundance at any given tavern."

"So it's a center of fine drinks?" Caspar wondered.

"Quite. Ales, beers, mead, wines, spirits, liqueurs, rums, and all that. Some is imported from coastal cities, who in turn import it from across the seas. Gnomes are working on a way to aid in reducing market prices: steam-powered waggons. The idea is to set up tracks between major cities, especially trade-centers. These steam waggons will (theoretically) move at a faster rate than horse or ox-driven ones, not to mention that their speed will keep them safer from bandits, and their efficiency should lower market value of imported goods to a price more comparable to local goods."

"By Cassandra! *Steam* power?" Caspar wondered. "Can such a thing really be done?"

"Oh, of course! We Gnomes have all sorts of steam-powered gadgets in our lands. Our people had just gotten approval from the

High King at Auschternople when I left to begin the test track. It will run from that fine city to the one south and west of it, Beacon Hill. The lighthouse city. Beautiful place, so I've heard. Not that Auschternople doesn't have lighthouses, but Beacon Hill is really the better port all in all, from what I've been told."

"What sort of things run on steam?" Caspar suddenly broke in, returning his friend to the subject.

"Eh? What? Lifts, for one thing; more efficient than stairs. And we already have a fine steam-powered transit system below the earth, where it's easier to use such things. It's this thing that was the basis for and the selling point of the new idea that we presented to Auschternople. If I was an engineer, I could tell you more; as it is, I'm only familiar with the popular ones; the lifts, the transits, and some factory and warehouse machines that also use steam. But to return to the city," Percy continued as they neared the inn, "Frostvale is also known as a center for mercenaries and smugglers; not that I advocate bandying such words about--you'd likely end up with a few holes!--but the town thrives all the same, mostly because of them as opposed to in spite of them. The mercenaries end up back here after work, and the smugglers are always in demand when the local Merchant Guild starts raising taxes on something or other. Heh. Half of them *belong* to the guild itself, *there's* irony for you." the Gnome went on, and Caspar chuckled softly as they came to a halt.

When the horse and the dog had been led to the stables for the night, Percy and Caspar headed inside, sitting in a corner of the second-largest commons in the inn. A gruff but jovial inn-keep took their drink orders, and Percy resumed his history discourse, which really did fascinate the young man. Frostvale, or its earliest beginnings, at any rate, was founded by a hops farmer named Farnham Frost and his wife Ethel. Good soil and good weather provided a stable farming environment, and eventually more farmers and herdsmen began settling the land, which had been claimed by the Frost's. They paid a tribute or rent to work the land, and Farnham eventually grew to be the unofficial head of the community; after his death, the rapidly growing town presented its charter to the king at Auschternople, naming themselves "Frostvale" in Farnham's honor. Even today the Frost family still had a good reputation, and Frost Malt Beer was a popular town favorite. It had been discovered by Frost and other farmers of his crop that this land was particularly kind to the hops and grains that were used in alcohol; hence the beverage trade had flourished here. Other crops did well in the area, but none so well as those used in fermentation, and even the royals and nobles of Auschternople sent regularly for the almost magical drinks that were found here. Caspar, taking a sip of the

Frost Malt Beer, had to agree. It was a fine brew indeed.

"Not that I advocate drinking as a regular habit, of course," Percy said, "but if one were to become a drunkard, this is the town I would recommend." he said with a shrug as he took a sip of his own mug, setting it down with a satisfied sigh. A band of troubadours was playing in one corner of the inn; Caspar enjoyed the experience of listening as opposed to playing for the night, and when they headed up to their rooms later that evening he was still humming one of the tunes. He fell asleep some time after Percy did, and his dreams were of Evelyn.

***

Morning brought a return of the sunshine so sorely missed by those walking upon the earth, and it was that morning that the two travellers set out again from their lodging to continue through Frostvale to the New North Road on the town's opposite side. Merchants and farmers were already milling their way about the city, and in the new sunshine Caspar could see that the city was indeed situated in a vale; a river ran through its midst, crossed by several bridges. He and Percy crossed one of the greater spans, and were almost to the gate some moments later when a figure in a hooded robe made as if to stop them. Caspar reined in Elvar at once, but Dusty barked, the faithful hound perturbed that anyone should accost his master in a strange land such as this.

"Hold, friend, I mean no harm." the mysterious stranger spoke.

"Then what do you mean, friend?" Caspar returned; the man suddenly flashed out a silver medallion like unto Caspar's own. This man was of the Order of Cassandra. Caspar at once paid closer attention. "The Order... what is it you would have of me, friend?" he asked curiously.

"By secret messengers we knew of your journey, friend; listen and I will tell you of a thing you may find useful. There is an ancient temple in the heights of the vales to the northwest. In this temple is a sacred relic, a relic from the ancient ages. We have not ventured in many a long year to retrieve it, for though the way there is not difficult the trials are. But... there was always something about you, young Caspar. We believe that it and you are connected in some way. Therefore I was sent to tell you lest you pass it by unaware." the man told him.

"The way not dangerous, yet the trials are." Percy snorted. "Fish-fosh-faddle! We've no time for this, friend Caspar!"

"Now hang on, Percy, I'm sure there's a good reason they've decided to tell me this... the Order would never do me harm, and he said 'difficult' not 'dangerous', after all!" Caspar said in reply, and the Gnome shook his head.

"Nevertheless I feel it is my solemn duty to be wary of hooded-- now hang on, where did he go?" Percy began, looking around for the mysterious man. Caspar too looked about, and saw no one like their friend in the masses coming and going from the gate in either direction. "Ha! See? Does that not convince you? Or is there some other excuse you would excuse him with?" the Gnome wondered candidly.

"As I'm sure you're aware, friend Gnome, the Order of Cassandra has a flare for both the theatrical and the dramatic." Caspar said as he nudged Elvar to continue on.

"As may be, but I still say stuff and nonsense!" Percy shot back as they exited the gate; the guards nodded to them, and Caspar nodded back before replying.

"Anymore stuff and nonsense than a human minstrel seeking an Elven maiden?" the young man wondered with a smile. "And with the help of a Gnome, no less?" he added before Percy could frame a reply. Percy had to think for several moments on that one.

"Very well, I'll have to give you that. This time!" the Gnome conceded. "So then! He said northwest into the vale heights. Shouldn't be too difficult to find a trail or something to a temple... and besides, side-tracking is always a good excuse to go cataloging flora and fauna in a region, to say nothing of the cartographic value for in-depth maps..." Percy chattered on, and Caspar smiled to himself as they wound their way towards the direction in which they had been pointed by the mysterious visitor. The man himself was now atop the gates, watching the odd little band of them head to the vale heights with a smile. He turned to vanish into the crowds once more, and was gone.

***

There were several trails in the northwest region of the vale heights, most of which seemed to be the conglomerated passageways of wildlife around the area. It took several hours to locate the right trail, finally distinguished by an old signpost found by Percy when the poor fellow almost tripped, yet again, into a rosebush. This had only happened because the Gnome, quite fed up with the search, tried to pointedly march over to where Elvar was grazing so that Caspar would see the sense in finally giving up the search. Not that Percy hadn't been enjoying himself for the first few hours; but there was not much to catalog, and by the end of a third hour he had found one or two repeat entries, and thus became less inclined to the search itself. But that was before he almost tripped into a rosebush. As he was about to fall, his hands smacked into something made of stone; not just any stone, but polished stone, he knew at once from the feel of the texture beneath his hands. Percy cleared away some of the brush, and saw an ancient language used by the races marking the worn-out and mostly faded path just nearby as that which would lead to an ancient temple. Partially annoyed but mostly intrigued, he called for his minstrel friend, and the little party began ascending this trail.

"What a piece of luck you stumbled on to this!" Caspar remarked.

"In a very *literal* sense, to be sure." Percy quipped back as they hurried along. It was not dark, but it was near evening, and they wanted to have as much light as possible for exploring the temple. "No sense going about it in the dark..." Percy said. "Dark is all very well and good if you're prepared for it, but we're not. Now a Gnomish Archaeological Expedition, to be sure, is *always* prepared for anything. Well, mostly anything. Not quite *everything*. But they've their fair share of contingencies readied; lights, medicinals, all-weather gear, moderate camp defenses to ward off wildlife and the bolder of two-legged fiends..." the Gnome went on, and Caspar listened with interest that eventually turned to a feigned interest as his friend continued on the subject. It did pass the time, however, for which Caspar was grateful; and it was not as if it was irrelevant. Indeed, the young man listened intently as Percy turned to the subject of ancient traps or puzzles in temples and structures such as these, wondering if there was something of the sort within the place where they were bound to. Percy's recitations made it more or less abundantly clear that the Gnome expected nothing less, and that he expected Caspar to expect nothing less as well. Which was, of course, expected. Even the mysterious figure had had implied that there were devices of some sort lying in wait for them.

It got to the point where, when they at last reached the temple, Percy was more than half afraid of going out onto the grounds of the ancient structure, having since convinced himself that there was more than likely a host of pit-traps and such strewn about at random intervals around the temple itself. Caspar hitched Elvar to a nearby tree to let him graze about, and, in an effort to convince the Gnome that there was nothing to fear, walked determinedly up to the temple itself. He reached the stairs without incident, and turned to look back at the Gnome, who gave a wry shrug and then followed hurriedly.

"Can't blame a fellow for being more cautious than free of care!" Percy remarked, and Caspar smiled. They headed up the stairs, and found a door that was sealed shut. It was ornately made, and the defined outlines of squares could be seen upon it. Upon further examination, Percy determined that these squares could be pushed in. "Some sort of clever and antiquated locking mechanism--not ineffective, considering we don't know the key, but it is an antique in the general sense..." the Gnome remarked. Caspar looked over the door thoughtfully, wondering if there was some clue upon the thing itself that could give them insight into the door's secrets.

In the fading light it was becoming difficult to see, but at length he caught on to there being a series of symbols on the outer frames of the door, symbols that matched ones marked on the squares or "pads", as Percy called them. There were thirty-two symbols around the door, and eight upon it; Caspar further noted, though it was hard to be sure as the sun went down, that the thirty-two frame symbols seemed to be composed of an ostensibly random selection of the eight on the door. "Could it be that simple..." he wondered to himself.

"Hm? What's that?" Percy looked up, wondering what the young man was thinking. He glanced at Caspar, who gave a shrug and turned away from the door.

"It's getting late. We should try this tomorrow, when it's light out and we've rested a bit more." the young man returned, to which Percy agreed after a moment's thought.

"Quite. No sense in bungling about in the dark." the Gnome replied. "After all, we're not a Gnomish Expedition." he continued chattering, talking on and on as they set up camp for the night. Caspar listened with a smile on his face, content to let his friend ramble on until they both fell asleep later that night.

Upon waking the next morning, Percy found Caspar had already gone back up to the door; he hurriedly shook off sleep and trotted up to it himself, and began to see what the young man himself had seen last night as Caspar traced the outer frames of the door. "Ah-ha!" he said in exclamation. "Of course! These eight symbols upon the door are to be pressed in line with this track of symbols on the frame; the resulting sequence then unlocks the internal mechanisms of the door, and we're on to the next puzzle. Ha-ha! Brilliant boy, simply brilliant!" Percy said with a smile.

"Yes, but, here's what troubles me, friend Percy: do we press the symbols in the manner from left-to-right or from right-to-left?" Caspar said, and the Gnome blinked. Of course! A further dilemma, key to the intrigue of the mechanism. In which way did the sequence unlock the door? Percy frowned, trying to look for further clues about the temple itself.

"Hmm... now let's see... this temple; it looks Astralatian in nature. That's an old cult, a group not dissimilar to the Order of Cassandra, except they were more mystical in nature. Ah yes, yes... I see it now... if you look above the door-frame there's the insignia of the Astralatian Priests and such." Percy mused, and Caspar looked up to see a symbol of a nude woman, holding the stars in one hand and a crescent moon in the other. "Now, the Astralatian Priesthood existed some five to six-thousand years ago; from the looks of things, this temple is one of their later constructs, so it can be approximated to at least five-thousand. At that time, most tribes of men around this area used the right-to-left mode--some still do!--but the Priesthood here was very secretive, as well as being mystical, and so they may have gone with a sequence from left-to-right... unless they were hoping that some would over-think their secrecy, as I may be doing, and simply used the norm of the times for their combination lock..."

"Whatever happened to them?" Caspar wondered.

"Eh? Oh, them. The times changed, mystic secrecy became more and more frowned upon. The Astralatians died out in a sense; the fanatics clung to their ways until death, the casual members left altogether, but the moderates continued on, eventually reforming and restructuring their entire group to that which became the predecessor to your own Order of Cassandra, at that time known as Cassandra's Faithful. Cassandra, contrary to popular lore, was *not* a goddess, but a priestess who was head of the reform clauses; her successors eventually decided to rename the group in her honor."

"So... this temple, in a way, is part of my own history." Caspar mused, and Percy raised an eyebrow.

"In a manner of speaking, perhaps." the Gnome returned. "But back to the question of importance. Do we start from the right, or from the left?" he added, pacing back and forth as he began to ponder this once more. Caspar himself, his attention brought back to the puzzle by the Gnome's words, also began to think. It was still morning, so they had time, but he did not want to be here for days on end puzzling out every last puzzle that came their way in this place. He pulled out his flute, and then suddenly noticed something further; the symbols upon the frame and upon the door were fashioned to resemble the finger-notations of the instrument he now held. More, upon the frame, some of the symbols were outlined in silver, some in gold.

Supposing that one or the other were meant to represent the higher scale notes, Caspar looked over the frame again, and began to follow the revealed notes upon the frame from right-to-left. After a couple tries, he found that the gold ones were the low ones and the silver ones the high ones. But the order did not make sense. Percy then looked over at him, suddenly realizing that Caspar was playing, and blinked in dumbfounded awe at the simplicity.

"Of *course*! What a daft fool I am! Listen, boy, as you know, there's only ever been one direction in which notation occurs." the Gnome began with a knowing look to his friend.

"Left-to-right." Caspar smiled, and then played the tune inscribed upon the frame in its proper order. It was, to his amazement, the first few bars of an ancient hymn still played by the Order of Cassandra. It must have been one of the Astralatian hymns long ago, he realized, and with that he went up to the door and pressed the pads in their proper sequence. The doors swung inwards, revealing a large interior to the ancient temple. The two of them headed inside with awe, gazing about in wonder at the almost mint (but very dusty) condition of the temple. Dusty also followed them in, the hound eagerly sniffing about as he followed his master and his friend.

"By the way, what was the name of that tune?" Percy wondered as he investigated an old vase, scribbling down observations in his papers.

"It's called the 'Bells of Chloe', one of the most ancient hymns of the Order; it must have come from the Astralatian traditions." Caspar told him.

"Hm! Fascinating!" Percy remarked excitedly.

"I wonder where our next puzzle lies, and what kind of artifact I'm supposed to find in here when this whole place would fascinate a whole guild of Gnomes and the entire Order..." the young man wondered aloud as he gazed about.

"Quite! You'd have the Historians Guild, the Archaeological Council, the Antiquities Committee, a detachment from the Sociology Board, not to mention both the Artisans Guild and the Department of Musical Theorems..." Percy returned in a casual and chipper manner as he went glibly from one artifact to the next. "Hard to say what exactly one might be looking for that stands out amongst all the rest when the object in question is quantified as 'artifact' in a trove of the same. Hm!" he continued. Caspar, only half-listening at this point, was wandering up to the altar; upon the grand lectern he found an old book, a book that was very likely the treasure they now sought.

The covers of the book were made of platinum, the borders and bindings of Dwarf-steel; its pages were of pure gold, the letters made of intricately-wrought silver, and its overall design exquisite to say the least--and to say the most, it was beyond words. Turning through the pages, he found a perfect copy of the "Bells of Chloe", if indeed this was not the original notation itself, wrought as it was in a book left behind by the original composers, as he could now say with some certainty.

"By Cassandra!" he said in awe as he read over it, tears coming to his eyes as he saw, for the first time, the hymn in its fullness; much of it had been lost, and only one of the verses and the refrain had remained to them after the long ages. Determining to keep this book, he could not, however, resist singing the hymn, now that he had found it; and what better place than here for its first perfect recitation in countless years? He hummed a bit, getting his voice ready for it as he looked over the ancient words. They were not that different from the dialect in which most of the traditionalist members of the Order sung it in. As Caspar began to sing, Percy stopped to listen, and even Dusty came to attention.

Pieae yex susas, susa nos quatra mostremu vas medin
Pieae yex susas, susa nos quatra nostemo vas ledin

Iz qua-queistro nos vemo nas alamando, si velivina triste
Si velivina triste yex susas alamandan, ilhe mistrimo
Vas mediana comtraya mohani il qua-questra nisteni
Salmandana vexis susas mostreni al-mandaro nosteno

Pieae yex susas, susa nos quatra mostremu vas medin
Pieae yex susas, susa nos quatra nostemo vas ledin

Al iz medinia frashca nostre mistrimo yex susas iedin
Al iz velivianio vex nosteno vas medin, vas nos trana
Qua-quastre novenmas frashcatingie nodmaarin faas
Izqe nicomaya nicomtraya si melmaladinio na yex eda

Pieae yex susas, susa nos quatra mostremu vas medin
Pieae yex susas, susa nos quatra nostemo vas ledin

Pieae yex susas, suso nos quatra mostrina vas medin
Pieae yex susas, suso nos quatra nostimu vas ledin

Y exclusio nos qua-questre hemonista lexus nos marim
Hy exima yex susas noco questra qua-quatra limona ex
Qua-quastra decumas frashcatingie nodmaarin faas
Yelin yex yariin-ma frashca nostra mostrimuus refhan

Pieae yex susas, susa nos quatra mostremu vas medin
Pieae yex susas, susa nos quatra nostemo vas ledin

Vosoclomos nuestra max ledin vosclometros simun
Ex caquestra nodmaar faastrin yex yeliin vasdras iz
Furitnos trania valma noedyuun yex susas max medin
Furitnos trenie noedyuunasa il iz yex susas max ledin

Pieae yex susas, susa nos quatra mostremu vas medin
Pieae yex susas, susa nos quatra nostemo vas ledin

Pieae yex susas, suso nos quatra mostrina vas medin
Pieae yex susas, suso nos quatra nostimu vas ledin

Iz qua-queistro nos vemo nas alamando, si velivina triste
Al iz medinia frashca nostre mistrimo yex susas iedin
Y exclusio nos qua-questre hemonista lexus nos marim
Vosoclomos nuestra max ledin vosclometros simun

Pieae yex susas, suso nos quatra mostrina vas medin
Pieae yex susas, suso nos quatra nostimu vas ledin

Pieae yex susas, susa nos quatra mostremu vas medin
Pieae yex susas, susa nos quatra nostemo vas ledin
Pieae yex susas, susa nos quatra mostremu vas medin
Pieae yex susas, susa nos quatra nostemo vas ledin

As Caspar held those last notes Percy was all but overcome from listening to such a performance, and would have gone on being overcome, but as Caspar's voice faded away a door behind the altar opened and grabbed the attention of the ever-observant Gnome. He at once raced up to investigate it, and Caspar, satisfied with his new "friend", carefully placed it in a pack he had carried in to hold such things.

"Fascinating!" Percy remarked behind him, and Caspar suddenly turned around to see that a door behind him was open. "This door here must have some sort of pitch-lock; theoretical up til now--quite possibly magical in nature. The singing of the hymn in such wondrous manner as you have done, my friend," here Caspar smiled and bowed, "must have been then key to the next puzzle. It's all to do with this hymn, apparently; that's the key to this old temple. Now that I recall it, Chloe was counted as a goddess, revered by the Astralatians; she was the figure above the door with the stars and the moon. And now!" the Gnome remarked, stopping before an impressively ornate chest.

It was made of a wood neither Percy nor Caspar could recognize, but its bindings were of fine Dwarven-steel, and these were patterned with golden ivy. There was a lock upon the chest, but it was no mystical lock; it required a key, and a key they did not have. Nor did a search of the room reveal one. They could, however, carry the chest, and they did so, bringing it out to the main hall of the temple. As they left this secret room the door that had been guarding it shut once more, and they were left with the mystery of finding the key. Percy blinked once, and then gave Caspar an inquisitive look.

"Here now! Let's have that book out again, friend--it may tell us of the key!" he said to the young man, who brought it out at once.

"Of course, Percy. How silly of me!" Caspar said in honest deference, chiding himself for putting it away so soon when there was still a mystery to be had. The two of them looked in the book carefully from the very first pages, scanning intently for any hint of a clue that might show them an answer. It was arduous reading, even with Percy's knowledge of the old language; the book was a priceless tome, detailing all sorts of historical, mythological, and of course musical anecdotes relating to the Astralatian Priesthood. It began with the mystical origin of their cult, when Chloe selected seven young women and five young men to dedicate themselves to purity, never to have intimacy with anyone, and to dedicate themselves to a study of the divine in all its aspects. Their numbers grew, but the High Priesthood forever remained at the fixed number of twelve, with seven women and five men. The ruling priest or priestess was elected amongst the twelve themselves, and the remaining eleven of them formed a sort of council, who made most of the decisions related to their order, save the most weighty matters, which the ruling ecclesiastic decided. Details of their practices, their studies, and their mythology were found in an orderly fashion throughout the book, but it was not until the very end that they found what they sought. In an ironic twist, the key to the chest itself was embedded in the back cover, and it needed a key to release it.

"Oh, hang it all!" Percy grumbled. "Of all the stupid..." he continued muttering as he got up to look about for a key to get the key to open the chest. Caspar watched him as he began his search, and then turned back to the book itself for a moment before putting it down reverently so that he could join in searching. As the day waned outside, Caspar and Percy sought out their last key (they hoped) throughout the length, breadth, and height of the temple and its grounds. Percy read hastily through volumes and volumes of old scrolls and tomes in several libraries they found, seeking out anything that pertained to the altar, the mysterious room, or the priceless book; he did not find what he sought, but he did find several other lore-books which he believed would be very handy or at the very least of scholastic value, and these he began organizing into an empty crate that still lingered about the temple.

Caspar, occasionally dropping by on Percy to aid the Gnome in his endeavors (such as reaching for books that Percy could not reach), made a more passive search of things. It was his experience that if you were looking for something deliberately, you would never find it; whereas if you only paid your objective but little mind whilst wandering about, it would invariably find you instead. This thought, tried, tested, and mostly true from his life on the farm, was something that Percy found intriguing but counterproductive. Caspar smiled to himself as he thought of this, and meandered into an old storage room, where there were hung clerical robes, adornments, and other such accouterments that had once been used so long ago. He gazed around with a sudden interest, and then suddenly his eyes alighted on a chain with a small key. There was no one else coming for it, but Caspar all but lunged for the key and its chain, lest it should somehow disappear and start their search all over again. He raced back to where the book still stood as he called for Percy, and the Gnome came rushing out as Caspar reached the book with the small key. It fit. The larger key was freed, and Percy clapped his hands as he smiled.

"Bravo! Bravo!" he exclaimed as Caspar took this key and used it with the lock on the chest. The chest opened, and inside lay several more books and a golden end-flute, traced with silver and platinum. "Well!" Percy said in awe as his friend slowly lifted the instrument out of the chest in a reverent manner.

"This... this *must* be the artifact... and these books here must pertain to its workings..." Caspar murmured softly as he gazed at the thing; the silver and platinum tracings culminated near the top of the flute to form the silhouette of a woman--probably Chloe, Caspar thought to himself.

"Yes... yes indeed..." Percy remarked, looking at the books with a renewed interest. "Well... this is going to get quite cumbersome..." he added, thinking about all the books and stuff that they were collecting. Caspar suddenly looked up and blinked, then turned to his friend.

"You know, while I was wandering about on my slow and steady search," he began, emphasizing the last few words with a grin as Percy returned it wryly, "I did see this old carriage stored away in one of the temple stables. Elvar's trained for such things, it's no bother to him; and I daresay it might be more conducive for your studies than sitting on my lap while we jaunt about the world."

"A carriage? Still here after all these years?" Percy said with a raised eyebrow. "Well," he continued, clearing his throat, "let's get our treasures out of here, and then we can fiddle with it--you never know, some fool or other may have simply abandoned it. No sense to that unless it's quite broken... although its being here would have meant there should have been some trace of tracks about the area... hmm..." the Gnome went on, wondering to himself what it was that lay in the stables.

When they had set their burdens down near where Elvar was grazing, they headed to where Caspar had seen the carriage, along with Dusty. Upon reaching this, the Gnome made a thorough inspection of the thing; it was of antique design, to say the least, but it seemed solid and hale. It seemed built to absorb shocks and jolts of the very extreme kind, and was made of a most resilient wood, its black paint more or less absorbed into the texture of the thing. They opened the door, and found it very filled with cobwebs and other such litter that had accumulated over the long years since it was last used. The two of them looked about the stable, and found items that could be used in cleansing it from such rubbish; Caspar and Percy spent the rest of the day doing so, lighting up some of the old lanterns that still hung about when it got dark so that they could continue. As they cleaned it, they gradually found the accessories that would hitch it up to a horse, and made careful inspection of these to ensure their viability. Whatever they had been made of, they were still strong and hardy. "It's as if they were made yesterday..." Caspar remarked.

"To be sure, to be sure..." Percy agreed as they continued examining them. By the time the night sky was in full swing, they had thoroughly cleansed the old carriage, and had brought their things and Elvar over to the stables so that they could rest for the night. "It's no inn, but it will do for now." the Gnome remarked as they set up camp.

"We'll set off whenever we're good and awake, after getting this thing hitched to Elvar, that is." Caspar said as he began drifting off.

"Quite so, quite so." Percy nodded back. "Very interesting, to be sure." he continued; having been so absorbed in cleaning and working earlier, he had not been talking much at all, and now it broke forth as if someone unplugged a dam. Caspar smiled as he did so, listening as the Gnome brought forth his long held-in analysis. "The structure of the thing suggests that it does indeed belong to the time of the Astralatian cult; the components, however, are unknown to me. That wood is the toughest and most durable I've ever seen; but the frame of the thing seems to be standard Dwarf-steel. Tough stuff, Dwarf-steel. We Gnomes have been analyzing it for years, trying to improve upon it. No luck yet, but there's breakthroughs here and there that seem to be promising. But anyway. I wonder what it looked like in its prime condition... obviously, it was black; but why black? It's antithetical to the color schemes of the rest of the temple, and indeed the entire Astralatian theological and philosophical perspective..." he continued, musing aloud upon his inquiries and observations until sleep overtook him as well. The night passed in peace, and just before noon that next day they were off on the road again, still heading steadily towards the north.

Chapter Nine: The Werecat

It was four days after Evelyn had retrieved the Sword of Magus from the Ogre's keeping. After the monks and Princess Hannah had bidden her farewell, she had resumed her journey at a quickened pace, feeling pressed for time on account of her diversion. But at least it had gotten her through the mountains, and now she was once again travelling in a forest region; at an outpost near the foothills she had come across a group of traders, from whom she had purchased some maps. One of these had given her to know she was in the Were Forests, where dwelt one of the more mysterious races of the great continent of Argorro: the Werecats. She would not encounter them most likely. They were prone to hiding as strangers came about; the bolder ones, those of the mercantile-minded or the mercenaries among them were usually found further south among the great cities. At home the Werecats were so well hidden from others, and so adept at staying hidden, that if you encountered one at all it was either a miracle or you were being hunted for inadvertently trespassing on a burial ground or sacred shrine below the trees; and thus Evelyn kept to the road that meandered its way through the forests, maintained by the mysterious Werecats so that they would not themselves be disturbed. Evelyn's meeting with the merchants had taken place two days ago now, and she was now in the heartlands of the scattered forests. It would be another day or two before she was out of Werecat territory, and then she would be in the Kingdom of Augusta, the capital city of which was Auschternople. It was an imperial confederacy made up of various alliances and vassalage, and the Great King ruled from his grand palace in the midst of his chosen city. But there was a ways to go yet before she reached this.

At the present moment she was absorbed in looking at the ancient jyuga-trees, their thick trunks extending high into the sky as they towered above the forest road. *I wonder if the Werecats dwell in such places...* she wondered to herself as she kept going. Were they even now gazing down upon her, unseen in the boughs above, watching in amazement as an Elf of all things traversed their forest? Evelyn smiled to herself. Elves had hidden themselves away for so long, it was no wonder people gazed at her in rapt awe. She was amazed to see that this forest was so untouched by the Demonic Hordes when so much else had not been spared; the Kingdom of Augusta itself was still reeling from the great attack in some places, its nobles and knights trying to tighten their alliances to launch an attack in response, the merchants had told her. From the northern edges that bordered the Were Forests, to the far southern Dukedom of Murana Day, and then again to the western reaches of various lordships and earldoms, all Augusta was alight with activity, centered around the central and eastern portions where the king at Auschternople was truly and without a doubt the supreme master of his lands.

A squirrel darted across the path, followed by a second, and then a third; the three of them then dashed up one of the jyuga-trees, pursued by a fox, who skidded to a halt at its base and began barking in frustration as its lunch bounded away up the tall tree. Smiling to herself again, Evelyn resumed walking, taking in other sights of the forest; there were strange birds and stranger creatures upon the ground, wildflowers and herbs that did not grow near her old home, fruit-trees that looked inviting but which were, as a merchant had warned her, poison to the first touch, and butterflies that flew about nonchalantly, as if there were nothing in the world but them. Small and wily fairies also fluttered about, their lithe forms unhindered by garments of any kind, save the small leaves and flower petals they put in their hair. Some of them were painted about their bodies to be either better hidden or wildly decorated, and Evelyn smiled at them as they flew by with a wave. So Werecats were not alone in their forest after all. One more thing to criticize her people for; the intolerance of anyone but themselves within their borders. *Let the past lie forgotten, and let the future come swiftly.* Evelyn said to herself as she continued along. At the end of the day she reached a river, and after bathing in this she settled herself in for a rest beneath one of the trees next to it.

It was as she was still asleep the next morning that the Werecat found her. He stood taller than most, though he was of average size for his race, and his fur was golden-brown with dark stripes like one of his true feline cousins. Dark-green eyes looked at the sleeping Elf with great curiosity. She was not an intruder, for she kept to the path masterfully; but what had brought an Elf this far south for the first time in almost two-hundred years? This was the question Ragya had in his mind as he gazed upon her; she was beautiful, for an Elf at least, but that was not the most interesting thing about her. Ragya's other question lingered on her sword. Unless he was very much mistaken, it was the Sword of Magus, that human-mage who had built such a powerful and charismatic reputation that even the Werecats had acknowledged him as one of their close allies. Ragya had seen the signs that the earth-spirits had given him; Magus' sword was in the hands of a new bearer, and he must follow this bearer to seek his destiny. Slightly suspicious about this being an Elf, he was nonetheless charmed to see that at least one of these mysterious, overgrown fairies had seen fit to grace the world with their presence again. *Well, not completely a fairy...* he thought to himself as he took in her green tunic and the soft leather boots that lay beside her. A finely crafted bow was also next to her, and a quiver of arrows lay just beside it; Elves were renowned for their archery. The rising sun cast a beam down through the thick boughs of the jyuga-trees to shine upon her, and she softly stirred. Ragya all but vanished, being extremely adept at hiding in a forest, as were all his people. He watched for a moment, and decided to approach and speak to her in the traditional fashion of his people; Evelyn stirred herself, and after she shook herself awake she stood up to stretch. She then unfastened her belt, and took off the tunic to put it away and exchange it for another; it was as she did this that Ragya approached her. "Greetings, forest-sister." he said in a soft and mellow voice. The response was instantaneous; forgetful of all else, Evelyn dropped the tunic, grabbed the bow and an arrow, and before Ragya could take another step she had him in her sights. He admired the inhuman speed of her response, and the otherworldly beauty that now stood before him. For her own part, Evelyn paused a moment; forest-sister was an honorific among the Werecats, denoting a measure of respect or friendship. Nonetheless she did not like being taken off-guard, especially while naked.

"Who are you, forest-brother?" she asked him in reply.

"I am Ragya; I am a druid of my people, and it is my fheas to seek the bearer of the Sword of Magus and travel with them, so the earth-spirits tell me." the Werecat returned, blinking at her curiously.

"The fheas... a sacred bond for a sacred journey." Evelyn said, equally intrigued as he nodded back. She lowered the bow, and removed the arrow to put it back in its quiver. She then stood up, crossing her arms over her chest as she addressed him again. "Do you always sneak up on women in such ways, Master Ragya?" she asked him with a grin.

"I come to you now because the sky-clad body is one of the few times my people say that truth cannot be hidden. It is a sign of utmost trust and respect." he said, and she then saw that he too had no garment on. "Besides, there is no one around. No one will be this way today except for me--and you." he told her, and then sat down. Evelyn sat down as well, her initial suspicions dwindling away.

"So your fheas is to follow me?" she asked him, trying to

understand.

"The earth-spirits told me that it is the bearer of the Sword of Magus I must follow to reveal my destiny. That is you--unless that is *not* the Sword of Magus." he returned, his eyes intent upon her.

"It is the Sword of Magus. With it I slew the Ogre that stole it and reclaimed a treasure of my family." she replied, and he inclined his head in reverence.

"Then you seem to have your share of honor. But tell me, sister, why do you travel?" he asked again, his expression one of wonder; Evelyn smiled, and sighed wistfully as she replied.

"I am seeking a mortal man, one whom I hope to love as long as the candle of his life burns with fire and passion." she returned softly, and Ragya blinked, looking at her with a new respect.

"An Elf seeks a mortal man for a husband... forsaking her people utterly?" he wondered in a mostly-rhetorical question.

"In more ways than one. I was a princess among my people." she admitted, and at that the Werecat inclined his head again.

"Then I am honored you have trusted me with this. And I am honored to follow one who does not let the old ways interfere with what her heart tells her to do." he said as he got back up, heading over to put on the kilt that marked his occupation and clan.

Evelyn then went back to putting on her tunic, donning a grey one, and then fastened on the rest of her accouterments. When she had finished, she saw Ragya had his own wayfaring gear upon him, including a great staff, and the Werecat bowed again as she smiled at him.

"You needn't bow to me, Master Ragya; I forfeited all claim to my heritage by simply running off for a mortal man." she said as the two of them began walking.

"Nevertheless." Ragya returned softly, implying that he would revere her as royal even despite her self-imposed exile. Evelyn looked over at him with a faint smile, and then returned her attention to the road. "And what is the name of this whom you seek?" he wondered as they made their way along the forest road. "There are, after all, as many tribes of men as there are races, if not even more than that." he added.

"His name is Caspar; I hope to find him travelling on one of these roads as well." she said to him, and he growled or purred thoughtfully.

"Caspar..." he murmured softly. "A name given by those in the far south to their boy-children." he remarked, and then halted to sniff the wind. Evelyn, intrigued, stopped also to see what he would do. After sniffing the wind, Ragya then opened a pouch, carefully selecting seven rune-stones from it; he drew a circle on the ground with his claw, and cast the stones into its bounds. Evelyn knelt down as he did, wondering what it all meant. Ragya purred as a small smile crept to his face. "He travels, child; and he is not alone. Good companions are with him, and there may be one more that will follow him in his own quest. We shall see. The stones point to the great city of Auschternople; see--the Royal Ixthus and the Sea-Queen's Mother align with the Lover's Cross."

"And the other four?" she asked.

"The Forest-boughs for we who dwell in the woods; the Rune of Cassandra for one of the south; and the other two are runes of chance. Chance in this case being that of companions." he told her, and she nodded, amazed at seeing one of the ancient arts come to life before her eyes. They resumed walking after Ragya had put away the stones, and forded the river; when this was past, the trees thinned out a bit, their foliage dwindling as they neared the edges of the wood.

"How did you become a druid?" Evelyn asked him, and Ragya smiled.

"My grandfather was a druid; I was always enraptured by the art, and when the time came I showed a strong gifting for it. My grandfather himself trained me to begin with, and after my initial apprenticeship I studied under four other consecutive masters, until at last I became a master myself. That was many moons ago; but as for turnings of the sun, it has been fifty and four since I was first introduced to the druidic art at five sun-turnings." he told her, and Evelyn quickly deduced that a sun-turning was a year; thus Ragya was over twice as old as she was.

"So it was a way of honoring family then." she remarked.

"You could say so." Ragya agreed. "It would not be untrue... but family was merely the first step. And what of you? What led you forth on your own quest?" Ragya then asked her.

"A dream." she said simply, and the Werecat marvelled that she should be chasing after a mortal man because of a dream.

"Dreams and portents; it seems we are both divinely appointed to the path we walk." he mused.

"Perhaps..." Evelyn allowed.

"Believe me, I can be somewhat cynical of even my own readings, but they are always true, in some fashion." he said softly.

"What does that mean?" she wondered.

"It means that the mystical is not so easily read all the time; one may take it one way only to find it is something different altogether. And that which is simple may be complex, or what is complex may be simple. It is not an easy art, but it is one I know well; our path is, whether we like it or not, appointed." Ragya continued, his constantly soft and patient tone one that kept Evelyn's attention more than anyone ever had, even Mala.

"Do you believe in fate then?" she wondered at him.

"If I did not, I would not be here." the Werecat replied simply, to which she smiled.

"Of course. Your destiny." Evelyn said in return. They continued conversing lightly as they made their way through the forests, and by that evening they were on what Ragya identified as the outskirts. Before them now was grasslands, sparsely treed here and there by some small yet determined member of the deciduous kind; looming beyond the grasslands was a great mountain range, the tops of which were just visible to them. Ragya let out a soft growl, and the two of them turned to each other.

"Are you as swift as I, forest-sister?" he asked her pointedly. "We must run as if we were the essence of the wind across these bare plains, for our safety."

"I am one of the swiftest Elves, though I do not know how that compares." she replied to him. "What is out here that seeks you or I?" she wondered.

"These grasslands are populated by roving hunters and mercenaries; but there is also the wildlife. Now is the best of times to race across to find a place of shelter, when all is still. Shall we run, sister?" Ragya said to her, and she nodded. They then began to run; Ragya dropped to all fours, and sped off at a hefty pace, while Evelyn began picking up speed to match him as her lithe form followed the streak of Werecat that galloped across the grasslands. They matched each other pace for pace as the moons began rising, all four of them shining some light down upon them as they raced through the tall grass of the plains. It was exhilarating; it was as if they raced for the stars in the heavens above, as if the four moons were great monarchs come to see them run. Small creatures darted out of their path, too obscured to be identified; owls flew overhead, seeking their prey within the tangled stalks; fireflies twinkled hither and yon about the plains; the night-songs of crickets and frogs came to their ears; a fox raced about with its young; and the deer bounded away with a family of rabbits. In the Forests of Alastria, nature was almost tame; here, it was wild, truly wild, and Evelyn exulted in the rawness of such a place.

She would have gone on in the heat of such a moment, but after several hours of their wild run she tripped on something and went sprawling into the ground. Ragya heard her as she let out a small shriek, and before a second had passed he had flipped around to aid her. She had fallen on to her side, and groaned softly as she tried to move. "Lie thee still." Ragya said softly. The howls of wolves and other predators suddenly rose up in chorus. The Werecat growled; he knew what they were. Not only wolves, but coyotes and some jackals were lingering about. He had to get her out of here now.

"Come, sister, put your arms about my neck." he then said, and Evelyn reached up to do as he said. He stood up, and she wrapped her legs about him. "Hold tight!" he said as another chorus of howls was heard; Evelyn shuddered this time, and he felt her doing so. She felt vulnerable, and was likely injured somewhere, though she did not complain of it yet. The Werecat raced off, but not soon enough--the packs gave chase.

He could see them racing after them, and he began murmuring in the language of his people; it took a few moments for Evelyn to realize he was casting a spell of some sort. She felt him shifting in some fashion, and then he let out a roar; she then understood. He had shifted to pure-feline, taking the form of a great wildcat to outrace the pursuing packs. Once again she was caught up in the exhilarating sensation of their flight, and she cast her cares to the wind, literally, as they raced away from their would-be attackers.

After ten minutes, most of the packs had given up; after another ten, they had all given up, and the two new friends continued on their way undisturbed. When several more hours had gone by, Ragya came to a halt near an ancient grove of stones, and here he set down the injured Elf so that he could shift back. When he had done so he knelt down beside her again; she was holding her right leg. He helped her take off the boot, and then began murmuring in the language of his people once more; it was a healing spell this time, and Evelyn felt the pain recede as he spoke the strange yet hypnotic words. She took a deep breath, and let it out slowly as the final sensations of pain left her, looking up at him gratefully. He nodded, and then left her side to start making a shelter for the night as she took her other boot off. "We will stay here the night; this is a well-hidden place where nothing should trouble us-- and if it does, we will have warning." Ragya remarked as he began a small fire.

"We must have travelled some distance." Evelyn remarked as she removed all but her tunic so that she could be more comfortable.

"Many leagues lie between us and the forest now. It is my hope to be at the mountains before two sunsets." the Werecat said, and she nodded.

"Sorry about the delay." she said with a wry smile, and he shook his head.

"It is nothing, little sister; do not worry over it." he returned with a soft grin. Evelyn's smile brightened, and she looked up at the night-sky; when the fire was steady, Ragya looked up as well. There was the Great Warrior, proud and hale as ever; near him were the Twin Angels of Light and Darkness; over yonder was the Sea-King; here was the Red

Lion; and near the four moons was a star of blue, famous to all the peoples of the world as Heaven's Light. Other patterns could be discerned in the skies, but she only knew these few by name.

"Do your people tell stories of the four moons?" Evelyn wondered. Ragya blinked.

"Do yours?" he asked in reply, and she shook her head.

"They are motifs only, a backdrop for the high-minded philosophy of isolationists." she told him, and he blinked again.

"A pity. They are of great myth to my people. See! The green moon, we call her Asai; she is the mother of the red, Luna, and of the silver and grey Tanisto. Crystolin, the orange, is their father. He then lay with his partner again, and made the stars. His daughter Luna then tricked him into lying with her, and she conceived the greater stars, the constellations and the Heaven's Light. And the stars lay with each other, and their seeds were planted all about this world, giving rise to the good races. Luna, in jealousy, then tricked her brother Tanisto into sleeping with her, and she again conceived, giving rise to the dark races. Then the parents came together again, and Asai then gave birth to the sun, so that those who were of good would not dwell in darkness forever. Tanisto then made love to the stars, and the spirits came of his unions; the earth-spirits, the wind-sages, the water-sprites, the mountain-boggles, the tree-fairies, and the fire-wisps. Asai then invited her son to sleep with her, and of their union came the legendary heroes who ascended later to immortality, becoming the deities that some worship. Then the four of them came together, chanting with their heavenly offspring in union, and this brought magic into the world.

"And so the four moons are the eldest, we say, the progenitors who still watch over our world along with all in the heavenly skies. When there is an eclipse, it is usually Luna; we say she is offering herself to her brother the sun. Only once has she succeeded, and this gave rise to the demonic beings. And when the four moons are all full at the same time, which happens only rarely, we believe they are once again singing in chorus with their heavenly offspring, renewing the magic in the world." Ragya told her, his gentle voice once again compelling Evelyn to listen as his narrative unfolded. "That, at least, is the brief summary of the Tanga-Mao-Rrsta, our earliest and most sacred stories." he added.

"I would love to hear the fullness of it someday." Evelyn told him, and he smiled.

"It takes four days to hear it in full." Ragya told her.

"Even so." she smiled back. After that, they ate a light meal, and settled themselves in to rest for the remainder of the night. Evelyn dreamed of the stars, and of her and Caspar dancing about them, dancing to the music of the heavens, which not even Caspar himself could match.

***

As Ragya had hoped, they reached the mountains in two days' time, ascending into the foothills as dawn began to break forth. They had spent most of their time across the plains in a silence, saving their energy for running as swiftly as they could to reach their destination. Now the two of them slowed to a walk, slowly catching their breath as they made their way into the passage that led through the tall mountains. When they had more or less recovered, Ragya began telling her of what lay in these mountains; there were giant creatures, creatures that were more or less similar in size or girth to those in the mountains near Riverdell, and a few villages of men. It was Ragya's intention to avoid these, and when Evelyn asked him why he simply replied, "For haste's sake." Evelyn accepted this, desiring also to come as swiftly as she could to Caspar, and so they agreed upon their course.

"Besides, your herb-lore and knowledge of the wilds should keep us out of trouble." she added as they resumed a quicker pace. The Werecat's face lit up in a faint grin.

"Indeed." he returned softly as they moved along. "And there is something else in these mountains I wish to see; the fabled Shrine of Asai." he added, and Evelyn nodded. She only knew who Asai was from their earlier conversation, but visiting her shrine did not seem too much of a detour--or, perhaps, it was no detour at all, but something on Ragya's determined path. Had he been down this way before? He must have, from how he knew the area. She decided to ask him anyway, wondering about him more and more.

"Have you been down this way before?" she asked. "You seem to know our way very well... are you a bit of a traveller as well as a druid?" she added as he turned to her slightly.

"Once upon a time, when I was young. My parents were merchants, and we were often found wandering southwards, where men trade for what they will. You have not travelled yourself, I take it?" he replied, wondering about her in turn.

"No, I have not." she said with a soft smile. "Not exactly... the Forests of Alastria were burned, and I was taken along with the other refugees that were fleeing our cities." Evelyn said, remembering the hazy images of fire and people screaming or weeping as the fabled forests met their doom. She let out a sad sigh as she remembered, and he blinked.

"It is a true sorrow that the Forests of Alastria did not go unscathed in the Great Raid, as my people call it. My own father fought in a skirmish those years ago; he fell in battle as he defended a young

102

woman, a human woman." Ragya said, and Evelyn looked up at him. "I suspect that, knowing what I know of Elven traditions, your parents were either separated from you or they were killed." he added; Evelyn could again hear the screams of death, the screams of her own family as they died and she was spirited away. She let her hair fall into her face, and slowly gave a nod in reply. "Forgive me, forest-sister." Ragya said at once in his calming voice.

"There is nothing to forgive, forest-brother." Evelyn returned as she took a breath to keep from crying. "It's in the past." she added with a faint smile, which he returned.

"From the past, we find knowledge in the present, to prepare for the future." he said just as softly. Evelyn reflected on his words, and nodded as they kept on their way.

"How far is it to the shrine?" she asked after a moment's silence.

"It is a journey of two days," Ragya told her, "and it lies on the other edge of these tall mountains. From there, a path descends, and we will find ourselves in the heartlands of Augusta, the grandest kingdom of men."

"The Legendary Augusta..." Evelyn remarked softly.

"The struggling Augusta." Ragya said knowingly. "They did not escape the wrath of the Sorcerer King's hordes. We will need to be on guard." he added, and she nodded. Silence then resumed, and they focused on making their way through the mountains, Elf and Werecat silently padding along the paths as if they were but ghosts. Nature indeed made no intent to stop them, and they dwindled in to its scenery as if they were indeed a part of it; if anyone saw them, no one made to come after them, and no one believed those who spoke of it. Two beings from the fabled forests of the north travelling south--it was impossible, was it not? Ludicrous, yes. Very ludicrous indeed.

***

There was little but silence between Evelyn and Ragya as they made their way towards the Shrine of Asai; if they spoke, it was to agree upon the next path they should take to avoid their being noticed. And so they made their way swiftly and silently through the mountains, as if they were two spirits of long ago come back to walk upon the lands once more. The wilds grew denser around them as they got closer to the Shrine; Evelyn found this odd, until Ragya softly told her that it was a holy place to the Werecats only, and a place avoided by most other races. Thus it had been overgrown, and its pilgrims had been content to let it do so, if it kept fools away from their sacred grounds. But Evelyn was also of the forest, Ragya added; a different forest, but a forest nevertheless, and she would be welcome here.

"Are there priests or holy-men there, then?" she asked him.

"There are some. Never more than twelve; never less than four." Ragya affirmed. "Do not think it strange that these guardians let the forest surround them; we embrace nature, perhaps even moreso than your own people do." he added.

"It is true." Evelyn agreed. "The Elves seek to reshape nature to their ideals of beauty."

"And we let it grow in harmony with what we make, or take what is given by the land, and ask no more than that." Ragya returned, then looked at her curiously. "You speak of Elves as if you are no longer one of them?" he wondered softly. Evelyn made no outward reaction, but in her mind the question struck to the deeps of her heart. She *had,* in a small, snide way, insinuated that she was no longer counting herself when she spoke of Elves.

"Perhaps I am not--not in the way they desire." she finally replied. "The Elves don't want change. I do." she added, and Ragya made a purring sound.

"Then we are both on the same quest, in a way. To learn from the world, to show that the races can live in harmony as the fates intended." he said softly.

"May that be so." Evelyn agreed. A silence then resumed, until at last they caught sight of the worn road-stones that led towards the ancient Shrine of Asai. They hastened along this path, which was very faded and in most spots was just plain grass. It was another hour before they got to their destination, and Evelyn caught her breath as she looked at the ancient shrine; it was well-weathered, covered in strands of ivy and with spurts of holly emanating from cracks in the walls, but it was still regal in its own right, regal and otherworldly. "Have I stepped in to a dream..." she wondered to herself softly as they walked towards it. Her attention was so fixated upon the sight that she did not notice five acolytes of the shrine suddenly standing there before them at its doors; it was Ragya who gently put a hand on her shoulder, calling her back to attention. He spoke to those before them in the language of the Werecats, and they bowed, moving aside to let them in. They entered, and were escorted by a sixth acolyte to a homely room furbished with homely-style furniture and some candlesticks lining the walls. A chandelier of antlers hung from the ceiling, and small tapestries covered the ancient stone walls. Evelyn looked over at Ragya, but the Werecat was now silently meditating on one of the patterned rugs upon the floor. Deciding to follow his example, she laid her weapons and her boots aside, and then sat upon another of the rugs in the room. She closed her eyes, and the scent of the candles grew stronger; *they're tinged with some sort of incense,* Evelyn realized as their fragrance grew stronger. She inhaled deeply, reveling in the lovely perfume that permeated throughout the room, and suddenly felt herself lifted into a whole other world.

***

Time revolved around her; life, death, the universe in chaos, in balance; a host of lives being born, dying again, returning to earth and thence to the celestial planes of Ragya's four moons; the heavens spun around her, the earth spun below her; was it an orb, or was it flat? Did it matter in this realm? What was this realm, exactly, where everything and nothing seemed to be converging on one point, one focal point, a centrifuge of all creation? How had she--wait... wait! There was Caspar; he was driving a carriage. Who was that beside him? A Gnome? Yes, yes it was a Gnome.

They were travelling through mountains, just as she and Ragya were; a great city lay before them. Was this Auschternople?--no; it could not be. This city was in the mountains. Auschternople lay by the sea, according to the histories.

Caspar was then beside her. Time stopped. The universe stopped. Everything stopped; all that was left was the two of them. Evelyn caught her breath, flushing as she stood before him in the drab tunic; he smiled, and the scene changed. They stood on the spires of a palace; both of them were in white, a white so pure it seemed as if the stars themselves had come down to clothe them. "I love you..." had she spoken, or had he? It didn't matter; their arms wrapped around each other, Evelyn reached up, Caspar reached down, their lips met, and...

***

"Forest-sister, awaken!" Ragya's voice called insistently; Evelyn reluctantly stirred, and found herself lying on the ground, drenched in sweat. The Werecat sat next to her, his face full of concern. She blinked in confusion, and he shook his head. "You were in the fastness of a dream; it is now the late evening." he told her, and she confusedly sat up.

"I was... what?" she asked uncertainly. "What was that?" she wondered vaguely, her mind more focused on where a bath might be.

"It... is a gift that Asai grants to travellers, on occasion. There are those who seek to have what you have had for years, and never receive it. You are remarkable, indeed." Ragya said to her. Evelyn slowly brought the thoughts together, trying to make sense of them.

"Will it come true? Is it a vision?" she asked him again. Ragya smiled.

"Remember what I told thee; everything comes true, in a fashion. It may not be true in the way that you expect, but it will come to pass, in one way or another." he told her, and Evelyn nodded.

"Was this the purpose of bringing us here?" she asked for a third

105

time, a faint smile on her lips.

"Perhaps." Ragya returned, smiling still. "But for a better purpose, there are supplies that the acolytes keep here for travellers such as ourselves, and rooms for a night." he added. "The baths are outside; go out this door and turn right. They are in the back of this shrine. No one will disturb thee." Ragya said to her. She nodded again, and went to go relax herself in a bath.

Later in the evening, she found herself in a room similar to the one from earlier; one of the sisters had taken her to it, and given her some additional clothes for her travels before she was left to rest. It was a peaceful night, all in all, and she woke up the next morning refreshed. A meal was left on the table for her, still hot. After eating it, she decided to put on one of the robes given to her as a way of saying "thank you" as they left, and when she at last came out she found four of them standing there with Ragya. They bowed to her, and Ragya gave her an approving nod. Each of the Werecats touched their noses to hers, and then she and Ragya were on the road again.

***

When they had gone some distance, Evelyn looked at the beautiful patterns upon the robe she wore, and a question began forming on her lips. Ragya saw it as she gazed over that which she wore, and at once made an answer before she spoke.

"It is a robe of Asai, gifted to those honored by a vision during their visit. You are now highly favored among my people, forest-sister." he told her, and Evelyn smiled.

"It's a beautiful gift, every part of it." she said softly in reply, and he nodded. He then looked ahead, stopping as they came to a ridge; below them was a wooded country, interspersed with meadows and fields, and two rivers that seemed to converge far off in the distance.

"Welcome to the Kingdom of Augusta." Ragya announced softly, and they began to descend into the valleys below.

Chapter Ten: The Valkyrie

At the time that Evelyn encountered Ragya in the Were Forests, Caspar and Percy were indeed in a series of mountains; the continent of Argorro was well known for its mountainous regions, from the fabled halls of the Dwarves to the towering heights where the Giants lived. This was neither of those, but no less regal in and of itself; the early spring air lent to its reaches a vitality that escaped it in the later seasons of autumn and winter, and the two friends were making quite good time. The hound Dusty was sleeping in the carriage that Elvar pulled, and Percy was chattering away as he made observations of their surroundings to Caspar, who half-listened as he watched the road. It was no slight to the Gnome, who was more or less thinking aloud anyway. Caspar's being there with him lent him simply gave a credence to talking aloud as opposed to talking to himself, as he might normally do.

From what Caspar had heard when he was paying more attention to his friend the Gnome, these mountains were reputed to hold a Valkyrie Enclave, hence their curious name: the Maiden Heights. Their major city was farther to the west, deeper in the mountains that they now travelled. From what scraps of their history were available, the Valkyries claimed to be exiled angels, as Percy had told him earlier; they were all females, and in addition to their great physical prowess in battle could call upon eldritch powers to aid them. Except for the Elves and the Sea-folk, they were the most beautiful of the races in the world, so stories said.

"Fantastical nonsense for romantic story-telling, but there you are." Percy went on. "Not that I doubt it a bit, but there are Gnomish lasses I would much prefer to some everlasting angel; intellect over beauty, Caspar, remember that! Though I don't doubt as you may have it with that Elvish girl we're trying to catch up to. But at any rate; the Maiden Heights. It was during the Great Awakenings of the races, when most of us 'awoke' from whatever primordial slumber was in the dark days before time was even a thought, that the Valkyries claimed to have descended to earth against the will of higher powers. They were exiled then, as they recall it, and cursed with mortality. Oh, they don't age; not from the outside, anyway. Their eyes, now; their eyes, like the Elves, are said to betray a sign of age, but they're so reclusive that most of what we know is all-out fancy and wicked, sensual desires." the Gnome continued.

"Some have it that they don't wear clothes, even in battle; I find that absolutely ludicrous, and so does the rest of the thinking world. What fool would go into battle without armor of some sort? And the ridiculously voluptuous depictions in ballads and so forth--no offense to you, of course--but it's rather demeaning!" he went on, and Caspar smiled. He had always made an effort to steer clear of such raunchy songs, and heartily agreed with the Gnome's outrage.

"And furthermore--" Percy was about to go on, but at that moment Elvar halted, whinnying when his master tried to make him go forth again. Human and Gnome looked around; Percy pricked up his ears to hear better, and Caspar was about to draw out his sword when a javelin landed with a loud "thunk!" just near his hand. He froze, and Percy's eyes widened as he caught sight of the thrower. It was a Valkyrie. Her piercing blue eyes gazed at them with a determined expression that was neither antagonistic nor friendly; her golden hair was wound in a braid, clasped at its end with a golden binding; gold was the armor upon her chest, and she wore a leather war-skirt with a pair of matching boots. She then smiled at them, and strode forward.

"It has been long since any dared to walk these passes. And now look; a Gnome, the most diminutive yet most clever, 'tis said, in the company of a human who has the look of a singer as opposed to a warrior, driving a carriage fit for a goddess through the mountains, even in its clearly antique state." she said as she halted near the driver's seat; the Valkyrie then pulled her javelin out with one pull, and beckoned Caspar to join her on the ground. Percy moved over to the side that they were on, and she cast him a curious smile as Caspar got down. "So. What forms this odd little band?" she asked as she caught sight of the hound in the carriage.

"Would you believe, it was a dream that began my path?" Caspar said with a faint and disarming laugh to try and win her over. She did not make a reply, but she did raise an eyebrow. "And forgive my rudeness, as I forgive you for that javelin throw. My name is Caspar, and this is my friend Percy." he added.

"Percy Von Daumer if you please, madam." the Gnome put in with a doff of his hat.

"The rebuke is accepted." she said with a faint smile. "I was rather rude, but it made such a fine target." she added with a wink. "My name is Kia Re. You are not trespassing on our lands, but it would be wise for travellers to be more wary, lest they find themselves doing so."

"Believe me, no intention of trespassing; just passing through the mountains to..." the young man began again, flustering as she looked at him intently.

"To... what?" Kia Re asked him, and Percy coughed.

"A rendezvous, madam. We've a rendezvous with someone on the other side of these mountains, possibly in the direction of Auschternople, and thus we took the most expedient route we could think of, seeing as how the sea-side towns are all in a fluster of late."

"To meet with someone." the Valkyrie said with a slow nod. "Very well. If you would prefer not to trespass, and if you would allow me to make full amends, we are not without our own hospitality. I bid you join us for the night and take rest from your travels." Kia Re then added, and Caspar slowly nodded.

"I... yes, I would be grateful... ah... Percy?" he returned, looking up at the Gnome.

"Quite! I would be ever so delighted, madam; you must know that as an investigator of the histories and some of the sciences, that it would be my utmost delight to accompany--"

"Yes, friend Gnome, you shall hear and see and learn all you can wish in a night." Kia Re said with a smile. She then nodded to Caspar, who got back up on the carriage; he was about to help her up, but he found that she had already gotten up without any effort at all, and she then took up the reins of the carriage. "It's easier if you let one who knows the way drive." she remarked as they set off, and the carriage began rolling again. A moment passed in silence, and then Kia Re spoke once more. "You are a singer of songs, are you not?" she asked again as they kept on, looking at him with a smile.

"I, well..." Caspar said with another fluster, feeling inadequate to answer.

"Forgive him, madam, he seems to have picked up a stutter of sorts." Percy said with a jab to Caspar's side. "I can assure you that, in his moments of confidence, he is a minstrel of the utmost quality."

"Indeed? And what songs do they sing of us, friend Caspar?--for so I shall call you." Kia Re asked him again.

"Well... fanciful ones; imaginative... most of them probably not flattering... I tend to try and avoid most of them for integrity's sake." Caspar told her.

"Then sing me one that is flattering, O Silver-tongue." Kia Re said with a faint smile.

Caspar blinked, and in that moment suddenly recalled one he had heard long ago during a festival at Murana Day, about an ancient and mythical war. He decided that, if nothing else, it might take his mind off of the strange feelings he was having at the moment, and so abandoned himself to his music.

> *Sing to me, O Muse, of that far-off and ancient time*
> *When the gods themselves gave no care for the world*
> *And the lusting darkness sought to conquer all;*
> *Sing to me, O Graces, of when the angels of heaven*
> *Rebelled for the sake of mortal men and came*
> *Upon the mortal planes to fight against the evil fiends*
> *Of darkness, driving back the ever-hating monsters*
> *In the night, in the long nights of long ago*
>
> *Sing to me, O Muse, of when the angels came down*
> *Shining in the glory of the heavens, ever-brightly*
> *And the gods themselves in jealousy looked down*
> *At the shining hosts of heaven's warriors racing*
> *Towards the battles of the ancient night*
> *Fighting for the right, and in noble sacrifice*
> *To avenge the hurt and broken and the lost ones*
> *Who could not yet fight for themselves*
>
> *Sing to me, O Graces, of how the gods in jealousy*
> *Saw the warrior-maidens of heaven riding fair*
> *Across the mortal planes in battles long ago*
> *And in such jealousy decreed that forever and ever*
> *On these mortal planes they would remain forever*
> *Until the final battles had begun in all creation*
> *Until the ancient Wyrm of the Waters rises up*
> *To devour the hallowed halls of the heavens*
>
> *Sing to me, O Graces, of that far-off day to come*
> *When the angels of heaven, restored to their places*
> *Shall once again ride the mortal planes in majesty*
> *And in beauty never known before, riding once again*
> *To save both of the worlds they love, to go forth*
> *At battle's call with shining sword and helm*
> *When the Valkyries of Valheilen shall ride again*
> *To battle and triumph for heaven and earth*

Caspar's voice faded away on the last notes, and he felt strange once again. He looked over at Kia Re, expecting at the very best a condescending smile and at the worst a dirty look. But she gave him neither. Instead, her face seemed sad, distracted, and a faint tear rolled down her left cheek, as if she was holding in some emotion she was unaccustomed to. Out of politeness, he did not comment upon it, and instead turned to Percy. The Gnome was fast asleep. Caspar softly let out a sigh, smiling at him as he slept the ride away. Kia Re then took his left hand, squeezing it; he looked over at her, and saw a grateful look in her features as she smiled at him. He smiled back, and then she removed her hand, returning her attention to the road.

***

It was not Valheilen, the fabled Valkyrie City to the west, but the city they arrived at was no less splendid, Kia Re told them. It was built to look like the mountains, earthy-colored walls and spires reaching up with gleaming-ivory tiles upon the roofs. The gates were heavy and wooden, set with strong, iron-wrought patterns upon their frames; these were opened to admit the carriage, and Caspar found himself in the City of Jotun-De. The stables were to their left, and it was to this that their carriage and horse were led; Dusty at once raced to sniff at a pack of dogs in the courtyard, who greeted him amiably enough as the other hound came over. Kia Re led her two companions into the main hall, where Caspar was not surprised to see there was indeed no man in sight anywhere.

Most of the Valkyries had blonde hair like Kia Re; others had red or auburn, and a few had dark colored hair. They wore white or silver robes, and others wore varying shades of red; they were told that this signified rank or seniority among their people. Percy was writing faster than the eye could see, taking everything in as quickly as he could. Kia Re then left them to one of her sisters, so to speak, and went to go and change. They were greeted cordially as they were made to sit, and refreshments were brought to them. After a few minutes had passed, Kia Re came back, and she wore a robe of dark red. The Mistress of the Hall looked up, and raised a cup to her; Kia Re bowed, and went to sit beside her guests.

"What is't thou hast brought back to us, sister?" her leader asked.

"Two travellers seeking their way through our mountains. A minstrel and a Gnome, as thou canst plainly see: neither more nor less are they." Kia Re replied.

"As thou sayest; they shalt be given the guest chambers, and thou shalt answer for the two of them in this place." the Mistress returned.

"Be it as thou hast commanded." Kia Re said, inclining her head as she raised her own glass to her leader.

"A bard, thou sayest--where is his harp? Or his lute? Sooth, what fool of a minstrel be this?" one of the others remarked, and some of them laughed.

"You have not heard him, Rhiannon." Kia Re said in reply. "He could calm the goddess of hate herself with his voice." she added firmly, and they looked around at each other. Their Mistress nodded towards Caspar, as if impressed with Kia Re's assertion.

"Then when thou hast refreshed thyself, take up thy voice and sing for us, if thou would be gracious, bard." she then said. Caspar inclined his head in reverence, and the Mistress then gave the Gnome a curious smile. "And what of thou, curious one? Hast thou thy questions and all thy queries prepared for such a visit?"

"Be assured, madam, that all knowledge can never be contained or retained in its full entirety; yet with such wit as I have, I shall indeed be very indebted to hear the truth of the matters in all that concerns your people." Percy told her, and she smiled at him.

"A wise head, and a gracious answer." she returned; the conversations around the table then resumed, and the three of them talked among themselves for a while.

"I did not ask, for I was too overwhelmed, truly; but where did you hear that song?" Kia Re asked Caspar eagerly, her eyes alight with admiration.

"Long ago, when I was a child." he said with a smile. "It was one of the songs that truly inspired me to my own music." he added.

"It is an old song; ah, but I forget: you are of the Order of Cassandra. Deny me not, I see your amulet, friend. They keep in memory many ancient things, indeed. Even the fabled hymn the Bells of Chloe, if only a small fragment of it." she returned, and he nodded.

"What was the Bells of Chloe about?" he wondered.

"Our people say that Chloe was one of the rebelling angels; but she did not fight in war. She gave love and hope, and was not counted among those who became the Valkyries. The hymn is the most sacred and most forgotten of her legacy; it sings of how she healed the world long ago after the great darkness, giving love, joy, and hope to those around her." she told him, and he gave her a faint smile.

"I've something to show you after dinner, if you will, dear lady." he told her, and she gave him an inquisitive smile.

"Very well, friend." she returned.

"Minstrel!" the voice of Rhiannon came again. "Let us hear thy voice that can charm the devils of hell, as my sister has implied--or are you merely a songster?" she asked with a snide smile on her lips.

Caspar at once stood up, looking her in the eyes. She was testing him in some way, he believed, and was determined not to disappoint her. He thought for a brief moment, and then began to recite one of the other songs he had found in one of the books from the temple; it was another song that dealt with the Valkyries, forgotten by him until this moment, but now he let his voice ring out with it as clear as a bell.

O angels, come, come and sing to me
Sing of long ago in the word of stars
Of the fabled halls of golden heaven
In the years before the darkness fell

Let them fly, and let them fly
Sing the story as it passes by
Let them roam, and let them roam
Sing as the story comes back home

Fabled heroes of yestreyear
Valiant deeds in the halls of light
Sing to me of those ancient times
In the years before the darkness came

Let them sing, and let them sing
Hear the story as it takes wing
Let them play, and let them play
Listen 'ere the story fades away

Hammers ringing in the night
Shields are gleaming as they ride
Swords and spears reflect the stars
To fight the darkness as it comes

Let them ride, and let them ride
See the warriors in their stride
Let them go, and let them go
Hear their story of long ago

O angels, come, and sing to me
Of valiant deeds done in the night
Thankless warriors of the hall
Who fought when the darkness fell

Let them fly, and let them fly
Angelic Warriors of the sky
Let them go, and let them go
See them as to war they go

Host of Heaven, ever flying
Off to battle, banners high

The silver bugle sounds its note
Against the darkness as it came

Let them ride, let them ride
See the warriors in their pride
Let them roam, and let them roam
Until at last they shall come home

Riding swiftly to their battle
Charging host of heaven gleaming
Banners high and weapons raised
To fight the darkness as it came

Let them sing, and let them sing
Hear their song as the battles ring
Let them play, and let them play
In the battles cruel and fey
Let them play, and let them sing
The Valkyries shall ever sing
In the hallowed halls of heaven's wings
In the hallowed halls of heaven's wings

Caspar's voice faded away, and there was silence across the room; most of those who heard were softly weeping, including Rhiannon herself, and those who were not were caught up as if in some memory of long ago. They were not immortal creatures, but they kept a long and steady history, and they could recall with accuracy the great tales of their ancestors.

It was a song that touched their hearts, and as Caspar sat down again the Mistress of the Hall raised her cup to him, as did many of the others. Percy gave him a pat on the back, and they spent the rest of the evening in merriment as the hall resumed its activity for the remainder of the evening.

***

Later that night, Kia Re led them to where they would be staying for their rest. It was in fact next to her own room, and she told Caspar that if he still had something to show her that she would be awake for a few more hours. He nodded, and when she had gone they settled in as they would for the night.

"Caution as to what you show her!" Percy said firmly. "You've won their hearts for the night, don't jeopardize that trust or give them reason to detain us."

"Oh, she wouldn't, Percy. Don't ask me how I know, I just do."

Caspar said confidently.

"Hmph!" the Gnome quipped back. "I wish I had your optimism." he shrugged as he settled into one of the chairs for the night, this being as big a bed as the diminutive Gnome could with for. "Good-night, good-night! Don't forget my warning!" he said as he went to sleep, and Caspar smiled. Percy was snoring within seconds.

He was about to get the Golden Book and take it over to Kia Re's room, when she herself suddenly walked back in and shut the door behind her. She put a finger to her lips, and came to sit on his bed.

"Show me here. I felt something, and it was not good; whatever you have, you may be in danger because of it." she said softly, and Caspar nodded. Perhaps Percy was right in some way, but Kia Re was not part of it. He sat down beside her, and reached to bring out the Golden Book from the temple. She gasped silently as he pulled it out, and he opened it to the "Bells of Chloe".

"It's a perfect copy. An original, perhaps." he said softly as she gently took the book from his hands.

"By the stars..." she breathed. He then pulled out the Golden Flute, and she looked at this with equal awe. She turned to him, and blinked in amazement. "You are touched by Chloe. They will all realize this sooner or later... we Valkyries believe that we are the only ones meant to have such secrets as this. Where did you get these?" she asked as softly as she could in her great excitement.

"At an old temple to the south of here." he said, and she nodded at him.

"They will want to keep you here, and these artifacts as well." Kia Re told him.

"I can't. I can't be held up." Caspar said. "I must find her."

"Who?" she asked him.

"Her name is Evelyn." he told her, and she blinked. That was an Elven name.

"You're trying to find an Elf?" she said in an almost soundless voice as she gazed at him in wonder.

"Yes... that's why I travel, to find her. Oh, Kia Re..." he said, turning to the window, "You are beautiful beyond compare, but so is she. And when I saw her, I knew my heart was hers and hers alone, forever, as long as I live." he said, his face enraptured as he spoke. Kia Re smiled at him. So *this* was the mystery behind the two of them.

"Well then, we must get you out of here." she said. "Take rest; I will wake you near the dawn-watches. We must get out of here during the change of the watch." she added.

"Wait--'we'?" Caspar asked her as they stood up.

"Yes, 'we': those songs you sang, they stir my blood, Caspar; I want to fight for the world as my ancestors did, and I can't do that idling in these halls. I may find the world and its people fools at times, and they may be pathetic and petty beyond belief, but I would rather see that good gets its chance to triumph over evil than sit by and do nothing until evil comes to us."

"Because sitting idly by is the greater evil in the end." he said solemnly, and she gave him a nod.

"Yes." she said, and set the book down gently upon the bed. "Now rest." Kia Re told him, and he felt the strange feelings again as she placed a hand on him. She smiled at him, as if she could feel his confusion, and then left the room. After a moment, he carefully packed the two artifacts away, and then placed them under his bed before turning in for sleep himself.

***

"No mortal bard could sing such a song unless he had seen one of the ancient books." Rhiannon said to the Mistress at the council.

"Nay, none." the other agreed.

"Shall I have him brought for questioning?" the red-haired Rhiannon asked her.

"Nay, let him rest; we will not break tryst. We will be honorable; but if he does have one of the ancient books, he must never be allowed to leave. Nor shall his friend the Gnome." she said, her dark-blonde hair obscuring her face as she made her judgment.

"Very well, mistress. I shall bring him when he is awake." the other said, and departed the hall. The other three looked at their leader, uncertain of what to say.

"We will not disobey the mandates of heaven. This young man must remain here." she said firmly, and dismissed them. They bowed, and headed out for their own rest. "And yet, if it is indeed a mandate, why do I feel so wrongly about this?" she wondered softly to herself.

***

Just before the change of watch, Kia Re awoke; still feeling disturbed by something, she went out into the hall, and found Rhiannon pacing around the foyer of the great hall. *Now why would you be here, except to try and detain Caspar and Percy, when you should be sleeping?* She wondered to herself. Deciding not to wait any longer, she went back into her room and quickly donned her things, taking up the travel bag she had made up to accompany the two of them. Softly she headed into the guest room, and quickly shook Caspar awake. He awoke swiftly, and all but sprang out of the bed, accidentally locking lips with her as he rose up. They both blinked, and Kia Re then let out a small sigh, shaking her head at him. She motioned towards the hall, and then tapped her spear. Caspar blinked in understanding. There was

116

someone waiting for them in the hall. He got up, and tapped Percy awake; the Gnome was about to start chattering when he saw his friend motion him into silence. Understanding came to him, and he nodded, quickly gathering up his things.

When they were ready, Caspar and Kia Re took down the curtains and took up some of the blankets, tying them into a rope. She then softly opened the window; it was dark, save around the outer walls, and there were few watching these. It was the shift change. At once she lowered their makeshift rope, and Caspar tied it fast to the heavy bed. She went down first, followed by Percy and then Caspar. There was, fortunately, no window below them, and so no possibility of being seen for a time.

"Now where?" Caspar asked without a sound. Kia Re looked about, and crouched down to head for a small pathway that led towards the stables. Caspar crouched down as well to follow; Percy, being short, had no need to do so, and indeed trotted ahead to scout their way so as not to be caught off their guard. The Gnome motioned for them to halt, and they got down on their knees.

"So that *was* accidental, yes?" Kia Re softly asked.

"Of course! I mean... I'm not being rude, really, but--" Caspar softly spluttered.

"Relax!" she told him, and then Percy motioned for them to keep going. They hastily reached the stables, narrowly missing a sentry as she passed nearby. "Besides, kissing is common among all of us. It's a mark of friendship, and not limited to intimacy." she added softly. Caspar felt some relief at that, but was careful not to show it lest she mistake his meaning. When the other Valkyrie had gone on, they entered the stables swiftly, and began making the carriage ready for travel. Dusty was in a corner nearby, and the hound woke up at the scent of Caspar; sensing some sort of danger, the hound leaped up into the carriage without so much as a command, impressing Kia Re. "Faithful beast." she remarked as Percy joined the hound in the carriage.

"Quite, madam; quite." he remarked. Kia Re and Caspar quickly and carefully hitched Elvar to the thing, resuming their own conversation.

"Besides, you may as well get used to it. I will call you my song-brother now, and you will receive double the affection than any mortal could wish for." Kia Re said to him.

"I spend my life avoiding the coarse talk that men make of intimacy with Elves and Valkyries, and now I am to spend my life in an intimate fashion with both." Caspar said in a soft and wry tone.

"Not too intimate." she returned.

"How *do* your people...?" he wondered hastily, hoping it was not too rude to ask.

"It... is not spoken of in general conversations... but since you ask, and do so out of a respect, we are capable of impregnating ourselves, and only on our High Festival days when the blessing of the ancients is at its fullest for us."

"So... it's an act of will."

"And of love... love creates a family after all, does it not?" she said as she finished with her task.

"Even so." he replied with a nod as he finished his own work. Kia Re then opened the door again, and found that there were but a few guards atop the gate. She turned back to Caspar, and gave him a serious look.

"I hope that you are truly as sincere and full of integrity as I feel you to be, for I am about to give up everything on what may be a whim. They will surely exile me for this, and I may lose all that makes me who I am." she said to him, and he came over to her, placing his hands over hers.

"I swear by the love I have for Evelyn that I will be a faithful song-brother to you all the days of my life and yours." he said to her, and she took a deep breath.

"Thank you." she said, and he let go of her hands. She then looked back up, and spoke again. "I am going to open the gates; it is no uncommon thing for one of us to get the urge to go out at any given time, but you must be on my heels the moment that gate is open."

"I promise." Caspar nodded.

"Then get up there and wait until you hear the gates are open." she said, and walked off towards them. He got up on the driver's seat, and waited. Kia Re's voice rang out, and the sentries seemed to accept her words, for the gates rumbled open. It would take them a full two minutes to open it, and another two to shut it--perhaps longer, if one or more of them tried to stop them. Caspar quickly brought the layout of the courtyard to mind; there should be enough time. The great doors halted. Caspar at once flicked the reins.

"Hya! Fly, Elvar, fly!" he called out, and the horse took off with its burden, racing for the gate as fast as he could run. The sentries saw within the space of a moment, and Kia Re cast her javelin into the mechanism that opened or closed the gates; she dodged to the side as Caspar and the carriage came racing through, and leaped upon it like a cat. Her fellow Valkyries raised the alarm as they raced away, but no immediate pursuit was made.

"Reins!" Kia Re said, and Caspar at once handed them to her. She steered the carriage along the northern passage, heading them in the direction of the Kingdom of Augusta. For the rest of that night and for most of the day they drove on; when it was late in the evening they settled in for a rest, the feeling of dread no longer overpowering their senses. *But why was there no pursuit?* Kia Re wondered to herself as Caspar and Percy set up camp. Why, indeed?

***

"Have they gone?" the Mistress of the Hall asked.

"Yes." Rhiannon said angrily.

"We should hunt them down!" another called out.

"We know where they go, all we must do is pursue!" a third said.

"Do we even know if he really had an ancient book? Perhaps it is best to let them be." a fourth returned.

"Oh, foolish sister!" the third returned.

"Silence!" the Mistress commanded. They fell silent, and watched as she paced about the hall for a moment. When she was still again, she lifted up her eyes; they were filled with a sorrow, and they knew then the judgment. "We will not waste our time following this minstrel and his Gnomish friend. They received some signal of our intention, and we would be dishonored in trying to force them back now. But as for Kia Re..."

***

As the evening wore on, Kia Re went to a nearby stream to bathe herself from the mad escape. She was just feeling refreshed from the soothing water, when all of a sudden a shock went through her body. A gasp escaped her lips, and she fell to her knees in the midst of the stream. A shudder went through her, and she felt sick; then she felt a hand upon her. She looked up; it was Caspar. "Are you all right?" he asked her, and she shook her head.

"They have... taken my power. I am... but a woman." she said softly, and he nodded gently. He was wearing only his breeches, having been preparing for rest when he heard her cry out, and he could feel himself inflamed with a passion at seeing her in the nude. She was broader of frame than Evelyn, but still very graceful in form, and her rose-tipped breasts were fair and large, as if twin orbs of ivory with rubies set into them. For her own part, Kia Re could see that he was no mere minstrel; his strong frame betrayed more than simple song-making. He had been a worker of some sort, or was at least no stranger to working when needed. His tanned complexion suddenly made her wonder what he had been before he chose to embrace the roaming nature of his true vocation, but the thought was drowned out as she realized that she was thinking of him in a deeper and... no; no, they must refrain. She could see him struggling with it as well, the desire to forget all they had known and--by the halls of Ice and Steel! They must not do this.

To dispel the mood, she buried herself in his arms as they stood there in the stream, and he wrapped her in a strong and full embrace. Holding him closely, Kia Re felt his body reacting to their nearness, and longed for there to be no Elven Maiden, that she might make him her own. They stood there for another few moments, and then she made let go, but not before she kissed him again. It was a fervent kiss, and when their lips parted she felt his hands on her shoulders, rubbing them softly.

"We should head back to the camp." he said softly, and she nodded.

"They won't follow. They'll be content with exiling me in such a way." Kia Re said as they left the stream; she picked up her red robe, and placed it around herself, putting out the spark of desire that had been tormenting them. "Evelyn will be fortunate to have you." she added with a smile, and he smiled back as they headed back to rest for the night.

Chapter Eleven: Wayfarers and Thieves

For two beings who had spent their entire lives in the forest, it was no great challenge to remain hidden from the possibility of unfriendly eyes as they approached a more civilized part of the land. The Kingdom of Augusta, once renowned as the greatest kingdom of men, had fallen from grace in the long years since the last great age. The Age of Kings had ended with the Demonic Hordes ravaging the lands of Argorro, from the Forests of Alastria to Vinduürhaf Mökr, the fabled halls of the Dwarves, and thence across the lands to the Kingdom of Augusta. Auschternople had not fallen, but it had taken a great blow; and though it was not in shambles it may as well have been. The militia and the armies in this part of the old Augustan Kingdom had their hands full and then some in dealing with the Thieves' Guild and its cohorts; the thieves had always been there, but in the two decades following the invasion they had risen to become more than a nuisance--they were a plague.

And there were now raiders about in small bands, picking away at the disgraced kingdom so that they might finish it off and usher in their own rule. They were, fortunately, concentrated on the heartlands of Augusta, so that places such as Murana Day and Idoma were free of their prominence; but the crown itself was weary and worn with them. It was into this decay that Evelyn and Ragya silently arrived in, effectively making themselves as shades or ghosts so as not to be disturbed or attract attention. Two days after they descended from the mountains they found a small village and a market; Ragya bought a cloak for Evelyn, who had remained behind in their tree hideaway. They were fast approaching more populated places, and staying away from cities would be a suspicious thing on their part; the cloak would keep Evelyn's ears from being seen, which, after some discussion, she had agreed to. No one would think much of a Werecat travelling with a human woman in these lands, but an Elf? They would have attention in no time, and thus Evelyn agreed to the cloak, not wanting such attention.

Ragya also purchased a steed, and had her mount upon it as they continued travelling on the road. If anyone questioned them, Ragya explained that she was his master and he her protector, and that they were on an errand of great importance; this persuaded most who came across them, though it was not a satisfactory reply for the guards, who nevertheless let them pass. They could not stop just anyone for simply riding around. And after all, they had enough issues without aggravating the Werecats. So it was that Evelyn and Ragya began their trek through the Kingdom of Augusta's borderlands, hoping to find what they sought as they travelled through its bounds.

***

"And *I* still say we should have taken the left fork!" Percy grumbled as the carriage rolled steadily along.

"The left fork was going towards Grange-upon-Downy, a cesspit and a hellhole from everything I heard about the north in Murana Day. I'm *not* going there, and neither will Evelyn!" Caspar returned to him at once. The debate had been going on for some time now, and Kia Re sat listening to it with a roll of her eyes.

"Oh, how do you know!" the Gnome said with a sly grin. "Elves don't trouble with the learning of other lands, especially human lands: she'll see one spot as good as another for finding you, m'boy!"

"Because my heart tells me so, that's how. You'll see, Percy, we're going the right way: literally!"

"For Oron's sake will you give it a rest?" Kia Re called to them from a window. "If it makes you both feel better, I agree with both of you." she added.

"Oh, very, *very* helpful, yes! Very helpful." Percy grumbled softly as he rolled his eyes.

"No, no, she makes sense." Caspar said to him, and the Gnome then cast him a baleful glance. Caspar looked back over at him and then sighed in exasperation. "Gods! Elvar, halt!" he said, and the horse and carriage stopped. "All right, Grump, let's have a look at the maps *again*..." Caspar said resignedly, and Percy hopped down at once. Kia Re sighed, smiling to herself as Dusty the hound barked. The beast was probably smarter than all three of them; the horse as well, she decided.

Caspar and Percy then began unpacking the Gnome's maps for the ninth time in two days, and they set the relevant ones before them to examine them again.

"Here we go again, hound." Kia Re remarked to the dog, who let out a bored whine.

"Now look, Percy, do look! Your own maps show that the direct path south towards these lands goes past this town called Riverdell in the mountains; she'll head straight south from there, or as straight as she can at least, and find the road to Auschternople--"

122

"Yes, yes, yes--but what if she doesn't go to Auschternople? What if she went west as opposed to east?"

"Auschternople is the great city of the kings; it's where I would go if I was unfamiliar with the lands and customs of men; what better place to learn than in that place where still yet clings some semblance of culture?"

"You're giving the Elves too much credit on that count. They haven't forgotten history; haven't you heard how your people once raped an Elven Ambassador? Do you think she'll head on straight for Auschternople after that?" Percy asked him pointedly.

"That was almost three-hundreds of years ago! And I daresay Augusta has paid for that and all the other incidents a thousand-fold!" Caspar returned at once.

"Elven pride, m'boy!"

"Really, Percy, what can it hurt to take this road above another road? At least we're heading towards safer lands this way."

"Moderately speaking, of course."

"Now hang on!"

"Boys!" Kia Re interrupted. "Really! This has gone on long enough! Why don't we play a friendly little game to settle this?" she said; they looked up at her and then exchanged a glance.

"Game?" Caspar wondered. She pulled out a gold coin stamped with a maiden on one side and a lyre upon the other.

"Best three out of five. Three lyres, we keep going Caspar's way. Three maidens, we pick a way *I* choose."

"But--but--but--" Percy spluttered.

"And if, somehow, against the odds, we get five lyres or five maidens in a row, Percy chooses." she added. The two of them exchanged a glance again. Caspar smirked, and Percy gave him a knowing smile.

"Oh, we'll just see now, won't we, m'lad?" the Gnome said to him with a chuckle.

"I'm warning you, friend Gnome, I was quite a successful luck-winner in Murana Day."

"Your luck, my friend, is almost out!" the Gnome returned cheerfully; Kia Re smiled as well, and as they sat back to await the outcome she flicked the coin in the air for the first round.

***

As Ragya and Evelyn came inside the inn from stabling their horse, a few eyes turned to look at them, especially Evelyn. The two of them sat at a small table near the fire as one of the waitresses came up to them, and she smiled cheerily at them. "Can I get you something, friends?" she asked.

"A kettle of hot water, and two cups with it; and some bread, dear lady." Ragya said in his soft but audible voice. She nodded, and headed off to fetch them. The Werecat scanned the room briefly; a couple men were still staring over at Evelyn, but he believed they were probably smart enough to leave her alone while he was with her. Not that she couldn't handle them; she had, as she had told him, bested an Ogre, but now they were in human lands, and they were not willing to draw attention. The waitress returned with their order, and Ragya placed two gold coins and a silver piece on the table for her. "And a room for the night." he added, and she nodded again.

"I'll tell the keep you'll be wanting one." she said to him, and headed off again as the Werecat put a few tea leaves in the steaming kettle. It was ready in a few minutes, and they began to relax a bit more as they drank this.

"I am dying for a bath." Evelyn said almost inaudibly.

"This is a more civilized inn than most; they shall have one in the room for our use." he told her in reply, and she nodded. She looked briefly over at the men who were still staring at her, and wished for Caspar with a choked sob.

"Why do they have to stare?" she breathed, and the Werecat kept his eyes on the table as he answered.

"It is a human trait; staring at one implies the desire to speak, or an attraction, or in some cases it is meant to ward a person off." Ragya told her. "In this case I suspect the second. You are a beautiful lady, after all."

"Maybe we should go to our room." she said nervously, and he nodded. They left the table, and the waitress directed them to their room as they left the commons. There was indeed a bath waiting, and Evelyn got in as soon as she could, sighing in relief. Reviewing in her mind what Ragya had told her on the road, she hoped again that Caspar was near; the Werecat hoped to be at a place called Barnesville in about a week's time, and from there it would be another week or so to the legendary Auschternople. Auschternople... and Caspar... life was about to really change for her. A knock at the door disturbed them. Ragya drew a curtain around the bath, and went to the door. Curtain! She had almost forgotten modesty, and was grateful for the Werecat's being here. As Ragya opened the door, his gleaming eyes fell on one of those from the commons who had been immensely interested in his companion.

"And what is it you want?" the Werecat said in a soft but firm voice. The man was all but taken aback, but quickly made a bold face of things.

"To show the lady a good time, if she's a mind for it. Not often we see such angels in these parts." he said brashly.

"Nor will you ever again. Good night." Ragya returned, and shut the door.

"Wait!" the man said, to no avail.

"I do not respect those who have no respect for the sanctity and privacy of my lady." the Werecat said in a darker and slightly louder tone, and the man rushed off. There was no getting past the Werecat; not here, anyway. It was time for the next plan.

Evelyn sighed in relief as she heard the door shut again, and Ragya placed himself in front of it. When she had finished bathing, she got on some night-clothes and went for bed at once, too weary from their fast and lengthy travels to do much else. The last thing she saw as she fell to slumber was her majestic and alert companion, watching the door like an unblinking statue as he kept watch. She smiled, and her dreams that night were dreams of peace.

***

Kia Re, victorious from the coin-tossing game, drove the carriage along with a smirk that would have shamed a tomcat. She had continued on a route that more or less matched that which Caspar desired to take, out of some sense that, somehow, he was right about what Evelyn was doing. Percy, partially mollified by her winning instead of Caspar, resigned himself to making observations of the world around them; he was atop the carriage, making notes and so forth on all that they passed by. It was mostly farm villages, such as Idoma in the south, but there were a few weathered but hearty keeps to be seen off in the distance. Guards and patrols waved as they passed by, and Caspar gave them a smile and nod as they rolled along. He was playing his lute, dispelling any other thought about them save that they were an eccentric little band travelling the countryside. Kia Re listened to him with a soft smile; she had adopted the ruse of being his sister, and no one asked questions of them--or if there was a question, it was usually a request for a song, or a "How d'ye do this fine day?" sort of question.

> *Says your man to the sheriff, to the sheriff says he:*
> *"There's no better man for your money than me!"*
> *Says the sheriff to your man, to your man he says:*
> *"That better be so for your claim to be the best!"*
> *And so your man and the sheriff*
> *To the village they did ride*
> *And the sheriff and your man*
> *Were struck with eyes wide*
> *And the mad old ogre raving*
> *As he swung his oaken mace*

"Egads!" your man he said,
"We've work to do in this place!"

Says the sheriff to your man, to your man says he:
"The devil are you doing? For he'll be crushing thee!"
Says your man to the sheriff, to the sheriff he says:
"You sought me out with money, for I'm the very best,
And so I'll take down yon ogre
With the pride of my own self
You'll see, my bonny bully
That I'm worth all the wealth
Of your money that comes forth
From such a gallant man
I'll have the ogre on his knees
And you'll have peace again!"

Says the sheriff to your man, to your man he says:
"Be off with ye then so, if you're the very best!"
Says your man to the sheriff, to the sheriff says he:
"I'll be off so and I'll be winning a grand auld victory!"
And he swung and he lunged,
And he parried and he thrust
And he darted about the odorous lout
Until the ogre was near to bust!
"By gads!" the fiend did quoth
"If you'll not be standing still,
I'll take yon bully sheriff
And make of him a meal!"

Says your man to the ogre, to the ogre he says:
"You'll never have the sheriff, for I'm the very best!"
Says the ogre to your man, to your man says he:
"Come and show it little devil, and triumph over me!"
So he swung and he thrust
And he parried at his will
So that the ogre in his folly
Could not catch him, even still
And before the fiend could think
There was the sword stuck in his chest
"By gads, you little mongrel,
You really are the best!"

Says the sheriff to your man, to your man says he:

"By all the gods, the ogre's dead--
your worth's now proved to me!"
Says your man to the sheriff, to the sheriff he says:
"I told ye so from the start, that I'm the very best!"
And so off he goes with money
And fame throughout the land
The Merry Rogue of Badger-Down
Yes, that's indeed your man
The Merry Rogue of Badger-Down
He's indeed the very best
And if in need he'll come to thee
And you know all the rest!

Caspar ended his song with a few more bars of strumming, and then sat back in the seat for a rest. Kia Re looked over at him, briefly feeling a pang for him again; but as she looked at his eyes she knew his thoughts were of Evelyn. Well, she would make sure they met. This was her brother, after all. Yes. A brother. Was he not...?

"Ah-ha!" Percy exclaimed triumphantly. "That's why the birds come towards all these regions in the spring-time; these ruddy and hearty little fruits! Ha-ha! Oh, take that, 'Guild of Orthinology' and all you other imbeciles under the mountain! Ha! I, Percy Von Daumer, Roaming Gnome, am now vindicated!" the Gnome chattered, and the two in the front exchanged a glance.

"Someone's having fun." Caspar said as he pulled his hat over his eyes.

"Very much so." Kia Re agreed as they kept on.

"I hope Evelyn found a travelling companion... wouldn't want her alone..." Caspar said softly as the sun's rays began to impose a nap on him. Kia Re reached over to pat his shoulder.

"I'm sure she's fine." she said just as softly, and with that the minstrel fell asleep.

***

On that same day, Evelyn and Ragya were on the road again. They had not gotten too far beyond the town they had just left when, upon a sudden, they were ambushed by a party of eight men; Ragya at once let out a low growl, and Evelyn brought her fighting reflexes to full alert as she took in the situation. A ninth fiend jumped down from the boughs of the trees, and this one removed his mask. Ragya's eyes narrowed. It was the man from the inn.

"So, failing to find thy amusement in a more or less polite setting, you seek to ravage her here where you think no one is around to help?" the Werecat intoned in a soft but menacing voice.

"Give it a rest, whiskers, you're out of town. The constables won't hear you here, and you two'll be dead when it's all said and done."

"Look to your own lives, fools." Evelyn said as she removed her hood. Her violet eyes flashed, and the men took a pace back.

"An Elf!"

"By all the--Rim, you fool!"

"Take them!" the lead man, Rim, said to them. Three of them fired their bows, but the two forest-dwellers were too fast for them. Ragya kicked one to the ground, and then shifted to wildcat form; Evelyn leaped from the saddle, drew her sword, and killed two of them at once in with an inhuman speed and agility. A third fell to her blade a few moments later, and Ragya broke the neck of one, then knocked out two of the others by picking them up and banging their heads together. One of those remaining managed to swipe at him with a sword; the Werecat then picked him up and flung him with a great strength towards one of the mighty oaks, killing him on impact.

The second to last ran when Ragya roared at him, but Evelyn speedily drew her bow and fired, killing him. Rim was left by himself, and he was now quailing on the ground. Ragya shifted back, and Evelyn put aside her bow to calm the horse down. The Werecat picked up Rim by the tunic, and glared at him.

"You were saying?" Ragya asked him softly.

"P-please... please don't, d-d-don't... k-kill... m-me..." the man stammered.

"Don't kill him, Ragya. There's enough dead on the ground." Evelyn said to him, and he nodded.

"The sanctity of life is disturbed enough. But I will not have you following us." Ragya said, and dropped him to the ground. He then whirled out his staff, and brought it down with a loud "thunk!" upon Rim's head. The man fell to the ground like a tree, and Ragya replaced his staff on his shoulder. The two of them then sighed in relief, and Evelyn remounted, placing the hood back over her face.

"Let's go quickly." she said, and Ragya nodded.

"We should expect more of that. Be wary." he added, and she nodded in turn as they continued on their way down the road to Barnesville. As they did so, Evelyn hoped that Caspar was having less trouble on his road, and that he did indeed have friends with him-- friends like Ragya, kind, gentle, and firm.

***

Later that evening, Caspar was now driving the carriage, and Kia Re was almost asleep beside him. Percy was inside it, fast asleep from his exuberant studies, as was Dusty, the hound curled up on one of the seats. They were about to enter into a heavily wooded area, when all of a sudden Caspar drew the carriage to a halt; Kia Re started awake as they stopped, and looked over at him.

His face was intent on the woods before them, and she looked them over as well.

"I don't like it. Let's go back to the village." he said, and she nodded. They were almost turned around to go back when an arrow landed with a loud report on the side of the carriage.

"Ho there! Leaving so soon?" a merry voice called out, followed up by a chorus of laughter.

"Can't have that, my merry fool!" a second called out.

"Give us a few rounds with the girl and you can pass on by!" a third, gruffer voice added.

"Aye, aye! No need to go back: we're all sharing friends here, mate!" the first voice said, stepping into view. It was a robber, clad in green, like one of Caspar's songs come to life. He was joined by two others, who were the source of the other two voices.

"Look at that angel, lads! Just the way we like them!" the gruff man said.

"Not bony and not plump--just right!" the second said.

"Oh, laddie, you've had some nights with her, haven't you?" the leader quipped, and a chorus of hooting laughter erupted from the trees again.

"She's my sister, Master Rudeness." Caspar returned, and this was received with yet another round of laughs.

"Ha! Incest going on here, lads!" the gruff man called back to make them laugh some more. Caspar frowned, shaking his head; at that moment the leader noticed his lute.

"Hi there! Shut it! Shut it! Damn your eyes, shut up! We've a minstrel here!" he called out, and silence fell over the cackling woods. Twenty or so others emerged from the woods, and Caspar blinked. Was this a good omen or a bad one? "Now then, my merry bully," the leader said again, "I consider my own self to be a lutenist of goodly quality, and many a man here agrees on that count--aye, lads?" he said, and to a man they all responded with an "Aye!"

"What's this got to do with anything?" Caspar wondered.

"Everything, laddie!" the man returned cheerily as one of those who had emerged from the wood gave to him a lute; he began tuning it, and continued talking.

"You see, though I'm fine, and just fine, I daresay, it's been a while since we've heard another minstrel; if you can best me, and all the lads agree on your besting me in a series of merry melodies, you'll go free! And if not, well: then the original offer will have to do!"

"And if it's a tie?" Caspar quickly asked.

"Well!" the man said, halting a moment to think before resuming. "Well if it's a tie, then I suppose we'll have to let you go back for the night, won't we lads?" he announced, and the others nodded, murmuring affirmations that this was indeed a fair result for a tie.

"Ready, lad? And remember: merry melodies; no dirges, laments, or slow airs and such!" he said as he gave his own instrument a strum. Caspar picked up his own lute; it was still in tune, and he got down from the carriage to be on equal footing with his apparent rival. Percy finally woke up from all the talking, and blinked as he looked out.

"What in--I say! A contest!" he said softly to himself as he quickly took stock of the situation.

At that moment, the outlaw leader began to play his own tune, a lively jig; when this was over, Caspar played his own tune, a reel that had them all dancing and capering about. The leader tried to recover himself with a merry ballad that told the story of an innkeeper's daughter beating an ogre, which Caspar followed up by reprising his own ballad of the "Merry Rogue of Badger-Down", which had even his rival smiling, for it was a well-known and well-loved tune of outlaws such as they were. For nearly two hours they played back and forth, playing jigs and reels and hornpipes that were as old as the hills, and then finally Caspar ended with a lively performance of the "Battle of the Narrow-Downs", an epic ballad of a great battle, and when he had finished they were all applauding. The outlaw leader looked very pleased indeed, recognizing that his young rival was a master of minstrelsy, and himself clapped the hardest.

"By all the trees!" he exclaimed with a smile.

"He's won it, chief, and don't you say otherwise!" another man called out, followed up by a quick chorus of affirmations.

"I wouldn't dream it! And for such a gallant performance we'll lead you through the woods our very selves, won't we lads?" he said, and they all agreed with another chorus of ayes.

Caspar bowed, and when they had shaken hands he got back up on the carriage, and the outlaws themselves led them through the woods that night. Percy chuckled himself to sleep as they drove on, and Kia Re smiled the whole way through the woods as they all chattered on as if they were old friends. She looked over at Caspar and saw that he seemed to be in deep thought.

"What are you thinking about?" she nudged him.

"Oh, I was just thinking." he said with a shrug.

"About?" she pressed him again.

"I was just thinking that this little incident would make a wonderful ballad itself." he said, and the outlaw leader, overhearing, let out a hearty laugh.

"Indeed it would, my friend! Indeed it would!" the man returned. The forest looked less grim and foreboding all of a sudden, now that they had won the admiring respects--if not total friendship--of the outlaw band.

Chapter Twelve: Paths Intertwining

Five days after their encounter with Rim and his fellows, Ragya and Evelyn were at another inn. This one was quiet and out of the way, and the only other buildings around were the stables, their host's house, and a blacksmith's shop. A small patrol of Augustan Knights were also visiting the inn, resting from their patrol; their leader came up to the two of them when they were mostly settled in, and the Werecat nodded at him. The knights, at least, were more honorable in this day and age than they had been. The commander returned the nod, and sat down at a nearby table.

"No trouble on the road, I hope?" he asked them, and Ragya blinked.

"Why, commander, where can one go in Augusta that has not trouble?" he asked slyly, and the man wryly shrugged.

"True enough. Robbers?" he asked again.

"Indeed. They were swiftly dealt with. They shall not trouble anyone for a while." the Werecat told him, and the knight commander nodded back.

"Good." he returned. "What brings you this far south anyway?" the man wondered.

"We have business in these regions; it is a private matter, friend, but it bears nothing ill for Augusta. Indeed, it bears nothing for Augusta at all; you may say that we are but passing on our way in pilgrimage." Ragya told him, and the commander nodded again.

"With all these wanderers and vagabonds about, you understand I have to make certain of these things." he returned. "But you're a Werecat. You don't go in for that mischievous lying habit that most others do. Enjoy your drinks, friends." he said as he raised his glass to them, and then headed back over to his men. The Werecat raised his own glass in politeness, and returned his attention to Evelyn.

"I cast the rune-stones this morning before you awoke." he said to her in the simple tone he always used, speaking of such things as if it was a common occurrence. For him it was, perhaps, but Evelyn was still somewhat unused to magic being a commonplace event in her life.

"What did they say?"

"That someone very important to you is going to cross our path tomorrow." Ragya said softly, and her eyes widened as her heart skipped a beat. *Caspar!* "Yes, Caspar." he nodded with a faint grin. That night, as Evelyn lounged in a bath again, she could not stop smiling. Caspar was close by.

***

After passing through several more farming communities throughout the countryside, Caspar had more or less constructed his new ballad, which he was calling "Battle of the Lutes", or "Dueling Lutes": he had not yet decided. They were approaching a town called Barnesville, not a very important town in and of itself, save for the fact that it was the first major settlement on the King's Road to Auschternople. The King's Road began there, and was fairly well maintained by all the settlements along its path. Soon they would be on their way to Auschternople, and, hopefully, would find Evelyn somewhere along the way. Such were Caspar's thoughts as they settled in for the night near a communal lodge.

Kia Re looked at him longingly as he lay asleep; he had gotten over their moment many days past now, and treated her as she had first desired, as a sister and a valued friend. Now she was in a regretful state of mind, for she could feel that, somehow, they would soon find Evelyn, and she was wishing with all her might that she could have something else to focus on. Caspar had been more than just another human. He was understanding, trusting, loyal, quick-witted, gentle, and courageous. It was not everyone who could outwit a band of forest thieves and then make up a song about the whole ordeal as if it was simply another part of life. She was about to go over and kiss him as he slept, when Percy came out to check on things. "Still awake, mm?" he asked curiously. She briefly started, and then smiled.

"Yes, still awake." Kia Re said. The wise little Gnome followed her eyes as she looked back at Caspar, and watched as a muted sob heaved in her chest. He came over to her, and sat down beside her. He let out a sigh, gazing over at Caspar himself for a brief moment; he knew, of course, what had happened. They had told him, and he had simply shaken his head.

Heat of the moment, heat of the moment; that's all it was. It'll pass. He had said then--*then*, at least. Percy then looked up at Kia Re, who was staring at the flames of their fire.

"You're wishing that there was no Elf-lass waiting for us along the road, mm?" he said softly, and she nodded. "Indeed. But of course, if there was no Elf-lass, and no dream, he wouldn't be on the road at all, and you might never have left to try and claim glory in a cause you believe is more than your people's idly sitting about in their halls."

"Why did it have to be her?" Kia Re wondered. "Why an Elf, immortal as the stars, and not one of Heaven's own like me? I'm mortal; I can grow old with him, and die with him; she'll go on, the poor girl, and her heart will be shattered in his dying."

"Perhaps." Percy allowed.

"And Elves... they're so skinny and frail-looking; is my form not pleasing to him?" she softly went on. "My body is pure, my heart strong and hale, my breasts firm and my eyes bright."

"And you both agreed that was the last time you allowed yourselves to be so intimate with each other." Percy reminded her, and Kia Re sighed, smiling ruefully.

"The High Festival of Kia De Mara approaches, our first queen; I would have him love me so that I might bear his child. I would have him to myself, with no Elf at all." she said, shaking her head.

"No... no, I must not have these thoughts--but, oh! Percy, it is so hard..." she added, and he patted her gently on the shoulders. "Do you even have an inkling of how I feel, Master Gnome? Is there no brave tale of sacrificial love, or the giving up one's own desires for the sake of the one you love loving another instead?" Kia Re asked him, and he gave her a knowing look.

"It was not merely outlandish contraptions and ideas that gave me cause for leaving home, friend; nay, no Gnome would exile another for such things. I chose exile myself after my grants ran out, for the one I loved did indeed love another, and she wouldn't have a fool. So I left, resolving myself to the life of a Roaming Gnome. Maybe I won't see the end result of it all, but I can rest my confidence in knowing that, what I did, I did for a noble cause thus far beyond my sight." he told her, and she nodded softly.

"I see." she said in understanding. "You are right. It is for a cause beyond us--maybe a cause even beyond their own understanding, these two lovers; but we must help them." Kia Re said again. "I... will recover. Thank you, Percy." she said, and he patted her again.

"Absolutely, absolutely." he said, and when he had seen to the fire he got back up in the carriage for his own rest. Kia Re did walk over to Caspar after she was confident of the Gnome snoring; she did not kiss him on the lips, but she did kiss him on the cheek.

"Rest, song-brother. We are almost to the one you love." she said, and headed for sleep herself moments later.

***

As Evelyn dressed that morning, she hummed to herself one of the songs that Caspar had played in their dreams; she all but skipped out the door, and Ragya had to give her a knowing look before she remembered to put her hood on. With a wry sigh she did so, hoping that, when she did find Caspar, the need for secrecy would be over. They paid their fare as they left, and within the next ten minutes they were off again. Still humming, Evelyn simply reveled in the prettiness of the day, and Ragya looked up at her with a curious expression. He had forgotten how other races were so prone to idle and silly antics as this when they were in love. A sign was on their right; it indicated that there was five and a half King's Miles to Barnesville. *Five and a half miles of... "humming"...* he thought to himself with a shake of his head. The tune changed after about half of a mile, and then she lifted her voice up in a song, a song that seemed to enchant the very birds--or was it Ragya's imagination?

> *Sing to me, and come to me*
> *My love, across the seas*
> *My one true love, my only love*
> *And put my heart at ease*
> *Under the stars of night*
> *And the moons above*
> *I pledged myself to you,*
> *My one and only love*
>
> *My heart is yours alone*
> *Yours alone forevermore*
> *In brightest day and darkest night*
> *And across the pearled shores*
> *So sing to me, and come to me*
> *And kiss me with your love;*
> *Kiss me love, and love me*
> *Like the stars of night above*
>
> *The singing birds, the whisp'ring wind*
> *They sing of love, and joy and peace*
> *At morning's dawn, and evening's night*
> *A song they sing to put hearts at ease*
> *Kiss me and love me, my love*
> *And sing to me our song*
> *Sing to me, and love on me*
> *While the days are young*
>
> *I sing of you, now sing of me*
> *And let the world with great envy*
> *Be envious of your love for me*

And envious of my love for thee
O, Love, my love, I come to thee
And thou I knowest come to me
Sing again, and sing prettily
Your love awaits, awaits for thee
Yes, I your love await for thee

Evelyn's voice faded away into humming again as they crossed a bridge, and Ragya felt his own heart warmed by the song. The sound of birds singing indeed rang out the stronger, and the Werecat wondered if it was not due to the Elven melody. Another sign caught his eye; this one read: "Three King's Miles to Barnesville". Ragya blinked. Three?

***

As the carriage rumbled along merrily, Percy was animatedly chattering on about all the sights and sounds they came across, sitting atop the carriage with piles of notes weighted down so that they were not blown away. Dusty had his head hanging out of a window, and Caspar was idly fiddling with his harp as Kia Re kept them steady. Just moments ago they had passed a sign that had read "Two King's Miles to Barnesville", and the two in the front seat now exchanged a smile as Percy's voice rose in excitement about some species of bird he had just seen alighting on a nearby tree-branch. "That wing-structure! And the grace of its flight--ha! I could invent a whole new aerial-glider based upon him, mark my words! Percy Von Daumer will be a respectable name in Gnomish lands again someday! Now, to recalculate known wind-factors with the variable of an exponentially sized wing, and the suitable mechanics thereof in tandem with the average mass and weight of Gnomes to start with, and then humans, Elves, Werecats... not Giants, too tall... and of Dwarves, Dwarves'll go for these things like mad! Ha-ha!" he chattered on, drawing out a detailed schematic of his idea as they approached a crossroads. This one had a sign indicating one and a half miles left, and they halted for a brief rest near here.

"You'll be all right, Percy, won't you?" Caspar called out as he went to go and look at a nearby monument while Kia Re headed off into the woods for a brief moment.

"Of course, of course!" the Gnome chattered back. He resumed his attention to the plan before him, making alterations here and there as he saw necessary.

***

Evelyn and Ragya were talking softly about their homelands as they travelled along, when all of a sudden the Werecat stopped. She looked down at him in concern, and his eyes then narrowed.

"There are more thieves about." he said softly.

"Are they after us?" she wondered.

"Nay--they are after that carriage there, with the Gnome on top; see! The poor fool, he makes an excellent target... nay, no Gnome shall die today if I can help it!" Ragya said, letting go and shifting to wildcat form as Evelyn cast off her cloak and drew out the Sword of Magus to follow hastily behind.

***

"And now, if I just invert this axis to recalibrate for the--" Percy murmured to himself, but at that moment an arrow lodged itself beside him. The Gnome's reaction was instantaneous. With a shriek like that of a Gnomish Steam Engine he jumped up and off the carriage, and then hopped into it, shutting the door behind him just in time. Seven more arrows landed on the thing, and Dusty began barking loudly. Caspar drew out his own sword at the sound of the Gnome's loud yell, and hastily looked around. Where were their attackers?

"Halt, friend!" a voice said as a sword touched him on the shoulder. "Now, if you'll just surr--" it began again, but at that moment it cried out in a strangled manner, and the sword fell to the ground. The body of an outlaw was then flung past Caspar, and he heard a menacing growl. He spun about, and saw a great wildcat going after a few other outlaws in the trees. Shaking himself back to action he rushed towards two others that were after the carriage; Kia Re was also in action, fending off three with her spear. A fourth figure entered the fray, but Caspar barely noticed as this one went to aid Kia Re.

Within moments most of the outlaws were fleeing, including the two that Caspar had charged at; one had received a slash on the cheek, and the other was suffering the loss of a hand. Those attacking Kia Re were all dead. The wildcat came out of a tree, and with a shrug and a yawn shifted form; it was a Werecat! Caspar gasped in awe, and when the majestic being had resumed its--*his* normal form, he bowed. Caspar bowed back and he could hear Percy sighing in relief as the Gnome thanked their surprise allies.

"By all the mountains and rivers in Argorro, thank you, *thank* you!" Percy exclaimed. Caspar then heard his name, and turned around to see Kia Re talking with the other figure, who had dark hair and pointed ears; pointed ears... was it...? the figure turned around, revealing violet eyes full of a joy and a passion that equaled his own at having found each other. *Evelyn!* Caspar dropped his sword, and they ran to each other, embracing heartily. Kia Re smiled, and Percy, who had been talking with the Werecat, stopped to look as his acquaintance also watched the first real meeting of Elf and Man.

"Thank the stars." Evelyn said, and then, for the first real time, kissed him joyfully upon the lips as he kissed her back. They held each

137

other again after that first kiss, and then stood there, oblivious to all else.

"Thank the stars indeed." Caspar agreed. When the moment was over, they found that the Werecat had brought the other horse up, and Evelyn laughed as he blinked at her.

"Ragya, you were right. It's Caspar!" she said as she leaned into his arms.

"Ragya..." Caspar repeated softly.

"Indeed. And well met, Master of Song." the Werecat returned.

"And though he may have forgotten us," the Gnome broke in, "I am Percy, Percy Von Daumer; and this is Kia Re of Jotun-De. The hound is Dusty." he said, and the dog in question barked happily at their new friends. Ragya, after tying the other horse to the carriage, blinked at the blonde woman and then smiled at her. Kia Re returned the smile, coming up to embrace him as a brother-in-arms.

"The legends walk the earth again, mountain-sister." Ragya said softly, and her smile partially faded. "Your strength can return, if you but believe." he added to her in an inaudible tone that only she could hear, and she nodded.

"Thank you for your words; I will reflect upon them." Kia Re told him.

"And now, where are we off to?" Percy said again. "Our reasons for travelling to the great city seem annulled at this meeting--or is there something I have missed?" he asked.

"Auschternople remains our destination." Ragya said to him. "The Royal Ixthus and the Sea-queen's Mother aligned with the Lover's Cross. It cannot now be denied without bringing evil upon us for disobeying." he added, and Percy blinked. A druid!

"Fascinating!" he said genuinely. "A druid? Oh, sirrah, I implore you, sit with me here and tell me more!" he said to Ragya, who smiled as he nodded.

"I shall converse with thee, Master Scholar, and Kia Re our friend shall join us, for I sense we three have much to talk about." he said with a wink at the Valkyrie. "But let us do so as we drive, and let our two lovers acquaint themselves with each other inside." Ragya added, and Percy, taking the hint, winked back.

"Of course, of course; I've my papers to recover anyway." he said as he clambered out to get on top the carriage again. Kia Re smiled, shaking her head. "Caspar! Get on board, boy, or we'll leave you two for the robbers!" Percy exclaimed. Evelyn and Caspar looked up and, seeing the front of the carriage fully occupied, got in the back with Dusty as they set off once more. Kia Re let out a soft sigh, but her thoughts were soon fixated on the conversation between Ragya and

Percy; the Werecat was driving the carriage now as he talked with the Gnome upon the mystical and natural aspects of druidism, a subject she soon found she had a great interest for as they rode along the road to Barnesville.

Inside the carriage, Caspar and Evelyn had resumed their own conversation, and Dusty was half-napping in the back seat. They went over their adventures to date, and Evelyn only gave him a smile as he recounted what had happened with Kia Re at the river.

"Caspar, don't give it any more thought. By the trees and stars, I might have even kissed her myself in that moment." she said with a twinkle in her eyes, and Caspar smiled at her.

"It was a strange moment to be certain." he said.

"And a beautiful one. It's not every mortal man who can attract an Elf *and* a Valkyrie in such a way, from all I understand." she said, nudging him teasingly.

"I suppose that's true." Caspar returned with a laugh. "But now, all of my kisses are for you." he added.

"All of your romantic kisses, that is." she said with a sly look. "I know about Valkyrie friendships and comradery. Don't be bashful about it!" she said as he flushed. "I'll probably end up kissing her too, and we'll be one happy little family--the five of us." she said as she leaned on to him again; he wrapped his arms around her, kissing her forehead.

"Let the world be envious of us forever." Caspar agreed softly, and Evelyn smiled as she snuggled closer to him. He was indeed the man of her dreams.

***

"And so--I say, is that Barnesville there?" Percy interrupted himself; on their left was a bridge crossing a river. The road continued on ahead of them, but there was a path on the other side of the bridge leading up to a town that almost looked as if it was part of the surrounding forest it was situated in. Ragya blinked, and turned the carriage to head across the bridge and into the town.

"Sharp eyes, Master Von Daumer." he remarked. "I might have missed it, for our own conversation was far more intriguing than the road." he said with a smile.

"Indeed! I only noticed from my constant habit of observation." Percy returned as they finished crossing; they headed up into the town, and two of the guards halted them.

"Business, please!" one of them called up.

"Hallo, hallo!" Percy called down. "We seek lodging for the night, and perhaps a stop at the local merchants this afternoon or tomorrow morning as the case may be." he said.

"Travelling merchants, is it? Very well, go on; inn's on the right, stables are further in town, but there's a horse-post at the inn." he said as he and his fellow moved aside.

"Thank you, thank you!" Percy returned, and they made for the inn as they headed on in. A sign in front named it as Creek Lodge Inn, and when they had seen to their horses and to the carriage they began sorting through their things. Evelyn was amazed at the cache that Caspar and Percy had found; and though Ragya did not show it too visibly, his eyes alighted on many of these ancient wonders with interest.

"These things are *priceless*!" Evelyn softly exclaimed in regards to the Temple treasures that Percy and Caspar had held on to. "You are *not* selling these to some common merchants?" she asked in a horrified tone.

"No, no," Caspar assured her. "They're probably better off with us until we at least get to Auschternople. Then we'll see if the royal antiquities and archives guild wants them."

"Well that's slightly better." Evelyn shrugged, appeased by the words. "Though you are *not* getting rid of that book. I don't care if the king himself offers to make you his heir for it."

"It won't stop people from trying to steal it if they notice it." Kia Re said as she raised an eyebrow.

"Which is why it remains in a leather pouch." Caspar remarked.

"Come, come, now... we can at least pawn off some of these fine daggers; maybe a goblet or two..." Percy remarked. "It would save us coin, and we need the supplies."

"We've coin to make a beggar of the Augustan king!" Evelyn said to him in a wry tone. "But you're right. We can pawn off the goblets, and a few of the daggers and other trinkets; we don't need them. But the books stay until Auschternople."

"And I have to replenish my herbs. Not that I can't do so in the wilds, but merchants carry them in greater store than I can find even in this time of year." Ragya added.

"Let's divide it up then. Now do we go to market tonight or wait until morning?" Kia Re asked, and they looked around at each other.

"Let's go now. I'd rather be off in the morning as soon as we can." Caspar said, and the others agreed with this.

"I'll go myself, and perhaps Ragya will come with me to carry the bag while I make use of my bargaining skills? Or Kia Re?" Percy said, and the Werecat exchanged a glance with the Valkyrie, who pulled out a coin.

"Maiden or lyre?" she asked as she showed it to him. Ragya blinked, and smiled.

"If lyre, I shall go."

"Fair enough." she smiled back, and flipped the coin; it was the lyre, and Ragya gave her a nod. When they had divided what they planned to sell from what was to stay with them, they split up, and Ragya went with Percy to the Merchant Gallery while the other three went to arrange a room.

"Two rooms." Kia Re said as they approached the door. "You two can have one, and I'll stay with the others." she said with a faint grin. Evelyn smiled as Caspar grinned, and they went inside. They arranged for their rooms, and requested for dinner to be brought up to them. When this had been arranged they gave the keep five gold coins and two silvers, and he went to see to their meals after showing them to their rooms. "I'll be in this one." Kia Re said as she went in to the one on the right. "Good night!" she added with a smirk, and the other two exchanged a glance before heading in to their own room.

***

"Oh, but surely you can do better than that? Why, see, friend! This artifact surely dates to the Age of Legends..." Percy said with a knowing glance; they were perhaps even older, but he was trying to be fair with his bargaining.

They had already sold off the daggers to the blacksmith; Percy had made his offer, and the smith himself trebled it, saying he had not seen their like in his entire life, and that they must have been Dwarven-made. They had accepted half of his offer, the Gnome not wanting to bankrupt the man, and the smith graciously accepted.

Now they were dealing with a Home Amenities merchant, a sly and clever man whose wit matched the Gnome's own. He also seemed to know that these were very ancient and very priceless relics, but affected a disdain for them to get the equally clever Gnome to go lower with his offer. "Yes, but see here--it bears the wear and tear of time, my good fellow. Though I do see the fine markings of a clever goldsmith here..." he remarked, examining it more closely. Percy, who had examined the artifacts deftly before they left, gave him a nod.

"Yes, you see them now, my good fellow; personally, I am of the conclusion that they are the insignia of Riaxus, the legendary Dwarven smith of the White Mountain, and that these goblets were the ones he gave to King Jona of the fabled Whiterock Castle in the far north."

"By the gods, do you think so?" the man said in a more eager tone. Ragya blinked. The Gnome was indeed a master bargainer.

"It is perhaps disputable, but those are definitely the vowelless mode of runes used in the early Age of Legends by the Dwarven peoples; and as we all know, Riaxus lived in such a time when the Dwarves still did not see the value of vowels. Makes translations difficult, you see, unless one is familiar with the finer syntax; but I

141

digress! My final offer stands; twenty gold coins of the realm for the lot of them!--or shall I carry them off to Auschternople to gather dust in some historian's archive?" Percy asked him, and the merchant at once pulled out his purse.

"Dratted historians, the lot of them... collecting things they never use! I'll give you an extra two pieces for them!" he said at once, and Percy smiled graciously.

"Done!" he said, shaking hands with the man. He and Ragya left the Gallery moments later with forty-seven gold coins of the realm, and headed back to the inn.

"Very clever bargaining indeed, Master Gnome." Ragya complimented him as they made their way back.

"My thanks, friend Werecat." Percy returned. They entered the inn, and found Kia Re waiting for them in the commons. She waved them over to where a meal was waiting, and the two of them sat with her. "All sorted, I take it?" Percy asked her.

"Indeed. I had our meal redirected here; Evelyn and Caspar are having theirs upstairs. We're in the room on the right at the end of the hall." she told them as they began eating.

"Quite, quite." the Gnome returned. The three of them dug in with a will to their meal, as if they had not eaten for a week. They conversed lightly about their plans for the future, and even told some stories to others about the room who had taken an interest in seeing a Werecat and a Gnome in the company of such a beautiful woman. They thoroughly enjoyed themselves, and were certain that Caspar and Evelyn were also enjoying themselves thoroughly.

***

After resting for a bit, an inn-worker had brought Caspar and Evelyn their meal, which they had eaten with the same gusto as their friends downstairs. Evelyn had then gone for a bath, and Caspar stretched out in a chair after washing himself a bit with a basin of water that was near the window. He was almost asleep when Evelyn came back out, and he woke up a bit more as she came near to raise him out of the chair, leading him towards the bed. They sat on this for a while, kissing each other as they talked some more, sharing secret passions and hopes for the future, and for their life together. Evelyn then parted her robe, and exulted in the touch of Caspar's lips upon her body. The tips of her breasts were as violet as her eyes, and with a longing sigh she laid down with him on top as he kissed her lips again.

"Not yet." he whispered gently.

"Then just lay here with me; let me lay myself in your arms." she whispered back as she wrapped herself around him, and he embraced her.

"Always." he returned, and they fell asleep in each other's arms.
**

On the next morning they were well-rested and ready to go; both horses were hitched to the carriage, and they set off after a hearty breakfast. Kia Re and Evelyn ended up in the front after several miles, and the two of them chattered on as they drove the carriage along. They talked of Caspar for a while, and then turned to other things, such as how they had forsook their homes for a mortal man.

"I don't know... I just felt it was right. As if I had to. My people are doing nothing in their hallowed halls of the mountains; I wanted to be doing something, and I sensed such greatness in accompanying the two of them." Kia Re told her newest friend.

"Neither do my people do anything that would truly aid the world; they seek after a past that is long gone and never to return. The very thing they hold on to is the thing that is killing them, a slow death under the last trees of Alastria." Evelyn said, shaking her head.

"If we were indeed former angels, as our earliest ancestors claim, then it is time once again to fight for the right. We came to do battle out of love for mortals; now they disdain them, and they do no battle unless threatened themselves."

"Now love has entered your heart again, and you will fight for that love; among all the races, there is no greater cause, or so I have always been told." the Elf-maid said softly.

"You speak truly." Kia Re nodded. "Love is the bond which must hold us and see us through; may it never fail us!" she added, and Evelyn smiled, leaning her head on the other girl's shoulder.

"Never shall it fail." she said in agreement as they drove on; after a few miles more, Ragya relieved them, and the two of them went back inside the carriage with Caspar and Percy for the rest of that night.

Chapter Thirteen: Kingdom of Augusta

"Doesn't he do anything besides scribe down observations?" Evelyn asked Caspar as they drove the carriage along King's Road as the Gnome cheerily kept on with his work. It was a field day for the diminutive scholar, and he was determined to capture as much as he could down in his stacks of papers for study. He had been atop the carriage since Ragya had been driving it in the early part of the morning, listening to the sounds of birdsong that rang out as the sun began to rise and the last host of the stars became obscured from view; now it was late evening, and Caspar had been driving the thing alongside Evelyn for at least an hour, having taken over from Kia Re to let her rest. Caspar shrugged, smiling over at her as they drove on; above them, they could hear Percy rambling on to himself animatedly as he took down notes on this, that, and the other.

"And besides that, all I've noticed he does so far is make target practice for potential enemies." Evelyn added in an inaudible tone. Caspar sighed. Her Elven pride was still with her, though she might have denied it if challenged outright. He settled for a middle ground in replying, crafting his answer with the calm and level compassion she had quickly come to admire him for.

"The strength of the Gnomes is in their minds and in their hearts; wisdom and insight over quick and hasty actions, however well-intentioned." he said just as softly, and she gave him a soft smile.

"You are wiser than you give yourself credit for." Evelyn told him.

"I don't know..." Caspar said with a grin. "It's just not in me to take things in by the outward appearance. There's always something more."

"Yes, there is. And that is why I think you wise: because you take the time to look for it where most of us might brush it off. Well, maybe not Ragya..." she continued, "but he is hard to read sometimes." she confided to him softly.

"The Werecats were always mysterious, even during the old days, tales say. He is a boon companion, to you especially." he remarked. Evelyn nodded back, and was silent for a few moments.

"He said once that it was his fheas to follow me wherever I went."

she then said, and Caspar blinked, raising his eyebrows.

"Then you are special to him indeed." he said. "Of all the Werecats in the history of the world, only one has done such a thing to a person not of the Werecats themselves."

"Oh?" Evelyn wondered, intrigued at the words and suddenly understanding the great honor that was upon her.

"Long ago, in the Age of Legends, a Werecat named Omysieus pledged such a bond to Mysten the White and Kron the Warrior. They killed a great dragon far to the west of us, on the other side of Argorro they say, and after that had many other adventures together until the two men died; his fheas fulfilled, Omysieus left the adventuring world and returned to the Were Forests, where he died at the age of almost two centuries." Caspar told her as she listened with rapt interest. Two centuries? Did the mysterious Werecats have such long lifespans?

"They live to be so old?" she asked him.

"So the tales said." Caspar replied, and Evelyn looked down, feeling a sense of awe come over her.

"Then he has pledged his whole life to me..." she said in understanding; Caspar said nothing, but he did smile, gently nodding as they drove along.

"Of course, some live longer." the voice of Percy came to their ears, and Evelyn perked up at once from her thoughts, realizing the Gnome was speaking to them. "Scholars from the Guild of Intercultural Relations (one of the most prestigious Gnomish guilds) have had the honor on several occasions over the years to be accepted among the Werecat peoples for extended periods of time; from what we've learned of their people, they can live extraordinarily long lives, especially the druids amongst them. Something to do with living in the harmony and closeness of nature. One of my second-cousins twice removed on my great-grandmother's uncle's side of the family recorded that the oldest Werecat lived to be over six-hundred years old; a remarkable age for their people. It's the more adventurous amongst them that live shorter lives; the wear and tear of the world affects them in a greater way than most of the other races, if they're not outright killed by some enemy or another." the Gnome continued, but Evelyn halted his thoughts on this train of lecture by asking a question.

"How long do Gnomes live, Master Scholar?" she asked him with a faint smile, now somewhat interested in his wealth of knowledge.

"My people have the distinction of living as long as the Dwarves, anywhere from three to four-hundred years on average. It's this common lifespan between us, as well as both of our peculiar habitat arrangements (of living in mountains, that is) that has given rise to the belief that, somehow, Gnomes and Dwarves are related. The notion is not received in any fashion by either of our peoples, but it is cataloged in the Gnomish Archives, the most meticulous and thorough library you'll ever find in the whole wide world." Percy told her. "I myself am one-hundred and twenty-nine years of age, though most swear I don't look to be over fifty." he added, and Evelyn smiled more visibly at that.

"I agree. You don't look so old." she told him, and he recovered himself with a cough.

"Well, I mean, ahem. If you say so!" he returned. "But as to the quality of not aging, your people have it best. And the Valkyries as well." Percy then remarked.

"The Valkyries are mortal?"

"Quite. They only live as long as mortal men."

"And the Giants?" she wondered, and Percy raised an eyebrow.

"There's quite a lot of debate on that subject. You see, it's very difficult to do anything scholarly or anything academically inclined whatsoever as far as those brutes are concerned. You see, well..." Percy began, trailing off; Kia Re's voice then rang out from the window.

"They're murderous thugs who give no thought for anything but battle, and if they catch you in their lands they either kill you outright or torture you until you beg for death." she said coldly.

"Quite." Percy nodded. "Makes it difficult to find out anything about them."

"Oh." Evelyn said, blushing as she realized that the question may have been a touch sensitive to the poor Gnome. "I'm sorry, I didn't mean to offend."

"Not at all, not at all." Percy said to her in reply.

Evelyn then gave him another curious look, and asked another question--in Elvish, which she was confident that the scholastic Percy would understand.

"Wasn't there a Valkyrie who once fell in love with a mortal man?" she asked him, and Percy thought a moment as the question translated in his mind. It had been a long time since he had either seen or heard Elvish, and when the question materialized he slowly nodded, bringing to mind the words of the flowing language to answer in kind.

"During the latter part of the Age of Legends, a Valkyrie named Mia gave her love to a mortal man; his name is unknown, but what is remarkable about the union is that it was the only time a Valkyrie ever gave birth to a male child, who became a legend himself. The father was slain by goblins, and Mia in her wrath wiped out three tribes of them in revenge; she and her son fought in the Ogre Wars, where he fell in battle valiantly. She died of a broken heart shortly after, having lost both son and lover." he said in Elvish, and Evelyn gently nodded, wondering if Kia Re knew the story--which was why she had asked in

Elvish, so that she would not upset the matter further.

Caspar was listening, but he did not seem to have understood any part of it; resolving to teach him sometime, Evelyn just smiled, shrugging as they continued on. When the moons were at their height, Ragya came to relieve them, and they shut off the lanterns; Ragya could see in the dark, and they did not want to attract the attention of unwelcome foes.

As they settled in for the night, Percy curled up for rest near Dusty, the two of them having grown fond of one another in their travels, and the other three huddled together on the other side of the carriage, wrapped up in a blanket. When he was certain they were fast asleep, Ragya, seeing that the road was smooth for some miles, urged the horses to a faster pace for two hours that night, halting once to let them rest until morning. The Werecat then sat upon the top of the carriage, looking around warily to ensure that no one was nearby. Kia Re woke up first, and she got out of the carriage to go and bathe herself; when she had done so she returned to come and sit upon the driver's seat, and Ragya slid down from the top to sit beside her. "It is quiet on this dawn today." he said softly to her, and she nodded, understanding at once. He was uneasy, despite his poised grace.

"No one disturbed me as I bathed." she returned to him, and he blinked.

"You were not truly alone; all know that a Werecat can come to a friend's aid before the blink of an eye, and I made no secret of my presence."

"Foolish, perhaps, if one's desire is to be hidden; and what could be odder than you of all people driving this carriage towards Auschternople?" she said with a faint grin, which he returned.

"Or perhaps my seeming foolishness made them second-guess themselves; why would I be so confident unless I was something more than a simple Werecat?" he returned.

"Let's hope we don't find out." Kia Re said in reply, and he softly nodded. "How long is it to Auschternople, do you think?" she asked him.

"In this carriage, I hope to be there before tomorrow's eve. I urged these poor beasts to a run last night, and that is why I have halted them for now." Ragya said, and Kia Re nodded back. "I trust that your rest was undisturbed by such a thing?"

"It was a good rest. The others are still fast asleep, except the hound. He stirs awake now and again."

"He is a watchful beast." Ragya said, suddenly stiffening and letting out a low growl. Kia Re was alert at once, her hand slowly grasping her spear, which she had with her. Ragya then sniffed the air and looked to their left, and then behind them; he stood to his full height, and let out a wild yeowl that set several flocks of birds to flight and sent other creatures scattering about for their lives. Evelyn and Caspar then woke up; Evelyn grabbed her bow and leaped out at once, an arrow in her hand. Caspar took up his sword and Evelyn's quiver, setting it on the running board of the carriage for her. Kia Re looked about intently, wondering where this elusive fiend had gotten to. A strange whistling sound was heard, and Evelyn at once fired in its direction; a grunt was then heard, followed by a sound of coughing. The arrow had hit its target. She put another arrow to the string just as a band of raiders jumped out to ambush them, and quickly fired it and a third as their battle began in earnest.

Ragya did not shift to wildcat form this time, but he did use the mysterious powers of the druid to hinder their foes, raising mounds of earth to slow them down as the others got organized. Kia Re lost no time, but at once cast her spear at two of those that rushed up; it pierced through them both, and she artfully tumbled off the driver's seat to retrieve it, pulling it out of them and then using it as a staff against two others before she knocked one out; before the other could blink, she had run him through, and was then moving on to a next target. Caspar was now fending off those that got too close to him or Evelyn, and Percy was hastily building something out of the components in his baggage, the Gnome having also been roused by Ragya's yeowl and the shouts of the enraged raiders.

"Was that a sword-thrust or do you think you're a lumberjack?" Caspar said mockingly to his opponent, who was awkwardly swinging a rusted axe at him, seemingly uncertain of how to use it. Caspar then hit the man over the head with the pommel of his sword, and he went down. He quickly dodged the blows of two others, one of whom went down with an arrow in his eye. The second dropped his weapon and ran off screaming, and a third came after the young man as he prepared himself for another round. Three more had fallen to Kia Re, and a couple others had been hopelessly stuck in clods of earth from Ragya's spells. The rest of them began clustering together, and then Percy reemerged with whatever it was in his hand.

"Hold!" the Gnome called to his friends, who halted as he tossed the thing towards them. It went off with a tremendous explosion, and the rest of their enemies were blown to bits. Ragya did not appear to be very impressed, but the other three looked from their dead foes to each other and thence to the Gnome, dumbfounded as to what had just happened. "Well now," Percy began, "let's let them rest in pieces."

***

After their skirmish, they all went to go and bathe again, and when they had eaten a breakfast they set off once more, with Kia Re taking the reins. Ragya sat on top the carriage with Percy, conversing with the Gnome about his knowledge of explosive devices and compounds; Dusty the hound, wide awake, trotted alongside the carriage on a lead as they went along at a steady pace; and Caspar and Evelyn sat inside the carriage itself. She was enraptured as he played his music, listening with contentment as he went from one melody to another, now playing a jig, now a ballad, and then a slow air. The others could also hear, and Kia Re felt her heart soar as he played; Percy would occasionally make an appraising comment, which Ragya would nod back at as they returned to their own conversation. Caspar then turned to a new tune, the tune he had decided to call "Dueling Lutes" after all.

> *Twas the dark of night as we made our way*
> *To the forest on the edge of town,*
> *And we knew at once that something was wrong*
> *For e'en the trees gave us a frown;*
> *But it was too late, and thence our fate*
> *To be caught by an outlaw band*
> *And the leader he says, says he to me,*
> *"Hey lad! Stay a while and be grand!"*

> *Says I to he, I says "Now see here matey!*
> *We've a long way to go on this night;*
> *And we'll have no trouble from you and yours*
> *If you'll let us go back all right!"*
> *Says he to me, "Not a chance, laddie,*
> *For you're in our kingdom now!*
> *And how to get out of this you'll see:*
> *I give you my merry vow!"*

> *Well at first he was wanting my sister fair*
> *And he accused me of the same*
> *On that dark of the night near the boughs of trees*
> *When he plied his merry little game;*
> *And after a laugh whilst the others quaffed*
> *He saw my lute was by my side*
> *"Hey-ho, my lads, I've another game!*
> *And this one will be my pride!"*

> *And he spoke of a challenge, a challenge indeed*
> *As to the lute itself you see:*
> *Whomever made the merriest music that night*

Would be on their way so free;
And I thought it o'er as the night went slower
And I made my choice aright:
"If I lose you win, if I win you lose:
And if a tie we go back tonight!"

The terms were accepted and the challenge given fair,
Then he brought out his lute from his side--
And I got myself down with my own faithful friend
My merry music for to be plied;
And he gave a strum, and I gave a hum,
And we set to our tunes straightway,
Two lutenists dueling under the stars
To determine the right of way!

Here, Caspar broke off from singing, and entered into a lengthy and lively instrumental with his lute, using his skill with the instrument to make it sound as if there were two lutes playing at times, and Evelyn laughed merrily as she clapped along. Kia Re exchanged a glance with Percy; he was embellishing some of it, but after all, that was the way of the minstrel: a merry tale for a merry gathering. Caspar wrapped up his "fiddling" some minutes later, and returned to singing along.

Well he thought he had me there for quite a while
Until the last few songs were played
And he fretted and he flustered and floundered at the last
When upon my lute was played
That epic crown, "Battle of the Narrow-Downs"
And with that his men gave a cheer;
"By all the trees!" quoth he in defeat,
"Here's a minstrel without fear!"

And for our fair gallantry and our contesting brave
Which the merry rogues did admire
They led us through their own woods themselves
As the night went on in the shire
And at the other side he said with pride
"I pray you remember me!"
Says I to him, "I surely will do that!
And a ballad I'll sing of thee!"

And sure that's the very song I've sung to ye tonight
About a minstrel and the outlaw king

Whereupon a merry contest was once won under stars
As the combatants did play and sing
And from hall to hall, from Spring to Fall
Let it be sung right merrily;
About the Dueling Lutes of the Outlaw Woods
On that night when they accosted we!

Caspar ended his song with a flourish, and Evelyn clapped again, laughing merrily at his musical tale. She had asked him about it earlier, but had not been able to coax it out of him until now. Percy called down to him, saying something about "stretching a few details!", but the young man did not hear--or care. He and Evelyn were sharing a kiss, and the two of them were oblivious to all else.

***

Later that evening, they took shelter in a thick copse of trees and brush situated atop a small hill; Ragya was telling them of the Werecat legends, a series of tales that had sprung up from long ago in the Age of Veiled Mystery. Percy, of course, was scribing down what he heard; where the Gnome got his perpetual sheets of paper, none of the others could figure out. Dusty was finishing off the remains of a rabbit, and Evelyn, Caspar, and Kia Re were huddled together again as they listened to Ragya's narrations. When the stories were over and the fire was low, Ragya went to go and rest, as did Percy and Evelyn, leaving Caspar and Kia Re to take the first watch. Dusty eventually curled up to sleep near the horses, and the other two went to go and sit atop the carriage as their friends rested.

The four moons were of a mixed lot tonight; two seemed to be waning, while one was almost full, and the fourth could barely be discerned. They looked at the moons in wonder, and at the stars dancing about them; without meaning to, Kia Re laid her head on Caspar's shoulder with a soft sigh, but Caspar did not seem to notice. Indeed, he himself unconsciously wrapped an arm around her, and Kia Re found herself taking his hand. She then blinked, and then let out a soundless gasp as she colored, letting go at once as she sat back up; Caspar too then realized what they were doing, but he softly smiled, laughing gently.

"I'm sorry, I was... I mean... we should probably focus on the woods instead of... well... I mean..." he said in a soft voice, putting Kia Re's agitation at rest.

"Never mind." she said with a faint glow, her blue eyes sparkling with a hint of longing as she let a small smile creep to her face. Caspar nodded back, letting out a sigh of his own as he softly laid upon the carriage-top to look up at the stars. Kia Re swallowed, her heart pounding as she--*well don't look at him, then!* She thought to herself, and turned away to focus her attention on something else. The hound and the horses were almost perfectly still; if they were calm, then there was most likely nothing but the beasts of the earth and the fowl of the air about them. Indeed, as her gaze rose to look over the trees she saw an owl or two flying about, seeking their prey on the ground below. Two foxes scurried about in the distance, the animals seemingly at play with each other; or were they courting, as animals did in this time of year?

The thought caused her to look back at Caspar, who was fixated on another part of the woods. She softly came over to him to see what he was looking at; it was a large bear, shambling through the woods with two or three cubs.

"Best not to disturb them at all." she whispered softly.

"No indeed." he agreed. "I've heard the hunters of Idoma and Murana Day both say, 'respect the wilds, and they respect you'."

"Wise words. Considering." she remarked with a faint grin. Caspar turned back to her with a wry grin of his own.

"Well you're as human as I, now." he said with a smirk.

"Yes, I am." she nodded, settling in beside him and laying her head on his shoulder once more. Caspar felt a pang, but quickly reminded himself of the other angel below, the one whose beauty had started him on his quest to begin with. "I'm sorry... I can't help but love you. And if I left I fear my heart would break to death; at least when you're near me I feel more in control of these feelings." Kia Re told him, and he put his arm around her again, drawing her closer.

"I understand. I think." he said, and she softly smiled.

"Where are we going? Why are we coming together like this? What path are we meant to take, and how are we to get through it all?" she asked him then, her face falling as she rose up from their embrace. She looked out at the four moons, and Caspar could do nothing but smile, albeit a sad smile, and one that made Kia Re's heart pound for him again as she turned back to him.

"I don't know." he said at first, but then frowned; his brow furrowed, and the words of old Simeon came back to him. "'The wandering bard goes to find love immortal on the day that danger breaks forth; a rushing tide, a vast wilderness through death's valley; forged companions make the journey true'..." he said softly as they came to his mind, and Kia Re looked at him with a curious glance.

"A prophecy?" she asked him.

"I think so." Caspar said, and she gazed out to the stars once again.

"Forged companions..." she murmured softly.

"We're certainly forging our companionship as we go... although I don't know what much else of it means."

"Except the first part." Kia Re said to him with a smirk, and he laughed.

"Except that." he admitted, thinking of Evelyn again. He then thought of Farmer Wells and his family, all the way back in Idoma; were they well? Had their guests adapted to farm life? And what of the burned town? Had any more news been heard on such a count, or anymore towns or villages burned? His agitation rose to his face, and Kia Re, unable to bear his face clouding in sorrow, reached over to kiss him. She kissed him on cheeks lovingly, and then wrapped him in an embrace.

"You're thinking of home." she said softly.

"I am." he admitted, wondering how she could know.

"I think of my own home as well, and it brings sorrow that I may never see it again; I cannot bear seeing such despair on your on face." Kia Re said as she kissed his cheek again. The moment lingered for a few minutes more, and then she let go. "You're weary from singing; I can see it in your face. Go and rest, song-brother." she said to him, and he nodded, too tired to argue. He entered the carriage moments later, and kissed the sleeping Evelyn upon the lips as he lay down beside her. She stirred, and unconsciously wrapped an arm around him as he burrowed in next to her. Her eyes opened briefly, and she smiled, then fell asleep again as Caspar kissed her a second time before falling asleep himself. On top the carriage, Kia Re softly wept, praying for strength to endure this trial she felt herself placed in, if only for Evelyn and Caspar's sake.

***

By the next afternoon, their carriage had wound its way to the great vale near the coast where Auschternople was situated. Ragya and Caspar were at the driver's seat, Dusty was on his lead, Percy was (yet again) perched atop the carriage, and Evelyn was in the carriage with Kia Re.

As the carriage slowed, the two of them gently climbed out to get on top the thing, wondering what was going on. Evelyn sat next to Percy, who was making sketches of something; it was a tower, she determined moments later. A tower?

She looked up, as Kia Re was doing, and saw gleaming spires in the distance: they were about to arrive at Auschternople, City of the Kings, the Fading Jewel of the Kingdom of Augusta.

Book Two: A Tale of the Dying Lion

List! Hearken! See the dying
Struggle in his throes;
a proud lion who once roared
at all who crossed his path
Dying slowly
Ever slowly
Venom and poison coursing
through his veins like a cancer
and the world spins onward
Heedless

The spawning of strife and shame
Came from his loins
and now repaid in full
the cost of treachery given back
a thousand times
Nay! Mourn not!
Damned be the Dying Lion
and all his spawn forever
Proud Augusta,
clinging,
clutching her ragged garments to her breast
hoping that the nakedness might be hid
if only barely

See her ravaged body, raped
as once she raped others;
the Dying Lion brought down,
humiliated
Augusta's ivory breasts, once tipped with rubies
now shorn of their splendor;
plain-looking are they
and sucked dry from rapine, like dead grapes:
the Demon-hordes did well their work!
Yet the Dying Lion carries on
and with faltering courage, roars

Chapter One: Auschternople

The fabled city of Augusta was walled on most of its sides, walls that formed a hexagon around most of the city, broken by the sea on one side. For it was a port city in its oldest origins, a port that was once grander than even Murana Day to the south, but now its ships were dreary and all but unkempt, and its proud walls still bore the marks of the Demonic Hordes. If one were to look at a map of the city, they would find it somewhat concentric in nature, with the palace of the king at its very center. The five-sided building was without question the largest in the city, if indeed not the largest building in the world.

There were six major districts in the city; on its northwest was the Barracks or military district, and here could be found the quarters for Augusta's armies and some of her weapon and arms merchants, along with the dungeons; in the north district clustered the scholars, as well as the famous Auschternople Wizard's Tower, in addition to the Hall of Records and a temple; the northeast district housed merchants of all sorts, as well as the royal gardens; in the southwest district was a residential area, which was home to the stubborn and determined people of Auschternople still fiercely loyal to the king, along with a few inns and taverns--but none more successful than the "Queen's Inn", said to have been established long ago during the Reign of Queens in the Age of Kings, when the eldest royal heirs for generations were all women; by nominal standards, the two remaining districts (south and southeast) were called the Shipwright's District and the Harbor District, but over the years the twain became conglomerated, and though ostensibly two districts they were really one, a place where the naval business of the King's City was conducted. It was also rumored to be right above the infamous Thieves' Guild, but nothing had ever been proven.

Just outside the city on its northeast side was the Valley of Kings, the entombment site for the monarchs of the Augustan Throne; it was a particular haunt for the thieves these days, who eagerly scoured for relics and such as they could find. The Royal Army made a patrol of the area every two to three days, but it did no good, insofar as it could be ascertained. Still, it humored the king, and gave his armies something to do besides loiter. On Auschternople's immediate east side was a great enclosure of farmlands and grazing lands; the walls had been hastily but carefully made after the Invasion, and were moderately deterring to all but the most cunning and determined thieves. Auschternople was situated upon a north side of the Bay of Paupalousas, in a harbor that had come to be called King's Bay; a solitary lighthouse sat upon the lone islet in the bay, but in these days it had little use, and was even rumored to have been taken over by raiders. These raiders, aside from the thieves, were the greatest threat to Auschternople in these days, vagabonds who owed loyalty to no one, preying upon what was left of the once-great city as it continued to crumble.

The party of friends approached Auschternople's western gate, coming up the King's Road in their carriage and taking swift counsel among themselves as Ragya drove on. They would arrive in about ten minutes, and they now debated as to their course of action--or at least the particulars thereof.

"Going in with the Thieves' Guild is ridiculous--they'd turn on us the moment we served their purpose!" Percy quipped.

"As if that king is going to do any better?" Kia Re returned at once.

"Nobles are honor-bound to promises; this king is much better at that than his ancestors by all accounts, or so I have on generally good authority." the Gnome sniffed.

"Why don't we play all sides of the game this time?" Caspar suggested, and they all looked at him.

"What do you mean, friend?" Ragya asked him curiously.

"I mean, that we gently prod about to see what's what, and work on what we see from there. There's bound to be plenty of opportunity to gain favor with the king and his subjects; and as for the Thieves' Guild--well, we'll deal with them as we find them. In the meantime, our most immediate concern is pawning off the last of the unnecessary items we have, including, perhaps, this carriage." Caspar said, and Kia Re nodded.

"He is right. We should go softly." she said.

"Selling the carriage?" Evelyn wondered at him.

"My heart feels pulled across the sea." Caspar said as he gazed over the somewhat ruined but still majestic sight of Auschternople, his voice almost a whisper.

Ragya then stopped the carriage, and got down. The other four got down with him as he pulled out his pouch, murmuring the incantations over the rune-stones which he held in his hand.

"We shall soon see what course we must take." Evelyn said, and Ragya cast the rune-stones on to the ground. He knelt down at once, scrutinizing the seven he had, at random, selected from the pouch fastened at his side.

"See! The Royal Beast is held by the grip of the Mischief Maker; the Mystic Ward and the Sword of Justice are his only allies. With the Mischief Maker is the Father of Chaos. These two work against the Royal Beast constantly, beleaguering his allies. And here, the Unknown Stone. It makes its way towards the Royal Beast, but for what purpose is unknown, other than that it moves towards the sea indeed, marked by the Sea-Queen's Mother." Ragya said after a few moments, and the five of them looked around at one another.

"The Unknown Stone. Us." Kia Re stated in recognition. "They do not know our full counsel or purpose; and neither do we, save for one goal."

"And that goal, one way or another, is to make our way to the sea, so it says." Percy added, shaking his head. "It's all very mystical, and not so helpful."

"Then let us do the right thing." Caspar said evenly. "Let us offer our help to the king." he added, and Evelyn nodded.

"He's right. We should do as our hearts tell us. Auschternople may have been petty, but now it deserves at the least our pity, and if we can do good to help those who truly suffer here, then we should do it. And we can only do that by helping the king." she said, and Kia Re let out a slow nod.

"Your words are of wisdom, sister. Let us do that, then." the Valkyrie said.

"I concur." Percy added.

"Then let us away to the gates, 'ere they close!" Ragya said, and they jumped back up onto the carriage, and began heading for the gates.

Caspar looked at Ragya inquiringly, and the Werecat glanced over at him passively.

"You did not say which course you would take, friend Ragya." the minstrel said to him.

"Nor do I wish to add to such counsel. I am here for the journey, not the decisions." Ragya told him, and Caspar continued reflecting upon the words all the way to the gate. When they got to this, the guards, after a brief inquiry, let them pass into the city, and at once they made for that most famous of inns, the "Queen's Inn", which had by far the best repute--even in a time such as this.

***

On the road still called King's Road, they labored through the concentric pathways of Auschternople; to their right was the residential district, where their destination of Queen's Inn was to be found, and on the left was the Barracks and Arms Quarter, where dwelt the soldiery of the king and many who crafted weapons and armor. Straight ahead of them was the legendary palace, towering over most of the city with its spires; but far off to the left they could see the tall pinnacles of the Hall of Records and the Wizard's Tower in the Scholar's District. After several minutes they made a turn to the right onto a road that circled about the perimeters of the palace, and then they made another right on a road called Anchor Way, for it bordered the Shipwright's District and Harbor. Several of those who lived in the city gave the antique carriage a second glance, never mind its occupants; a young man and a Werecat sat at the driver's seat, and on the top was Percy, scribing down notes as they wound their way through. In the carriage itself they saw two ladies; Evelyn had put a hood on over her ears to disguise her being an Elf, but all could see she was exceptionally beautiful, as was Kia Re beside her. No one molested them on their way, for Ragya was a formidable sight to them; Werecats were still seen about, but they were mercenaries all, and it was unwise to trifle with them.

As they reached Queen's Inn the Werecat halted their carriage. The stables lay just next to the inn itself, and here they consigned their carriage and horses until they had decided as to what they should do with them. Queen's Inn itself was, on this level and the two above, triangular in shape, with a four-sided fourth floor on the very top. Stairs to the door were in the middle of the side facing the street, and the six of them (including Dusty the hound) headed inside once they had their carriage and horse secured. There were a few patrons at the bar, and the innkeeper greeted them cordially. Ragya handed her six gold coins as he softly requested a room, and she nodded, at once leading them to the corner stairs on their left; they headed up these, and were led to one of the middle rooms.

"These six gold coins'll see you through about a week and a half; are ye to stay here so long?" she asked them.

"We have no immediate plans other than resting a while from a long journey; I shall add to the coinage as becomes necessary, should we stay longer." Ragya told her softly, and she nodded.

"Right you are then. Welcome again to Queen's Inn! Dinner is at the sunset hour, and ring the bell if you need the baths!" she said, and bustled off to the common room once more. The six of them settled in, and sat about the room to talk. In an hour's time they decided to keep the carriage instead, hoping that it would be of further use across the sea. With that settled, they made a great sorting of all that was necessary and unnecessary, and when this had been decided upon, Percy went with Ragya once more to see about pawning it off in the Merchant's District. The other four headed down to the common room, and Caspar led Dusty to the stables to stay with the horse; when he had come back in, Evelyn and Kia Re both escorted him to an out-of-the-way table, and he gave them both a quizzical look.

"Caspar!" Kia Re whispered softly, nodding to a notice on one of the supporting beams of the inn; he looked at it with scrutiny, and then understood. It was a conscription notice. *Hearken ye citizens of Auschternople: All young men between the ages of fifteen and twenty-five summers are hereby ordered by the king's decree to report to Chief Watchman Boris for the training of arms in the King's Army. If thou shouldst find thyself failing to do so, ye shall spend a half-year in the dungeons on quarter-rations; if there is aught in the way of reason that thou shouldst be granted pardon and clemency in the way of this decree, in the case of illness or other reasonable excuse, make thou thy case before the king himself 'ere thou find thyself the object of his wrath. By Royal Decree, King Michael XIV, Lord Protectorate of the Realm, Executor of Justice.* Caspar took in the words carefully. There was a way out of it, so the notice read; now if only the king was as fair-minded as Percy had implied.

"No fear. I'm a minstrel." Caspar whispered back, and Kia Re gave him a serious look while Evelyn shook her head.

"You can't sing your way out of every cage, bard." Kia Re told him.

"This one I can." he returned.

"Are you sure?" Evelyn asked him warily. "Because if not, then--"

"Ragya's stones were clear: we are meant to leave, all of us together. I have no fear." he said to her.

"Very well." she nodded back. "But let us do make haste to seek out the king as the notice says and state your case." she added. Caspar nodded in agreement, and the three of them talked of lighter things until Percy and Ragya returned; they then had a good supper, and retired to their rooms afterwards.

"One thing's clear," the Gnome said as they sat down once more, "this city is in a very fragile state indeed. I don't suppose you saw the conscription notice?" he said with a wary eye as he looked up at Caspar.

"We'll see about it tomorrow." the young man replied.

"Indeed you shall! Can't have that on our heads." Percy nodded.

"And then I'd like to visit the Hall of Records." Caspar added.

"An excellent idea!" the Gnome agreed enthusiastically. "I could use a brushing up on the lands beyond, myself. As could we all."

"Books are not my strong-point." Kia Re returned with a frown.

"As for me, I would rather stroll about and see what exactly is going on in this city so that I can learn what is best to do in the way of helping." Evelyn said.

"Very well. Ragya?" the Gnome wondered.

"I shall stay here until our course is decided. Then I shall add my skills to whatever road we take." the Werecat said, and with that they concluded their little council. Percy and Ragya took the bunk on one side of the room, and left Caspar and the two ladies to decide upon the bed and couch. Evelyn then noticed the Sword of Magus seemed to be humming, and she took it from its sheath to see what was going on. The sword now slightly vibrated in her grasp, as if a great power had awoken; what power lay within the ancient sword of the world's most powerful mage?

"It sings to me..." she said softly.

"The Song of the Blade; it is potent." Kia Re nodded.

"I wonder if the Wizard's Guild here knows anything about it?" Caspar wondered.

"I shall venture and see them tomorrow." Evelyn said. The sword stopped humming and vibrating, and when it was plain to see that it would do so no more (at least today), she put it back in the sheath, and the three of them then flopped on the large bed together.

"Never mind an order. We're all family here, now." Evelyn then remarked as they bundled together for rest. They fell asleep within moments, and slept in a dreamless slumber until dawn peeked into their window.

***

Morning brought rain, and through the streets of Auschternople the four companions hurried on towards the palace despite it. Straight up the road they went, and navigated through two intersections to reach the elegantly paved pathway that led to the grand doors of the imposing and still-grandiose palace; here, they were admitted by the guards, who gave the hooded Evelyn a second glance. Was she an Elf?--no, she could not be. What Elf would come to Auschternople after all these years? And so the four of them headed across the palace grounds, and thence into the palace itself. When they were let in to see the king, they found his hall filled with several other minor nobles, as well as guards about the room, guards about the balconies, and several around the throne itself; two of them were near the doors, and there were indeed two guards at all five doors that led into the audience chamber.

"What doest thou here, boy? Send thyself to the barracks and thence to the Chief Watchman!" the king said at once, discerning his youthful age as he descended from the throne. "Or hast thou reason I shouldst leave thee in peace? Art thou a citizen of mine kingdom, or a wanderer from distant lands?"

"Your majesty." Caspar returned, kneeling as he stepped forward. The other three also knelt. "I am indeed as you see me; Caspar of Idoma, near to Murana Day. I do seek exemption though, great king;

for I am also a traveller, a wandering minstrel by trade, and it please you, your majesty." the young man said, and the king raised his eyebrows, looking over him and his three companions.

The ladies could have been of the noblewomen at his court; the Gnome was an odd companion, but then again, these were odd times. Small wonder if one of the little folk should join this young bard--as he claimed to be. But ah! There was his harp. Was it for sham and show, or was he of the craft indeed?

"Thou bearest a harp: bearest thou the craft? Rise and answer!" the king demanded.

"Majesty, I will add that I am of the Order of Cassandra." Caspar added as he rose, and for the first time the king noticed the amulet.

"Trinkets and thievery are common about this city, boy. Shew thy craft or mine guards shalt escort thee to the dungeons for contempt!" the king said again. Obediently, Caspar took up his harp, and knelt down to play; he recited a tale from the Age of Legends, a heroic tale about a young knight who fought a great giant, a massive ogre, and then a terrifying dragon to save the lady of his dreams. At the last, the knight was mortally wounded by the winged fiend, who also fell that day, and his lady never loved another man after. The king had since sat back down on his throne in amazement; Caspar's gift for music was exceptional, and Evelyn and Kia Re found themselves looking at each other reprimandingly for doubting he could "sing his way out" of a situation. When the last notes faded away, there was silence for several minutes; the king then rose again, and went forward to Caspar. He stood the young man up, and then looked around at his court.

"If anyone hast a doubt that this young man is anything but a bard, be damned to you! He walks freely in my city, he and all his companions! I shalt not impose upon thee any conscription; but do thou if thou pleasest come again someday, and entertain us at our feasting!" the king said, and Caspar bowed low. They were then escorted out, and once outside the palace grounds they breathed easier.

"Well, I take it back. You can indeed sing your way out of things." Kia Re said with a smile.

"Yes, yes, yes... let's on with it then--we've work to do!" Percy said, and they headed along towards the Scholar's District. When they were about there, a young lady brushed up against them in seeming accident, but then Caspar noticed his pouch was gone.

"Hoy!" he called, and dashed after her. Kia Re followed, and Percy stopped with Evelyn at a fruit stand while their two friends dashed after the thief. Kia Re, suddenly feeling a burst of anger, tossed her spear with a yell towards the young girl; it landed where she intended, just near her head so as to frighten her, and with a scream the young lady collapsed to the ground and sat there quivering. Caspar caught up to her while Kia Re suddenly caught her breath; she could feel it in herself, her powers were returning. With a glow, she strode forward to reclaim her spear, pleased at finding out such a thing was possible. Caspar gently reclaimed his pouch from their quarry, and helped her up.

"Now see here! There's no call for that." Caspar said to her in a soft tone; she looked up at him with tears. "Oh, now! Come along; whatever it is, we'll help--but not by letting you steal from us!" he added, and the three of them went to rejoin Evelyn and Percy. The Gnome took one look at the new girl and raised an eyebrow.

"Qi Wengo Wan; gliski nama touske?" the diminutive scholar said with an inquiring tone.

"Iiyao; tousk Weishuune: nama tous Ji Mao." she returned.

"As I suspected." the Gnome nodded cheerily, and she smiled back at him.

"But they call me Jenna." she said.

"Indeed! And we shall give you your proper name, Ji Mao." Percy said. "I am Percy; this is Caspar leading you along, that is Kia Re who frightened you, and here is Evelyn; our fifth companion, Ragya, is at Queen's Inn."

"Weishuune?" Caspar suddenly realized, looking over the young lady again; her skin was bronzed, her eyes a dark brown, and her hair black, bound back in a pony-tail; she was indeed of the Weishuune, though her outfit suggested otherwise.

"I am." she returned softly, conscious of her loose clothes as she crossed her arms over her chest. "I am sorry for my actions; they taught me to do such things, though I am always remorseful about it."

"And I am sorry for frightening you." Kia Re said gently, and the other girl smiled.

"Who are 'they' and what do they teach you to steal for?" Percy wondered, and then shook his head. "No, never mind; I understand perfectly now." he said.

"She's of the Guild." Caspar said as he caught on.

"Yes, I am. Though I would happily get away, if I could." Ji Mao told them. "But they are always in a position to strike back at those who would cheat them." she added; the four of them exchanged glances. Here was someone who might help them in their endeavors.

"And if they could not?" Evelyn asked her softly; Ji Mao's eyes widened, and she made a quick glance about.

"Then I would be happy. But how can you say such things?" she asked.

"We'll see, won't we?" Caspar told her. "Come with us; are you hungry?" he asked her, and she nodded. They bought some fruit from the stand, and continued on. A man in a hooded cloak tapped Caspar on the shoulder, and he halted while the others went a few paces more before realizing he was behind. "What do you want of me, sir?" Caspar asked; the man flashed the silver medallion of Cassandra. It was a fellow adherent.

"You are new here?" the man told him; his voice was soft but firm.

"Yes, we are. We seek a way to find passage across the sea."

"And how do you intend to do that?" the man asked him curiously.

"Hopefully, by gaining favor with the king and his followers." Caspar told him.

"I see. You must listen carefully, young one." the man returned; Caspar gave him a curious look as he began.

"Why?"

"I am a seer, friend minstrel. I see many things; on one vision I have seen this city in ruins, and in another I have seen its restoration. Augusta can never return: the kingdom is dead, though its noble king still clings to hope; that hope is not entirely in vain, though. There is a hope, but it is not the hope he wants; it is the hope we need." the man went on, and Caspar listened with careful attention. "At the height of these visions I have seen you and your friends, even this one with you now, if she continues to follow her heart instead of her head. You will change this city for good--or for ill. Every choice you make has ramifications; choose wisely, and choose in great caution. Trust none but those who love you."

"Sound advice for anyone in these evil days." Caspar said in reply.

"Indeed." the man nodded. He looked up at the sky, gazing out across the tops of the buildings. "For thousands of years this has been the City of Monarchs; the city will endure, but the monarch may not. Hopefully the circumstances will be benevolent, and this city transition by a more peaceful process than violence. You can ensure that happens." the man told him as he looked back at the younger man.

"How?" Caspar asked softly.

"You already know. Follow your heart. You are a good person; I can feel it. When the way seems doubtful, just trust the words of your heart." the man returned, and as mysteriously as he had arrived he vanished, and Caspar was at a loss to explain the conversation to his friends, when he had caught up to them. They took it as an omen for good, and continued on their way. Ji Mao, Caspar, and Percy headed to the archives, and Kia Re decided to stay with them while Evelyn went to the Wizard's Tower. She was more concerned about keeping an eye on their new friend than she was about making sure Evelyn was safe; after all, the Elf could take care of herself. *She fought an Ogre with that sword.* Kia Re said to herself, smiling as she headed in to the archives with the other three.

On almost the other side of the district, Evelyn approached the Wizard's Tower, and was greeted by two novices. They ushered her in at once, explaining that her visit had been anticipated. "What?" she said at once, wondering why or how.

"The Master of the Tower felt the presence of that which you bear." one of them told her, and Evelyn understood. The Sword of Magus' strange vibrations last night had echoed in the magic realm. Why had it done so? She was about to find out--hopefully. The tower was tall, and many rooms were on the many floors of the structure as it rose up into the air; they at last reached the top, and here Evelyn was ushered in to a private lounge, where the Master of the Tower was waiting.

"So. You are now the bearer of the Sword of Magus." he said, and she nodded. "Spare me the disguise, simple as it is. I know you are an Elf." he added, and Evelyn removed her hood.

"So you know that as well." she remarked. "Do you know why the sword did what it did last night?"

"Because you are not a magic-user. Yet." he said as he turned to her, raising one of his eyebrows at her.

"Yet?" Evelyn wondered.

"You have the sword. It has let you carry it this far. But unless you take the appointed path as its bearer, you may have to leave it behind; for it will not always cooperate as it did with the Ogre. Already you have known its power; did it not excite you? Did you not want to know more of the sword itself, to unlock its full potential, and yours?" the master said to her, and she withdrew it from the sheath, gazing at its tapered length; subtle runes of magic were inscribed upon it, and they seemed to reflect the light, as did the red gem in its pommel. "You hear it again; you hear its song, longing for the days when it was a weapon of power, when its first master, the great Magus, wielded it in the Age of Legends long ago." he said with a soft smile, and she let her senses revel in the sensation. *Her full potential...*

"My full potential?" she wondered softly.

"Elves have the capacity to be the greatest of magic-users, when they choose to do so. And you: I sense great power in you. It is waiting for you to find it. We can help you. We do not seek to bind you here, only to guide you, to set you down the path that will let you and the sword become one together in battle. Will you take our offer?" he asked her.

"What must I do?" Evelyn asked in reply.

"There are standards that all magic-users adhere to; even Magus, though he was more of a free-spirit, abided by such standards as we have and use. They are no great burden, and they are acceptable to

Elven custom."

"I forsook Elven custom." she returned. "I am willing to bind myself to such standards as you may have, however, if it means I can help my friends."

"Indeed. And you may help them better in learning what we can teach you, though we may not have much time. You are needed with your friends. But enough of this: what say you to the offer?" the master asked her, and Evelyn re-sheathed the sword.

"I accept."

***

Ji Mao's revealing outfit was a touch of a distraction for Caspar at times, but he at last managed to absorb himself in a book about Derghak, a somewhat mysterious continent far to the east of the High Seas Regions; Percy was focused on several books detailing this region, where the Sea of Chloe, the Sea of Tears, and the Aubrnos Ocean mingled about a scattering of islands. The meeting of the waters had caused a great storm to arise, the Eye of Balkris--at least, that was the current theory of the Gnomish Oceanographer and Meteorology Guilds; it had been referred to the Board of Queries for inspection and verification on account of a complaint from several other guilds, most notably the Anthropological Society and the Historiographer's Guild, whose own conclusions relied upon the local folklore of the High Seas Region's native Weishuune peoples. The Oceanographers and Meteorologists scoffed at this, but allowed the query to proceed anyway.

Kia Re was not reading books, but she was watching Ji Mao, who turned to Caspar every now and again with a longing look. The Valkyrie was not unsympathetic to her glances. Had she not also desired the young man? A pity there was only one of him... she soon fell asleep in a chair next to Percy, who smiled at her as she slept. Caspar then went to put his own book away, and Ji Mao went with him. She gazed at the books in awe, but then her eyes returned to Caspar. He looked over at her, and smiled gently as she came over.

"You really hold nothing against me for earlier?" she asked him softly.

"I do not." Caspar shook his head. "It's not in me to bear a grudge. We'll forget about it, and go on as friends, eh?" he said, and she smiled at him.

"I am glad, then." she said, reaching out to hug him. "I do want to get out of this place. I am tired of being their servant. Take me when you go; don't leave me here with them!" she said to him, and Caspar held her gently.

"We'll take you along; don't worry about that." he said, and she kissed his cheek before heading back to the table where Percy sat. Caspar, thoroughly flummoxed, headed out of the old building to seek the Wizard's Tower.

He found the tall tower some minutes later, and was ushered in to its foyer with great welcome. They set out refreshments for him to eat at his leisure, and told him Evelyn would be down after some time. This ambiguous figure gave him a weary feeling, but it was better than tormenting himself with thoughts of yet another girl as their companion. No; no, shake them off. There was no need at all to think of such things. She was very grateful, and happy at a prospect of escaping what was probably a very wretched life; there was no reason to suspect she had any feelings for him at all. With that thought firmly in mind he settled in on a divan, and fell asleep himself moments later.

***

"Probably went to check on Evelyn." Percy remarked as they exited the archives.

"True." Kia Re agreed.

"In that case let us return to my house. I need to get some things from there." Ji Mao said as they began walking towards the inn.

"Let's head to the merchants, first. If that's all right?" Percy returned.

"It is acceptable." Ji Mao nodded, and they headed off towards the Merchant Quarter of the city; here, they found a store called "Marta's General Goods", and made a purchase of clothes and food. Kia Re found herself enchanted by a dress in another shop, and after a touch of cajoling added it and a couple of dancer's costumes to their purchases.

"You never know when such things could come in handy." Kia Re said with a wink, and Percy rolled his eyes.

"Of that I am thoroughly in doubt. But have it your way." he remarked. Ji Mao at once put on one of the new sets of clothes, and when their purchases were packed away in a parcel they headed to the other side of the city for Ji Mao's house. It was just down the street from Queen's Inn, and she gathered only a few things indeed from the small abode; two daggers, a book, and an amulet that Percy softly told Kia Re was a family insignia. "Last personal relic of family, I might imagine. The Weishuune were brought here as slaves originally, until the islanders themselves gave trouble to the Augustans and demanded their people's freedom; she must be descended from those who remained in the city." he said, and the Valkyrie gazed at their new friend with a new wonder.

"I did not realize Augusta was so depraved as to commit acts of slavery..." she said to him softly.

"Well, long ago, at any rate. Now they themselves are being taken

168

as slaves by these raiders in the hills. A sad irony, but perhaps deserved, in some respects." he remarked.

"Perhaps: but I will say that no one truly deserves such penalty, even if it is merited in some fashion. And if there are slaves around here we should free them." Kia Re returned.

"I heartily agree." the Gnome nodded.

"All right, I am ready." Ji Mao said with a soft smile.

"Very well! Let us hie back to the inn." Percy returned, and the three of them returned to the inn; Ragya greeted their new companion with a great respect, for their two peoples were both people of mystical rituals and of family, and Ji Mao was honored indeed to meet one of the fabled Werecats.

"But where is my forest-sister and her chosen love?" he wondered.

"The Wizard's Tower." Kia Re told him as she lay upon the bed.

"Hmm..." he returned, frowning thoughtfully. "Her destiny is much altered." he said after a moment, and they looked at him.

"What do you mean?" Kia Re asked him.

"I mean, that the Sword of Magus is now in the hands of a true magic-user."

***

"This is the Ring of Chloe." the shopkeeper told Caspar. "It is said that there are other relics of her about, but we keep this one here." she told him.

"It is an odd chance; I have what seems to be the Golden Flute of Chloe that I found at an old temple to the south." Caspar told her, pulling it out for inspection as her eyes widened.

"Lords! So it is! See here, it's these faint runes about the base of the mouthpiece that show it." she said, pointing to the almost unseen markings.

"I wonder if the Ring is useful with the Flute?" Caspar said as he looked at the old but still marvelous instrument in a new-found wonder.

"So the legends say." she grinned at him mischievously. "Would you care to buy it and find out?" she asked him. Caspar returned the mischievous look, leaning upon the counter as he did so.

"How much?"

"I'll start at... fourteen gold pieces."

"Come now--I've shown you a rarer trinket than you dared hope to see from a merry fiend such as myself. I'll go to seven." he retorted, and she looked at him with a sigh.

"You're such a handsome thing. I'd sleep with you in an instant. Twelve."

"I'll be faithful to the one I love. But since you speak so complimentary, I'll go up to eight." Caspar returned.

"For being faithful to the kisses and love of such a fine woman as I'm sure you have, I'll go down to ten, but not a penny less." she told him.

"If I show you something else will you go to nine and a half?"

"It better be damned good." she said with a smirk. He then pulled out the Golden Book of Chloe, and she gazed at it in wonder. "You weren't kidding! Did you find this with the Flute?" she asked him after flipping through a few of its pages.

"Indeed. At an Astralatian Temple somewhat to the north of a town called Frostvale." he told her.

"Ah! I had wondered about those rumors; but it's so dangerous to go travelling anymore through these lands. Especially if you're a woman." she said with a nod.

"That is truly a shame." Caspar said genuinely. "We should all be free to go where we will without fear."

"You speak it well. Fortunately I have the Tower to keep me safe." she smiled. "I do believe that's seven gold pieces." she said with a wink, and Caspar smiled back.

"Then I'm grateful to you, dear lady." he said, and with that he paid the final price, and went back to wait for Evelyn. *The Ring of Chloe...* he said to himself; *what on earth will it do?*

After another few hours of waiting, Evelyn came down at last; she had her own book, and when she had kissed Caspar she began telling him all about her day. He listened with rapt awe as the two of them headed back to Queen's Inn; her initiation had ended with her being given the Book and Ring of Magus, which had been kept in the Tower of Auschternople faithfully in the long years.

"And it feels so--so right! This is our path, Caspar, you and I; together we will travel the lands, and we can begin to make things right for all peoples."

"I certainly hope so." Caspar agreed. "What of your bow? Shall it sing again, or is this to be your more prevalent occupation now?"

"I may keep the bow." Evelyn shrugged. "But this; why fire an arrow when you can cast a bolt?" she added with a wink.

"Such is true." he smiled.

"And what's that? You have your own little trinket, I see?" she asked him.

"Something the mage-ware's keeper was telling me about; Chloe's Ring, she said."

"Really?" Evelyn remarked with a funny look. "I didn't know the goddess had a ring."

"Well, we'll see now, won't we?" Caspar smiled back. "It's not every day such relics come your way."

"And now we have a fair parcel of them." she sighed. "What are we to do to keep from being stolen from?"

"We'll figure it out, I'm sure." he returned. They reached the inn around dinner time, and found that the others had ensured dinner was brought up to the room. "Good thought." Caspar remarked as the two of them sat down to join their friends.

"Indeed." Percy agreed. "Long day of it at the Tower, eh?" he asked Evelyn.

"Very much so." she nodded back.

They ate in silence for a time, eagerly diving in to the repast before them after the day's events. Then Percy began to tell them of what he had read in the books at the Hall of Records; he had focused only for a time on the journey ahead, feeling a stronger necessity to study more recent events.

The Thieves' Guild was more preeminent in the city than they had thought, to which Ji Mao gave an affirmation. There was a hidden lair in the city itself, and the thieves were in collaboration with the raiders in the hills.

"And so they go about looting, stealing, and so forth; it appears that there are indeed raiders occupying the lighthouse in King's Bay. But the royal fleets are grounded by order of the king; he seems to think there is enough trouble in the city itself without trying to recapture the lighthouse--and he may be right." the Gnome told them, shaking his head as he finished his little synopsis of Auschternople's situation.

"So where does that leave us?" Caspar asked him.

"In a difficult position, should we seek to somehow alter all these circumstances to our favor." Percy said to him with a shrug.

"Yet we must change it."

"It is our purpose perhaps to do so; but in what way was not clear." Ragya remarked.

"Let us then start with the simple things." Evelyn suggested. "For my own part, I must keep up with studies at the Tower for a few days. It shouldn't be much for the rest of you to do some small things here and there. We don't *have* to go after all these villains at once." she added, and they agreed with this.

"But when we do get to those villains," Percy put in, "we must have some sort of plan for them. I shall stay here and work on my devices; they may come in handy when and if we get to the point of being a force in the area instead of mere observers. For now let us be content as those mere observers, however; there's no need to draw more attention than we need to." he said with a knowing look at all of them.

"This is also true." Evelyn agreed.

"In that case, let's try and get started on the morrow. For my own part, I want to see what's what at the harbor." Caspar said. "Maybe we can lend aid there in some way." he added.

"Sound thinking, m'boy." Percy nodded. "And what of our new friend? What would you suggest we do along the way, I wonder?" he asked, turning to Ji Mao. The girl thought for a brief moment, somewhat troubled by the question.

"I would try to find ways to weaken the Thieves' Guild from within." she said in a very soft voice, as if afraid of being overheard. "They have ample opportunities for those who would align with them, opportunities a clever person could use against them somehow, if one knows how to play such games."

"And do you?" Ragya asked her, and she shrugged.

"I do not claim to be clever in such ways. But I can get you in, if you so desire." she said in reply.

"Then perhaps I shall see these thieves, and use my wits against them." Ragya said to the others. "A Werecat will intrigue them, and be above suspicion, perhaps, on account of my people being mercenaries outside the forest."

"It is well spoken." Kia Re nodded. "I shall go with Caspar and aid him." she added, and Evelyn smiled.

"Keep him out of trouble for me." she said to Kia Re, who smiled back.

"Always." she returned, and with that they began dividing up the room for sleeping. Percy decided upon a chair for tonight, being the smallest, and so the top bunk was left to one of the others. Ji Mao, being smaller than Kia Re, simply shrugged as she smiled and headed over to the divan. The blonde Valkyrie smiled back and headed to the top bunk as Caspar and Evelyn took to the other bed again; she looked over with a pang at the two of them, and then turned to the wall. Within moments, she was mercifully asleep, dreaming of otherworldly things and places. As for the two lovers, they were asleep the moment they were clasped in each other's arms, content to know rest for the night.

Chapter Two: Androcles

When Ragya was awake, he discovered that Ji Mao was already prepared, dressed in her rogue's outfit once more. She nodded to him softly, and he blinked; it was time to go. Neither time nor thieves waited for anyone. The Werecat hastily prepared himself, and then he and the young girl headed out of the inn; it was still early morning, and Auschternople was just waking up itself. As the two of them made their way through the streets they stopped briefly at a bakery for a light but filling breakfast, and Ji Mao then resumed her course; they kept on towards the Shipwright's, but Ragya suddenly got the impression that they were going about in circles. He was almost certain of this when they suddenly stopped at a house near the main road that divided the residential part of Auschternople from the Shipwright's District.

Here, Ji Mao softly knocked, and received a muffled answer in reply. She spoke a strange word, and the door opened to admit them. Ragya was not accosted, but he was greeted with wary glances, which he returned in kind. Ji Mao spoke to one of those who seemed to be in charge, and he nodded after several moments, then turned to the tall Werecat beside her.

"She speaks well of you. We thought we'd lost her the other day when she didn't show back up; nice of you to take her under the wing and all." he said. "I'm Tomas Red. And you?" the man then asked him.

"I am Ragya, a simple Werecat who has just recently arrived in the city; I seek employ and profit, and it please you, good Sir Red." Ragya told him.

"Jackie said he came in with that 'uge carriage, boss." another returned.

"My companions are of no concern; we travelled together, and here we parted ways." the Werecat returned, his soft and confident voice dispelling most of the doubt the statement had brought up.

"Travelling companions; not so uncommon, 'specially with the likes of us around, eh lads?" Tomas remarked, and the others laughed. "I'll wager you've killed a few of my mates out in the countryside, eh there, Ragya?" the man added with a cunning look.

"Perhaps." the Werecat returned to him. "What is that which men say? 'All in war is counted as right'?" he said with his own piercing gaze, and Tomas raised an eyebrow.

"Something like that, yeah. So now, whiskers, what can we do ye for? Employ, is it? We've a tidy lot to get through, and no end in sight for the main goal." he said in answer. "I've the idea to test you, though. Nothing hard, if you're as good as you say... just this: there's a mate of mine in the dungeons. I want him out. Name's Aron; he's the owner of this here house." Tomas told him, and Ji Mao looked up at the Werecat. There was no hint of anything on his placid face, only the perpetual calm she had first noticed.

"Very well. I shall see to it." Ragya said.

"Dungeons are in the Barracks District. Watch you don't end up in them yourself, eh?" a third voice said as Ragya and Ji Mao turned to go. The Werecat did not reply, but he did glance back, giving the man a curious look, as if he had said something very silly. In moments the two of them had blended back into the streets, and were on their way towards the dungeons of the great city.

"And how do you plan to free this man?" Ji Mao asked him.

"We shall see." came the response, and she had to content herself with this answer.

***

When Percy had awoken, he found that all save Evelyn had gone off for the day; the Elf-maid was just drying off from a bath, combing out her hair before she got dressed for the day. Percy found that there was a good quantity of breakfast still on the table, and dove in to this to start the day. As he glanced over at Evelyn he could see she was distracted, although by what was unclear to him at the moment. The kindly Gnome halted his repast after a few moments, and cast a quizzical glance her way.

"I beg your pardon; but good morning! And how are you faring on it?" he said to her, and she turned to him with a smile.

"Good morning, little scholar. I am well enough; the day's prospects have already worn me out though, and I have not even begun them." she returned as she finished with her hair; she then stood up to dress, and the Gnome returned to his meal.

"Understandable. We did task ourselves, after all." he agreed. "Nothing we won't be able to handle, I'm sure." he continued, and she smiled faintly as he went on. "After all, Werecats are renowned for their ingenuity; Ragya will have no trouble making puzzled fools of the Thieves' Guild. And I shall have no trouble here--once this breakfast is eaten!--a Gnome is a Gnome, as the saying goes; but there is aught else that seems to distract you, I dare say." Percy added; this unexpected halt in his talking left Evelyn at a blank as she began fastening the laces of her boots. And yet, he was right; she was distracted by something else.

"It's probably nothing." she remarked after a time. "After all, they're just friends. And we promised each other. All three of us." she went on, and Percy raised an eyebrow as he reached for a mug. *Oh-ho, is that it now?* He thought to himself as he took a sip.

"Nonsense, of course. Kia Re is true to her word; she'll not try to come between you and Caspar. Even if she can't help casting a glance his way every now and--"

"But that's just it!" Evelyn said to him. "She can't help it. I know what she's told me, but sometimes I wonder just how far she--"

"Have you ever heard the tale of Kira the Song-Maiden?" Percy interrupted her, and she blinked, turning to him.

"Who's that?" she wondered.

"She was a Valkyrie who lived during the Age of Legends, early on, that is. She fell in love with a mortal man, a man who saved her life. But the man was already married, and though he did love her, in his own way, he could not and would not betray his love for his wife. Kira could not but love him, however, and she fought by his side at every chance. He remained faithful to his wife, and she honored him for it, her love for him giving her strength. But eventually, when the battles became less and other heroes began wandering on to the scene of time, she could stand it no longer, as is recalled by the Valkyrie's 'Lay of Kira and Genoron', the tale of these two heroes, made at the dawn of the Age of Legends:

> *A thousand lives my soul may have lived,*
> *but may they live no longer!*
> *My heart was his, and always his,*
> *and love made it beat the stronger;*
> *but here today, my heart is broken,*
> *and shattered forevermore--nay,*
> *speak not to me of Valheilen's walls,*
> *and the proudly carven door!*
> *Here, at last, on the mountain heights*
> *in the cold, pale gleam of morn,*
> *the heart between my breasts shall stop,*
> *for a love lost and forlorn!*

"Then she went up to the highest peaks of the mountains, taking only her spear and sword, and when she had laid the spear beside her, she fell upon the sword, desiring her life to end rather than continue on with dishonorable thoughts of coming between the man and his wife. And thus perished one of the great Valkyrie warriors of the age; her people built a tomb around her, still there to this day, and in time the man himself came to lay his own sword at her tomb. His wife also came, and laid twelve pale roses on her tomb for the twelve great battles Kira had fought alongside him, and when the two of them had passed away they were laid to rest by the Valkyries in Valheilen itself." Percy recited, and Evelyn looked at him in true amazement--and horror.

"You... you don't think Kia Re would... *kill* herself... do you?" Evelyn said as she took in the story.

"Oh, no, no no..." Percy returned chidingly as he shook his head. "But a Valkyrie will keep their word at any cost; honor means more to them than life. Something the Elves might know a touch about." he added, and Evelyn nodded.

"Duty, rather than honor, whether the duty is honorable or not. But perhaps it is the same in principle." she agreed.

"There we are. Now! I've held you up long enough, and I need to get to work myself--hie away, dear friend, and we'll see you back here tonight!" Percy said, and Evelyn smiled, then headed out the door with her things to head for the Wizard's Tower.

***

Choosing simple, nondescript clothes for the day's work, Caspar and Kia Re had gone to the harbor after a good breakfast with Evelyn; they had left a good bit for Percy, who would be most likely working in the room throughout the day, and after Caspar had kissed Evelyn farewell they had set out. In the Harbor and Shipwright's District, the King's Bay broke the geometric walls of the city, and if one could see it from the air it might resemble a biscuit that has been half-eaten. The water lapped up happily along the shore, and gulls and other water-fowl lingered at its banks, scavenging for food; what cared the birds for the trouble of men in this city? Here there were ducks; there a pelican; to another side were geese, and far in the distance was a heron squabbling with some of the gulls over a meal. Ships stood in the bay, some of them encrusted with barnacles and such; still proud they sat there, even in a bedraggled state, and even Kia Re had to admire the weathered vessels. The Harbormaster soon caught sight of them, and headed over to them to see what they were about. "King's orders: no ship to leave the bay until crises are dealt with." he said as he neared them.

"So we've heard. And we've no intention of trying to coerce you into disobeying." the young man returned.

"Well, what be you about then? Hm?" the Harbormaster wondered.

"It's like this, sir; we're travellers, but there's nowhere to travel, now, so we thought, begging your pardon, if we might seek employ here at the harbor, if there's aught we can do to help out? There may be no sailing now, but when there is, these ships look as if they might need some maintenance done?" Caspar said to him, and the Harbormaster seemed very intrigued by the offer.

"Looking for work, is it? Travellers, eh? Seeking to mind the boats and mayhaps get a touch of insight into their workings in case your travels take you to sea, eh? I like that. I like it a lot. Shows initiative; foresight; all that. Tell you what," he went on, "we'll start with this here sloop, eh? She's got the worst of it, and I don't deny I could use some willing hands to get them all back into ship-shape. Come on then, lubbers! Off we go! And mind the planks on the dock, some of *those* need reworking too, if I can get those lazy carpenters down here!" he said, and he took the two of them over to the sloop in question, where they began work for the day.

***

The dungeons of Auschternople were a formidable looking sight; two wings connected to a main hall, and above the hall was a second floor, probably for the guards. And this was just the visible part of it. Ji Mao told Ragya that there were two more floors beneath this, two massive floors nearly filled with prisoners. The King's soldiers and enforcers were not totally useless; they *had* caught as many as could be caught, but for some reason that seemed to engender more and more miscreants rising up. It was said that the king was planning on building a second dungeon, but who really knew with all the things that the palace was occupied with these days. If Ragya had a plan in mind, he did not tell the young girl, who was fairly nervous as they made their way closer to Auschternople's dungeons; she quickly swallowed the tension, however, for the Werecat, bold as brass, went up to the door of the dungeons and knocked. The surprised guards let them in, and they were ushered to the top floor, which, as Ragya suspected, was a quarters for them.

"Now what do you want?" the chief guard inquired.

"Good master, I seek to inquire about one Aron of the Shipwright's District." Ragya told him, and the chief guard grunted, flipping back through a book on his desk.

"Let me see, let me see... ah, here he is... Aron; brought in five days' past for stealing a good quantity of bread from a stall, as well as being found to have had two stolen casks of ale in his house; raised quite a row when we caught him. Four of my men are still at the infirmary." the man said to him. "What do you want with him?" he asked in a bored tone.

"If I tender the value of the goods to their owners and pay damages, may I have him released to my care?" the Werecat asked. "It would be counted a great favor to those of the Were Forests."

"What! Release him?" a man scoffed.

"Now hang on there, sergeant." the chief returned. "It's a fair offer, and I don't need to remind you that all these prisoners in here are more a burden to us than a boon for the city." he said, and the other man spat.

"Say what you like, chief; loose Aron and we'll lose a key player of the Thieves' Guild. Mark my words!"

"As you were, sergeant!" the chief told him. "Out with it then, whiskers. Full value of goods: thirty silver and sixteen coppers. Damages: three gold pieces. You got that? Bring it, and I'll tender the money where it needs to go and you can have your petty thief." he said to Ragya, who pulled out a pouch and counted out five gold pieces.

"Consider it interest on my part, and a token of goodwill for the king's men." he said as the man's eyes lit up at the number of coins.

"I'll do that, and no mistake! Right then, downwards we go. He's on the lowest floor, all in a nice cell by himself." the man returned, and when the money was put in a safe he led them down with two others; the floor just below was not so big, but the next and lowest floor was massive indeed. There were prisoners and prisoners, men and women and children all, just as on the previous floors. Guards patrolled about, but did little to stop anything that went on in the cells; there was a fight going on in at least three, and women being used or abused in several others. Ji Mao felt her face flush and a sense of anger come over her at the passiveness of the guards; Ragya gave no hint of what he felt. At the far left corner of the room they found Aron, all by himself as was told. The guards stood aside as their chief unlocked the door, and Ragya went in to the cell to greet the prisoner.

"Who the blazes are you?" the man wondered. Ragya's eyes glowed at him, and the man suddenly recognized Ji Mao (or Jenna, as he called her) standing behind him. The Werecat was a friend. Was he going free? "Ah, never mind that; finally come for your old friend, eh there, whiskers?" the man said with a grin.

"Indeed. I have paid for your abuses; now you must tender service to me, old friend." Ragya returned at once.

"Fine, fine. Help us up then." Aron returned, and when he had got up they headed out of the cell and thence out of the dungeons. Ji Mao blinked back tears as she saw a girl her own age being forced into pleasing her cellmate, and she did not even notice when they were back out on the streets of Auschternople; at least, not until the voice of Aron spoke again. "All right, all right, you've had a go of it and got me out; thank you very much, but who are you?" the man said.

"I am Ragya. This is my passage to joining your reputable organization." the Werecat told him with a small bow.

"Oh, that's the game, is it? Tomas has gotten desperate, hiring strangers to get his mates out of a mess." Aron shrugged.

"Whether or no, you are free, and I am the one whose wits have saved you from a decidedly indefinite fate in a prison." Ragya said just as calmly as ever, and the man shivered.

"Cold, isn't he, Jenna?" he said to the young girl. "But here now: maybe you'll believe us all about them prisons now, eh? Told you the guards don't care about women being used in there. They enjoy the sight just as much as the other prisoners. I've heard they raped them theirselves, when there weren't no male prisoners about." he added, and Ji Mao flushed again.

"Come now, we have no time for delays." Ragya said, and with that Aron shut his mouth. He led the way back to his own home, and Ragya placed a paw on Ji Mao, looking at her with a compassionate expression. Ji Mao smiled softly. He did care. He was just wise enough---and strong enough--not to show it when he knew he didn't have to.

When they returned to Aron's house, the same house that Ji Mao had taken the two of them to earlier, he opened the door and went in at once. No one started; only Aron would do such a thing. Tomas and the others welcomed their comrade back heartily, and after a lunch they began to talk of more serious matters. "See now! Jynax had his glory day, but he's on for more as soon as can be. This fresh blood ought to be the tipping point of it." Tomas remarked.

"What? Us stealing the crown wasn't good enough for him? Scattering the horses, kidnapping some of the people? He wants more already? Can't the bastard wait?" Aron fumed. "I've already paid time trying to get supplies for his fool schemes, least he can do is wait!"

"Don't talk like that! You don't know who might be listening!" another said.

"Damn his eyes, and damn him! Ever since those raiders took root it's been one thing and another!" Aron thundered. "Where's old Brian, I'd like to know? Those were the days! I liked those days: no strange, over the top headstrong plans for kingship; just simple thieving and a bit of mischief! That's what we signed on for in the old days, not this foolery!" the man went on, and Ragya listened to his tirade with interest.

The Thieves' Guild did not see eye-to-eye with their new allies; some of them, like Aron, wanted to go back to the way things were; others were trying to balance the act, and others had gone full-steam with the raiders' plans for Auschternople and, possibly, Augusta.

"And what are you going to do about it?" Tomas said to him with a raised eyebrow. Aron flushed angrily, and sat back down grumbling.

"Now, our spies tell us there's a caravan on the way; we all know what that means, don't we lads?" he continued, and they chuckled. "Means there's plunder on the horizon. They'll be on the road from Murana Day; get the stuff ready by evening, that's when they'll be along-- double quick!" he ordered, and they all took off at once. "And you, Ragya, go and spy out the location double quick; southwest gate, get going!" he added, and Ragya nodded. Ji Mao went with him, and she gave him a look as they departed.

"What are we going to do?" she asked him.

"I will do as I am told. However, that does not mean you can't slip off and find Evelyn or Kia Re and Caspar; if their plans are not to be until the evening, that should give plenty of time for our friends to do something--or, perhaps, even to tell the king's guards about it." Ragya said softly, and she nodded.

"I will go and find Caspar and Evelyn; they are nearer to us." she replied.

"As you say, dear sister. Now hurry! I must away." he returned, and they split up. The Werecat was soon out scouting the countryside about Auschternople, and Ji Mao was slipping through the streets towards the harbor. She found Caspar and Kia Re taking a break from their new vocation; the Harbormaster was asleep. She came up to them softly, and Kia Re nudged her friend as she came up.

"Ji Mao? What is it?" Caspar asked. She looked around; there was no one in sight.

"The Thieves' Guild is going to seize a caravan this evening. Ragya told me to find someone to help stop them, or to warn the guards." she said softly, and Kia Re nodded.

"Where?" she asked.

"They are coming from the southwest road." Ji Mao told her.

"I'll go and help." Kia Re said to Caspar, "You stay here, bard, and keep tending to the ships. And you, dear one, hie back to Percy and see if he needs help. I'll come with you; I need my weapons." she said, and the two girls rushed back to Queen's Inn as quickly as they dared. As Kia Re dressed for battle, Ji Mao explained the situation to the Gnome, who had inquired about their being back; he heartily agreed, and before Kia Re left he gave her two of the explosive devices to aid her.

"Careful! Just you remember how I used them before!" he said, and she nodded to him.

"Elvar is in the stables?" Kia Re asked.

"Of course. I just brought both horses a lunch." Percy remarked.

"Well, he'll earn it tonight." Kia Re returned, and headed down; within moments she was riding for the gate herself, and Ji Mao decided to go back to the docks and help Caspar.

She found him finishing up work on the sloop, and soon joined him, the Harbormaster not picky about who helped him in maintaining the ships--so long as they were willing. Back in normal clothes, the work felt relaxing to the young girl, and she soon forgot about most of the trouble of the day as Caspar began singing to ease the burden of work.

***

Ragya sat perched in a tree alongside the road; there came Kia Re, fully dressed for a battle as she rode down the road upon their horse. He did not escape her sight, and she reined in as she caught sight of him in the branches. Ragya pointed down the road; the caravan was a ways off yet. She nodded, and he jumped down from the tree.

"Ride on; I have done what I came to do, and I must go and report. As far as I know you were just out for a ride." he said as he hastened back to the city, and Kia Re smiled to herself. She stretched, and spurred Elvar back to a gallop to reach the merchants in time. In the meantime, Ragya deftly vanished from sight once inside the gates again, and went straight to the nearest guard-captain. This man agreed to keep a watch out for the merchants, and to send a patrol near evening, and with that the Werecat slipped off to the guild.

***

Later that evening, Evelyn arrived back at the inn to find Caspar half-asleep on the bed. Ji Mao was already unconscious, and Percy was still working away on his devices. Evelyn smiled, slipped off her boots, and kissed Caspar as she got in the bed with him. He rolled over to kiss her, and relaxed in her arms as they lay there.

"Where's everyone else?" she wondered.

"Out and about, I suppose. Percy said something about a caravan, and Kia Re went off to see about it."

"And Ragya?"

"Probably mingling with the guild." Caspar shrugged.

"Hmm." Evelyn sighed. Caspar's eyes began to close again, and she kissed him once more. "The harbor took your offer, I see." she smiled.

"Yes... never imagined... oh, well... tomorrow it begins again..." he said with a yawn, and with that he snuggled her closer, falling asleep as she gently caressed him. Evelyn was then content. He was definitely hers.

When he was decidedly asleep she went over to Percy and asked him where the raiders were coming from; the Gnome told her what he knew, and she hurriedly put her boots back on to go and see if she could also help, getting the other horse from the stable as she left. Just as the guards were setting out she got to the gate, and they accepted her offer of aid as they set out.

***

Ragya, in the meantime, was being shown about the guild. Under a rug in Aron's home, there was a subtle door; this door hid a ladder, which led down into the first level of the guild. There were four rooms in this first section, and a hallway to the next big room, which held two smaller rooms and a staircase; down the staircase was a row of shelves stocked full of parchments and scrolls--the thieves kept records and such, after all--and behind the door on the right as they came down was yet another long hall. Behind the door at the far end was a sleeping quarters, and on the left was a door that saw a short hall behind it, and behind the next door was the armory. Rows of crossbows, quivers of bolts, swords, maces, axes, leather armor, and several rows of fine daggers lay about the room. Another long hallway saw a room with a stairwell at the end of it, and down this was another sleeping quarters, with some parts of the room set aside for storage, and at the far end of this room was a large door with a sealed lock. It was the Thieves' Vault. In here were kept their greatest prizes, Aron told him.

"Not the crown, though. That Jynax has it to himself up in the caverns, damn him." the man said with a shake of his head.

"And how did that get stolen?" Ragya wondered with genuine interest.

"One of those girls in the prison now, she was a maid in the king's household. She was 'persuaded' to lift it one night, and she did so right enough, but not before she got caught handing it off to one of us. She's been there ever since; pleading the belly for her sentence now, as it were. Most women there end up doing so whether they want to or not." he shrugged.

"And what do you consider most valuable in here?" Ragya wondered with an air of boredom, suggesting he had seen finer treasures.

"Doesn't know what we have, do we? Heh. Let's just say the king would have a fine day of it if this lot somehow ended up back in his hands. But there's loads of us between him and the vault, and the vault is no child's play." Aron told him, knocking on the solid door to emphasize his point. There was no echo. It was solid, and likely packed full.

"Indeed." Ragya returned, and with that they returned to the main hall on the first floor of the guild proper.

"I suspect we'll see more added to it tonight; after the raid and all. If those damned cave hooligans let us have our proper share, that is." Aron snorted, and Ragya said nothing. By now, Kia Re had undoubtedly reached them, and they would be on their guard.

***

It was now late in the evening; Kia Re had indeed reached the caravan, which had five merchant waggons and a host of eight guards about it already, but they welcomed her help and her warning. Lanterns were lit brightly to keep an eye on the road and for the inevitable attackers. They were just reaching the line of trees bordering the roads when they heard rustling in the brush; the guard-captain blew his horn loudly, and to his surprise a horn answered from the opposite direction.

"Dammit, the King's guards! Have at 'em, boys!" a voice called, and all at once a band of raiders appeared. Kia Re, once again feeling something well up inside of her, let loose a strong yell, and waves of mystic light surrounded her and her allies. Their attackers stumbled back, and the guards seized the initiative as they fought their foes with a will; in moments, thirty knights of the King's guard had galloped up to join them, and with them was Evelyn.

Her mage-training had not been without use; she drew the Sword of Magus, and whirled it about to create an icy chill about the raiders, some of whom fell over in shock and were then set upon by a guard or knight. She then cast a bolt of lightning at a group of them, and Kia Re threw her spear at a second group with such force that it passed through five in a row and then split a tree in half. Seven of their foes then surrendered, while another five ran off into the hills. Ten knights went to pursue them while the others rounded up the wounded and the dead, and the short battle was over. When they had gotten to the gates, Evelyn and Kia Re were heartily thanked, and the captain of the knights then took them aside.

"By the by, if you've the mind for it our stable-master could use a hand. He's up in the Great Enclosure east of the city. Don't bother going now, he'll be asleep--just keep it in mind is all I'm asking. You've done a great service for us tonight, and we'll all sleep better for it. Well," he said in amendment as he glanced over at the prisoners, "most of us will."

"We will keep it in mind." Evelyn told him. "Good night to you, sir." she then said, and with that they parted ways; Evelyn and Kia Re took the horses back to the stable, and when they had seen to their well-deserved suppers they headed in themselves. "And you, you seem to have gotten back some measure of your own power." Evelyn said to Kia Re with a faint smile.

"Simple skills." Kia Re said with her own smile. "But yes, it is coming back; a feeling rises up in my soul, and I feel it again, and I have no choice but to let it loose." she added. "And you? That was fairly more impressive than what you told me of the Ogre."

"It was invigorating." Evelyn admitted. "I feel... as if it was meant to be." she remarked as they headed up the stairs, and Kia Re nodded.

"Yes. I feel the same. We shall do great things together, the six of us, dear sister." she said to Evelyn, who nodded back.

"I know we will." the Elf-maid agreed. They kissed each other goodnight when they had gotten to their room, and joined the others in slumber soon after.

***

In the morning, Caspar and Kia Re went back to work at the harbor while Ji Mao and Evelyn went to see the stable-master. Just as she had been told, they found him east of the city in the Great Enclosure, tending to a group of young foals as he started his day.

"Here now--hie! Relax, my friend; they'll not harm ye." he said to one of the foals, who had started as they came up. "Pay no heed, missies; he's had a rough go since the others were stolen."

"Stolen?" Evelyn wondered.

"Horse-thieves came and rustled off six of my good friends nine days ago now." he said to them. "I'll not be denying I'd be right glad to see them all back. I've petitioned the king, but gods only know he's busy with this, that, and the other."

"This city does seem to be awfully wild for the center of civilization." Evelyn lightly quipped, and he chuckled.

"You've hit on it right enough, miss. I don't suppose you'd know a thing about finding horses?"

"If you think you can tell me where they've been taken, I might try and find them for you." she returned.

"Well, that's something, anyway..." he remarked. "I hear they do a lot of raiding in the north marches; *tomb*-raiding, mind you, and that's what they've the horses for. Pack-horses. Pah! My beasties, treated as common pack-horses; these are king's beasts, meant for his knights!" the man ranted indignantly.

"Hmm..." Evelyn frowned, looking northwards.

"Not that the Valley of Kings is far off; but they keep their proper camps in the march beyond the stream. You go on, you'll see what I mean." he said, and returned to work. With that, the two friends headed back out, and Ji Mao took Evelyn aside.

"He is right; I remember now hearing something of this horse-thieving. They take all they can get from the tombs since there is no one to guard them anymore. Better to watch the living than the dead, they think." she told her friend.

"Can you think of anything we might use to our advantage?" Evelyn wondered.

"On the northwest side of the valley is an unbroken tomb; the Tomb of Rogar. He is a legendary king from Augusta's early days, they say, one of the first kings. They plan to strike at this one next." Ji Mao told her. Evelyn thought quickly. This could be a double opportunity.

"We could beat them to the prize and take the horses back, if we did it right." she said softly as they walked along.

"You could take the horses. I could take the relic. Who better to outwit a thief than their own kind? I am trained for such things." Ji Mao suggested.

"That has merit. But I don't like splitting up." Evelyn told her worriedly.

"They do not know I am against them, that is my advantage." the other girl returned, and to that Evelyn had no reply. "Besides, it would break your friend's story if you showed up to aid me in getting the relic." she added, and the Elf nodded. She should have thought of that.

"Very well. But please be careful!" she said, and Ji Mao nodded, smiling. With that, they hastened off to the valley, and once there the Weishuune girl headed down into the valley while her friend stayed behind out of sight to wait for the right moment.

Ragya was also with the group of thieves planning to break in to the tomb; he had made sure to be gone with this group before the dawn so that he could not at once be taken in to account for the failure of last night's raid, though some back at the guild were murmuring about this even now. Was it a coincidence? No one could say for certain; and in any case they knew better than to trifle with a Werecat. And so Ragya had been unhindered in his joining the tomb-raid; he caught the scent of Ji Mao, and turned to find her coming up to him. She sat down on a box beside him, and relayed her plan. The Werecat nodded softly, and they returned their attention to the old tomb. "Now..." their leader began, "how to get in and find this thing..."

***

Percy, having finished up with anything that needed doing on his own count, decided to head down to the harbor to see if Kia Re and Caspar needed help in their endeavors. He found the two of them working on a caravel, and eagerly joined in. The three of them spent most of the day working on this, and after a time they explored more of the ship, eventually finding a curious craft below decks that Percy recognized at once.

"Why, bless my beard! It's a Gnomish submersible!" he exclaimed with delight.

"That it is, little master, and ye'd know more of it than I, I'll warrant." the Harbormaster remarked as he came down.

"Of course, of course. This must be the craft that was shipped off to here some thirty or so summers ago." Percy remarked as he studied it closely.

"Aye, indeed. Thirty-two, from the records."

"Indeed! And it's kept aboard here?"

"Not much else to do with it; couldn't have it rotting in the bay, so I keep it in here. I don't mind saying it'd make a mighty fine escape boat; begging your pardon, Master Gnome, but there it is. Fits nicely and all, and I've this caravel specially built to accommodate it; she can set it loose and haul it back in again, that's the thing of it." the man said, and they then noticed that the hold was indeed rigged and customized to do just as he said it would do.

"All tested, I presume?" Percy wondered. The man started laughing--almost chortling--at the question; not out of meanness, though, as they soon found out.

"Ain't nothing to do *but* test it since the order came to keep all ships here. She works fine enough, I daresay."

"Indeed. How very fascinating..." the Gnome went on, and Kia Re went with Caspar to go and clean some of the quarters while the Harbormaster and the Gnome went on with their own conversation. She sighed, and Caspar looked up from his scrubbing a moment to see a look of boredom upon her face.

"Done with it already?" he said with a gentle laugh.

"Working in a harbor is not the glory I hoped for."

"Battle will come, perhaps. For now, the small tasks are ours, inglorious though they seem." he returned. Again she looked at him longingly; how did such words of wisdom come to him so easily? She quickly averted her gaze, and they went on with their work until the evening, when the Harbormaster sent them off home for supper. Percy still chattered on about the Gnomish craft, and while Caspar listened to him with interest, Kia Re went off for a bath to wash off from the day's work and, hopefully, to forget about wanting Caspar for a time. At least they had done some good so far; Caspar was right. The menial tasks were inglorious, but necessary. There, she was thinking about him again. *Gods!* She swore, angrily drying off as she got out. Kia Re headed up to the room; Percy and Caspar were both asleep. With tears in her eyes, she went over to kiss the sleeping Caspar, and then went to bed herself.

Chapter Three: Tomb Raiders and the King

At the time that the others were heading to rest in the inn, Ragya and Ji Mao were silently making their way to the door of the tomb. Quick messages had passed between them and Evelyn, who was preparing as agreed to seize the six horses and ride with them back to Auschternople; this would allow the Werecat and the rogue to open the door of the tomb and gain a head-start on the others. Ragya had already figured out the combination of symbols to press; all he needed was a good distraction so that they could slip in without their "friends". Evelyn was now within sight of her goal; the horses were all tethered together, and one was tied to a worn stump of a tree. It would be a simple matter to loose the knot and ride off with them; nonetheless speed was needed. It would not do to be caught; or perhaps it might... no, no; brush aside that thought.

There were forty of the thieves here tonight. She was not strong enough. Silence was her friend at the moment. Well, until she had the horses running, anyway. Within moments Evelyn had the knot undone, and she quickly jumped up on the horse's back; she nudged him and dug in her heels, and with a whinny he rode off. The other five followed--having no choice, tethered as they were; the whinny managed to grab the attention of the thieves, and most of them chased after the fleeing Elf and the horses. At the entrance of the tomb, Ragya smiled; he made quick work of the door, and headed in with Ji Mao. The door shut behind them, and with that they were inside the Tomb of Rogar.

***

Evelyn, in the meantime, was having a fine time riding back with the horses; they all seemed eager to head back to their pastures, as if Evelyn's gentle nudge of the one she now rode had been a cue for them. At least twenty of the raiders were chasing her, but these all halted once she was in sight of Auschternople and the guards on watch. With grumblings and cursing they made sure to keep out of sight, and worked their way back through the darkness to the tomb to bring word. Evelyn thus brought the horses safely back to their pastures, and was well-thanked by the stable-master. She then retired to Queen's Inn, thoroughly exhausted from the experience. Caspar was awake again, waiting for her to return, and she went with him to the baths after they kissed.

"And where's Ragya and Ji Mao?" Caspar said between kisses as they lounged together in the bath.

"They've probably gotten into the tomb by now." Evelyn returned. They stayed in the bath together until the water grew cold, and then they went to dry off and head for their room.

On the other side of Auschternople, in the Valley of Kings, the frustrated raiders had discovered that Ji Mao and Ragya were no longer in their company, and that the door had been opened and closed--or so they presumed from the Werecat's paw-prints upon the ground disappearing into the wall of cliff. Ji Mao's soft prints were just beside his, and they vowed revenge if they were cheated out of this prize.

***

The Werecat and his Weishuune companion, having got inside, were suddenly faced with a new challenge. While Evelyn rode the horses back to Auschternople, Ragya, with his night-sight, carefully studied the room about him. There were many statues around the large room. He counted slowly and carefully; there was a total of eighteen. Ji Mao looked up; there was a catwalk above them, but it could not be reached without a rope. She pointed up to this, and Ragya blinked. The catwalk reached to the other side of the hall, where two diverging staircases spiraled down to either side of the next section of tomb--or so he presumed from the door at their terminus. He also now discerned that there were rows of ancient caltrops and spike-traps about the floor, carefully placed so that they formed neat walkways towards the statues.

"These statues must be a key of some sort or another." he mused softly.

"I am looking at them; and I seem to see that there are twins." she said, holding her torch steady. Ragya looked again; there were indeed twins. Nine pairs of statues. Somehow, they were the key.

"I wonder..." he mused, motioning for her to stay while he went to the nearest one. Its face was towards the far side; its twin across the way was facing the right-wall. Ragya gently pushed the statue; it did not move. He tried to turn it, and it remained fast in place. He went to the other; this one moved. Ragya studied the other statue again, and maneuvered its twin into a like position. The eyes of the statues gleamed with a green light.

"This, then," he began again, "is the puzzle: one of each of these twins moves, and we must align it with its sibling as I have done here with this one." he said, and Ji Mao nodded. They puzzled out the

188

remainder, and the door at the far end opened when all of them were aligned. Behind the door was a number of traps, or so it seemed from the pressure plates on the floor. Ragya let out a growl of frustration, a rare thing for him to do.

"This does not look good." Ji Mao remarked.

"You are lighter than I; slip around them, if you can, and see if there is not some device that stops them on the other side." the Werecat said, and she slipped off her boots to softly pad through the hall, barely avoiding the plates at some intervals. When she was almost through she slipped, and fell on to the last plate. At once the devices started up, and Ragya sprang back as Ji Mao jumped back up with a shriek as a blade snatched at her shirt and narrowly missed wounding her as she slipped out of it; just as the Werecat had thought there was a lever, and she pulled this. The traps ceased, and Ragya cautiously stepped on the plate; nothing happened. Not willing to press his luck, however, he dashed across, where the young girl was flustering in embarrassment as she gathered the remains of her torn shirt. She put it on as best she could in its state, and they resumed walking.

"Do you think anything else like that is here?" she wondered.

"Possibly." he allowed. "But see now! We have a new riddle. These appear to indicate stairs," he said as he looked at the glyphs on the wall, "but they are hidden away by some ancient device."

"Maybe this lever here?" Ji Mao suggested, and the Werecat glanced at it. He went over, and cautiously pulled to see if it would move. It was stuck fast.

"I dare not force it." he said. "We may bring some ancient trap upon us. Let us now to the riddle at hand." Ragya then said, and they looked at the glyphs carefully, puzzling out their meaning. Ji Mao figured this one out after several long and frustrating moments, and a stairwell was revealed that led down to the next floor. As Ji Mao's torch had gone out when she slipped, Ragya lit up his staff to see what was in this new room; there was a gaping pit full of deadly spikes placed at intervals of a hand's breadth in any direction, and they were each the height of a man. There was no immediate clue as to how to get across. The Werecat blinked, and shook his head.

"They must have had some clues as to this place. We did not think to search the tents for them." Ji Mao said to him.

"We should have, yes; but I feared to arouse more suspicion than necessary, trusting in my own wisdom. Perhaps that was a mistake." he allowed.

"We shall yet see, friend." she returned. Ragya looked up; there was nothing. His gaze returned to the pit. There was a twinkle of something reflecting his light. Intrigued, he lowered the staff so that it would catch a glimmer of something near, and in this way he discovered that there was indeed a reflective source of some kind here; what was it? He went over, and looked carefully at it; it was a heavy piece of glass. He tapped his staff so that its crystal shone brighter, and at once he could see; the glass was a transparent bridge across the pit. "See? There we are!" Ji Mao said with a smile.

"Indeed." Ragya agreed, and they slowly headed across this to the next door. It was yet another puzzle.

"It has to do with the seasons of Auschternople: look, the harvest is here in the corner of the relief." she said.

"And up here is the planting of seeds." Ragya agreed. "I must think carefully; the Old Augustan calendar is just different enough from the current one."

"Ah! I did not think of that." Ji Mao said as she stepped back.

"Yes, see here: currently there are four seasons, but in Rogar's time there were three only that men counted, and the year was divided into thirteen moons. We of the Werecats still use a similar calendar, but now Augusta uses a different one, based off a Gnomish model." he said to her.

"The Weishuune of the Isles are said to use a three-season calendar as well." Ji Mao said.

"So I also have heard." Ragya nodded. "Now... let's see..." he frowned thoughtfully, and after several long moments of thought he made his guesses; the door opened, and a there was a descending staircase revealed to them. This led to another stair case, which led into a hall, that led to an ascending staircase, this one leading up to a narrow ledge. "And why not into the room?" Ragya wondered, stretching out his staff to look at what was below; on the floor below were many writhing and wriggling creatures, and Ji Mao almost gagged as she saw them cannibalizing each other. Eggs and more eggs lined the walls, and some were hatching, revealing more of the queer things as their progenitors either laid more or seeded each other to lay more. It was a most hideous cycle of life, and Ragya dimmed the light so that only the nearer things could be seen, such as the ledge.

"Let us not fall in." Ji Mao said with a shudder.

"Indeed!" Ragya agreed, his tone of disgust overshadowing a look of fear in his eyes. The ledge was worn, and crafted to be unstable--so they found as Ji Mao almost slipped. Ragya quickly grabbed her, and swung her around to the other side of himself as they went on. The noise of the chittering creatures was now louder, and the young girl felt her insides churning at both the sound and the rising stench emanating from below. One of the things jumped, and was almost at their height when it fell back down, and was devoured by its own kind.

"This is like a nightmare of hell!" the young girl said fearfully, but Ragya said nothing in reply. They were almost across when she slipped again, and Ragya quickly leaped to catch her, using his staff to hold himself in place as he held her hand tightly. She quickly reached her other hand to grab his, and he was about to pull her up when one of the creatures grabbed her by her leggings. Ji Mao screamed, and at the opposing force Ragya pulled her up hard. Up came Ji Mao, and down went her leggings and her boots with the creature. Ragya then flung the two of them into the hall, where they lay resting for several moments.

Thoroughly disgusted with the tomb, Ji Mao recomposed herself, and went onwards with Ragya following. She took off the ripped shirt, and Ragya handed her a cloak, which she belted around herself. The belt with its daggers and its pouches had been around her shirt, and had not been lost to the creatures, thankfully. Now they came to the tomb itself, and in its wide hall lay many treasures of old. There in the far-right corner of it was a door, which hopefully led upwards and outward to some forgotten exit. It was well into the night, if they could have known; outside the tomb, the thieves and raiders had almost figured out the first door, and were preparing to enter themselves. As if he sensed this, Ragya headed back to the pit, and with his magic collapsed the stairs on the far side to prevent anyone from following. It also collapsed the ledge, and he hastened back in to the tomb as this fell into the pit of writhing creatures.

Ji Mao was already collecting things and placing them in a convenient chest, and he took out a few bags to put smaller trinkets in. After nearly an hour of deciding what to take and what to leave, and of packing that which they would take into the chest and the bags, they heard the sounds of screaming echoing from the other side of the tomb; some of the raiders seemed to have fallen into the pit by accident, or were they on the level above being pierced by menacing stakes? It did not matter. The rest of Rogar's treasures would be safe. Ragya took up the chest, and Ji Mao the bags, and they headed for the door. It was indeed a secret escape, a slowly rising set of stairs that led to an exit far beyond the valley of kings; by the time they reached the other end it was almost dawn, and when they came at last to the northwest gate the guards had just exchanged watches. They were let in with many a stare and confused look, and after they had taken their burdens to the Hall of Records they set out to a clothing merchant on the other side of town, and Ji Mao exchanged her borrowed cloak for a soft dress. They returned to the inn, and settled in for a long sleep.

***

When Ji Mao woke up, she found that she was alone with Percy in the room; the Gnome told her that the others had already gone off for the day. It was high noon, after all. Ji Mao nodded, feeling very hungry indeed.

"Well, there's plenty here." Percy told her, gesturing to the still-warm luncheon on the table. "It was sent up only some moments ago; Caspar and Kia Re are down at the harbor, as usual, and Ragya and Evelyn are being accorded an audience with the king at his palace. Something about a commendation. You should have gone, but you were worn out." the Gnome shrugged, and Ji Mao suddenly swallowed what she was eating and dashed off. "I say! What's the matter?" Percy wondered, but she was already gone, running through the streets of Auschternople in her dress. She ran straight to the palace; *a commendation?!* Surely not! Had a word of her and the companions' doings been reported to the king already? She was halted just as she got near the palace by a familiar face; it was Aron.

"So! Thought you were clever, bringing in spies, eh? Treacherous little wench! Should have known it was you and that overgrown cat what messed us all up! I hate Jynax as much as the next honest thief, but you've gone too far now!" he thundered; unfortunately for him, he was too loud.

"Halt!" a voice commanded. It was the king himself. He was surrounded by twelve of his guards, and Ragya and Evelyn were with him.

"This is the other of whom I spoke, great king. The young Weishuune girl we rescued from the streets and straits of crime." Ragya said in his soft voice, and the king nodded.

"Thou sayest it well, but didst not tell me she were so pretty a girl; seize yon churl, and bring the fair maiden to the palace and refresh her!" he commanded, and the guards seized Aron, and the grumbling thief loudly protested.

"Hoy! Lies! Deceit! You'll pay for this you over-growed cat, you! Damn your eyes! And damn Jynax! Curse him, curse him, and all the raiders! You backstabbers, you--" and on he went as the guards took him away. Ji Mao was led to the king's palace, where she was bathed and re-clothed in a fine dress indeed. Caspar, Kia Re, and Percy were extradited from their own tasks, and the king ordered a celebration for their deeds in his city.

"The Tomb of Rogar, mine ancestor, preserved from desecration and its most sacred relics brought to mine city; a caravan that hast made it through the fiends for the first time in many months, horses stolen brought back to the city; thou hast made a fair name for thyselves thus far! Shalt we not celebrate?" the king said as they protested, and they relented. It was, as he said, a much-needed excuse to celebrate. The Thieves' Guild had been thwarted of its recent antics, and in confidence

Ji Mao related the workings of what lay below Aron's tricky house in the Shipwright's District. A small army of a hundred soldiers or so were sent there, and the guild's secret hall was soon unearthed and a fierce battle fought underneath the streets of Auschternople; after several hours the king's soldiers emerged victorious, and Tomas their leader was brought up in chains. The door of the vault was blown open by devices from Percy, and inside lay many things which many folk of Auschternople had missed. These were returned to their owners, or left to be found by their owners, and the Thieves' Guild of Auschternople were all ratted out by those captured and then rounded up for the dungeons.

"If I'm going, they're all going!" Tomas swore.

"Fine by me." the chief-captain returned to him. By the end of a second day, the affair of routing the thieves was finished, and the companions still being honored in the palace. Caspar and Evelyn eventually slipped out to the royal gardens, and after a time the two of them became lost in the floral labyrinth, content in each other's company as they meandered through the maze. They talked of hopes and dreams for the future, wondering what the days would be like when the lands knew peace again; they tried to guess the names of flowers, and those of the singing birds in the boughs of trees scattered throughout the gardens; they sang songs, or danced in the corridors of the hedges as they wandered; and by and by they came to the center of the gardens, where the most beauteous sights of all had been meticulously place for an exquisite scene.

The hedges about formed an oval, and in the midst stood a great fountain, a fountain with seven maidens and seven pitchers which poured out into the tiers of basins below; this was surrounded by flowers and herbs and grasses of many kinds, and the birds and butterflies flew about it. Several fruit and nut trees were also flowering around the edges, and there were three stone benches near the fountain; a rose bush grew near one entrance, and near the one they had come in grew a solitary pine. They halted here on one of the benches, and continued talking in soft voices, as if they feared to disturb the peace of the garden. A kiss passed between them, followed by several more, and after a time they then fell asleep on the bench together.

***

"And where, oh where, are our two young lovers?" Percy asked Ragya pointedly as the festivities in the palace kept on. The Werecat looked out of a nearby window that faced the royal gardens, and Percy followed his gaze as Kia Re and Ji Mao came over, both resplendent in gowns of white and red, respectively.

"If one were to traverse the lengthy corridors of the King's Gardens you might find the two of them there; they headed out quite a while back, and I do not doubt that they are quite well." Ragya returned softly, as he always did.

"Well, we've plans to make regarding the future, that's all!" the Gnome replied in a quiet but irate tone. "I don't suppose you could find your way through that?"

"The patterns are simple, for those with the wit to see it; I believe I could come to the center--if that is where they are." the Werecat told him.

"Why disturb them at all?" Ji Mao asked with a soft smile.

"We're not out of this yet by a long shot; and now the king has firmly entrenched us on his side. That may be a help, or a hindrance." Percy told her. "We need to convene and make our plans more carefully."

"I'll go with you, Ragya." Kia Re said to the Werecat, and he nodded; the two of them then slipped out, leaving the Gnome with Ji Mao. She sat beside him as he clambered up into the bay window, pacing about furtively as the liveliness went on.

"Dear lady, wouldst that thou might honor me with thy dances, if it didst but please thee!" the king said to the young Weishuune girl.

"And how shall I refuse the king such an honorable request?" she said to him in reply, and excused herself to take his offer. Percy glanced at the king warily, but his thoughts were then disturbed by one of the royal scholars coming over to converse with him. The Gnome happily obliged the man, and soon they were deep in conversation about the finer points of philosophy.

In the meantime, Ragya led Kia Re on their search through the maze unerringly, as if he had spent his whole life in the gardens; they noticed in passing that there were several large stones placed throughout the maze, and they were carved in characters from an ancient Augustan dialect. "Riddles, indeed." Ragya remarked as he stopped briefly to examine one.

"Riddles?" Kia Re asked in surprise.

"A human fancy, it may be; if one is going to be lost in such a place as this, one may as well have something to occupy his mind other than the innumerable names of plants. I wonder if Evelyn and Caspar are not even now puzzling over one instead. We shall see, if they are not at the center." he said.

"Riddles and songs are for the hall, not idle fancies and follies." she said with an airy disdain.

"Indeed." Ragya assented as they continued on; after a much briefer time than their two friends they arrived at the center, and found the two of them asleep on the bench. Ragya, feeling disturbed by some inner sense, nudged Kia Re to go and wake them while he carefully selected seven stones. When the other two were awake, they found that Ragya had pulled out the Royal Ixthus, the Lover's Cross, the Rune of Chance, the Royal Beast, the Father of Chaos, the Mischief Maker, and the Common Earth. "Would that we had brought Ji Mao and Percy with us." Ragya said in a soft tone that had a tinge of worry or irritation in it.

"Should we go back and get them?" Evelyn wondered.

"No time. I must cast them now. See!" Ragya said, and he tossed the seven runes onto the ground. He knelt beside them for several long moments, carefully studying their patterns. Kia Re, who had started picking up on the basic sense of the runes, and who had heard of castings in her home of Jotun-De before, also looked at them with a scrutiny.

"The Lover's Cross and the Royal Beast seem as if they are in conflict." she remarked.

"Indeed. You see it well, sister." Ragya agreed. "And the Common Earth is pointing to the Royal Ixthus; the Mischief Maker is subdued-- see! He lies upside-down; but the Father of Chaos yet runs free. Above all, Chance rules; whatever lies before us we must be cautious. Percy is right, we need to get away from these festivities and make our future plans."

"Mischief Maker--the Thieves' Guild." Caspar understood. "And the Father of Chaos is whomever leads the raiders." he added.

"Indeed; that is how I read them." Ragya nodded.

"Then the Royal Ixthus and the Common Earth; the nobles and their serfs?" Kia Re wondered.

"Yes... the Common Earth points to the Royal Ixthus, but with what intent I cannot yet say. It might be violent, it might be less so, as Chance makes it."

"And the first two." Kia Re said softly, looking up at Caspar and Evelyn. Ragya looked up as well, looking at all three of them in turn.

"This Chance is a deadly chance; which is why I said we must be cautious. I am always cautious about taking sides, unless I see a clear benefit to aiding one or the other--or if I see a way of disrupting something that should not be." the Werecat told them. "Now quickly; let us go back to the palace and collect our other two friends." he said, and when he had gathered up his stones again they headed back to the palace.

***

Ji Mao was now back with Percy at the bay window, and thus they were when the other four came back to them. They hastily told the two of them what they had seen in the gardens, and the Gnome, though of a more practical mindset regarding mysticism, nonetheless agreed that it was indeed high time they got out of the festivities to go their own way. They were almost to the door when the king's voice came again.

"Leavest thou so soon, and thou wouldst not give me the honor of dancing with yon dark maiden of surpassing beauty?" he said, and Caspar felt a tinge of anger at the words.

"Begging your pardon, sire," he said as he turned back, "we find ourselves in need of rest, and would return to a quieter scene for doing so." he said, and the king raised an eyebrow.

"Give thou to me but an hour more, I pray thee, and thou shalt leave then as thou seest fit to do so." he said, and they looked at each other in agitation. They acquiesced in reluctance, and Evelyn did indeed dance with the king, while Caspar looked on in a dark mood. The hour went by slowly, and at its end, Caspar, Ragya, Percy, Ji Mao, and Kia Re were told to go back to the inn.

"Where's Evelyn?" Caspar asked as they began leaving.

"His lordship says the lady asked for a tour of the castle." the guard told him.

"Lies!" Caspar loudly retorted. "Where is she, damn you!" he asked again.

"Hold on there, lad!" Percy called as Ragya held him back. "Let's... just get ourselves sorted, and then we'll go back and clear it all up, eh?"

"Clear it up now and have done! What's going on, fool?" the young man demanded of the guard, who scowled.

"It's the king's wish, young sire; you lot are to be sent to the inn and the Elf-maid stays here. Those were his words to me." he said, and Caspar flushed angrily. "Now get on, and mind yourselves lest you find your new lodgings in the dungeons!" the man added, and the palace doors were shut. Caspar wriggled free, and began banging loudly on the door.

"You have no right to do this! We helped you! We risked our lives to help you! And this is how you repay us? What sort of king betrays his people in such a manner?" he called.

"An Augustan King." said a voice behind them. It was the mysterious man Caspar had met a few days ago. "I told you; the hope needed is not the hope wanted. And though this city will go on, its monarch may not. His crown is gone, as now you know, and who can say what those in the hills have done with it? Find it, and unravel the last threads of Augustan tyranny: or give it back to him, and let the city erupt in a wave of violence to make the Great Invasion peaceful in comparison. Shall they die in a violent death, or shall they make a new order from the fading ashes of what is left to them?" the man said, and then headed off.

"I don't know where to look!" Caspar called after him.

"I've already told you--follow your heart." the man called back.

"My heart is locked away in this damned palace with a petty tyrant!"

"You are stronger than you think, Caspar, son of Malachon!" the man said as he then vanished into the streets, and Caspar blinked.

"Malachon?" he wondered softly to himself. "Who--that's not the name of my father!" he said with a shake of his head. "His name was Caspian!" he remarked as they headed back to the inn with reluctance.

"Are you sure?" Ragya said softly, and Caspar looked over at him.

"That's what Farmer Wells always told me; Caspar, son of Caspian and Miri am I, and I have known of no other relatives but they." he returned; the Werecat said nothing, but nodded in assent to the answer.

***

"And where are my friends?" Evelyn returned darkly.

"On their way back to yon inn." the king told her.

"You are not making as fine a ruler as we thought. Perhaps we should have let those of the Thieves' Guild win this little war." she said to him airily. "I will not comply with your demand. My heart belongs to Caspar, and I will die before I betray him with a petty king!" she added in a more forceful tone; but the king's eyes darkened as they gazed at her with a deep-seated rage.

"Thou speakest above thyself!" the king warned her.

"My blood is more royal than yours will ever be; I am descended of the Ancient Elven nobility, and I could have been their queen, if I had chosen! Your pathetic Augustan dynasty is as nothing to the nearly unbroken Elven Royals: and a thousand times over tainted with innocents' blood!" Evelyn retorted at once, and the king stepped back. Power was revealed in her; she had indeed been studying at the Wizard's Tower! Perhaps it was wise to let her go; but Augustan pride held this thought away.

"I shalt leave thee here. Power thou hast--but the wizards serve at *my* command. Think thou on such matters before thou triest to escape!" he said as he left, and the door shut behind him. Evelyn, exhausted from her tirades, stripped off the fine gown and tore it to shreds as she shrieked in rage, and sobbed herself to sleep, thinking of Caspar all the while.

Chapter Four: An Unexpected Siege

Caspar spent his night out in the stables in the carriage; one by one, the companions all came down to join him, Kia Re snuggling next to him as he silently grieved. Ragya sat near with Ji Mao, and Percy sat with Dusty just next to them. None of them (except the hound) slept that night, and none of them said anything. When morning came, Kia Re and Caspar headed off to the harbor to aid the Harbormaster again, and the other four milled about the city. Percy went to occupy himself in the Hall of Records, and Ragya took Ji Mao with him to the Great Enclosure, curious to see the herd animals and perhaps barter for some herbs and such. Caspar and Kia Re did not stop working until the late evening, and when at last they reached the inn Caspar returned to the carriage; Kia Re, feeling her heart go out to him, followed him to it. He sat down where he had the night before, and she sat with him; she then put a hand on his cheek, and kissed him.

"Caspar, talk to me. I know I'm not Evelyn, but I love you, and I want to help you." she said softly, kissing him again; he let their lips linger together for a time, and then she wrapped him in her embrace.

"My heart wants to storm the castle grounds, seize her out of the king's grasp, and run off; let Auschternople be damned--if I had known that they had learned nothing, I would have ignored the runes to my peril!" he said, choking back a sob as she kissed his neck.

"We cannot run now. We must face it; we will prevail, Caspar, I know it! I don't know how, but we will!" Kia Re told him, holding him tightly as he fell in to her embrace.

"Lend me but a part of your strength and I can face it." he begged of her as they let go and he looked into her eyes.

"I had no true strength until I found you." she returned to him. "Any I now have is from you, Caspar." she told him. She kissed him again, and though he reveled in her touch he longed for Evelyn's lips upon his.

"Oh, Evelyn... thy lips are lonely... and I, here am I drowning my sorrows like a fool in the arms of a friend. Unhappy wretch that I am!" he said as their lips parted, and Kia Re gently smiled at him.

"It does seem ungracious. But I can think of nothing else to say; all

I know is what I feel." she told him.

"I know." Caspar nodded back. "When we have her back we shall all share our kisses, and let the world be envious of it!" he said as he laid back, and she lay down beside him, kissing his cheek. He stared up at the ceiling of the carriage until he fell asleep, and Kia Re fell asleep gazing at him as he slept peacefully. She dreamed of the three of them dancing in a secret glade of unmatched beauty, and the stars were wondrous in the night sky above them.

***

That morning brought them strange tidings indeed, tidings that the companions did not know what to do with. During the night, a war-host of Dwarves had come up to surround most of the city, and a host of Valkyries were with them. Ragya, Ji Mao, and Percy joined the throng of people that were heading to the walls to see what the king's answer would be to such a thing; Evelyn was with him, surrounded by many guards. She glanced over at them, and Ragya blinked at her softly. He had not foreseen this. Or had he? Had they mistaken the runes' meaning? *The Common Earth points towards the Royal Ixthus...* Dwarves, though not entirely common, were of the earth, so legends said. Perhaps there was a double meaning? Or was this the Rune of Chance coming to haunt them? What sort of chance was this? A strange one, to be sure. Only a few days had gone by since they came to Auschternople; had this mighty host been behind them all the way, or what tidings had brought them hither?

"I am Grand General Frigund of Vinduürhaf Mökr." the leader of the Dwarves called out suddenly. "At my left is my second-commander, Gromond Red-Axe, and at my right is the esteemed Battle Sage Briana of Valheilen. We are come to your walls with the authority of our respective leaders to tender terms as we will." the Dwarf said; Evelyn, recalling her old lessons, understood this as the polite way of saying, "You are now under siege"; but what reasons could they have?

"General, I am King Michael, the fourteenth of that name in Augustan dynasty, and am Lord Protectorate of the Augustan Realm, the Executor of Justice in this mine city. I ask thee for thy purpose in coming as if to war before the walls of Auschternople, Crown Jewel of Augusta?" the king returned. Another polite diatribe; "Why the hell are you here?" was its essential and most poignant meaning.

"Be it known to the King of Augusta--what little remains of it--that after great and long counsel together, the other peoples of this land Argorro have found thee wanting, even after thy imposed penance of twenty years long gone. We are here to ensure that thy people are dealt with fairly, and that they henceforth deal with others fairly! Raiders lie about thy realm, assailing whom they will; thieves plunder your city;

your armies outside the wall butcher and bully others, even your own people; and thee sit in thy castle fiddling as it all burns, they say. We come to the aid of Augusta's people, to redeem them from gross injustice!"

"And what is this beside thee?" Briana called up. "My eyes can tell the falcon from the eagle twelve leagues away through fog and mist; what is this Elf doing in your walls, O King?" she asked.

"This is mine guest but recently arrived." the king returned.

"Let her speak for herself!" Frigund said, and at once two Valkyries and ten Dwarves nocked arrows to their bows to reinforce the demand.

"As thou sayest." the king relented, knowing he would never hear the end of it now.

"My Lord Frigund, my Lady Briana," Evelyn addressed them, "I am Princess Evelyn of Alastria; I came to this city as he said, some days ago, in the company of strange companions. We gave our aid to this king in hindering the thieves and raiders of which you rightly spoke, and I have been repaid by being wickedly stolen away from my friends, one of whom is my betrothed in promise." she called down, and the Dwarf exchanged a glance with his two associates. They returned their glances to the wall in but a brief moment, their expressions dark.

"History repeats itself." Briana said snidely. "Will another defenseless Elven Maid be raped in Auschternople's walls? Hast thou a Valkyrie here also, and thy guards forcing themselves upon her in gross indignity?" she demanded.

"Be damned to you!" the king retorted at once. "I shalt not be so foolish as to repeat a history of woe! But I do not deny that I hath indeed kept this one, desiring peace between mine kingdom and hers!"

"A forceful marriage will carry the remnants of Alastria to your walls, O King!" the Dwarven General said to him in reply. "This much I know of Elves. Their own king, Thadolin, but recently told me of this one and her flight, seeing mine armies pass by his realm, and he asked that if I should come across her, to give her aid in her flight. I mean to do so, and I declare you in no uncertain terms to be under siege henceforth until you are surrendered by conditions we shall tender to you at a time of your choosing!" the general said; horns blew, and those that had come up to address the city departed to their camps.

The citizenry of Auschternople retired from the walls, murmuring against the king's words as they headed back into the city.

"Then henceforth I declare this city under martial law! There are to be no more foolish exemptions to the conscription! Search every house, every inn, every building, and see thou that thou hast a grand army to match this force!" the king said, addressing his guards; Evelyn paled. *Caspar!* But no--the others had already departed. She could see Ragya

200

racing through the streets with Percy and Ji Mao on his back. Her guards were gone. Without stopping to think, she raced away into the mess of people, and before the king could return his thoughts to her she was almost gone. A hefty guard managed to stop her, however, and she angrily struggled with him as several others came up. The poor Evelyn was then dragged back to the palace, kicking and screaming, and when she was again shut in her room she broke down again.

***

The three companions wasted no time, but hastily packed all their things away and ran to stow them in the carriage; when they were certain that all they had brought was in the carriage, they then quickly hitched up their horses, and drove through the streets towards the harbor, finding Caspar and Kia Re at work on a frigate. They hastily explained the situation to their friends, and the five of them took quick counsel as to what to do. They could do no more in the city. The king's order would see them all in martial service to the city unless they somehow fled.

"And we're in the perfect place to do so..." Caspar suddenly realized.

He looked around hastily; the caravel with the submersible was the furthest away from the main docks. Kia Re took his meaning at once, and she looked about for the Harbormaster.

"He's there with the troop of guards. He seems to be trying to get them to lay off of his workers--including us." she said as she espied him at the other end.

"He won't succeed. Get the carriage aboard that caravel there; I'll cut the lines." Caspar said, and Ragya turned the thing around, and then drove it quickly to the caravel in question.

They hastily secured the horses and carriage to the deck as Caspar cut the lines; they then hauled up the anchor, and it was not until they were pulling out that they were suddenly noticed. With a great clamour the guards and the dockworkers ran towards them shouting for them to stop--too late! They turned the ship to a south by southwest direction, aiming for a point just beyond the walls. Ragya, who knew the basic points of steering a ship, kept them on course as Caspar looked back in sudden anguish; Evelyn was still with the king. Kia Re put a hand on him, and Ji Mao looked over at him in pity as she calmed the horses down.

Percy climbed up to the crow's nest, seeking the best point of land to weigh anchor at. To the east he espied the lighthouse; to the south he saw the forests and hills where the raiders were said to be; to the north, of course, was the now very agitated city of Auschternople; and to the west he saw more of the city; a host of Dwarves and a few of the

Valkyries were coming to besiege the southwest gate.

"Ragya!" the Gnome called, whistling to get the Werecat's attention. "That point there, about three-quarters of a Gnomish mile beyond the gate! That little inlet!" he said, and Ragya gave a nod, heading their new vessel for the place in question. They weighed the anchor on the southern side of this inlet, halfway in-between the two major stretches of forest, and as they lowered the plank to shore five Dwarves and two Valkyries came up to them.

"Hold!" one of the Dwarves said. He was grey of beard and hair, but his eyes glinted with a hale and fierce light.

"A moment, friend Rogak," one of the Valkyries said; "recall the words of the captive Elven Princess: she said 'strange companions'. See how strange is this company!"

"I am inclined to agree, lieutenant," one of the other Dwarves said, "but I shall follow your lead. Do we make prisoners of them or let them go?"

"How about allies?" Caspar asked them. "The Elf you speak of, Evelyn, is my heart's queen, and she is yet in the city. I will not leave until the king surrenders her!" he added.

"This is her betrothed? A mortal man?" the other Valkyrie remarked. "Strange indeed; but that was not the half!"

"And what's this? A Gnome and a Werecat?" a third Dwarf said with a quizzical eye.

"So it seems." the one identified as Lieutenant Rogak nodded. "Out with it! Were you let go, or is this some bold escape?"

"Less bold than others, I may say." Percy told him. "Say rather it was a stroke of good luck for once; the pendulum swung in our favor today--at least with escaping martial law." the Gnome added.

"And why did you not head out to sea at once? Hm?"

"Did you not hear the lad?" Percy wondered at the Dwarf. "The Princess Evelyn is yet there! Do you think he would leave her?"

"Let us take them to the General and the Battle Sage." the first Valkyrie said.

"Yes, let us do that. You two, guard this boat and their belongings!" Rogak said to two of his Dwarves, who nodded.

"Stay with them, Mina. They may need you." the Valkyrie said to her sister, who also nodded. The five companions were escorted to the camp, and Dusty barked after them for a while before settling in again near the horses, who were let loose to graze. The hound kept careful eye on them, and every now and again looked towards the place where his master had gone, the faithful beast being commended by those guarding him.

***

"The betrothed of an Elven Princess? Who are you, mortal, that an Elf should give her love to thee?" Briana asked him.

"Not only an Elf but a Valkyrie as well." Kia Re added. "I am Kia Re, recently exiled from Jotun-De." she added, and the two leaders exchanged glances.

"These are indeed strange times." Frigund remarked. "But the question remains: how is it that you ended up with this company, boy?" the Dwarven General asked him again.

"I am naught but a humble minstrel in love, seeking my way through the world and doing what I can to right its wrongs, however small my impact may be." Caspar told him simply, and the Dwarf shook his head in wonder.

"And I go with him on his quest, seeking to reclaim the glory that is ours by right in helping him." Kia Re added.

"Percy Von Daumer, at your service! I, too, go with this my friend Caspar on his quest, lending my aid and knowledge to his travels!" the Gnome said with a bow.

"I am Ragya, a druid of the forests; I swore my fheas to Evelyn, and I will not break it. I will aid in recovering her, so that she may continue on with the one she has chosen." Ragya told them in his ever-soft voice.

"And I am Ji Mao. I was of the Thieves' Guild, but these found me, and I decided to cast my life in with theirs. All we wanted was to make a difference for the bettering of Augusta, and now we are cheated by the whim of a king." the young Weishuune girl added, her emotional distress overcoming her shyness. She had, Percy believed, gotten the worst upheaval of them all so far in the past few days. The Dwarf and Valkyrie looked over them with wise and scrutinizing eyes, taking in what they had heard. After a lengthy silence, Frigund shook his head, and Briana gave him a look of inquiry.

"I believe their tale. It is too strange to disbelieve! This is my judgment on the matter: that they be allowed to roam freely and aid as they will. But they are not to return to the city unless as part of our invasion force." the general said.

"I will concur with this judgment." Briana nodded. "Let them return to their ship, since we have no more tents to spare. And let a troop be there with them; we do not know where these raiders are, and I am not willing that they should have a ship!" she added.

"It is well spoken. Let them be guided back." Frigund nodded, and the five companions were taken back to the ship. The two commanders then returned to their battle plans, and their aides came back in to help them.

When all that had been ordered regarding the companions was done, Percy returned to making his devices, Ragya began sorting through his herbs, and Ji Mao went back and forth to aid either Percy or Ragya as needed. Caspar idly strummed his lute, and Kia Re went through her weapons and armor. Eventually the lute was set aside, and the young minstrel lay upon the cabin bed, gazing out the window that faced towards Auschternople. Kia Re softly looked in on him, and then went up on deck to stare out to sea herself. The afternoon was wearing on, and there had been no hint of battle yet. Yet. *Give it time, it will come...* Kia Re thought to herself.

By the late evening, there had been some minor ranged skirmishes, but little of great consequence. Caspar was on deck, plying the strings of his harp as Ji Mao, Ragya, and Percy were focused on a game of stones. Kia Re sat with Caspar, listening to him play as she rested her head on his shoulder. He did not sing, claiming that his heart to do so had been stolen away from him; she did not doubt it, but she would have given anything to hear his voice in song again. She gently kissed his cheek as he continued playing, all his being focused on the melody.

In the castle, Evelyn looked out the window of her room; it was on the south side, and from the reports she had heard she knew that her friends had taken a ship from the harbor and gone but a short way-- possibly to join the besieging army. A tear escaped her eyes; she could swear that she heard the strings of a harp in the far, far distance, and she knew that Caspar was as torn as she was. She fell to fantasizing about him as she lay in the bed, desiring to kiss him and to love him and have him close. It was now strange to have been gone from him so long; indeed it was a very disturbing sensation to her, and she wept as she curled up into a ball beneath the covers of the bed. *Caspar...*

***

The next morning, Percy was summoned to the leaders' pavilion to lend his aid in regards to refining plans and strategies of attack against Auschternople and its king. The Gnome, who had spent a great deal of time in the archives of the city and who had a penchant for being able to remember extraordinary details, obliged them by drawing what he could recall of the sewer systems and catacombs beneath the city. General Frigund then had his own engineers team up with the clever Gnome to formulate a way of getting at these subterranean passageways so that they might come up from under the city and surprise the king's armies. In the meantime, Battle Sage Briana made use of Ragya's skills to scout about the land to look for raiders; in this way, they managed to find seven more merchant caravans that had been intending to go to Auschternople, and these were brought in to the war-host's camp, where they would stay for the duration of the siege. Ragya was then able to confirm that, from the signs about the southern reaches of the city, the raiders were indeed in the hills. They made a note of this, and returned to camp content with their efforts for the day.

A band of Werecats came down from the north later that afternoon, and, upon hearing of the situation, acquiesced to joining the host gathered before the walls of Auschternople. Inside the city, the king was growing more dangerous and less subtle, and he almost cut the head off of one advisor who suggested surrender. Evelyn went about with an escort, and the Elven-maid felt as if she was dying a slow death in the walls of the city. She only ate and drank to keep from truly fading away, desiring not that Caspar should find her in a weakened state. Today she went to the gardens, and the guards contented themselves with guarding all the entrances. There was nowhere for her to escape in them, after all, except by coming out one of these.

Just as it was turning dark, a legendary and formidable sight appeared in the field near the west gates of the city; it was a Dwarven catapult. On the advice of the Gnome, they had set it up for a shot at a target he knew would have a defining impact: the dungeons. He had spent the day making meticulous calculations, and was very confident of these as he now had them load it with a great and heavy stone as they cranked it back. The guards on the wall of the city sent a report to the king about this new development, but there was nothing they could really do about it. Evelyn, overhearing this report, went to a window on the west side of the palace to see what would happen. The lamps of the city were just being lit. All at once, something with an intense glow was seen out in the field; it was the stone that was to be tossed into the city. Evelyn gazed at it intently; where would it strike? The flaming thing was launched into the air, and it came down in the Barracks District--the dungeons! As Percy had intended, the great stone bore down heavily on the walls of the dungeon, cracking some of the cells open. The prisoners lost no time. There was a revolt at once, and guards were dispatched to quell it. Content with their mischief, those besieging the city did not attack again, leaving Auschternople to fend off the surging fire and the escaping prisoners. Evelyn turned from the window, and retired to her "cell", as she called it, not intending to dignify it as anything more than that.

***

From his vantage point on the ship, Caspar had seen the fiery stone launched; he saw it go down in the northwest part of the city, and smiled to himself. It had probably been intended to crack open the dungeons. When he did not see another one, he looked again; flames were now spreading, or so he guessed from the rising glow he could discern in the distance. The stone had done its work one way or the other, and that was all the intent of the besiegers this night. With a longing sigh he retired to the cabin, where he found Kia Re waiting for him. She was looking out of the window, combing out her long, lustrous golden hair as she sat upon the bed in a soft gown. He came to sit beside her, and she smiled over at him as he sat down. Kia Re set the brush aside, and wrapped him in her arms; he returned the embrace, running a hand through her hair as they sat together. They fell asleep that way, and were awakened by the sound of gulls crying on the shore.

***

Morning saw the end of the prisoners' revolt, and those who had not been slain were being either taken for executions at once or being forced to aid in rebuilding the broken section of the city. When some of the nobles at court complained of such harsh treatment, the king had them stripped and sent to aid in the reconstruction. Evelyn retired to her room soon after that, and when the king tried to come in and see her she cast a spell upon the door. Fuming, the king returned to his own chambers with a servant girl, who served as the object of his desire for the day. She wept throughout the affair, and when it was over he had her sent out to aid in the labor as well. The king was fast losing the respect he had hard won in the early days of his reign, but the city was yet under his control--inside the walls, at any rate. Outside, the besiegers were content to starve him out, and that day they seized the Great Enclosure, blocking off the original gate and breaking up a wall on the northeast side for a new entrance. All that the city now had left were her stores.

Chapter Five: The Lion's Roar

When dawn came rising up with the sun from the sea's horizon, those in the war-camp saw that bodies had been hung from the wall; there hung all those who had executed, and a fair few from those who had been laboring to repair the damage, including seven of the nobles and the poor servant girl. Incensed at this new outrage, they let loose more catapult stones into the city, and before the second hour of daylight eleven stones had been hurled in, some striking the Barracks District and some in the Harbor District. One struck near the palace, and glass shattered around the point of impact. The besiegers then began to implement their plans for tunneling into the city, when upon a sudden a sound of strange horns came to their ears.

They had not gone unnoticed in their march to Auschternople; a host bearing the banners of Murana Day came up from the south, and they halted just out of arrow range from the Dwarf and Valkyrie host. Their leaders met in the midst of the field, and Duke Melchior of Murana Day refused to talk terms, believing the king well within his rights to do as he pleased in his own city. General Frigund gestured to the walls, but the Duke smiled wickedly.

"I would do far worse to my own citizens, should they murmur against me with an armed host outside my walls." he said, and with that Frigund stormed away in a fury. Briana did not let the Duke get away so easily, for he had made suggestive comments to her throughout the brief discourse. With an inhuman speed she drew her sword and slashed him on the cheek, and then turned away herself as the Duke stormed off in anger for the wound.

Only moments after they were back in their respective camps a new battle began; it lasted for several hours of the day, and the king even managed to send out a few of his most loyal knights to aid those who had come up from the south. They fell valiantly, even by the standards of their enemies, but they succeeded in killing Gromond Red-Axe, and the second-commander's death was a heavy scar for the Dwarven General, who had fought with him against the goblins or giants many times. The host of Murana Day was driven back by a sudden onslaught from the Valkyries, who were joined by Kia Re, Ragya, and Caspar. Caspar indeed gave the Duke another scar for the day, and the angered nobleman, recognizing his former subject, vowed vengeance.

"Thy family from the farms of Idoma shall all die by my hand for your insolence, knave! But not before I bring them your head!" he swore as he was dragged away from the battle by his knights. Caspar then fit an arrow to Evelyn's bow, which he had brought for the battle, and shot at one of those aiding the Duke; the man fell dead, and with that Caspar slung the bow back over his left shoulder and resumed combat with the sword, taunting his enemies with skill.

Heartened by the young man's display of courage, the Dwarf and Valkyrie host set back into their new enemies with a will, and a contingent of them was set off to fight a second wave of Knights from Auschternople that had just been set loose. By the late afternoon, the armies from Murana Day had retreated from the field, setting up a camp further south than they had hoped, and the victorious besiegers held a brief celebration, after which they held a vigil for those who had died that day. Ji Mao, Ragya, and Percy joined their allies for these two functions, but Caspar and Kia Re headed back to the ship at first. Intoxicated with the thrill of being in a battle, and with the spells of Valkyrie wards and blessings from the day's fighting still lingering in their blood, they began kissing and kissing, stripping off weapons and armor as they got inside the cabin. Kia Re unbound her hair, and kissed him furiously as she undid his belt, and he began undoing the straps of her armor. It wasn't until they were nearly to the bed that they realized what they were doing, and in shock they halted.

"What are we doing?" Kia Re said in a daze, letting her hair fall over her breasts as she sat down on the bed.

"I have no idea..." Caspar said, sitting on the floor next to the nightstand as he caught his breath. "All I could think of as the battle was won was you. There was a potent magic in the field of battle when our new friends charged again." he said as he slowly recovered himself.

"The Valkyrie chants of battle." Kia Re nodded. "They were indeed potent today. And I, too, could think of nothing but wanting you inside me as the battle dwindled. It would be a perfect end of the day to me." she said as she adjusted herself to lay down, and Caspar came to sit beside her.

"And we would have felt very miserable afterwards, I'm sure." he added, and she let out a sob. He kissed her then as he laid down beside her, caressing her side as their lips lingered together.

"I wish you were with Evelyn, trapped in the king's palace with the one you love." Kia Re told him.

"I would be in the dungeons if he had caught me, and possibly hanging from the walls." Caspar returned.

"That is true... I did not think of that..." Kia Re admitted as their legs intertwined. They lay looking at each other for several moments, and the potency of the spells from the battlefield dwindled away.

"We should get up and get dressed for the vigils tonight." Caspar said.

"We should." Kia Re nodded as they caressed each other. Still yet they lay there, and as the potency of the Valkyrie wards finally dissipated, they still lay together, caressing each other as they shared another kiss. "Did you go to find love with one who is immortal, or one whose love is immortal?" she said softly.

"I feel so sure I love her, and yet I feel sure of my love for you as well." he admitted. "Why should it not be both?" he wondered, and she smiled at him.

"You were right the first time. We would be miserable. And you were right the second: we should get dressed." Kia Re then said, and he nodded. But neither of them moved from the bed, and their eyes lingered on each other; a knock on the door finally broke the spell that they themselves had woven with each other, and Kia Re hastily covered up with the sheets as Caspar donned his leggings. Ragya was at the door.

"Ragya!" Caspar said in surprise. "I'm sorry, we were worn out."

"It is understandable." the Werecat nodded in agreement. "Are you coming for the vigil tonight? I came back to look for the two of you." he wondered.

"Yes. We'll be ready in a moment, friend." Caspar nodded.

"As you say." Ragya nodded back, and went to go and wait for them at the gangplank. Caspar and Kia Re hurriedly got dressed into something appropriate for the evening, and were walking with Ragya to the vigil moments later. They walked on either side of the Werecat, hoping to shake off the heat that had risen up between them; a cool breeze blew from the north, and the young minstrel looked over towards the city of Auschternople. *Evelyn... forgive me...* he pleaded silently as they walked along. They reached the site of the vigil some minutes later, and found the dead arranged on funeral pyres, friend and enemy alike being honored in the time-honored ways of battle. Prayers and songs of battle were spoken and sung, and then the pyres were lit. May the dead, who died valiantly this day, never be forgotten.

Evelyn, watching from her window on the north, saw the pyres lit, and murmured her own offerings of peace to the dead. The Master of the Tower came to stand beside her, watching as the rows of pyres lit up the night. He shook his head, and Evelyn looked at him curiously.

"It is insensible. The monarchy will never gain back respect after this. Do you know what he has done, my apprentice?" he asked her, and she shook her head. "The king bedded one of his servant girls; then sent her out naked to help in the labor at the dungeons, and then had her hung on the walls dead. That's the legacy of Augusta's last king. And he will be the last--mark my words!--no one will follow a king in this city evermore, and Auschternople may well fall to the dust." he said, and Evelyn gasped in horror.

"Why have they not revolted!" she wondered in dismay.

"Because the king's soldiers and knights are just as cruel as he is, for the most part." her mentor told her. "Now come with me, young Elf, there is something I have to teach you, and I have persuaded the king to let me do so. Come along, quickly!" he said, and they hastened from the palace to the Tower; he took her up to a secret chamber, and a crystal ball lay on a stand in its midst. It shimmered with a swirling light, and she looked at it curiously.

"This is one of the fabled Stones of Alastria!" she said in recognition.

"Indeed. One of nine, as I recall it." he nodded. "I thought you would know it. Now look!" he said to her, and she looked; there were her friends by the pyres, the solemnity of the day heavy in their faces; the image faded, and was replaced by a yawning cavern. Ragya was heading in, and there was Ji Mao coming up just behind him; the other three were already inside it, and they seemed to be in a battle. Again the image changed: Auschternople was being rebuilt; but in another image it was burning, burning to the ground, and people were murdering each other in the streets. Children were being murdered, women raped, and the king's head was upon a pike.

Now it swirled again: there they all were, the six companions out at sea, just as they had hoped. But it was a tainted victory, for they all seemed somber and regretful, as if they had left the city in ashes. It shimmered, and the ship and its little crew were bright and lively; Auschternople, she knew, had been rebuilt in this vision. Now it changed again; she was with Caspar, making a passionate love; then Caspar was with Kia Re, and the two of them were just as fiercely making love; Evelyn felt a pang of sorrow and of jealousy at this. Then the image changed again: now she herself was with the Valkyrie, and they kissed and caressed one another.

Blushing, she realized she did indeed have some measure of love for her--but then the image changed again. Forests, swamps, mountains, deserts, towers, castles, foes uncountable passed before her eyes; a great lion roared, and a hawk scratched the eyes of the beast. Then she came to a barren land, a land beyond tormented and twisted heights of a great mountain chain; a dark castle sat upon a hill, and on its throne was a succubi with her latest victim. The castle faded away, and she came to a tower, a large tower; it was the Tower of the Sorcerer King. Two eyes lit up the Stone of Alastria, and then the visions faded. She slowly backed up into a chair to sit down, trying to make sense of it all.

"Do not try!" the Master said as if he guessed her thoughts. "It shows you what it will, as well you should know, whose race crafted them in the Age of Veiled Mystery." he told her. "The secret hopes and fears of your heart are all mingled in its depths, and you may well miss the true meaning of what it shows." he added, and she nodded.

"I do love her. Or I want to love her. And, oh, my... how I love him... and does he indeed love her?" she wondered to herself.

"Beware trusting the orb as a guide for your heart." he told her.

"Then how am I to deal with these images?"

"Let your heart be that which guides you, and not the orb. All the orb shows is what may be, and what could have been; will you let the world around us fall into darkness, or will you give it light as best you can?" he asked her, and the orb lit up again; there was Caspar, holding aloft the king's crown, and the monarch himself was on his knees in surrender. Was he to die, or was he to make other penance for his crimes?

"I will remember the wisdom of your words." she said at last. "I would have this end in a way of peace, and not in bloodshed." she added, and he smiled knowingly.

"Blood will be shed; but we can ensure, at least, that it may be the right blood." the Master told her, and she nodded again. He led her back to the palace, and she fell asleep thinking of Caspar. No; she did not feel doubt in her heart. He loved her--but he also loved Kia Re. The three of them seemed fated to love each other. She smiled, only wishing that she and Kia Re might have traded places; was Kia Re thinking the same? Perhaps. Her eyes closed in slumber, and she dreamed the dream that Kia Re had but lately reveled in; the three of them dancing together in a far country, far from all the troubles of the world.

Outside the walls of Auschternople, the companions retired to the ship. Exhausted from the day, they all fell asleep moments after they arrived back at their new "home", and their dreams were just as pleasant as those of Evelyn's.

***

Morning saw another, lighter skirmish between the opposing forces, and several more erupted throughout the day. Ji Mao and Ragya went scouting in the hills around the noon hour, and Percy went with them to create sketches of maps regarding enemy activity they might come across. The Gnome came armed with his explosive devices, and the three of them stealthily went through the woods, seeing no sign of anyone save the animals. When they got to the foot of the hills they rested, and quietly discussed among themselves what they had seen so far.

"They must not come this way often." Percy remarked. "And I daresay that two huge armies would send them crawling for their hideaways at any rate."

"I feel this is true." Ji Mao nodded. "They must be reinforcing their hideaways in the hills. I heard rumors of great caverns, caverns that lead down to an underground lake that leads into the King's Bay."

"This is sound to my mind as well." Ragya agreed. "We must see if we can at least find the entrance to these caverns--but we must be wary! We are only three, and we do not know the full number of those arrayed against us."

"Quite." Percy nodded. "Onwards, then?" he asked, and they softly got up, cautiously picking their way up into the hills. Ragya caught sight of a worn track, and they followed this for a long way; it wound around the tallest of the hills, and ended about three-fifths of the way up at a ledge. Ragya hoisted the Gnome into a nearby tree, and then joined him as Ji Mao also shimmied up into its branches. They examined the area closely from their vantage point, and the Gnome made meticulous drawings of their observations. "It seems as if there is some sort of artificial obstruction they use for a door, carefully groomed to resemble the ground. Hsst! There!" Percy said softly; just as he suspected, the "door" opened, and two raiders slipped out; these headed in a different direction than the path, and when they were out of sight Percy nodded again. The three of them then carefully slipped down, and hastily raced off to where their ship lay anchored. When they got there, Percy began refining his maps and notes, and Ragya was called away to aid in a skirmish. Ji Mao went to go and aid with the wounded, and the diminutive scholar was left to his devices, happily scribing away. When he was finished he and Ji Mao went to deliver his refined notes to the commander's pavilion, and they were asked to stay and give report.

While Ragya aided in a skirmish on a more westerly side of the battlefield, Kia Re and Caspar returned from a skirmish nearer the ship, once again feeling intoxicated from the battle and the spells of the Valkyries. As they got to the ship, a series of flaming arrows and debris touched down in the camp on shore, and those that were stationed about the area reacted at once, including the two of them. Kia Re charged into the fray with the rest, but Caspar grabbed his lute and ran to get up in a tree, from which he sang a scathing song to infuriate their attackers. It was a mockery of an old duke of Murana Day, who foolishly sent his troops out to fight the ghosts of his own imagination.

He inserted Melchior's name into the ballad instead, and in anger their opponents got worked up into a frenzy which betrayed them in the end: the unbalanced forces of Murana Day were routed by the Valkyrie-Dwarf alliance, and they sang many songs of victory. When the dead were brought back for yet more pyres, Caspar and Kia Re again returned to the ship, now doubly intoxicated.

Kia Re drew out a sword, and with a playful look tossed another to Caspar. He smiled back, and the two of them began teasing each other with sword play about the deck of the ship. Back and forth they drove each other, until at last they got near the door of the cabin. Kia Re then disarmed them both, and, opening the door, shoved him inside. Here, she did not give him a chance to get up, but at once jumped down to wrestle with him. He shrugged her off and leaped up as she did; they eyed each other intensely, uncertain of how long they wished to keep up this little sparring flirtation. They then ran forward to try and catch each other off guard, and by luck Caspar managed to grab Kia Re in a headlock; she then arched back, spun around and flung him onto the bed. Winded, he had no resistance left to him as she stripped off her battle-skirt and softly climbed on top of him, kissing him with a will. Again they slowly divested each other, content with kisses and the gentle caress of each other's hands upon their aching bodies. They had fought in a total of nine skirmishes that day, nine out of a total of fifteen across the field, including the one near their ship. Caspar fell asleep from weariness, and Kia Re sighed to herself; perhaps it was not meant to be after all. She covered them with the blanket, contenting herself with being near him.

***

Ragya stared intently across the field as the night wore on; the skirmish at the western part of the fields had ground to a standstill, and he did not like it. A Valkyrie named Fiona was with him, and the red-haired warrior did not like it either.

"They toy with us. See! There is no one about those fires." she said softly.

"Indeed." Ragya blinked. He then frowned, scanning the area. To his right he looked, and suddenly grabbed his companion to roll the two of them out of sight. Fiona, understanding that something had caught his attention.

"Where are they?" she asked softly.

"They are circling about and coming up from the west--let us hie to our friends!" the Werecat said, and with that they slipped away as fast as they dared, bringing news of this sneak-attack to the nearest host they could find. The forces of Murana Day, thwarted from their surprise moments later, had a hard time of getting back to their friends and allies, and eventually some of them surrendered while others ran off into the west or up to the north. Ragya and Fiona were then escorted to the great pavilion, where Percy and Ji Mao were discussing their little spy-mission with Briana, who desired to go after the caverns at once. Frigund warned against this, however, and suggested that a smaller force should try and invade them.

"We need to keep an eye on these dogs--that little trick from the Duke just now has me on alert, and I wonder indeed if these raiders are worth the trouble in comparison." the general said, and Briana accepted this.

"Perhaps not." she allowed. "But we cannot ignore them forever. They are part of our goals here, my friend." she told him, and he nodded back.

"Indeed! But the Duke of Murana Day was not--and we must deal with his forces 'ere we come back to our original plans."

"I hear the wisdom in your words. Very well; we shall let these raiders be for a time, and give our battle to the duke."

***

On the next day, Evelyn spent most of her morning looking out the window to the west, her violet eyes intent on where she was certain she could see a ship on the southern shores of the bay. Was today the day the besiegers would break through, she wondered? So far they had been content with what the catapults could ruin, and with cutting the city off from its supply of food; and of course they had the king's ally the Duke to deal with now... perhaps there would be no rescue today. Several battles were reported to the palace throughout the day, and on the next day the king announced that the city would be on rationing to conserve their food supply. Any and all who protested this were killed, and their bodies hung from the wall. On this day, the Duke's forces made a dent in the besieger's ranks, and after a bitter struggle that lasted until noon of the next day the battle waned once more.

Outside the walls, Ji Mao and Ragya were both aiding with the wounded, and Percy was hard at work with some of the Dwarves, devising a means to quickly but carefully dig into the city. The young Weishuune girl almost broke down at times, but Ragya was always there to speak an encouraging word or to simply place one of his paws on her in consolation. One of those who had died that day had been Fiona, and the Werecat was not immune to losing a friend, however short a time he had known them.

Caspar, numb from all the bloodshed, sat in the cabin of the ship alone until Kia Re at last came in from her most recent battle. She divested herself of armor and weapons and lay on the bed, weary from the long struggles. Caspar fell asleep in the chair, and she looked at him with a longing in her blue eyes; she fell asleep thinking of Evelyn, wondering if their hostage friend was thinking of them. Evelyn herself gazed out the west window yet again that evening, and saw all about the walls funeral pyres lighting up. It had been a bloody two days indeed, and the king's murdering of his people was not the least crime of death. Wishing she knew how to escape, the Elven-maiden fell asleep, once again dreaming of her and Caspar dancing with Kia Re beyond the furthest shores. Dawn rose with colors of red the next day, and the carrion-fowl gathered about the area, eager for a share in the carnage.

***

Caspar spent his day slowly riding about the war-camp, playing his harp as he rode to try and liven the spirits of those around him, since he could not find solace himself. He went about in this manner for several long hours, until at last a skirmish rose up again--a short but intense skirmish. The Duke himself was out again, and he was about to bear down on Kia Re, who was locked in combat with two soldiers. Caspar's heart almost stopped, and in anger he called out to Duke Melchior, who turned to see his former subject charging at him with sword drawn; the Duke spurred his horse towards Caspar instead, and tried to cleave off the young man's head, but as his hand was upraised Caspar quickly slashed, and the Duke lost sword and hand to the minstrel's blow. He stared in shock at the stump of his arm, and rode off for his own camp at once. The two soldiers, distracted by the sight of their liege-lord being so bested, fell to Kia Re's spear moments later, and she jumped up behind Caspar as he rode over to her; she kissed him on the cheek, and they continued through the battle together, until the Duke's men retreated, disheartened by the injury done to their leader.

Elvar bore them back to the ship, and the two of them dismounted so that they could unburden the faithful horse of his accouterments. He was let off to graze, and the two of them then headed in to the cabin, divesting themselves of weapons and armor as they got inside. Kia Re then embraced Caspar from behind, and he placed his hands on hers.

"I thought I was about to lose you back there." he said to her.

"And I thought the same when he lifted his blade against you." she said in a trembling tone. "I don't think I could have lived if he had killed you, never mind dear Evelyn--she would be well within her rights to kill me if anything happened to you on my watch." she added, and Caspar turned around to hold her.

"We will think no more of it." he said as he kissed her forehead. "We're alive, and we can both laugh at it sometime in the distant future; and we'll laugh with Evelyn, and Ragya and Percy and Ji Mao, too." he added, and she reached up to kiss him.

"Yes, we will." she agreed, relaxing in his embrace. They stood together for many long moments, and then sat down together on the bed, still holding each other. "Oh, how I miss her... I got so used to her company in that short time, never mind you yourself." Kia Re said softly, and he nodded.

"I hope she's well; I wish I could come to her rescue right now..." Caspar said in a barely audible voice as he turned to look out the window. Kia Re let go of him, and looked at him fondly as he stared towards Auschternople. After a few moments, she took his hand again, and kissed it. She then got up, and pulled him along with her to go and wash off from the skirmishes of the past few days. As they returned to the cabin they saw only a few pyres being lit, which they took as a good sign. When they were inside once more Kia Re began kissing him again; he kissed her back, and they half-danced, half-walked over to the bed. She removed the towel she had been wearing, and as she lay down upon the bed she pulled Caspar's off as well. With a smirk she then pulled him down to the bed, kissing him again as she gently pulled him on top of her.

"We should yet refrain." he said as their lips parted, and she kissed him again.

"I know." she said. "But I want you." she said as another kiss passed between them.

"I know." he said, and with that they lay there again, gazing into each other's eyes with a barely restrained passion. "We should stop now." he said even as their legs intertwined, and she nodded. But instead they kissed again, and a second and a third kiss followed this one.

"Don't stop." Kia Re softly pleaded as she kissed him again.

"I can't." Caspar returned. She smiled, kissing him once more as they caressed each other with feeling. "I wish someone would knock at the door." he said as they went on kissing.

"I wish there was a battle, or that we could go and storm through Auschternople to find Evelyn..." Kia Re said as she kissed him. "We should stop. I can't do this to you." she said, and for a moment they paused, their eyes lingering on each other. They both thought of Evelyn, and they both wished desperately that, somehow, Ragya and the others could have saved her from the walls on the day the besiegers arrived. Caspar could still see the moonlight on her small, violet tipped breasts, and Kia Re could hear her gentle laughter; a tear fell from her eye, and Caspar brushed it away gently. "I shouldn't even tempt you. I have been in the wrong." she said, trying to convince herself further.

"We've both been in the wrong. I should be stronger." he said in kind, but still they lay together.

"We'll be miserable." Kia Re said, and then wondered if it were really true.

"We'd deserve it." Caspar agreed, but she kissed him again anyway.

"I want to grow old with you. Am I not mortal as you are?" she then said, rubbing him on the back as they lay there.

"You are. Your skin is like fair ivory, your eyes twin pools that reflect the skies above, and your lips as sweet as honeyed-mead." he said, and she faintly smiled.

"I am reddened by the sun, and the ivory turns to bronze."

"Perhaps. But still lovely." he said, kissing her again. "We need to stop now." he said, his voice shaking as he rolled over to look out the window towards the city. Kia Re softly nodded, and contented herself with lying next to him, listening to his heart as the night wore on.

***

The last skirmish of the night was another brief battle under the stars; Duke Melchior, thinking to avenge himself doubly upon Caspar, led an assault towards the caravel. But he did not count on being intercepted by a larger force that had espied his movements, and as Caspar himself lay soundly asleep with Kia Re at his side, General Frigund slew the Duke's horse, and then fought the man himself in single combat while the smaller force of Murana Day was wiped out by his army. The Duke, struggling to fight with his left hand, was given honorable combat by the Dwarf General, but was nonetheless outmatched after several minutes. Frigund bashed in his knee first, and when the Duke was bent before him on the ground, the Dwarves' general brought his war-hammer down upon his head, and the Duke perished. His body was put on display before the west gate of Auschternople, and in the morning a report of this was brought to the king, who came to stare in disbelief. Later that day, a second report came in; the forces of Murana Day were either surrendering or retreating. Enraged, the maddened king began plotting a wicked revenge, and sent his guards up to Evelyn's chambers at once.

As soon as the guards got to Evelyn's chambers, they heard a whistle from behind them. Turning, they saw the Master of the Tower, who spoke a single word of command; at once they fell over dead, and the Master then entered Evelyn's room. She gave him an inquiring glance, and he took her out to the hall, where the eight guards lay dead on the floor. Evelyn stared in shock, but had no time for the scene and its implications to fully register, for the Master then hurriedly escorted her through the halls. Down a disused stairwell they went, and when they exited the palace they made for the Tower. He brought her to a different room this time, and set her upon an upraised platform, handing her a few books he told her she would need.

"The king has lost his mind. He was to have you executed. Do not say you owe me your life; it may be true, or I may be sending you to a worse fate. But I am sending you away, and he will have a devil of a time trying to get in here." the man told her, and she nodded.

"You're teleporting me to my friends." she realized. She had heard of such a thing, but had never known it could truly be done.

"You should arrive just near the ship." he nodded back. "I know for a certainty that your Caspar will be overjoyed to see you. I have been scrying the battlefield, and he has been resisting the advances of your friend Kia Re quite admirably. They love each other, but his heart is immovably yours." he added, and Evelyn smiled. That was all the confirmation she needed.

"Then I shall give him myself this very night. And thank you, master, for everything you've done." she said to him, and he returned her smile.

"Use what time gives you for the benefit of all, and I will consider myself thanked." he said, and with that began his incantations; his voice rose to a crescendo, and the world swirled all about her; she felt as if she was passing through heaven itself as the spell took her out of the tall tower--perhaps she was!--and then she felt the whirling sensations of light slow, and when she could see straight again she found herself standing near the ship, just as the Master of the Tower had hoped.

"Evelyn!" Caspar's voice came, and she dropped the books as she felt his arms wrap around her; they kissed several times, and he held her tightly. "How!" he asked in wonder.

"The Master of the Tower and his magic." she said with a glow; he helped her pick up the books, and they headed in to the cabin, where Kia Re greeted her with a kiss.

"Thank the stars! Now we can truly decide our course." the Valkyrie said as they all gave each other a hug. "Are we to leave, or do we yet feel honor-bound to stay and help?" she said as they let go; the others, having seen Evelyn materialize outside, came in to give her their own greetings, and after they had made a mini-celebration of her return to them they came back to Kia Re's question: should they leave, or stay?

"I would stay." Ji Mao said. "I still want to see the right thing done, and I don't think that all this violence will do that."

"I agree." Evelyn nodded. "The Master showed me a grim fate for this city, and I feel it is right that we try to find a civilized way to end this conflict."

"I admire the sentiment, but we seem to be getting nowhere on such counts." Percy remarked. "We should stay to gather supplies, certainly, but then we should be off--we are of no use here."

"Master Gnome, I believe you are wrong this time: we *have* been of use, and of aid, and I feel yet some task undone." Kia Re told him.

The four of them then continued debating the issue; Ragya said nothing, but Caspar's mind began working. A task undone... what was it that the mysterious man had told him? Something about a crown... the king's crown; he thought harder, his brow furrowing as the words came back to him: *this city will go on, its monarch may not. His crown is gone, as now you know, and who can say what those in the hills have done with it? Find it... find it...* find the crown; where was the crown? The raiders had taken it. Where were the raiders? In the hills. Those in the hills had taken the crown, and if the city was be at peace, the crown of kings might bring an end to the conflict. But who was he to make them all stop fighting?

"Caspar?" Evelyn called, lightly patting his cheek. "Are you all right?"

"Yes, fine... I was just thinking..." he said in a hypnotic sort of way.

"Thinking about... what?" Ragya wondered.

"The crown... the raiders have the crown. We can find the crown, and perhaps finding it may be the start of bringing order back, and then peace." he said, and the others looked at each other. Percy gave him a knowing look, as if the Gnome knew something further, but he did not say what it was just yet. "But who are we to make demands of them, never mind having the thing..." he said in a resigned way, and with that Percy went over to a shelf where he had been stowing his parchments. The Gnome brought out a book he had somehow snitched, and unrolled one of his own papers as he opened the dusty volume.

"A question I was intrigued to look up on the day that we got into *this* little mess." he remarked. "Since our mysterious man named you with a different father than you recall, I was compelled to seek out the name of your mother." the Gnome continued, and Caspar perked up. "Assuming that this Miri is the daughter of Rowland and Giselle, native to Murana Day?"

"That's what the Order of Cassandra and Farmer Wells both told me, but I never knew my grandparents either. They must have been slain in the Great Invasion." Caspar nodded.

"Actually they passed away only five years ago, according to these records." Percy said with a shrug, and Caspar blinked, his jaw wagging as he tried to process this.

"Moving on! As I progressed through the genealogy of your ancestors (fascinating stuff, really! Your great-great-granduncle on that side of the family was a knight), I discovered that, approximately some eleven-hundred years ago (judging from the generations), your mother's side of the family were in fact the original claimants to the Augustan Throne. A distant cousin manipulated them out of the picture, but the family records were preserved by a faithful scribe. Their being royalty was forgotten some six-hundred years ago, for the family found that a simple life was all they really needed after all, and thus your immediate ancestors passed from being kings to serfs. And thus your great-great-granduncle's knighthood the very least the duke of the time could do; indeed he seemed to have a knowledge of it. But there we are. You, my friend, are the last heir of the Augustan Throne, for Michael the Fourteenth has no wife and thus no children."

"That's insane!" Caspar cried out. "How could it be so forgotten? And how could my family forget such a thing? No clues? No keepsakes? No family heirlooms to prove it? Just these records?" he wondered all at once. Evelyn looked at him with great surprise, and exchanged a glance with Kia Re; they were in love with a prince?

"As I explained, those of your family who were originally exiled fell in love with the simple life, and left weightier matters to their greedy cousin. And when I made queries about them the Grand Keeper swore up and down that these were original books and records, and that the matter of the dethroning was well-known in Augustan history, even if the family itself faded away into mere rumor." Percy told him.

"But what does that mean?" Caspar wondered in a daze, feeling overwhelmed by the thought of it all.

"It means, my dear boy, that the crown is yours, according to your mother's side of the family." Percy replied.

"And the kingdom as well..." Kia Re softly added, looking at him with a new wonder and love in her eyes.

"No wonder you bear up so nobly; it is in your blood after all, my love." Evelyn said as she smiled at him.

"I felt you were something more the moment we met." Ji Mao said quietly.

"As did I." Ragya agreed.

"As for myself, I was not very much surprised. This sort of thing has happened before in the histories of men, and it may happen again." Percy remarked. "But now that I know for a certainty, I say to you, my friend, that I am doubly at your service no matter what course we take." he added, and Caspar rubbed his eyes as Evelyn kissed his cheek. They all looked around at each other, and slowly began smiling at one another.

"Well, whatever I am, we should still go after the crown." Caspar said.

"That we should--if our intent is to stay." Percy nodded.

"It is. It would be wrong to leave them to destroy each other." his friend returned, and the Gnome nodded once more.

"Very wise." he agreed.

"Then let us rest this night; they will not miss us should we venture out, now that the siege can go on without interference." Kia Re said.

"Agreed." Ragya nodded. "Tomorrow, we should pay our... 'respects'... to those who prey on the weak."

"I would chose the late afternoon to start such a quest." Caspar added. "Let us use the night against them as they use it against us."

"Agreed." the Werecat nodded.

"I think we can call that settled." Percy said as he went to put away his books. "Now if you'll excuse me! I've a tunnel to see to." the Gnome said, and headed back out to where the siege engineers were breaking ground to begin tunneling in to Auschternople. Ragya and Ji Mao left as well, and the other three were left to themselves. Evelyn smiled, and held out her hand for Kia Re, who came over to sit beside the two of them on the bed.

"The Master of the Tower also told me that you two have been teasing each other." she said softly, and Kia Re flushed as Caspar let out a wry smile.

"It was foolish to do so, and I'm sorry." he said.

"As am I." Kia Re added.

"I love you both." Evelyn said as they linked arms together. "Let's not fight about it; right now, I just want to love you both. Tonight." she said, kissing Caspar as she laid him down on the bed. Kia Re let out a laugh, and Caspar gave his beloved a funny look.

"Both? Tonight?" he asked nervously.

"I think tonight I should go and walk under the stars." Kia Re began as she stood up, and with a laugh Evelyn stood up to give her a hug goodnight as she departed. She then returned to sit next to Caspar, who smiled at her.

"A test?" he wondered.

"Perhaps." Evelyn said softly as she kissed him. "But I do mean to have you tonight, if you promise yourself to me alone, now and forever." she added with a second kiss, and he wrapped his arms around her.

"Then I so promise; let me be all yours, dear Evelyn, now and forever." he returned just as softly, and with that they settled in for a night of passion; the world was in chaos, and yet here they were, making love in the midst of it. Kia Re sat atop the crow's nest of their ship, looking out over the bay at the sight of the four moons encircled by heaven's host of stars. It was a beautiful night, she thought to herself, and still more beautiful for it being a night of lovers reunited. She sighed longingly; she and Caspar had passed their test. True love would not fail, and neither would the love of friends.

***

> Sing to me, O stars, of lovers reunited;
> Tell me when the whispering wind wafts
> Through a dream of trees, softly singing
> A melody of bliss; Ah! The sweet caress
> Of your lips on mine, and the touch
> Of your hands upon my breast; my heart is full
> And my soul content. You are my delight, and
> You are my joy; the light of my eyes is you:
> Open the secret joys of your heart to me,
> And I will share with you my own.
> Let us have done with sorrow, and sing
> Only of that which is beauteous to the heart,
> Yours and mine--mine and yours; O!
> How I love you; beautiful, beautiful man,
> Strong of arm and hale in body, let me see
> Your heart, the heart that beats with my name;
> See! I give you my own heart; hear it beating
> As you lay your head between my breasts
> And kiss me goodnight; goodnight, my love
> And every night, I will love you.

I love him; he is as my brother, yet I love him,
My song-brother, he who loves a love immortal.
I gave him my heart freely, and he did not spurn
The gift I gave him; but I lay my desire aside:
For his love for her is stronger and truer;
Yet still I love him--the taste of his lips
The ruddiness of his form, the gentle voice:
Hear him sing--O, immortal maiden, love him
As I love him, and never give him up,
For I fear lest aught should come between you,
Even myself; and I bind myself with love, that
I might not do so. O! Man, beautiful man;
My heart is full of you, and so desired my body
To be full of you; but now give her the passion
So long denied you; for days are as years
Where love is concerned, and hope springs ever
From the fountain thereof: the Fountain of Love.
I will not be jealous, but still I love you.
I love both of you, and I always will.

All the melodies I have ever played, of romance
Doomed, blessed, cursed; rejected, despised, or
Embraced, I never truly knew what drove them on;
A thousand ballads I sang of love, yet love
Never I knew in person--until you came along,
Immortal maiden of my dreams, now with me forever.
And another love I know; she calls me her brother,
And in her heart beats a love
Just as pure as mine for you--
So I gave it back to her, giving her the love
She asked of me; do not ask me whom I love more
Or whom I love best; for our love is a sacred love,
And my love for her a special love
Gifted by the stars above that I might understand
More fully what love really is; faithfulness
To you is all my desire, and to be faithful in
My promise to her, to love her as a brother.
Is it not strange? A mortal such as I
Has captured the heart of not one but two
Maidens who rightfully belong among the stars,
And I will rest content with their love
All the days of my life.

Come to me, and sing to me, love me
My dearest and best; you who followed
On the whim of a dream, who dared to believe
He could find me among the wide lands
Of these far countries; are you not most beloved
For doing so? What tales do they now sing
In your home now so far away when they
Think of you? And ah! What tales do they
Sing of me, whom I rejected for you and you alone?
We both left family to find family, and
Family we have been given back again;
The trust we gave each other is fully earned
And you have not despised my love, but
Steadfastly you sought to be faithful
I love you both for such a thing--and
If any should ask, you are both a part of me
I will cleave to you and to her who is my friend also
And not leave her to be alone; she is one
Who deserves our love, forsaking her desire
So that we can share our dream of love;
Should we not honor and love her for it?
Her heart beats with your name on it;
Her lips murmur your name as if caressing you
And her eyes shine at the sight of you:
It is not hidden from me! O, how she loves you
With a passion that equals my own.
Let us love her, and honor her, for her love
Will be the tie that binds us together.

I thought I could not go on without him;
But now I see--under the light of moons
I see clearly; love increases where love is true,
And their love is true indeed.
I am not going on without him,
He is honoring his promise to me, which
We swore under the sacred mountains;
And I shall honor my promise to them both:
Their love shall be remembered for all the ages,
And may my love for them be also remembered;
Let it never be forgotten, that we three
Gave each other love, and honored the commitments
We made to each other
Under the sacred sight of stars.

O! love, love so beautiful--how I love them
How I long to give myself to them--to him!
To her--is it not strange? A shield-maiden
Such as I, desiring to love a mortal and immortal
Both, whose own people have all but rejected
Those outside our sacred halls? Call it what
You will; I will call it love, for it has proven
Strong, and true, and noble; now consummated
In beauteous pageantry under the light of moons

Love, like flowers, blooms in its season
And only grows when given nourishment:
Tend the garden of flowers, and they thrive;
Tend the garden of love, and love grows;
Cast aside the flowers, and they die;
Cast aside love, and it withers.
But we will do no such thing; for love
Has become to us what water is for all peoples,
A nourishment for the soul and for the heart
I choose to love you, and to love her;
I will honor my vows to both of you throughout
All the days of my life, and may they be long
For your sake, immortal maiden,
So that the spark of my life is more bearable
When at last I go to the halls of my fathers
And am gathered to rest, to await the final end
And our reuniting--but fear not, beloved!
For I am never alone in love; are not the three
Of us bound by love? We will both await you
At the end of days, when the world is made new,
And all that is good
And all that is lovely
And all that is wonderful
Springs from the ashes of what was, to create
That which is yet to come: the best,
And ever so shall our love be,
Awaiting the best
At every turn of the year
And treasuring that which was
As we rejoice in that which is

I love him...
I want him...

I love him...
I need him...
I love him.

Chapter Seven: Raiders of the Lost Crown

Dawn rose slowly over the seascape's horizon, a mist rising up steadily from the ground as streams of sunlight began casting their brilliance upon the earth. Kia Re watched as the birds began to stir, and then the animals came alive; was that a dolphin there in the bay? Perhaps it was. A brilliant wave of pinks and reds came trailing with the sun like a bridal cape, clouds following in the wake as morning began. Ragya was behind her on the deck, murmuring in the strange, guttural, but also musically rhythmical language of the Werecats; it was a prayer or incantation of sorts, she decided to herself as she listened. Percy was making breakfast, and Ji Mao was helping him; Caspar and Evelyn came out on deck in a merry mood, and the two of them joined Kia Re on the aft deck behind the helm as she continued gazing out at the sight of the sunrise. She felt their arms upon her, and she smiled at the two of them as she returned the gesture.

The sight of a sunrise over the waters of the bay seemed entrancing to Evelyn; Kia Re did not blame her. Neither of them had lived near the sea; she had lived in the mountains, and Evelyn in the forests. Caspar had dwelt near to Murana Day, so the Duke had implied with his threats on the field of battle; had he ever seen a sunrise over the bay? The young man seemed as allured by nature's own painting as the two of them. Perhaps he had not. The sound of crashing waves came to their ears, and a sound of gulls crying out echoed throughout the bay. It seemed to have a profound effect on their minstrel lover, and for the first time in several days his voice lifted itself up in a melody. Slowly it began, as he hummed a soft tune as if nature were the melody, and he the harmony; it rose into a wordless and tranquil melody, if indeed it was not some eldritch tongue from forgotten years, and then at last he finally transcended into words.

> *Upon the shores, upon the sea,*
> *in morning's dawning light*
> *Beyond the years, beyond the fears*
> *of darkness in the night*

I sang a song of golden fire,
and crimson in her trail
The night was gone, now comes the dawn,
farewell to stars so pale
O night! O night, the moons
and stars are your delight
But day is mine, the sun divine,
and the clouds of ever-white

Unto the sea, unto the shores,
as dawn brings forth the sun
The night it dies from hither skies,
the song of stars is done
Now sings the sun, now laugh the clouds,
with colors in their wake
And all the birds, with soundless words,
in singing do partake
The boughs of trees with
flowered crowns awake
with blissful joy
O night! O, night, your faint delight
is naught to that which we enjoy

Now lives the day, now sings the dawn,
and the sun is in her train
Farewell to night, and fading light,
and farewell to moons that wane
The tranquil sea of blues and greens,
its waves crash on the shore
In harmony with dawn's own plea
for a music of evermore
And here the sun! Now there the clouds!
The colors rise again
So let us sing, and may music ring
from the hills 'til day shall end.

"Now let us eat! A meal complete! So that we may reach day's end! A fine repast, but not meant to last, come get it now my friends!" Percy sang out from below in imitation of Caspar's song. Evelyn burst out laughing with Kia Re, while the young man himself turned to look at the Gnome with a wry grin.

"Ve-ry funny." he said to his friend, but the Gnome doffed his hat, bowing.

228

"I thought I was in perfect pitch, thank you very much. Now do come along! We've work to do this day--and not the singing kind!" he said in reply, and with that the six of them all joined together for breakfast. It was a merry affair for them, for they had not been gathered all together around a meal for some time, and they talked more than they ate; but the food was indeed eaten. It was late morning when they had finished, and as the Valkyrie and Dwarf war-host geared up for a renewed siege, the companions made their own plans for the day. Thus far, there were two things they agreed on: they knew the location of the raider's hideout, but they did not know how extensive it was nor how many of them there truly were. There might be twenty, or there might be ten times twenty. With that Percy drew up an inventory of his devices; he had been hard at work indeed, for he counted off twenty-three devices rigged to explode as needed. Evelyn had her bow and a quiver full of arrows yet, if her magic should tire her out. They had all been supplied with arms and armor from the merchants who had been absorbed into the host, so they had these at their disposal, and there were several potions for their usage that would aid them if needed. It was agreed that all the potions should be taken along (and their instructions carefully read), and with that they geared up with their chosen armaments to set out for the day. One of the host's sentries asked them where they were off to, and the Dwarf was about floored when he heard that their intent was to deal with the raiders in the hills. He looked them over and shook his head, but acquiesced nonetheless.

"Very well! But on your own heads be your deaths: whether by their hands, or by ours if ye should prove traitors!" he said solemnly, and with that the six of them took their leave of the host to head up softly into the hills. Clouds gathered about the sun, and the day's fair light was soon hidden for a time behind the billowing curtains of white.

***

"Doesn't look like much..." Kia Re remarked softly as they approached the site of the door.

"Neither do most of us, at first glance--Ragya maybe, but there we are." Percy replied to her. "Now I must get close and see about this door!" he said, removing his hat so that the rest of his camouflaging attire blended in with the hills; the diminutive Gnome then slipped right up to the thing as if he were no more than a rabbit, and began examining the place where he, Ragya, and Ji Mao had seen the door open. He tapped the side of the hill softly, and then scraped away a layer of dirt, stopping as his scraper hit something solid; he carefully brushed aside the earth, and found it was a surface of wood. *Oak, likely as not...* Percy thought to himself as he observed the texture of it. He pulled out another tool to listen inside; there were faint sounds, but they seemed to be going away rather than drawing near. When he was certain there was no one about, he waved his companions over. Ragya then softly clawed away the earth over the door, and when it was all uncovered they found it was five feet wide and six tall, by the Augustan standard. There was a handle on its right, but this had been very obscured by its camouflage. Now they pulled at it, and the door opened outwards with hardly a groan; seeing the hinges, Percy set to work again, and in a few moments the door was laid aside by the Werecat so that the caverns stood open to all comers. Peering inside, they saw a yawning cavern indeed, with a tunnel at the far end; there were two platforms, one above the other, which could be reached by ladders. These were holding supplies and such, but there were no guards about.

"I dare say the crown might be hidden here." Caspar remarked softly, hoping his voice would not echo. "Ragya, Kia Re, go and guard that entrance there. We'll search the supplies for aught in the way of clues and such." he added, and the two of them headed swiftly to the door to watch it while their companions moved to ascend the ladders; they searched through the crates and barrels as softly as they could, but found nothing of immediate interest. At length Percy found a map, and Caspar brought out one of the lanterns they had found so that they could examine it; it was a map of the caverns. There were seven major caves connected by smaller passages, and the seventh and lowest was an underground lake that led into King's Bay.

"This one is marked 'supplies'; the next 'armory', the third 'prisoners', the fourth is noted as 'quarters', as is the fifth; the sixth is named as 'great hall'--a subterranean inn and tavern, I shouldn't wonder--and the seventh, of course, is named 'harbor'." Percy read, and replaced the map. "Fairly straightforward. Nothing tricky. They don't suspect anyone of being clever enough to get in, let alone raid them." he sniffed.

"Then let's upset that mindset now." Caspar said, and with that they dimmed the lantern and descended the ladders. They nodded to Ragya, who went first as they entered the descending passage; the Werecat could see in the dark at need, as could Evelyn, and so they made their way down without need of light. The passage wound about in a spiraling curve before depositing them at the armory, where they halted just out of the light. There were five raiders, one of which was just near a door at the far end. None of them were facing the passageway. With quick and silent motions, the six companions silently slipped in, taking up positions to make quick work of their foes. Before the raiders knew what had hit them, two of them were dead, including the one near the door, felled by Evelyn's bow. Ragya knocked one up against the wall with a hefty swing of his paw, rendering the man unconscious, and Kia

Re ran a fourth through with her spear as Evelyn shot the last one. They then took quick stock of the armory; seeing nothing of value here either, they opened the next door, and found a steep staircase leading in to the third cavern.

"Percy, scout it out carefully." Caspar said to the Gnome, who at once obliged him. As if he were no more than a ghost, he soundlessly descended the stairs, and in moments was seen coming back up.

"Door." he said quietly. "I took a look through the keyhole; they've twelve guards in the room and twenty or so prisoners that I could see, including a child. There's another trapdoor like this one near the far end." Percy told them.

"Twelve visible..." Kia Re murmured softly.

"And just below this next is a cavern full of them, if the map was right." Evelyn sighed.

"We have to get to that door first, somehow." Caspar said.

"I agree." Evelyn nodded.

"Leave that to me." Ragya said, slipping off the hefty pack he was carrying and setting it on the ground. He took out one of Percy's devices, removed the pin, and tossed it down. He then shifted to Wildcat form, and dashed down after the device; it went off with a bang, and they heard the sound of shouts and screams, not the least of which was Ragya's own wildcat call; they rushed down after their friend, Percy dragging the pack along as best he could. Kia Re, in the lead, saw what was going on first. The door of course had been blown to smithereens by Percy's device, and the Werecat had charged through straight to the other door. He was now fighting ferociously as the guards of the prisoners tried to bring him down; there were at least thrice twelve, but thankfully none of them had ranged weapons.

Kia Re charged in as she took in the sight quickly, yelling to distract some of them. Ji Mao slipped in behind her, and artfully began slipping in and around the scattered crates to slip her daggers into an unsuspecting raider's backside. She vanished from sight again, and a second then fell to her sneaky maneuvers. Caspar emerged just after her, racing over to join Kia Re with his sword and buckler, and Evelyn used her new-found magic to blast five of their enemies back. Percy then tossed two of his devices towards these five, and a tremendous "bang!" saw them and three others incinerated by its impact. Ragya, having downed five of his own, picked up a sixth and hurled him towards three others, then picked up a large, heavy barrel and set it atop the trapdoor to keep their allies from emerging, if any had heard the battle from below--which was likely. He was covered in bruises and a few cuts, but he was still a fearsome force to be reckoned with. Kia Re then lifted her spear, and a dazzling light filled the cavern. She then bashed one in the face with her shield, and Evelyn let loose a burst of static energy that killed seven others.

Ragya let loose a wild and blood-freezing yeowl at that moment, and several of their enemies cowered down in fear, as did some of the prisoners. He tore in to those who had been frightened, and those who were stronger of heart were soon distracted by his companions. Ji Mao snuck up behind two and made quick work of them, then tossed both of her daggers at a third, who fell down dead. She then retrieved the keys from one of those she had slain, and quietly slipped about to go and free the prisoners. There came a banging sound from the door. Most of the guards who were left were now scrabbling to get to the other door and flee, leaving Ragya free to open the one he had blocked off. He shoved the barrel aside, opened the door, and let loose another spine-chilling yeowl; a scream was heard, and the sound of people falling backwards down a flight stairs was heard, intermixed with other other screams, shouts, and expletives from below. Ragya then slammed the door shut again, and shifted back to Werecat form to make use of his druid skills.

There were now only fifteen raiders with them in the cavern. Wait! Thirteen. Ji Mao had struck again, having freed two prisoners and handing them the keys so that they could continue freeing themselves. Most of the guards who had been trying to escape up the stairs had been downed by the vigilant Evelyn, and there was a pile of dead raiders near the door; she brandished her sword to intimidate a couple of those still living, and one accidentally slew the other as he turned back in fright. His companion was then struck by a bolt of energy from the Elf, and he then joined his comrade in death. Now there were ten. Five were being held at bay by Caspar and Kia Re, two were being watched by Ji Mao and Evelyn, and the other three were being entangled in vines that Ragya had summoned up from the earth.

"How many escaped?" Kia Re asked.

"Five or six." Evelyn said.

"We'll bind the others together; give those we rescued their weapons." Caspar said as the remaining guards surrendered, and a few moments later these were all shackled together.

"Thank you! Thank you!" one of the captives said with a grateful heart.

"Now we can finally get back to Auschternople!" a woman said in a near-faint.

"Auschternople is being besieged, but the host surrounding the city will give you aid." Caspar told them. Their faces registered surprise, shock, and disbelief at the pronouncement given to them.

"What!" one of the men cried.

"I knew it--that damned fool of a king has shown his colors at last!" a second called out.

"You speak treason, Jarius!"

"Ha!"

"Never mind all that!" the woman said. "Whatever's going on, we need aid; and if we can only get it from those besieging our fair city, then so be it." she said as the child came running to her arms.

"They'll give you more aid than you might expect; they came here to deal with these fiendish raiders themselves, but Augusta has been more of a problem than they anticipated. You will find your king less noble than you may remember." Percy told them, and the freed prisoners murmured amongst themselves at these tidings.

"You're armed, and your captors are now your captives. Go free." Caspar said to them, and this was the one thing they could agree to do. They departed the caverns with those who were now their captives, and with that the companions gathered around the next door. Ji Mao saw to Ragya's wounds, which were fairly minor compared to what they could have been, and Caspar opened the door slowly; there were grumblings and expletives still emanating from below.

"They were so flustered by Ragya's prank they don't dare come back up." Evelyn said with a faint smile.

"Would you come back up if a wild beast had shoved its ravenous face into yours with a great howl?" Caspar grinned back, and she shook with silent laughter.

"Never mind that!" Percy said, and dropped two more of his devices down the stairs now revealed to them. More shouts emanated from below as they went off, and the caverns shook from the impact. He tossed a third down, and when this had gone off with a great bang there was silence; the silence continued for several moments, and they then decided to head down. Caspar started down first, followed by Evelyn and then Kia Re; Percy came fourth, while Ragya re-shouldered the great pack as he followed Ji Mao down.

A smell of sulfur and cloying smoke filled the room; the smoke was dissipating, but it was still obfuscating, yet there seemed to be no signs of life in the room. As Evelyn's eyes adjusted to the dimness she could see that it had been fairly blasted apart by the three explosives, and there were dead bodies or body-parts strewn about the floor in bloodied heaps. They examined the room carefully, and when they had found nothing of value they proceeded to the next door. This led them down into a tunnel that spiraled downwards for a long time before terminating at a door. They heard voices behind this one, and they stopped to listen.

"What in the blazes is Jynax is doing with that sorcerer up at the lighthouse is what I want to know!" one of them said.

"I heard it was a *sorceress*--in which case there's no need to guess!" a second said, and there was laughter at this.

"We've got our own problems here, anyway--didn't you feel the caverns shake? And what the 'ell was that banging sound, and all those screams and such?"

"The boys upstairs are having a row of it like as not; you know how they get."

"I swear I heard screaming, like a ladies' scream..." one of them said.

"You know how those women prisoners get when we slip up their shafts."

"Naw, that weren't it--'twas a devilish scream of terror, as if 'ell had popped up all a-sudden. Don't tell me you didn't hear it!" the cynical one returned.

"You're hearing things! Come on, let's go for a drink."

"Aye, a drink!" several others echoed, and Percy looked through the keyhole; twelve figures descended into a door at the far end of the room. He motioned to Ji Mao, who fiddled with the lock for a few moments to get it open, and they headed inside. There were five asleep. These they tied to their beds securely, and then cautiously headed down the other flight of stairs; below them was the great hall of the raiders, a large cavern that was indeed, as Percy suspected, a tavern for them, where they would meet for meals, celebrations, and the planning of raids and such.

All of those who were gathered in this cavern were clustered upon three upraised platforms, where tables, chairs, and bars were set up. Musicians and a dancer girl in a revealing costume held the attention of those on the lowest of these, and there were similar things going on above them on the other two. The apparently muffled sounds of battle in the caverns above had not given them cause for alarm at all.

Caspar tapped Percy lightly on the shoulder, pointing to the great wooden beams below the lowest and largest of the platforms. The Gnome nodded; taking these out would destabilize the platforms. But he was reluctant to do so. He found himself wondering if the poor girls were slaves or willing entertainers, and Caspar's sudden change of expression seemed to indicate he was now thinking about that question as well.

"If we take out the platforms, we'll be killing *all* of them." the Gnome whispered furtively. "If those poor creatures are innocents, I'd never forgive myself!"

"Bluff them." Kia Re said, taking up three of the explosive devices and striding out boldly into the hall before they could stop her. "Hail,

234

murderers!" she called out, and all of them turned to face her and her companions, who came up behind her. "Set free those you have taken as slaves, or die together in vain!" she said as she held aloft one of the devices.

"And what, pray tell, is that, that we should fear your words, wench?" one of them called out. She tossed it into a pile of barrels, and it exploded loudly, destroying the pile of them. The raiders gaped and stared in fear, and their slave-girls screamed in terror.

"Surrender!" Caspar ordered. The scantily-clad women needed no second bidding; they all raced down to the ground and then out the door past the companions, while the angered raiders began taking up arms.

"You think you're so clever! You got this far, and you've made a right mess of our 'ome like as not, but it ends here!" one of them said.

"Fight fair!" a second called out.

"Aye, no more tricks!" a third added as he took up a crossbow.

"This is no trick." Caspar said as he and Kia Re held aloft several of the explosives. "This is a trap." he added, and they tossed the things towards the great beams; in moments the platforms came tumbling down in heaps as the caverns were shaken again, and those raiders that survived the devastation resigned themselves to surrender.

Twelve had survived out of fifty-nine. Ji Mao was sent back up to report to the War-host, and after an hour's time a troop had been sent to aid in searching the caverns more thoroughly, and to collect the prisoners. Caspar and his friends spent the time diligently searching through the wrecked caverns, but found no hint of the crown. They questioned one of those they had captured, and he sneered at them.

"Clear out the caverns, save the prisoners, reclaim the treasures-- pah! Pathetic fool. The crown's not here. Jynax has it. Just you try and take it from him!" he said, and was then led away by one of their allies. The companions descended from the great hall down to the last part of the caverns, the underground lake with its subterranean harbor; here they found several small sail-boats, and they could see daylight at the far end.

"If he's not here, then where is he?" Evelyn wondered.

"The only place he could go would be the lighthouse, if his intent was to stay around this area as an enforcing figure." Percy remarked.

"The lighthouse..." Evelyn frowned.

"There's got to be some sort of trap about it, or some sort of signal to get close to it." Caspar mused, shaking his head as he thought of using the boats.

"Never mind it for now." Percy said with a shrug as he began starting back.

"Never mind it? Never mind it!" Caspar turned to him with exasperation. "What did we do this for, Percy? This was your idea, after all! Are we giving up now?"

"I did not say that--I said never mind it *for now*; where can he go, Caspar? Look at the boats behind you: do you think they would last outside this sheltered bay?" he said to the young man, who looked back at the boats. None of them was larger than twenty feet by Augustan count, and none of them had sails, only oars. "Those are lake-boats, my boy. They are meant for travel in sheltered waters such as these, not the open ocean, nor indeed the more tumultuous churning of the larger Bay of Paupalousas, of which this is only a small inlet indeed. No, my friend; Jynax, as he has been named to us, is quite trapped in the lighthouse. Though I daresay he has the royal navy trapped as well: ancient Gnomish mechanisms stand upon the isle that could incinerate a vessel, and thus the king's wise ban on sea-travel. Jynax knows he cannot get out, and thus he has taken refuge in the one place where he knows he can make it night impossible for others to get out also." the Gnome told him, and Caspar sat down, feeling foolish. Percy smiled gently, coming back to give him a pat on the shoulder before heading back out of the caverns himself, along with Ragya and Ji Mao. Kia Re stood staring at the boats in silence, wondering if they could use them by night to sneak up on the lighthouse, while Evelyn sat next to Caspar. The Valkyrie then let out a "hmm", and turned to come back and stand near them.

"Perhaps they would be of use in our next move, if that move means assailing the isle in this bay." she remarked.

"Perhaps." Caspar nodded. "Right now, Percy's right: we can let him be for now." he said as he got up; Evelyn rose up as well, and the three of them departed the caverns to catch up with their friends.

When at last they returned to camp, they found that the prisoners (totaling twenty and three altogether) had been secured in a newly constructed wooden hut near the central camps, and that those who had been freed from the caverns were being cared for with diligence. Little had gone on about the main fields of the siege; indeed, the cavern raid had been the highlight of the day, as far as battle went. A few ranged skirmishes with guards on the walls had come and gone, but little else; one of the catapults had (again) smashed open the dungeons, and the city was in an uproar, insofar as they could tell.

It quieted down for certain in the late evening, and they could see the guards tying more naked bodies to the walls. The king had indeed lost his mind, but the guards seemed more reluctant than usual in their task; indeed, they could swear to hearing the sound of weeping as they went about their grisly task, and began to feel some measure of pity for those within the walls of Auschternople.

**

Later that evening, a sound of unfamiliar horns was heard. From the west, a small host was approaching; there were five banners born aloft under the light of moons and stars. One was the banner of Riverdell; the second and third were the signets of the Gnomish Diplomatic Corps and the Gnomish Guild of Intercultural Relations, respectively; the fourth was that of Murana Day; and the fifth was the royal insignia of Alastria.

The newly arrived hosts settled in for the night at a respectful distance, but in the morning their representatives came forth to greet their counterparts; the companions were summoned to this meeting, on account of Percy's and Evelyn's peoples being two of those now gathered on the field, and Evelyn flushed as she caught sight of the now King Thadolin with his queen; Mala was with them, and the matriarch raised her eyebrows as she caught sight of her prodigal standing with her lover hand-in-hand. The two Gnomish Guilds greeted Percy with great amiability, and the Earl Jeremias and Hannah his daughter, along with Abbot Geron, came to greet Evelyn, unknowingly shaming the Elves for their lack of greeting her. Evelyn, however, knew it perfectly well, and gave Thadolin a sly smile as the king now flushed in humiliation; he and Mala then came to greet her, and the matriarch more willingly than the king.

"Thou hast thy dreams, I see, and what what hast it cost thee?" she asked softly.

"Nothing that I would not gladly pay again, dear Mala." Evelyn told her, and Mala let a great smile come to her face. As long as Evelyn was confident in the choice she had made, that was all she cared for. As greetings and introductions were being finished, General Frigund invited their new guests to the great pavilion; they graciously accepted, and the company then made their way to the place in question, where they were all given a seat in a wide circle. This was done by the rule of Gnomish diplomatic standards, which required all parties to be given an equal voice and stature in such functions as these. It was a time-honored tradition, and one they could all agree was a fitting practice, for the six races had not had such a meeting for many a thousand years; and now here they all were, gathered together before the very gates of the city that most held to have caused their division to begin with. This ironic setting was remarked upon by the Elves, and the Valkyries laughed in agreement.

"Well," General Frigund began, "here we all are. I do not claim preeminence at this setting, but I will say that this venture you have come to is an agreed course of action settled upon by mine king and the Valkyrie Queen Dana. I would therefore submit the question as to why these new arrivals have come, and for what purpose?" he said, and the Werecat leader, Oga, nodded at this.

"It is a very strange thing to see our friends of the forest coming forth from their realm at last," he added, "and I do not doubt some great purpose behind it."

"News of your plans travelled faster than thou didst, General Frigund." King Thadolin told him. "We hath come forth, agreeing by general council ourselves, to see if we cannot aid in this venture and so bring a final end to the menace of Augusta." he said, and one of those from the party of Murana Day gave him a look.

"Diplomatically, as I might hope." one of the Gnomish ambassadors put in. "Violence you have had in good measure, so I have heard and seen from yonder bodies on the walls; should we not give them opportunity to surrender?"

"They hath made their choice." Briana said darkly. "The Mad King will not hear sense. It is by his whim that bodies are hung naked from the walls of his own city to dishearten us and his own people. He deserves only death!"

"Aye, and there is no remaining royalty of Augusta to treat with in such matters." the Dwarven General remarked with a shake of his head. Percy then coughed.

"Not quite true, General Frigund. If I may?" he began, and the diminutive scholar was allowed to step forward into the center of the ring. "I had a feeling a discussion of this type would be soon coming, and therefore I brought along some relevant documentation. Now," he continued as he set the book open to the correct page and laid his parchments in order just beside it, "As all or at least most of you know, some eleven-hundred years past, a cousin of the Augustan Royal family managed to depose them, and sent them into exile." he said, and they nodded at this.

"Well, the family did not die out. Indeed they thrived in peasantry, and they were quite fond of farming, judging from the records I have found. They eventually found their way down to the lands about Murana Day, where, though the nobleness of their family had been forgotten, the names were not. Indeed, we have an unbroken line of succession all throughout those eleven centuries." he said, tapping the table that held the book and his parchments.

"Are you saying there is yet a member of the original royal family, long obscured by time, that stands alive to treat with us?" Thadolin said as he rose from his chair. "And why should we not hold them hostage, bidding the one who sits on their throne to come forth and make his amends under threat?"

"Fool Elf, do you think that this Mad King, as he has been called, will act in any sense whatsoever to anything we say, save for the possibility of holding a sword to his own neck?" Mala said to him, and Thadolin sat back down at the chiding words. "Pray continue, Master Gnome. I would hear thy conclusions." she then said, and Percy resumed.

"As I said, the line of the original family was uninterrupted, just as the usurpers went on in unbroken succession. Content in their lowly status, they soon forgot all about being noble, but there were indeed meticulous family records, which marvelously and miraculously escaped being incinerated twenty years ago. These records were sent to the crown but lately, and those faithful and meticulous scholars in the Hall of Records transposed what was sent to them, adding it to what they had, to reveal this uninterrupted lineage. This leads me in to the identity of the current heir." Percy said, and Caspar took a deep breath as Evelyn took his hand. "Although in the presence of my companions this individual has had the identity of his father obscured, there is no question as to the identity of his mother and her own parents, who are the last two generations recorded in this book." Percy continued. "This lady is named as Miri, who was the daughter of one Rowland and his wife Giselle, who passed away five years ago. Miri was slain by the Demonic Hordes, and her husband Caspian with her. Their son was left orphaned, and he was taken in by the Order of Cassandra at Murana Day, and later worked for one Farmer Wells of Idoma. His name is Caspar, and he sits before you with the Princess Evelyn, who has claimed him as her own betrothed for life." the Gnome finished, and those in the pavilion turned in surprise to the young man. Caspar did not flinch from their looks, but his heart was troubled. What would they do?

"And what would this obscured heir of a disgraced kingdom speak of on behalf of his people, should he chose to claim his inheritance at the fall of the current king?" Thadolin asked darkly.

"I do not seek to rule." Caspar said in reply.

"Lies!" Thadolin retorted, jumping up again. "All humans seek power--thou art no different than any of thy greediest ancestors!"

"You insult us, friend, whose realm lies but a week's journey from our own." the Earl said, and Thadolin looked at him darkly.

"Humans brought the Great Invasion upon us; we paid for the sins of Augusta, not our own!" Thadolin insisted.

"You incestuous Elves were never much better. Every time there was a problem it was somehow everyone else's fault!" a Dwarf challenged.

"Peace!" one of the Gnomes called out. "We are *not* here to exchange insults, we are here to decide the fate of a kingdom!"

"Kill the king and the young man: that is my decision!" Thadolin said at once.

"We should not usher in what we hope to be an era of peace with bloodshed!" his wife said to him.

"I agree with these words." Oga nodded. "Your wife is wiser than thou, friend."

"Ha!" a Dwarf chuckled; it was well known that, among Dwarves, calling a woman wiser than a man was a great insult--and a great mockery. Thadolin, who also knew this, gave the Dwarf a baleful look as he sat down.

"This man is different." Kia Re said softly, and all eyes turned to her. "His heart is pure as new-fallen snow; he knows neither guile nor deceit, only love; he knows naught of mockery, and does not give insult or abuse to those around him; he is as patient as the unchanging mountain, wiser than the oldest sage, gentler than the meekest lamb, yet stronger than the boldest lion. He may be one in a thousand, one in ten-thousand, or even one in a thousand-thousands, but he is different than any man I have ever heard tell of; he cares not for himself, but as his calling of a minstrel leads him to inspire others with songs of hope, so he does with his life, working to try and inspire peace and unity, never seeking for himself but always seeking to give of himself so that others might know peace." she said, tears brimming in her eyes as she spoke. Though none but the other Valkyries gathered about could feel the full sentiment of her words, they all knew that her praise was not lightly given, whose race seldom reveled in any achievements but their own. The Elven King Thadolin gazed at Caspar in new wonder, wondering indeed how he had won the love and loyalty of the fiery mountain maiden. *The same way he did with Evelyn, no doubt.* Thadolin thought to himself.

"By the Hammer of Gos, a Valkyrie giving praise to a mortal man..." Frigund said with a shake of his head. "What a time to be alive!"

"And who shall deny these words, spoken as if in love?" Briana said to them. "Our love and loyalty is not lightly given. This young man has earned her respect, and for that he has mine." she added as Mala stood up.

"This young man has also won the heart of she who should have been our queen by all the Elven customs of law and tradition. She has forsaken them for him, seeking to win his heart as surely as he won hers, all for the sake of a dream, as she told me. The old wounds that Augusta gave to our two peoples I consider as healed by the joining of these three in their fellowship." the matriarch said, and Briana inclined her head.

"Your words are well spoken." the Battle Sage of the Valkyries said.

"And let us not forget this our fellow Gnome who has so valiantly argued his case!" one of the other Gnomes put in. "We are an amicable people by nature, but not even a Gnome will make so fast a friend without good reason. And are not even men, whom we get on with fairly well most of the time, renowned for their mockery of us at times?" he added, and they all agreed that this was so. "Yet I see this my fellow Gnome putting forth a case for one whom he seems to think of as a friend more than a colleague-in-arms, as one might say."

"And he has the friendship of a Werecat." Oga said with a nod.

"And of me." Ji Mao said, coming to stand behind Caspar with Ragya.

"A Weishuune? By the trees and hills, all those races unjustly treated by Augusta are here!" the Gnome remarked, "And one of each stands behind this young man for love or for the sake of comradery."

"As for myself," Ragya said, "I swore my fheas to Evelyn; she has betrothed herself to this young man, and for that my fheas extends to him and to my other companions here, and their heirs, for as long as I walk the world."

"That, too, is not lightly given." one of the other Valkyries noted with awe.

"But see now! Let us examine the proofs." one of the other Gnomes put in. "I do not doubt the research of our fellow Gnome, as all Gnomish scholasticism is thorough, but let us be thorough ourselves." she said, coming up to the table with several others from around the ring of chairs, including Mala, who knew well the history of Augustan nobility. She confirmed the first four generations of exiles was an accurate recording, and two of those from Murana Day gave confirmation as to the rest of them.

"These records are known by all the officials in our dukedom by the sea." one of them said, "But are rarely recalled to memory, as those recorded were, as the Gnome suggested, content in their status as simpletons instead of bearing the weight of a kingdom. We let them in peace, and they indeed prospered until the final generations before the invasion. I did not know that Rowland and Giselle had passed away; they would confirm these records, as my father and grandfather both knew them well, and had many a long discussion about family histories." the lady said. "You look like your grandfather, Caspar son of Miri." she said with a smile, and Caspar smiled back.

"Then I need no further confirmation than that." Frigund nodded. "We indeed have the true heir of Augusta with us. And what, I ask, is his will for this kingdom? Will he take up his throne to rule justly? Or will he do otherwise?" the general asked, giving him a keen look as they all sat back down. Now Caspar rose up, glancing about uneasily as he was unused to attention (save for when he was singing); he looked around at all those watching him, and shook his head.

"No." he began softly, and they exchanged glances with each other, wondering at the word. "In this city before us there is a seer; hear his words to me: 'the hope needed is not the hope wanted. And though this city will go on, its monarch may not. His crown is gone. Find it, and unravel the last threads of Augustan tyranny: or give it back to him, and let the city erupt in a wave of violence to make the Great Invasion peaceful in comparison. Shall they die in a violent death, or shall they make a new order from the fading ashes of what is left to them?'--those within the city hope for a better king; that is their dream, but this man implied to me that as long as there is a king, tyranny will go on, and I will not rise above what I consider my station to continue this legacy." Caspar continued.

"Though there is only one thing that will bring the Mad King to heel: his crown has been stolen, and if this is found, he may well recover from his madness just enough so that we may treat with him as a man and not a beast." he added.

"What! Give it back to him? But you said--" Thadolin started in a splutter of words, quickly cut off by the young man.

"I did not say give it back: I said find it." Caspar said in reply.

"Yes, yes! I see!" the Earl exclaimed. "The mere sight of the crown may recall to him his senses, and we may well get him back to the grounds of negotiating."

"Insanity is a strange beast." the Elven King nodded. "Perhaps this idea has merit."

"And what will we do, should we succeed in doing this?" Oga wondered.

"Yes, what indeed? What shall the last heir of Augusta do with the crown, aside from tantalizing his distant kin with it?" Abbot Geron remarked.

"I will shatter it." Caspar said, and they all gasped.

"What!" Percy exclaimed, aghast at the words.

"That crown, though a symbol of folly and wickedness, is a priceless relic!" Frigund said. "It was forged at the beginning of the Age of Kings by our greatest smith of the time: do you mean to shatter something that has withstood the ages of time?"

"And would you not shatter the last grip of sanity that this king has?" Oga wondered.

"How else to unravel the last threads of Augustan tyranny so that something new may come?" Caspar said to them, and to that they had no answer. "It has been said that Augusta is a dying lion; let it die, therefore, and let something new rise from its ashes! That is my will for this kingdom, and it seems indeed one of the few ways to end this siege peacefully."

"One can do that without shattering the crown." the lady from Murana Day told him. "There are long-forgotten clauses in Augustan Law that lend themselves to a situation such as this; my colleague beside me, and several of these good Gnomes may know of what I speak, for I do not know it by heart." she said, turning to the man in question, who nodded as he looked over at one of the Gnomes.

"Good fellow, aid my memory; but if I recall the exact words, they say thus: 'in the event of there being no legal or willing claimant to the throne of Augusta, including cousins up to the eleventh degree, then the kingdom shall pass to a general council until such time as a monarch can be installed from a lesser family'--is that not what it says?" the man said to one of the Gnomes next to him.

"Certainly there are no cousins left; Duke Melchior had no children, never mind the fact that in the past five centuries the Augustan monarchs did away with all but their closest relatives, as far as they could determine." the Gnome said. "And as to your memory, it is quite right. A council is to be established, drawn from all walks of life in the city: merchants, farmers, workers, and all others considered as 'peasants' by the statutes of Augustan feudalism; the captains of the armies, navies, and the cavalry must be present, and the Master of the Tower with his council must also be there. In theory, this council could rule for an indefinite time, and there need never be a monarch again."

"A Council of Burgesses." the Earl nodded. "In Riverdell I rule alongside a similar sort of council."

"Then could not this young man rule in harmony with such a council?" one of the Elves suggested.

"He has already said he wishes not for power; ascending to the throne in any such way would prove him false." a Dwarf returned.

"Then we must at least take thought for where the crown is." the Elf returned as Caspar sat back down.

"Indeed." a Gnome agreed.

"But in the meantime might we not give this current king cause for doubt?" Briana said to them, and Frigund gave her a knowing look.

"What? As in announcing that we have our own Augustan King who challenges the legitimacy of his reign?"

"Say rather that we have him, and that as he comes from the truer lineage, the people in the city may revolt against Michael to surrender to us without needing the crown as proof. It is only the king who would need to see it, is it not?" she wondered.

"Do you forget that such claims only mean things to those of Auschternople with proof, whether noble or not?" Frigund reminded her.

"Still, if announcing his lineage would give them cause to revolt, should we not do so?"

"Nay." Hannah shook her head. "They will be stubborn unless there is proof; I have seen it." she added, and with that the delegation from Riverdell was convinced.

"We must get the crown." her father said.

"And where do we look, hm?" a Dwarf asked him. "We searched that hell-hole of a cavern top to bottom and found no crown."

"It's at the lighthouse." Caspar said, and they turned to him again. "The raiders' leader Jynax has it with him at the lighthouse, and Jynax has a sorcerer of some sort there with him."

"Augusta is crumbling indeed if a petty raider can seize the lighthouse!" Briana said with a laugh. "Magic-user or no, it would take treachery for an enemy to capture the lighthouse, or so all the stories say."

"The stories are true." the older man from Murana Day nodded. "Not even those of the Demonic Hordes could seize the lighthouse; not even the dragons could near it. I remember well that siege, where I lost my three sons and their sister fair." he said with a shake of his head.

"Well then if a petty raider can seize the lighthouse, surely this long-lost son of kings can take it back." Thadolin sniffed. He allowed for the legitimizing credentials of lineage, and he could plainly see the effect of love and loyalty that surrounded Caspar, but it did not lessen his opinion of the young man. The Elven pride in him was too strong.

"Your words are of darkness, and darkly given." a Valkyrie said to him with a glare. "He would be well within his rights to challenge you for such a slight."

"Hast he then another mountain maiden lusting for his chambers?" Thadolin quipped, and the Valkyries, including Kia Re, all rose up, as did the Elves, save for Thadolin and his queen.

"Take it back, leaf-spawn!" Briana spat at him.

"Better a leaf than a fallen flake of snow from the mountains!" Thadolin returned as he stood up.

"Your pride damns you, Thadolin!" Evelyn called over to him. "I cannot believe that the one who let me go willingly instead of raising alarm in the village would stoop to such low insults at a gathering of peace!" she said, and Mala looked at Thadolin in outrage and surprise.

"What is this!" she said in exclamation. Thadolin raised his hands at once to her with a stern look, and she subsided.

"Let me fight him for honor and glory, and we shall see whether or no the fallen angels are truly weaker than these wilting flowers!" the insulted Valkyrie called over.

"All of you to a woman forsaking immortality for love of mortals! Pah!" another Elf sniffed.

"In the name of--halt this at once! We have standards to adhere to!" a Gnome called.

"This was a mistake, trusting Gnomish diplomacy over our own laws!" the Elven King shook his head.

"Your laws cry for the death of anyone who so much as spits at you!" Frigund said to him darkly, and the king glared at the general. "The Gnomes are revered and respected for their tact: not so the Elves! Unless it is in dealing with their own kind, and not even then, as I can guess from the words of the Princess!"

"This council is fast coming to blows!" Ji Mao whispered to Ragya, who blinked.

"Indeed." he murmured back.

"Why, you--" Thadolin began as he stormed towards the general, but upon a sudden he was knocked to the ground by a strong hand; bewildered, he looked up to see Caspar standing over him.

The young man had a sword drawn, and he indeed looked the image of a king, despite his humble cloth. Caspar raised the sword to eye-level, pointing around the pavilion with it until they all sat down; Thadolin quickly headed back to his seat, suddenly afraid of the young man. When they were all quiet once more, Caspar sheathed the sword, and shook his head.

"Is this the grace of the Elves?" he said to Thadolin and his followers, who flushed in humiliation at the words. "Is this the strength of the Valkyries?" he then turned to Briana and her warriors, who exchanged glances of embarrassment. "Is this the honor of the Dwarves?" Caspar then said to Frigund, who bowed his head in shame, as did his followers. "And the rest of you--what is this council to you? Does it mean nothing? Was it merely in gesture that you came, or did you mean to accomplish something by joining together?" he asked them all, and they all looked at each other, searching the faces of their nominal allies as they tried to think of an answer. "If you have heard anything today, I would think you should recall the words of my friend, who is also my battle-sister; unity comes from understanding and from compassion, not from holding on to anger or judgments." he told them, and Evelyn came to stand beside him.

"You sit here accusing Augusta of that which you are still doing yourselves!" she said to add to his words.

"And a mighty fine heir you yourselves make to the legacy of pain."

Kia Re said as she too came to stand beside him.

"I do not believe this council is here by chance." Ragya added as he came forward to join his friends with Ji Mao and Percy. "We are brought together for a purpose, and unless we wish to see the unraveling of all our lands, we must bear patiently with each other. There is still an enemy greater than either Augusta or these raiders--and he will not be so easily quelled."

"These are not mere years, or decades, or even centuries of prejudice to overcome. But they can be overcome." Caspar told them. "What would you have? Friends to look to if the dark tides come again? Or would you burn all alone, holed up in some forgotten part of the world as you yourselves are forgotten?" he asked them. The six companions looked at their audience for a moment longer, and then returned to their seats. No one said anything for a long time.

Then, King Thadolin stood up, drew his sword, and went to place it on the table. Briana did the same with her spear, and Frigund laid his hammer next to theirs. Oga the Werecat laid his twin-blades near these, and Earl Jeremias laid his own sword upon the table. The Chief Gnome sat his small dirk upon it as well, and with that, those around the pavilion began clapping as their respective leaders began making peace with one another. Content with their actions, the companions slipped out as the discussions turned to the drafting of alliances, and began planning their own adventures.

"We still have a lighthouse to raid." Kia Re said as they neared their ship.

"But we cannot get there in this ship." Percy reminded her.

"Then let us take one of those in the caverns by night, and so surprise them." she said.

"I can see well enough by the lights of the night to row or to steer us there." Ragya told them.

"And what of Auschternople?" Evelyn wondered. "What will we do with them when we have the crown?"

"We will grant them the mercy they denied to others." Caspar said, and with that they boarded the ship, preparing themselves for the next stage of what they now knew for certain was their quest. This, they deemed, would be their last act in Auschternople, and perhaps even Argorro itself; whatever else awaited them, it lay across the seas.

Chapter Nine: The Last Vestige

The companions spent the rest of their afternoon aboard their stolen--
or, as Kia Re preferred to say, "liberated" caravel, making careful plans
for their moves against the lighthouse. Percy, with one of the spyglasses
from the cabin, was examining the site from the crow's nest; he
carefully made note of what he could see, and formulated what he
considered reasonable speculations as to what he could not see. There
were two of the long canoes drawn up near the pier, and a path led up
to the lighthouse itself, diverging partway to head off to another
building, a small house on the southeast corner of the islet. As to the
lighthouse itself it was fairly tall, reaching a height of nearly one-
hundred and ten feet by the Augustan Measure; there were six visible
flying buttresses that gave support to it, and Percy could reasonably
conclude that there were two more on the far side. At its crowning
height stood the ancient but well-kept mirrors that reflected light out
into the bay, and, as Percy knew well, there were seven Gnomish
devices at intervals about the isle that were capable of launching a
breath of flame against an incoming enemy ship. These had most likely
not been used for some time, and he hoped that, in the interval, their
workings had been forgotten. *Perhaps not all so very likely, but there
we are; and I daresay that even the threat of their being there keeps
sober-minded sailors from venturing out,* the Gnome thought to
himself. *Best we approach in darkness all the same. Aside from that
they don't seem to know how to light the great-beacon at its height.*

When the Gnome had finished his meticulous observations later in
the afternoon he came back down, and at once set to work on refining
his stratagems and diagrams. Ragya, who had also been observing the
islet in his own spare time, lent Percy a hand with this, and by the time
the sun was going down they had all agreed on their course of action
regarding their planned attack. They geared up for battle once more,
and softly headed back to the caverns. It was an emptier series of
caverns they came across this time, for the war-host had reclaimed a
great deal from its holdings. All the wreckage and carnage had been
brushed off to the sides, but as yet a scent of death, never mind the

lingering tang of sulfur, still filled the air. They quickly descended to the lowest cavern, and loaded themselves and their gear into one of the boats. Evening had now come in strength, and the lingering shadows cast by light of sun had gone. The four moons and the stars now shone dimly above in the night; and to their benefit and disadvantage both, clouds were coming in from the south to cover the land in a fuller darkness. Benefit, because it would truly obscure them from watchful eyes; disadvantage, because the night-eyes of Ragya would be hard put to keep their course straight.

Not minding this, they rowed out anyway. They floated for a few moments until the Werecat was certain of their direction, and then Ji Mao and Percy were set to the task of holding the tiller steady while the other four used the oars to row them softly towards the islet. As they rowed away from the mainland, they could discern the fires and camp-lights of the war-host burning brightly in the night; hopefully, negotiations had not soured during the day. Caspar shook his head softly; was that not a likely possibility? But then, hopefully, his actions and those of his friends had made more impact on the council than they fully knew. It might not happen overnight, but a beginning had to be made somewhere. Perhaps indeed the pride of isolationists like the Elves was willing at last to bend just enough so that this beginning could bear fruit. His thoughts strayed over to Evelyn, and as he looked over to where she sat beside him, he knew she was thinking of him also, for she too was smiling over at him. The night was on their mind, the night of passion and of love's ultimate expression, and it took a cough from Kia Re behind them to startle them back to the task at hand. The Valkyrie smirked softly to herself as they began rowing in rhythm again, and Ragya shook his head softly, a faint amusement upon his features. In this way, they reached the small islet of the lighthouse in the half of an hour or so, their slow and steady course accurate to the last King's Inch.

As Percy had explained at various points during the day (here recounted in an orderly fashion), a lighthouse of some sort or fashion had always been posted on the islet in what was now known as King's Bay, originally known as Titan's Cove. Its earliest incarnation was a great beacon that had its heyday in the Age of Dawning Light; by the Age of Kings, this had progressed to the more sophisticated lighthouse, and when Augusta was in its prime it had been rebuilt to its current state. The Gnomish devices used in defense of the bay had been specially ordered, and had taken the Gnomes the better part of five decades to complete. During the Great Invasion, not even the Demonic hordes could seize the thing, as they had already heard once before; but in the aftermath of the invasion much that was secure fell into the hands of the wicked and the mischievous, and so it was with the lighthouse. Now the companions intended to reclaim it, hoping that their silent attack was as close to treachery as needed to seize the ancient thing.

No lights were lit in either the lighthouse or the smaller house next to it, and as far as Ragya could see, there was no one out and about. It was not cold, but the night air was cool, and so perhaps lent itself to keeping the brigands indoors. And for what, after all, did they have to be worried about? It was a clouded night, and a fog was rising up on the bay; who in their right mind would be boating at this time? But they neither knew of nor reckoned of this little band of friends, audacious perhaps in their antics but also determined. They tied their boat to the pier on the south side of the islet, and softly crept up the path to the little house first of all. There was a window on the east side; they peered in, and saw inside several sleeping brigands and three women locked in a cage. A fireplace was visible on the north wall of the house. Percy then had Ragya hoist him on to the roof; the little Gnome softly scrabbled towards the chimney, and carefully lowered himself down while his companions went around to the door. Thankfully there was no fire lit; the ashes were cold indeed, and the scent of smoke faint.

Percy slipped towards the door without anymore noise than a mouse might make, and softly unlocked the door. In came the companions. Ropes and good cloth they found, and with these they swiftly bound and gagged their prisoners. In but a few minutes, the raiders were the prisoners, and the three women set free of their cages. These three told them of more women being held in the lighthouse itself, and also that there was indeed a sorceress among the ranks of the raiders. They in turn were told to wait at the house, and when the companions were implored to stay it was decided that Percy should remain with them. The Gnome assented to this, and his five friends then softly made their way up to the lighthouse. Ji Mao then silently picked the lock open, and they headed inside.

On this ground floor, the lighthouse was empty except for shelves of books and a few chairs and tables scattered about. Some of the books looked to have been mangled, singed, or otherwise disrespected, and there were empty bottles of who-knew-what lying about, some oozing the last remains of their contents as they lay on their sides, some lying in pieces on the floor, and some having taken the place of the books on the shelves. A narrow, iron-wrought stairwell was in the center of the room. It led up and down; Ji Mao, being the lightest of them, was selected to go and scout the downstairs. She did so, and found that there were nine more women being held prisoner; one of them seemed as if with child, and four of them had babies cradled next to them. When Caspar heard this he strode down softly but angrily, and the others followed after them. There were only five guards, who were hastily tied up and secured in a closet; Ji Mao then brought their freed captives out of the lighthouse and to where the others were waiting before rejoining her companions as they began their ascent.

It was a long, long stair indeed; Ragya could barely fit, and he softly growled at this but kept on determinedly nonetheless. They halted for a brief moment when they were three-quarters of the way up, and spoke in soft tones to each other about their progress. "This seems almost too easy." Caspar remarked in a soft tone.

"I agree." Ragya said. "There must be some sort of trap ahead."

"If not merely the presence of the sorceress herself?" his friend returned.

"If not merely that, indeed." the Werecat agreed.

"Perhaps some of us should go back down and look around the islet to see if they've more about?" Caspar suggested.

"Indeed. I should go; I cannot abide these closed stairs any longer!" Ragya said.

"I'll follow you, friend." Kia Re nodded.

"The two of us will be enough. Caspar, you, Evelyn, and Ji Mao should be fine on your own--but beware this sorceress!" Ragya said, his eyes looking up at the young man intently. "You have seen my power, but it is of the earth; and you have seen Evelyn's, but she is as yet newly trained. This one above us may be a master, or they may not: but either way you must never, ever underestimate a magic-user." he said with soft but firm emphasis, and Caspar nodded back. The Werecat and Valkyrie then headed back down the winding stairwell, and the other three resumed their ascent.

***

As Ragya and Kia Re hastily exited from their quick descent, they softly nodded to each other to search in opposite directions, carefully seeking any tell-tale signs that might confirm all was not as it seemed. Ragya went to the boats, and found that all three remained as yet tied to the pier. Kia Re looked to the house; Percy was chattering on about something, and the women were eagerly listening, grateful for someone who would talk to them instead of using them. On a sudden impulse she knocked for them, and told Percy their fears; the Gnome agreed that it was a bit convenient, and he also agreed to take one of the boats and head back to shore. They found the Werecat still at the pier when they arrived, and he nodded at this counsel.

"Go quickly, master scholar." he said, and when the Gnome and the women had set off across the bay for the shore the other two again began their rounds. Kia Re then flung herself down, and Ragya flopped beside her at once. There were shadowy forms rising up from an unmarked door in the earth between the lighthouse and the small house, and they were heading for the lighthouse.

"We must distract them." Kia Re said, and Ragya nodded quickly. "Valheilen!" she shouted out in challenge, raising her spear for attack as her words grabbed their attention. "For the Mountains!" she called out again, and their assailants, revealed as flesh and blood by a fireball from the Werecat, began fighting for their lives against the two companions.

***

Caspar and the others had just made it to the top when Kia Re's voice rang out below; all, indeed, was not as it had seemed, and there had been some sort of trap--now foiled by the vigilance of their companions. They nodded softly to each other, and exited the stairwell to find themselves in an oil-chamber below the main fixture of the lighthouse; not a sound could be heard but the sounds of battle far below them. On the north side of this room was a staircase leading up to the fixture. There were three sleeping forms at its base. Or, at least, they had *been* sleeping.

"Hrmph... 'sat? Hear it?" one of them murmured, blinking awake as the sound of battle stirred them.

"Urf... what the--hey! Below!" a second suddenly shouted. "We're under attack here! Jynax!" he shouted, and the three companions reacted instantly. Ji Mao tossed her dagger at one, catching him in the forehead; Evelyn blew one out the window with a blasting spell, and with a terrible scream he fell far to the ground. Caspar tripped the third as he reached the stairs, and the poor fool tumbled down their length to the very basement of the lighthouse. A sound now came from above, the sound of a woman shouting harshly and receiving a harsh answer in reply. Her partner in arguing was, they presumed, Jynax, and they heard the door open as heavily booted feet descended the stairs. The man himself had obviously been ordered down, which Evelyn took as odd; human males were not usually so compliant with their females. Jynax was nearly as tall as Ragya, and broad of frame.

"So." the man himself said as he caught sight of the dead bodies. "We have intruders, do we? Well, I know the tune for intruders. Won't be but a minute, lady." he called upstairs.

"Shut your braggart mouth and kill them, fool!" the woman's retort came.

"Yeah, yeah..." Jynax shrugged, drawing out his sword. Caspar, sensing the man's pride was at a state where he might boil over in rage, at once began taunting him.

"So, the leader of the raiders; mighty Jynax, the orchestrator of Augustan ruin, being ordered about by a woman." he said, and Jynax glared at him darkly. Evelyn bit her lip to stop laughing, but Ji Mao looked at her friend in concern. Jynax was not one to taunt lightly.

"And you are?" the man asked him.

"A merry minstrel making many mischievous mockeries of mayhem's master." the younger man returned wittily.

"Oh-ho, minstrel, is it?" Jynax raised an eyebrow. "You'll be singing a different tune when I'm through with you--I'll make lute-strings out of your own guts and make you play them!"

"And a merry tune will sound forth from it, I'm sure!--about as merry as your own self is right now, taking cues for battle from someone who's got you over a barrel. Do you massage her at night as well? Or did we interrupt the night's ritual?" Caspar quickly returned, leaping out of the way as the man charged him; the sword he intended to take off Caspar's head with clanged loudly against one of the oil pots, almost wrenching it from his hand. A nice dent was made in it, and he swung again, missing once more; the force of his swing carried him into a twirl, and he reeled from the motion. "Tut-tut! This is a sword fight, sirrah, not a ballet!" Caspar called over.

"Stand still, dammit!" Jynax thundered as he rushed the young man again. Just in time he saw a dagger whirling for his head; he ducked down, and the thing lodged itself in one of the beams. He looked over to see Ji Mao vanishing from sight, and too late he turned back to Caspar, who slashed him hard on the cheek before Jynax could manage to start parrying his attacks.

"By thunder!" the man roared. They fenced back and forth, and then Caspar managed to trip him up a bit; he tipped one of the empty cauldrons over so that it covered his head, and pounded loudly upon it. When he had done with this little trick, the raiders' leader stumbled about, angry and very frazzled from the experience. "Mmf! Garn! Ears... ringing... damn... boy!" he stammered out, and a dagger sliced him on the other cheek as it whirled by. "Yeargh!" he said as he finally regained his balance, and then rushed over to the young Weishuune girl. She dove out of his way, and her Elf friend tipped a full cauldron over so that the man slipped once more. He fell down on his back with a thunk, now quite sick and dizzy from the ordeal.

> *Jynax! Jynax! Lost his feet and lost his wits!*
> *Children three, simple we be, content to see*
> *Jynax--Jynax! The raider-king in dire fits!*
> *Here we are, come and see!*
> *The raider-king is a fool indeed!*

Caspar's witty rhymes made the man himself jump up at once, only to slip again, this time full on his face. Ji Mao was laughing now, and Evelyn did not restrain herself either. "Hi now to you, friend fool! Where's the crown?" Caspar asked him.

"Crown? Crown! Be damned to you, boy! You'll not get it from me!" Jynax said as he slowly got back up; he then leaped to a dry part of the floor next to the young man, and Caspar parried his blows with great care as the enraged raider drove him back. Feinting to his right, the younger man then slashed the other's right knee, and Jynax fell back onto the floor. "Garn!" he swore again, grunting as he made another swing; the sword was knocked from his hand by a hefty blow, and Caspar raised his own blade to the man's neck.

"Now, the question again. Where is the crown?" Caspar said as he caught his breath.

"Oh-ho-ho, no; not from me, boy! You've a worse fate if you get through me!" the man said with a sinister chuckle as the other two came up. Jynax then fell back and kicked the young man's legs out from under him, and then quickly got back up, seizing Ji Mao as he ran to jump out the window with her. The young girl shrieked, and just in time Evelyn caught hold of her. But Jynax also held on, clutching at her belt. Hanging precariously from the heights of the lighthouse, the young girl tried not to look down as she kept her focus on Evelyn's eyes.

"That's it, keep looking at me!" Evelyn said soothingly. Jynax tried pulling harder, but Evelyn's strength was much more than he realized. For Elves, aside from Werecats, Giants, and the Dwarves, were one of the strongest races in the world. Quite accidentally, however, he did loosen the belt; Ji Mao, holding tightly to her friend, kicked back hard several times. He held to his death-grip on her belt despite this, but the belt itself (and the breeches) were pulled off, and he fell to his death as Caspar now managed to get up and help Evelyn hoist their poor friend up.

"That was close!" he remarked as they caught their breath.

"Blanket." Evelyn pointed to the stairs as Ji Mao crossed her legs. Caspar went over, and tossed it to her; she wrapped it around herself, and they then halted to listen carefully. There was no sound from above.

"The crown must be upstairs." Ji Mao said softly.

"Caspar, take her back down; I'll handle this." Evelyn said.

"Did you not hear Ragya!" her lover returned at once. "We can't underestimate her!"

"I am aware of that--and do not you, my love, underestimate me either!" she said in reply.

"You should have listened to your friend." the woman herself said, her voice seductive and chiding at the same time. "Oh, do excuse the wrongful introductions of Jynax and the others. You see, these pitiful fools were only correct to a point--I am not a mere sorceress, I am something far more..." she said as the three of them turned to her; she was beautiful, tantalizingly so, but there was a sickening quality to her being so. Evelyn, her learning in the Tower having been comprised of such creatures, put a name to the one before them at once. It was a succubus. Her pale skin became wholly visible in its pallor as she divested herself; her hair was red, as were her eyes and her lips, and the tips of her breasts were black. She wore now only soft sandals, and even the two girls had trouble concentrating. Caspar was almost under her spell, and her wicked fangs showed forth from her mouth as she licked her lips. "So... young! All of you--and darling, why that poor, patch-worked blanket? You look so much better without it..." the succubus said with an inviting quality, and Ji Mao found herself undoing the blanket, and then undoing her jerkin as this fell to the ground. As soon as the thing had her attention focused on the Weishuune girl, Evelyn's willpower grew much stronger, and she drew her sword; Ji Mao, her jerkin mostly off, suddenly gasped as the thing then turned its attention back to Evelyn, and she reddened. Evelyn now found herself in a contest of wills with the creature, but with her focus renewed the thing had a harder time trying to have its way. "I remained behind all these years, forsaking my kindred for a more... stimulating site of prey... Elves are so luscious and ripe, especially the young ones like you..." the thing began.

"Silence, devil-witch, and fight with honor!" Evelyn said.

"As you desire!" the thing said with a laugh, and with a wave of her hand sent Evelyn flying towards the edge. This snapped Caspar out of his own trance, and he leaped to grasp her hand as their opponent returned her attention to Ji Mao, who was shivering in confusion. "Oh, dear and sweet little girl, don't cover up so; give yourself to me, my darling, my love!" she insisted, and Ji Mao tried to resist as her jerkin fell to the floor next. She stepped back, covering herself as she took deep breaths; the succubus advanced slowly, and began wrapping the girl in an embrace. "There... relax... feel the heat of our bodies as one..." the succubus soothed, and Ji Mao felt her will-power drained. She was about to succumb, but at that moment a blade came up between the breasts of the succubus, who let out a gasping shriek as the sensation of pain rippled through her. The thing reverted to its true form, a rotting corpse of a woman held together only by the dark magics of the abyss. Caspar withdrew his sword, and the succubus crumbled to dust. He then went over to Ji Mao, holding her gently while Evelyn picked the blanket back up to cover her with it.

"I was so... so..." Ji Mao said as she shivered.

"We know." Evelyn said softly, kissing her on the cheek.

"Let's think no more of it." Caspar said, and they agreed to this. They headed up the stairs, and Evelyn had her arm about Ji Mao as they ascended to the final height of the lighthouse. There, just beneath the reflective fixture, was the Crown of Augusta. Caspar picked it up, and tied it to his belt after looking it over. It was certainly ornate, and very tough to the touch; Dwarf-work indeed, Caspar thought to himself as he smiled. The three of them headed back down, and then on an inspiration Caspar took a tinderbox and lit the lighthouse as a signal to all who could see it. Its light illuminated the bay; the king saw it from his palace, the war-host and the council saw it as they gathered outside to see what the light was, and Percy and his charges caught sight of it just as they landed.

"Hmph! The absolute atrocity of that timing!" he grumbled, and several of those with him let out a laugh, the first real laugh they had laughed in weeks, if not months or years. In the meantime his friends slowly gathered back down at the pier on the islet, and exchanged embraces or kisses as the mood took them. None of those raiders who had fought had been captured alive, and they found the man who had been tripped dead in the basement.

"Let us leave this place." Kia Re said as she helped Ji Mao down to the pier.

"And what did we find at the top of the tower?" Ragya wondered to the other two.

"Jynax. We had a falling out with him..." Caspar remarked, and the Werecat gave him a faint smile.

"I saw."

"And there was no sorceress--well, not a *typical* one, anyway..." his friend added.

"What do you mean?" the Werecat asked.

"It was a succubus." Evelyn told him, and his eyes widened as he nodded.

"Then you are fortunate. Few survive such encounters. And I assume that accounts for the blanket?" he added softly, and they nodded back. Getting in to their boat, they set off at once, guided to shore by the lighthouse's radiant brilliance.

It was fully two hours later before the companions were reunited, and in the meantime some of the war-host was sent out to secure the lighthouse and the prisoners. Ragya and Percy attended the ensuing celebration, as did Kia Re, but the others retired to the ship's cabin. Evelyn and Caspar shared the bed with their friend, and the three of them fell asleep as soon as they were all bundled together under the blankets.

General Frigund and Battle Sage Briana looked out over the bay at the lighthouse, and the Dwarf once more fingered the crown in his hands that had been presented to him by Kia Re. "A Dwarf crafted this long ago; it might be fitting if I was the one to hold this before his mad eyes when we call on him." he remarked, and Briana shrugged.

"Perhaps." she said. "In the ironic sense, at least. But a statement would be made if it was either myself or this King Thadolin." she added, and Frigund grunted in agreement.

"There is that. I had not discounted such a thing." he said. "Or, perhaps, we should let family sort it out." he then remarked softly, and Briana raised an eyebrow.

"That would be fitting as well." she agreed, and with that they turned back to the great pavilion. "Let such be decided at the conclusion of tomorrow's council, however that shall turn out." she then suggested, and Frigund nodded, albeit wearily.

"Twenty tons of solid granite--ha! That fool Elf knows less than he thinks about my people. And Granite is nearer to *your* mountains, not the grand marbled halls of Vinduürhaf Mökr! Bah!" he grumbled as he set the crown on the pedestal, leaving their most trusted guards to watch over it.

"It was the original floor material used for the--" another Dwarf put in as the leaders passed him by.

"Oh, be quiet!" Frigund said to him with a weary chuckle, and the other shrugged.

***

"And so a succubus remained behind in Argorro." Percy mused as he and Ragya talked back on the ship. "Most disconcerting, to be sure. There's dragons in Argorro, but they've *been* here. One of the more demonic creatures is a disturbance that needs looking into with scrutiny." he added.

"Perhaps." Ragya remarked. "But for now this one is dead, and perhaps she was all that was left of them."

"One could hope, and hope is almost as rare as Ilax stones these days." the Gnome shrugged.

"Then we are wealthy indeed." the Werecat returned, "For we thrive on it; indeed, we seem to be giving it away as if it were the trinkets of a king."

"True, true." Percy agreed. They continued to other venues of conversation, while in the cabins Kia Re took one of the other rooms for her rest, smiling as she caught her three friends asleep together. Ji Mao certainly seemed to get the short-stick in these escapades. It was good that they all watched over the young girl. She fell asleep just as the lighthouse beacon was put out for the night, and the sounds of the sea followed her in her dreams.

Chapter Ten: White Shores, Black Sea

The sounds of the sea carried Kia Re into a dream of seas; she swam under the mighty depths of the oceans, and saw ancient castles and eldritch creatures. Coral reefs opened up their vast and colored expanses before her, and schools of fish uncountable swam before her as she was swept along in their wake. Ah! The freedom of swimming, unhindered by cloth and raiment as the water, cool and refreshing, rushed along her body like a soothing oil-balm. She reveled in the sensation, wondering if she was awake or dreaming. Up, up, up she swam now, seeking the rays of sunlight that broke upon the surface of the water in hundreds of shining diadems; she surfaced, and the crystal blue of the ocean was before her eyes. Still up she went, and she felt as if she was flying; wings she had, and as she caught sight of herself she saw herself as a bird, a great osprey of the water flying across the sea. Kia Re laughed, but the sound of her voice was as the cry of the bird, and that was not strange to her. That which was strange was, only moments before, she had been a Valkyrie. But what did one have need of beauty that attracted others when one had wings to fly? Ah, the graceful sensation of flying through the air; it was like swimming--yes, she was, in a sense, swimming through the air. Or did she fly under the water? Down she dove, and the bird was shed for her own body once more. There was no need to hold her breath as she swam down, down, and still more down into the depths; was that not strange?

Down and down she continued, until all felt strange and disorienting; then she felt a mighty rushing current propelling her upwards, the force of its tide irresistible. *I only hope I once again emerge as a bird!* Kia Re thought to herself, but it was not to be this time. This time, her legs stuck together, and they became scaled, with a fin taking the place of her feet. She was a mermaid this time? Oh well. From a beautiful female to another beautiful female. How could she complain? And the siren-song emanated from her lips; she rose up from the sea to sit upon a rock, and sang her heart out. The sea was as clear as glass, and she leaped into the air once more to be a bird; through the air she flew again, and the wind carried her far, far away, further than she ever imagined the world could be. What lay beyond the High Seas? Beyond the unexplored parts of their world? Was it flat or round, or some other shape? She could not tell. What she did see was a sea of black; not a murky, foreboding, or disgusting black--more like unto a sea of onyx, or was it obsidian? It was smooth and comely, and its waves lapped up on a white shore, so white that the memory of snow in her mind seemed dirty. She descended to earth again, and was once more her own self, naked and unashamed as she ran about the shore with a laugh. *Where am I?* Kia Re then wondered as she lay upon the beach; a figure was striding towards her: *Caspar!* She thought in recognition; unafraid, she approached him, and their lips met in a kiss. There was no one but them, and there would never be anyone but them. She kissed him, and kissed him, and pulled him down to love him.

On the pearl-white shores near the shining black sea they made love, such a love as had never been before nor would ever be again. *Just love me forever... oh! Forever!* Kia Re thought to herself as she felt the heat rising in her body. With a sweet sensation of pain their passion ended, and they lay caressing each other, kissing each other with tenderness as the passion faded--or did it begin again? She did not know, and she did not care; he was now hers, and she exulted in his touch, his nearness, his embrace; he was all her world.

"I love you." she said.

"I love you." he told her.

"Love me again, and let us go on loving." she begged.

"Always." he said again, and the dream turned; now they were on the heights of a tall tower. Slain enemies lay before them, and before the wide plains overseen by the tower. Kia Re turned; Caspar was lying dead, and she screamed.

"Your love betrayed him to his death." a cold voice spoke; she turned again. It was a tall and foreboding figure in a dark robe.

"Liar!" a familiar voice called out. Evelyn struck at him, but he killed her with a word.

"And you betrayed her as well. Betrayal; adulterous lust; is this the honor you seek to reclaim?" the figure mocked.

Kia Re screamed in anger, and the dream turned again.

An endless wheel turned before her; who was she? What was she? Valkyrie or woman? Warrior or queen? A mermaid, an osprey? Did time have meaning, or was it an illusion? Pangs, sweet pangs, sweet caressing and sweeter kisses; the stirring of passion in its height; sunrises of gold, sunsets of red, and the four moons shining with the endless host of heaven. Now she was standing over the Sorcerer King; he was dead by her hand. She had lost her friends, but Caspar's child grew within her. There was Ji Mao; she had fallen saving Percy. How did she know that? Evelyn was curled up beside Caspar; in death, they would never part again. *How could I betray her so...* Kia Re sobbed to herself.

A wheel turned before her again; forests, jungles, oceans, mountains, prairies, deserts, and all sorts of wondrous, unnamed and innumerable vistas spread out before her, blending in harmony and yet all different. Where was she? Where were her friends?

Death...

Betrayal...

Folly...

Lust...

No!

Kia Re screamed out the word, weeping and weeping as the other four rang in her mind and heart like a bell. "I love him: I will give up everything for him, even my own life! But I will not betray them!" she cried out, touching her growing belly.

Now she stood, and there was no longer a child in her womb. She looked up, and there was Evelyn, nursing a child at her breast. The young one had the same violet eyes as its mother, and golden hair. Was it a boy or a girl? The child fell asleep, and Evelyn kissed her baby as her lover Caspar came over to her. Kia Re felt empty. How could such a--

But the wheel turned once more, and she felt herself rise, truly rise, on angelic wings. She was of heaven's host, and her kindred welcomed her back home.

You fought valiantly, sister. Now rest with us at journey's end in eternal peace; the others will join you in what will seem as no time at all. They said to her, and she believed them. She would wait, patiently, until all her friends were reunited with her. That was a more blessed thing than any she could wish for, even to have Caspar as her own was a pale figment of the mind to the thought of having this instead.

Wake up...

I don't want to.

You are needed... you are loved.

Love me. Feel my heart. Feel my lips upon yours.

Kia Re...

"Caspar!" she gasped as she felt herself lying on the beach again, the height of love's ecstasy reached; the sweet pain was released, and she caught her breath with him as they gently kissed. It wasn't a beach; it was a beach-house, and they were upon its roof, lying on a divan for their pleasure. "What is this place?"

"Whatever you want it to be." he said.

"Where are the others?" she asked him.

"Evelyn is at rest. The others took their leave of us long ago; it's just us three." he told her.

"Ragya wouldn't leave..." she wondered as she kissed him.

"His fheas was fulfilled. He gave his life for us. Percy and Ji Mao are exploring the world; Evelyn's baby is growing, and now we may have another to look forward to." he said, and she smiled, wrapping her legs around him.

"Oh, Caspar..."

"Kia Re...

***

In the early morning hours she awoke. A faint and pale hint of dawn peeped in to her window, and she woke reluctantly. *Why, oh why...* she grumbled to herself as she slowly got up, wrapping a blanket around herself. She cried softly, shaking her head at herself. *Kia Re, you dear, silly girl; you know you'd never forgive yourself for it! And unless by some miracle Evelyn wasn't jesting the other night there's never to be a chance – so forget about it, and focus on being a sister to him... a sister he's seen naked... and almost made love to...*

"Oh, by all the spears of Jotun-De..." she sighed to herself.

"You all right?" Caspar's voice came to her. She turned with a gasp. "Sorry! Didn't mean to frighten you." he said with a laugh.

"No, it's fine!" she said, wrapping herself in the blankets more fully. "You're awake early?"

"I thought I'd surprise us all with breakfast for a change." he said, and she smiled as he continued on his way with his own smile. With a silent groan she laid back down, curling up as she felt a pang to love him. *And kissing a pillow is simply not the same,* Kia Re thought to herself ruefully, and fell back asleep into a dreamless sleep until the full light of dawn roused her a second time from her bed. As she looked out the window she blinked; the shores had seemed white for a brief moment, and the bay had been as black as polished obsidian.

Chapter Eleven: Leo Moritur

The companions ate the first meal of the day with relish, and then sat about on the deck of the ship for most of the morning as they continued talking or finishing off what was left of the food, a small item indeed. Most of it was light conversation meant to cheer their hearts after those several battles they had been fighting for the past week or two, but some of it turned to events that were soon to be at hand, and still more of it turned to wondering what lay ahead--what course would they set together, now that they could indeed set off where they would? Would they head out to another part of Argorro, the large yet mysterious continent they all called home, or was it indeed across the sea they would travel, seeking other lands, other peoples, other trials? Or why seek any trial at all, they wondered; why not settle for finding a land where all their hearts could rest?

"The runes were clear on one thing only," Ragya said softly, "it is our destiny to leave these shores."

"Is the fate of our choice-making, or was it inevitable?" Caspar wondered.

"Such questions are difficult to answer." the Werecat shrugged. "Is all we do indeed foreordained, or is it merely the paths that are set, paths that will be walked whether by us or by another, if we refuse them? That is a question which many have sought the answer to for all the countless years under the skies."

"For my own part, I believe it is only the paths that are ordained." Kia Re remarked. "If there is no choice to our lives, then it is not a life at all."

"Perhaps it is so." Ragya nodded.

"As a scholar of all disciplines, I find it difficult to accept there is no such thing as choice, when all the wide world and its wonders give testimony to every and any possibility and probability that ever could be." Percy put in with a shrug. "I see the runic mysteries as merely a guide to help us. But even they are not infallible." he added with a knowing look, and even Ragya gave him a subtle nod.

"And for what--wait, there; our friends approach." Evelyn began, catching sight of a few guards heading their way.

"Our counsels can wait. This looks important." Caspar said, and they stood up as they agreed to this. The Dwarves and Valkyries halted just before the gangplank, and the companions gathered at the port side of the ship to hear their words.

"Thee are summoned to the great pavilion, and instructed to don thy most formal attire for the day's events." the lead Dwarf said, and Caspar nodded. Their visitors then departed, and with that the six friends looked around at each other.

"Well. Let us see indeed if we have anything that matches their words in regards to attire..." Caspar shrugged, and they headed back into the cabins. When they had found what they hoped was appropriate and had dressed themselves in it, the six of them then headed for the great pavilion, where they found the council awaiting them.

"Good, good! But now, see here: one last thing." General Frigund said, and one of his Dwarves came forward bearing the Crown of Augusta on a velvet cushion. "I ask again, Caspar son of Miri, of the ancient lines of Augusta, are thee of a mind to accept thy birthright, or shall the monarchy of Augusta fade at last, and the people take up rule for themselves?" the general asked, and the Dwarf bearing the crown halted in front of the young man. Without even looking at the precious heirloom Caspar shook his head.

"I will let the people decide their own laws and customs. I will not take up the throne." he said solemnly, and with that the crown-bearer stepped back.

"Be it as you say; but for the sake of formality my servant, Gromak son of Dorn, shalt accompany us at your side this day. Today, we go once again to the gates of the Lion's Den." the general said, and Caspar bowed. The company and their guards then made for the west gates of Auschternople, and the trumpeters sounded their greeting.

"Be it known to his majesty, King Michael, the Fourteenth of that name, royal heir to the Augustan Throne, who names himself as the Lord Protectorate of the Realm and the Executor of Justice, that the peoples of Argorro, under their respective leaders, have gathered before his gates to call him to parley." one of the heralds shouted up, and they saw one of the guards leave the wall. In the half of an hour the king was brought up to the wall, and he gazed out at what no one in Argorro had ever dared think to see; the banners of all the races gathered together in peace. Even the flags of Murana Day were now borne against him, and he took it as an ill-wind indeed to see the dukedom rallied against him in the company of those who besieged his city.

"What, ho! Villains! Hast thou come to give me more excuse to hang corpses from my walls?" he called down in challenge.

"You speak like a false king, son of usurpers." Frigund returned to him. The king's face darkened at him.

"Hast thou more than insults to exchange, or for what wouldst thou parley?" the king answered him.

"The matter of your kingship is what I would parley. Behold, O king! The symbol of your realm!" Frigund said at once, and Gromak hoisted the crown upon its cushion for the king to see. Their adversary stared at it in amazement; so *this* is why the lighthouse had been lit last night. The war-host's forces had taken it back from those miserable raiders. And now *they* held it; thieves stealing from thieves!

"Thou hast stolen from thieves indeed; and thou art now what mine laws might indeed consider as thieves, if thou shouldst withhold this thing from me! How shalt thou makest me to barter for mine own?" he said aloud.

"Because you are the son of usurpers, and the true heir is here before your walls." the Dwarven general returned to him.

"Thou sayest in jest!" the king laughed. "Long ago wert mine far-off royal cousins sent grovelling into obscurity; what proofs hast thou of thy claims?"

"Bring your own scholars to the wall, and have them recount the line; for it was kept in records indeed, and all we have here was copied from your own books, O king, by this scholar, Percy Von Daumer, a Gnome of quick wits and discerning intellect." the general told him.

At once the king turned to a soldier on his right, and gave him a few swift commands. The man ran off, and then the king turned back to those before his walls.

"See now! I shalt come down, if indeed this be parley; I and these scholars thou hast named, with their books, and ten of mine guards." he said. "I grow weary of shouting from the walls."

"Be it as you say; but it is not we, O king, who will break parley, for parley has been our intent from the first. But it was thy own pride that kept our ends from bearing fruit!"

"Then let us halt our accusing of each other, general." the king returned as he left the walls. Some ten minutes later the gates opened, and the king and his party stepped out of them to treat with the war-host. They all retired to the great pavilion, and chairs were found for the king as they gathered about to hear the scholars of Auschternople recount the lineage of the usurped. They recounted it in full, from the dethroning of Auschternople's original king, to their taking up the occupation as farmers, and then as wandering merchants who came for a season to Frostvale, and thence they traced the lineage of the family as they travelled yet further south, ending up once again as farmers in the land of Idoma, with connections to the Order of Cassandra.

It was in this way that the last heir had been taken into the Order's custody, for the second-to-last generation had perished at the hands of the Demonic Hordes, and the third-to-last, Rowland and Giselle, had spent their last days in a small cottage west of the monastery at Cloverdell in retirement. They had thought their grandchild dead, and so had never thought to look for him, and so the Order had raised this last heir until a farmer of Idoma took him on as a hired hand, where he had spent most of the last eight years working as a man of the soil and a man of music until he had departed on a journey northwards.

"And thus, the lineage traced, the record stands as final; Miri, the daughter of Giselle and Rowland, gave birth to a son Caspar, son of Caspian, her lawful husband. Are these the records of which you have mentioned to our king?" the acolyte inquired, and those about the room slowly began nodding.

"They are indeed." Briana nodded. "And you, King Michael; have you never heard of this record before?" she wondered.

"I hath never had time to delve into ancient history with raiders and miscreants in and about mine walls, and thou thyself might be counted therein; have a care!" the king said with a frown.

"My apologies." she returned with a faint smile.

"But in these last few days you yourself have become more of a plague to your people than those same raiders..." a man remarked, one of the king's own guards, in fact, and murmuring was heard about the pavilion. The king frowned darkly at him, but the man remained calm.

"Bring thou forward this Caspar, son of Caspian and Miri. I wouldst look upon this contender to mine throne." the king said, returning his attention to the council. Caspar stood up at once, and the king stood up in amazement. "What! Thou? Thou art mine contender? I shouldst have had thee slain at once, and not merely cast out of mine palace!" he said, seizing a crossbow from one of his guards and shooting it before he could be stopped. Caspar fell with a bolt in his shoulder, and at once the king's own guards turned on their mad monarch, who drew his sword in answer. Evelyn and Kia Re quickly raced to Caspar, holding on to their friend as the others faced the treacherous king.

"I told thee that treachery would be of thy own making, fiend!" General Frigund spat at him.

"Treachery? Nay, justice! If Augusta's lineage ends today, it shalt be mine hand: and at last I hath revenged myself upon the last member of those who disgraced mine ancestors, who in their wisdom deposed the petty king and rightly cast him aside!" the king roared.

"Thou speakest like a fool!" Frigund returned. "You are guilty by all the laws of parley and diplomacy in this act! You shall be seized for judgment and sentenced for this and all your other crimes!"

"Nay: mine death is my own to command!" the king returned, and, dropping his sword, took a dagger from under his cloak and slit his own throat. He fell dead to the ground, and the Elves made the sign against evil as his blood flowed.

"Blasphemy!" Thadolin hissed.

"Sacrilege, indeed!" Mala said with an intake of breath, putting her veil over her face. The king's guards turned to the other leaders, and Frigund nodded at them.

"Do as you will with the body. We must tend to our wounded." he said and four of the guards took up the body and departed in the company of another five, while the tenth remained behind. It was the man who had spoken against the king.

"I am honor-bound," he said, "to remain at the side of the true king--for such is the oath I took on becoming a captain of the guard."

"Then stay, if you have a mind to!" Frigund said. "We will see that he is cared for." the general told him, and with that Caspar was rushed to the healers. Blood flowed freely from his wound, and he was faint and pale as they set him upon a bed.

***

"He still fades. That was a deadly bolt, indeed!" one of the Gnomish healers said with a shake of her aged head as she came out. Stars were now in the sky, and Evelyn, torn apart by Caspar's seemingly imminent death, wept in the company of Ji Mao. Ragya stood nearby, trying again and again to discern the runes. Percy then came running up, and the diminutive scholar's face was grey with worry.

"Too deadly," he remarked as he caught the words of his fellow Gnome. "Alas, my dear Agatha, the thing was poisoned with Iver's Blood." he said with sorrow.

"What! The villain!" Agatha returned as she clasped Percy's hands in her own.

"Oh, yes; it took me and the others too great a time to figure it out. It is deadly, after all, and only a tiny bit is needed for it to--to..." Percy continued, trailing off as he remembered Evelyn was nearby. Already he saw her head turned up, and those tear-streaked eyes of violet brimming over yet again as she caught his words. The Gnome shook his head, and Agatha nodded in understanding. There was no time for an antidote to work. Ragya came over to them, and sat down to talk with them.

"I have tried my own healing arts on him; I am not as skilled as I should be. He fades yet, though I have managed to ease the pain." the Werecat said softly.

"Yes, that you did." Agatha agreed. "He sleeps peacefully enough, and he will be at rest when he goes the long road to the stars." she continued softly. Kia Re, who had been pacing all about the camp for several hours now, suddenly brushed past them and headed in to the tent where Caspar lay dying.

Evelyn was weeping again, convinced she was about to lose Caspar.

They cannot save him; all these people and all their wisdom, and they cannot save him, and I cannot even comfort the one I love with my love, but he must be sent to the world of dreams to die ignobly... she thought to herself in wretched agony.

Kia Re closed the curtains behind her as she entered, her mind and her heart made up. Caspar would not die this night. She placed her hands on his face, feeling the strength and power build up within her as love filled her heart. It was enough to aid her for this one task. Perhaps that love would be given back to her only as the love of a brother, but that would not stop her from loving him--or Evelyn.

There was a moment's more hesitation; what she was about to do was irrevocable, and she could not undo it. Kia Re's thought was to bind herself to him, forever joining her heart--her soul--to his, if not his to hers, and in that way she could save him from any death as long as she herself lived. It was the greatest gift a Valkyrie could give to one of their own kind, let alone one not of their race. Was it right to do so? Was she going too far, even for the sake of love that should increase? She looked up at the ceiling of the tent; a calm came over her, as if those in the high halls of heaven itself were lending approval to her for her intentions. And with that there was no more doubt in her heart. The words of Caspar's song came back to her, filling her heart with love overflowing.

> *O angels, come, and sing to me*
> *Of valiant deeds done in the night*
> *Thankless warriors of the hall*
> *Who fought when the darkness fell*
>
> *Host of Heaven, ever flying*
> *Off to the battle, banners high*
> *The silver bugle sounds its note*
> *Against the darkness as it came*

"I will not let you die this night, my love, my only love." Kia Re said, and with that she called down an aurora of light; the light filled the tent, and those without wondered what it was. Ji Mao gently shook Evelyn, and the two of them stared in wonder. Inside the tent it was as if all the colors of the world had descended in shimmering candles to visit Caspar and Kia Re. "In love, I bind myself to you, my song-brother, and I will not let you go." she said, reaching down to kiss him.

Light filled her, and light spilled over into him as she kissed him. The light reached a great crescendo of brilliance, and when the kiss faded, so did the light. Caspar's color began returning to him, and he breathed easier; Kia Re, worn from her actions, knelt down by the bed, still clasping his hands in her own.

The companions and Agatha ran in to see what had happened, and they saw Caspar sleeping peacefully, color restored to his face, and Kia Re kneeling beside him as if worn from some great struggle. Evelyn ran up to her side, and kissed her several times before wrapping her in an embrace. Ji Mao also came over to hug her, and the three girls sat together holding each other with smiles of joy.

"I don't know what you did, but thank you." Evelyn said, kissing Kia Re again.

"I love you too, my friend." she returned to the Elf, and they leaned back to relax. The Werecat and the Gnome exchanged a glance; they both could make a fair guess, from their different yet similar backgrounds of learning, as to what Kia Re had done. She had bound herself to him. The Werecat gave the Gnome a solemn look, softly nodding his head towards the door; they headed out, and Ragya closed his eyes to take out three stones at random. He tossed them on the ground, and there they sat as plain as day under the light of the moons. The Lover's Cross, the Rune of Chance, and the Rune of Desire.

"Well. This is going to be an interesting journey." Percy remarked.

"Indeed." the Werecat agreed.

***

By noon of the next day, Caspar was recovered enough to be led into the city. With the death of the king, the citizenry of Auschternople had effectively tendered their surrender to the war-host, and the leaders thereof now gathered in the palace. The dead king's body was burned on a pyre, and the heir-apparent was made, despite his reluctance, to sit on the throne. Caspar's first, last, and only act as king was to abdicate at once, and he gave control of the city to the appointed council, as decreed by Augustan Law. This council then voted to accept his abdication, and to continue working on reforms to govern what was left of their kingdom. The Lion of Augusta was dead. A new thing was about to begin, one that was to alter the fate of Argorro forever; but they did not know it.

Chapter Twelve: Phoenix

The first thing the council decided on in the presence of the commanders of the alliance was to reform the Kingdom of Augusta into the Dominion of Augusta, keeping the prescribed structure of the council as dictated by Augustan Law to oversee the affairs of the reforming country. This was agreed upon by the new-formed alliance, who, having accomplished all they really needed to have accomplished, began sending the larger parts of their forces home and requesting that diplomats and ambassadors be sent to entreat with the new Dominion. In the meanwhile, the companions yet remained around Auschternople at the request of their allies, and they honored this request. Their ship was returned to the docks, and as a last favor to the king-who-could-have-been the Council of Auschternople voted to give the ship to him with all its accouterments. This was accepted by the Harbormaster, and the companions then decided to call their ship the *Aurora*.

The Council's third major act was to make the legendary phoenix their new flag and symbol; a golden phoenix on a field of green trimmed with red was their design, and it was almost unanimously accepted. There were some who still preferred the Roaring Lion, but as this signet was more specific to the now-ended line of kings most of them voted against it. The first of these banners was finished in a day's time, and it was hoisted atop the tall-tower of the palace, now a gathering chamber for all of the Council and its representatives. Proudly it flew over the heights of the city, and Auschternople cheered at their new flag waving in the winds. It was one of the first pleasant ceremonies for many days; they had already spent a good deal of time mourning and seeing to their dead who had been hung ignobly upon the walls. Over the course of a week, the Council continued to restructure their new nation, building upon the best of the old system and doing away with its worst; at the end of that week the diplomats and ambassadors from the other races arrived. Even a Giant came, the tall and imposing chieftain's curiosity aroused at the rumors of the wind that Augusta's kings were no more. When his questions were answered satisfactorily, he departed with a promise that the Giants would leave them be for five winters at least, at which time, if the Dominion was still flourishing, the Giants would open further negotiations.

It was a Gnomish ambassador, Abe by name, who at this time plucked up the courage to propose that the new Dominion not only include the tribes of men, but all of the other races as well. The Augustan Council opened the proposal for discussion, and the motion to do so was then carried forward by the acceptance of the Dwarves, the Werecats, and, ironically, the Elves. Skye, the Valkyrie's diplomat, was not so certain of her own stance on the matter, but had not spoken against it. She seemed rather to want to wait and see exactly what such an alliance would mean. The diminutive Abe was called to the center floor to expound upon his idea, and the attention of all assembled was on him. "I mean, my good people, that in the interest of common good and the furthering of good relations begun a few days past with the Laying Down of Weapons in the grand pavilion," he began, "that I and several colleagues see the potential for a unified Argorro. I do not mean to dismantle the sovereignty of our respective peoples in any way--not at all!--I merely propose that, as we have begun, so let us carry on, and combine our sovcreignty for the benefit of all concerned, that we might stand against the true enemy, this Sorcerer King who has invaded all our lands, whose full motives and intentions yet remain unknown. Should it not be to our benefit to join together as one voice in response to his actions? Have we not spent enough time casting the blame about, whether well-deserved or ill-earned?" the Gnome said, and many clapped at these words, even Mala, who had been chosen as ambassador for Alastria. Skye inclined her head with a smile, and spoke out.

"This is a proposal I believe my people would accept; and I see that even the Elves think of it without malice. I am willing to continue negotiating terms of such a confederacy, if we are all agreed on the principles of what this our colleague has presented to us?" she said, and the motion was again carried.

"So be it. Let it be entered into the records that, on this moment, we the Council of Augusta, in conjunction with our allies, have agreed to discuss terms on the broadening of this new government for the purpose of allying in the common good and interests of our respective peoples." the head councilman said, and from there the discussions went on long into the night on how to lay more specific groundwork for such an alliance.

***

As those now gathered within the walls of Auschternople took counsel together for the future, the companions took their own counsels together on board their ship. Time felt pressing to them, and they now rued every moment they lingered about the city; even the patient Ragya was eager to be gone, if only for the sake of not disturbing the runes, as such a thing was taken as an ill-omen amongst his people.

Percy was the most vocal about leaving, his scholastic desire for adventuring into lands he had so far only read of growing stronger; and after all, they had since accomplished their true goal: they had found each other, and their plans to leave should no longer be hindered for the sake of politics. Ji Mao was eager to see her ancestral homeland, and now that she had been gifted along with her friends the means to do so, she meant to do so, and to continue on with them, if they would let her. Kia Re seemed distant, but when the question came to her she agreed; it was time to go. There was nothing left for them do do here, and so much more to be seen and to be done across the waves; let their path unfold across the sea. And as for Caspar and Evelyn, the two of them, having been the first to begin the journey, were eager to continue, and afraid of stagnating in one area.

"We have done enough here." Caspar said to them. "It is time we made our own path; they don't need us here, they just want us around." he added, looking over at the palace.

"They may not let us go so easily as we think." Ragya returned. "And surely if they do, they may do so with a goal of their own in mind: to send us forth as ambassadors, hindering what may be our true purpose. Let us not allow ourselves to be constrained as representatives of their new-found alliance, save perhaps in principle. I at least wish to remain outside the control of any one ruler or governing council, no matter how well-intentioned. Our own hearts should guide us, not the will of those who know not what lies outside their domains."

"Then our goal is as I might hope; to be explorers and ambassadors of goodwill in our travels together." the Gnome remarked. "And at any rate, they have taken precious time from us as it is; if we must leave, let us not petition them, let us simply leave!"

"But we cannot simply leave, Percy; now that the city is under lawful control again we are under that law, and simply leaving without notice would be counted as a fine against us, if we ever returned." Caspar told him.

"No... we will never see Argorro again." the Werecat said, looking back towards the city as they looked at him. "Whether this journey claims our lives or not, none of us will ever see our ancient homes; not the warm climes of Murana Day, nor the hallowed mountains of Valheilen, nor the jyuga-trees of the Were Forests, or the fabled Woods of Alastria, the comforting halls of the Gnomish mountains, nor even this, the legendary city of Auschternople." he said softly, and Ji Mao then looked from him into the city, and then slowly turned to look eastward.

"And where will we end up?" she wondered softly.

"White shores..." Kia Re murmured softly. "White shores of pearl and alabaster, and a calming sea beside, and a great villa..." she continued as her Weishuune friend turned towards her. Caspar and Evelyn exchanged a glance; it sounded beautiful, but was the price too high?

"Can we really turn our backs forever on this, the home of our people, our ancestors, who lived or fought or died here, never to return?" Caspar wondered as he turned his own gaze to the eastern horizon.

"We can. And we shall prove the stronger for it." Ragya said to him.

"The voyage across the ocean, no matter the destination, is one of months, our choices not withstanding." Percy told them. "We shall need to be well-provisioned. You were right of course, Caspar my friend; there is no sense in leaving immediately. We need time to prepare."

"Then let us do so, and make our leaving certain so that those who might think to try and hinder us will second-guess themselves." the minstrel returned, and with that they at last got up. The hound perked his ears up as they began walking back into the city, and followed his own master faithfully as they went out for the day.

It was at least a week in truth before they were adequately prepared for a voyage across the ocean, never mind the constant repetition of pleas and bargainings to try and make them stay. In the end, the Council had no choice but to grant their petition to set sail as soon as they were ready to do so, or they risked appearing as the kings of old, grasping and ungracious. And so it was that those who were debating the fledgling alliance found themselves convinced at last of its sincerity, even the stubborn Elves and the proud Valkyries, and the grace of Auschternople on such a matter as the companions' intention to leave was accounted a mighty atonement by many. Even so, it was as Ragya had thought; the full council tried to make them representatives of the new alliance. Percy argued long and hard against this for the better part of two days, saying that, as a group, the companions were stronger without the hindrance or burden of being bound to such a thing; his points were taken up by various members from all sides of the council, and eventually the case for their being independent was accepted, even if it was, to some, recorded in a fashion that was somewhat ambiguous.

"Let it be entered into the records on this day that, on this moment, we grant to the last heir of the Augustan Dynasty sovereignty over his own affairs and that of his companions. They shall be counted by us, the Council of Argorro, as their own representatives, and shall not be bribed, hindered, or otherwise obstructed in any means by any of our own, no matter what part of the world they may find themselves in." the head councilman declared.

"This, of course, will be difficult to announce throughout the world." one of the others, a Dwarf, remarked. "It is therefore my proposal that we create a charter establishing that they do indeed have sovereignty over their own affairs, and that it be signed by the most notable among us to validate their independence to those of our people beyond this continent of Argorro--I mean, of course, those on the distant continents of Derghak and Akanimastra, should these sail so far."

"The point is taken." the other nodded. "I shall now make the motion that we nominate qualified persons to draft such a charter." he then said, and the motion was carried; the committee was then formed, and sent off to create the charter while the companions themselves carried on in preparing to leave Auschternople. When Caspar himself heard the words of the head councilman as to the condition of their leaving, he shook his head.

"I never counted myself a king, and find it frustrating that they do so still. But if this is how they choose to convince themselves of letting us go, then for that at least I am grateful." he remarked, and Percy nodded.

"Quite so, quite so." the Gnome agreed. "Now, on to our little Gnomish craft... which was inadvertently ceded with the ship... it would be wise to gather some hard-stock provisions to store there, in case of some emergency that might end up destroying the caravel."

"Hmm. Then I trust you know what's best for such a thing." Caspar said to him with a smile.

"Oh, indeed; I just wanted you to be aware, so that you are not taken off guard by the decline of coinage at our disposal!" Percy remarked, and Caspar laughed.

***

Eleven days had now passed since the companions had decided that it was high time to be gone. The charter validating their self-sovereignty was being signed, and their provisions laid up in good store on the *Aurora*. Evelyn and Ragya were making a final visit to the Tower to see if there was anything they had inadvertently left out that was necessary for their craft; Ji Mao and Percy were taking a last stroll about the Merchant Quarter before heading to the palace to retrieve the charter; and Kia Re was strolling up into the hills south across the bay, seeking for Caspar, who had gone up into the hills earlier that day himself. She found him sitting beneath a great tree, lost in thought as he stared out over the bay. He smiled faintly as she sat down beside him, and she smiled at him in return.

"You never told me what you did." Caspar said softly as the first stars began appearing in the late afternoon sky. "To heal me, that is." he said in answer to her glance, and she then sighed, looking at him longingly before returning her own gaze to the sea. "Kia Re?" he asked quietly after a few moments more, and she looked back to him.

"Among my people, there is a sacred bond, a bond that is irrevocable, a bond of love." she said to him. "It is the closest thing our people have to a marriage; and it is so much more than that, from what I understand. You are human, and so you may never fully understand its full and purest meaning; but my heart is now bound to yours, my life is linked to yours, every tear, every pain, every joy will echo in my heart." she continued, and he gazed at her in wonder even as his heart went out to her in love. "I couldn't let you die. This bond... this bond that I have made with you--*for* you, it allows me to save you even at the point of death. That is how I healed you. With love. A bond of love." she finished, her heart beating faster as she felt a thrill of emotion rise in her soul. She quickly looked away, but Caspar gently turned her face to his.

"Then I swear again, as I swore that night in the city and again in my heart by the water, that by the love I have for Evelyn that I will be your true and faithful song-brother all the days of my life and yours." he said to her gently, and a smile broke through her face as tears fell from her eyes. "Kia Re..." he said to her softly, caressing her cheek; without realizing it their lips met, and they lingered long in kissing each other before simply holding hands as they gazed at each other deeply. She looked at him, her heart at peace, and he looked at her, his own heart full of love for her. Kia Re knew it; she could feel it emanating from him, and she did not know whether to stop what might happen or to let it happen. Caspar was struggling as well; she could feel that much in his heart. He was truly pure, without guile, without any thought of deception or betrayal; he wanted to love her as much as he wanted to love Evelyn, to give back to her what she had given him without thought for herself. Now tears came from both their eyes, and slowly they reached over to kiss again. But she did not want to let him go further than a kiss, though she buried his head against her bosom as she held him. His right arm wrapped around her back, and his left hand very gently caressed her breast as he kissed it; she wrapped her own arms around him, and held him close.

"The others will be wondering where you are still." she said to bring them back to their senses. "We should return to the ship; you know anxious Percy gets with schedules and keeping to them." she said with a laugh, and Caspar laid his head in her lap as they let go, staring out at the bay once again.

"He said something about an inescapable farewell feast tomorrow night." Caspar told her, and she sighed in frustration.

"How much longer can they find excuses to keep us here?" she said with a slight hint of venom. He smiled, and playfully shoved her back on to the ground as he rolled to lay beside her in the grass. She gave him a smirk, and sighed again. "I can't stand this idling. I know that, on a ship, it won't be much better; we'll be stuck together in an even more confined space for who knows how long?--but at least then it will be a doldrums of our own choice, if doldrums it must be." she said, stroking his hair as they lay there.

"And we'll all be tormenting each other before we reach the Isles of Weishua, the way Percy talks of it." Caspar added, and she gave him a wry smile.

"Tormenting how, I wonder?" Kia Re said softly, and Caspar reached over to kiss her again.

"With love, I hope." he said with a second kiss.

"This is unbearable." she said as she gave him a third kiss. "I would rather hate you." she added with another kiss.

"But then I might have died." he said softly, letting her sit atop of him.

"And I would have died with you." she told him with a solemn look, a look not unlike one she had fist greeted him with.

"Died hating me, or loving me?" he asked her with a similar expression.

"Hating to love you and loving to hate you." she told him as she turned away quickly, the color rising to her cheeks.

"And now?" he asked in a voice barely above a whisper as he kissed her cheek. Kia Re sighed longingly, tears in her eyes.

"There is no hate. There never was." she said as her voice broke. There was silence then, a silence of two dear friends communing in the stillness under the stars of night beneath the four moons of Argorro; only that, and nothing more.

"And there was never hate in my heart for you, either." Caspar said at last. Kia Re could not but smile, and the silence resumed itself again until Evelyn came to join them.

"There you are!" she said with a smile upon her lips, and the other two got up to greet her with a warm embrace. They then sat down all three together, hardly daring to disturb the peace of the night save with soft voices. All the while Kia Re's face slowly lost its cheery countenance, her soul deeply tormented by what she might have done, had there not been some restraint of great power over them that night. Evelyn reached out to take her hand, and the Valkyrie looked up into the face of her friend whom she loved. A guilt tinged her eyes, and Evelyn gazed at her with a heart of concern. "Kia Re, what is it?" the Elf asked her with a look of confusion. Caspar quietly took in a deep breath as a lull of silence greeted his lover's words, and then Kia Re answered.

"I am distressed in my soul, in my heart of hearts. Oh, Evelyn! I didn't mean to do this to you, but I had no choice, I couldn't let him die!" Kia Re told her, tears flowing freely. Evelyn then put a hand on her cheek and a finger on her lips. She understood now what had happened, how Caspar had been healed, and why her friend was downcast. Kia Re had made what the Elves knew as a soul-bound with Caspar; the Elves, too, had the capacity to do such a thing, but theirs was nowhere near as potent and as life-saving as that of the Valkyries, the Angels of Heaven now exiled to the world. Evelyn drew her friend closer, and held her as she wept freely, and Caspar put his arms around them both.

"I understand, dear friend. I will never hold it against you. And I swear I will never let such a thing destroy the friendship we have with each other. Oh, Kia Re, I swear by all the living trees of Alastria we will always be friends!" Evelyn told her as tears flowed from her own eyes.

"And neither will I--I swear by the Bells of Chloe and the Crown I have forsaken forever." Caspar added; muted sobs from the Valkyrie were the only sounds to be heard apart from the sounds of night after this, and the three of them sat there holding each other as if they were a carven statue, unmoving from their embrace as the crickets and tree-frogs sang their nocturnal jubilations.

Across the fields, at a distance that only Evelyn could see, if she had been alert and attentive, their Werecat friend sat in a tree of his own, casting the rune-stones. He had done so seven times, and each time the three stones fell to earth in the exact same alignment with the same meaning: doom. Wherever their journey made its final paces known to them, one of these three was to die at the end. He looked over at them, loving on each other without guile or restraint under the stars as the night went on. Any potential rifts between the three of them were now and forever sealed; this much Ragya believed without any doubt. They were determined to love each other in equal strength, and to bear with each other in that love as they left their old lives behind. Would that love be strong enough to endure the penultimate test that he now knew would come? Seven times he had cast the stones, one cast after another, angry at their reading; but seven was a number of significance to his people. It was a finite symbol, a number that could not lie. He caught the glint of moonlight on their distant forms, and the light of their eyes reflecting the light of heaven's stars as they held each other. No; it was not for them to know.

"This I vow," Ragya began, "and I call upon the Four Moons: Asai the Mother, Crystolin the Father, Luna their Daughter, and Tanisto their Son as my witnesses, that I will never tell these three or the others of what I have read this night. And may the Runes be at last defied in their reading, when this fateful test shall come at last!" he said to the night, and then raced back to the ship, his lips sealed. All that was needful to know, they already knew. *Let their love guard them on this night: yes, and every night after; and may the children of Evelyn and Caspar be as warm and compassionate as they are, and the spirit of friendship between these three and we six together be a symbol of what can be in all the wide world now and forever,* Ragya thought to himself, and with such thoughts in his heart he went to rest.

***

Far away, across many leagues of ocean and many miles of lands beyond the realm of Auschternople, a fell tower gleamed in the light of the moons. And high upon the open roof of that tower, under the light of those four moons, a lone figure stood gazing in a crystal ball; the wind wisped through his hair and beard, and he smiled mysteriously as he took in what he saw. Three friends; three lovers; three races. They had sworn a bond of eternal friendship; but oaths were made to be broken. So thought the Sorcerer King, beholden to none but himself. The image faded away, and the man returned to the inside of the tower through a door on his right.

Chapter Thirteen: The Bay of Paupalousas

Of that last day in Auschternople, there was little of consequence that happened until the feast, when the companions were honored for a final time. But even that celebration was not notable for them, grandiose though it was to all the others gathered there. Had there been many speeches, or had it all been one, long, unbearable monologue? None of the six of them, not even the clear-minded Gnome or the attentive Werecat, could precisely recall, so anxious were they to be gone from Auschternople at last. There was certainly good food. Ji Mao remembered the food well, for it was much more splendid than any meal she had eaten, even after joining up with those who were now her friends. She was, however, feeling disturbed that her lithe figure was becoming not-so-lithe; Ragya shrugged, saying that, among his people, plumpness was very attractive, though litheness was not despised. She blushed as she smiled at this, and forgot her fears over eating too much.

There was music, and dancing, and the crowning dance of the evening was a Valkyrie and an Elf; there was much applause for these two, and they returned to a table with blushing but happy faces. None of the companions danced, but Caspar was persuaded to sing again, and once more he brought forth music into the great hall, his voice gently accompanying the melody of his harp as he played its strings. For a time, it was a wordless song, and his voice softly accentuated the music from his harp; but as was the way with Caspar, he eventually rose to words, and a song rose up from his lips that gave them all to know that he was indeed a true bard, for the song he sang was the Bells of Chloe in its completion.

Only the Elves, and a fair few of the Gnomes, could understand the words, but all knew the tune and its melody, and all fell silent as they recognized the ancient hymn. Mala, who had only heard the song once in her long lifetime, broke down in soft weeping as she listened, and Evelyn, to heal the last of the rift between them, came and sat with her, tears in her eyes also. The song, as Mala and the Elves heard it, ran thusly:

Hear all ye the Bells,
the Bell for us is ringing purely in the night
Hear all ye the Bells,
the Bell for us is ringing sweetly in the light

Long under the stars
lay we all in confusion, with hearts beating sadly
With hearts beating sadly
the Bells rang in Harmony, in truest light
Listen all of you
to the sound of purest joy under the hosts of night
To the sound the Bells
are ringing in the guileless and pure melody

Hear all ye the Bells,
the Bell for us is ringing purely in the night
Hear all ye the Bells,
the Bell for is is ringing sweetly in the light

In love and in beauty forlorn
the bells rang clearly in eventide
In grace and in sweet caress of night,
we woke to hear them sing
Under the starry host we saw
beauty singing sweetly as to a king
And in beauty and grace
we sang along, and for love's joy we wept

Hear all ye the Bells,
the Bell for us is ringing purely in the night
Hear all ye the Bells,
the Bell for is is ringing sweetly in the light

Hear all ye the Bells,
the Bell that in purity rings through the night
Hear all ye the Bells,
the Bell sweetly singing under the starry light

And hearken to the starry host
as you look to the sea beyond
Listen well to the Bells
that sound purely under stars and over wave
The host of heaven's regiments

in matchless beauty, a king crowned
With the sound of the Bell
and its beauty echoing ever and ever

Hear all ye the Bells,
the Bell for us is ringing purely in the night
Hear all ye the Bells,
the Bell for is is ringing sweetly in the light

In majesty of old we heard
the sweet majestic sound in the night
And in conquering darkness
we crowned a king to the sound of joy
Calmly in the long darkness
we awaited the sound of the bells at night
Calmly in the fading twilight
we sang for the harmony of bells of light

Hear all ye the Bells,
the Bell for us is ringing purely in the night
Hear all ye the Bells,
the Bell for is is ringing sweetly in the light

Hear all ye the Bells,
the Bell that in purity rings through the night
Hear all ye the Bells,
the Bell sweetly singing under the starry light

Long under the stars
lay we all in confusion, with hearts beating sadly
In love and in beauty forlorn
the bells rang clearly in eventide
Now hearken to the starry host
as you look to the sea beyond
For in majesty of old we heard
the sweet majestic sound in the night

Hear all ye the Bells,
the Bell that in purity rings through the night
Hear all ye the Bells,
the Bell sweetly singing under the starry light
Hear all ye the Bells,
the Bell for us is ringing purely in the night

Hear all ye the Bells,
the Bell for is is ringing sweetly in the light
Hear all ye the Bells,
the Bell for us is ringing purely in the night
Hear all ye the Bells,
the Bell for is is ringing sweetly in the light

Thus the song was heard by those whom knew what the ancient words meant; it was a mysterious song indeed, and it spoke of mysterious things regarding the even more mysterious Chloe, as Kia Re had told Caspar on that night in Jotun-De. Few indeed recalled that full meaning of the song, and fewer still had even heard its name, let alone the song itself. Mala embraced her one-time fosterling with love, and then bid her well on her journey.

"I did not understand, even as he lay dying, even as he spoke at the councils, why you love him. But now I do: and I say to you, daughter of my heart if not my womb, that from your love I sense an even greater one shall spring." Mala told her, and Evelyn inclined her head as she smiled. The rest of the night for the companions was spent aboard their ship; Percy and Ragya plotted out their course through the bay as Ji Mao sat to watch, and as for the other three they went to rest at once. They had already made much of sleepless nights, and so settled in to recover from the lost hours the night before. Dusty the hound stayed below decks with the horses, and the carriage was fastened securely to the deck; their supplies were in good order, and were meant to last for some months; they had the best Auschternople could offer for sea-gear, and had been hard pressed to force the merchants to accept payment, for the merchants had been intent on simply giving away things to those they now claimed as heroes. They would hear none of it, and though the night passed with continuing celebrations in the city, dawn brought them new tidings: the *Aurora* had sailed off.

***

Ragya remained at the helm of the ship throughout most of the day, the Werecat being careful to keep their course straight east once they had passed the islet. By the late afternoon, the waters of King's Bay began to mingle with the Bay of Paupalousas proper, a great expanse of sea-water that at the end of its northern reaches was bordered by the fertile farmlands of Aridian east of the River Dane, the longest river of Argorro, and bordering at the end of its southern reaches lay a great forest, the Forest of Dyn, which lay near the town of Dyn, a simple manor and keep on the edges of the wood. The River Dane passed near the eastern borders of the Were Forests, and its most northern beginnings reached even beyond the Forests of Alastria, to places where even the hardy explorers who had mapped most of Argorro dared not to travel. Its southern delta that fed in to the bay was a wide area indeed, and most general maps concurred on an area of sixty King's Miles as its final width before the waters of the river finally merged with that of the bay. As to the Forest of Dyn, it was a great forest indeed; some held it to be the largest consecutive forest in the land of Argorro, now that much of Alastria had been burned to the ground. Others contented that the forests of the westlands beyond the central mountains held greater forests, forests which made this one seem as if it were a farmer's orchard. However the case, it was, as most now generally said, the largest forest in Eastern Argorro. The companions could not yet see it, as it lay at least a day's more voyage ahead of them, and indeed they might even be too far to the north, as Percy said earlier in the day. But it was, so folk said, a marvel to behold: one of the few lands that as of yet remained without taint, even from the Great Invasion.

When the winds began to blow against them later that evening they furled the sails, and they let the steady current carry them gently east. Ji Mao, always fascinated by maps, came to the side of Percy as the Gnome began scanning the charts once again. It was a general map of the High Seas Region, so called because it was at this point that three distinct oceans converged--or so it was said by sailors and cartographers. The matter was in dispute among the Gnomish Guilds, some of whom held that there could be no true distinction between waters of the ocean. For now, however, where the Bay of Paupalousas ended the Sea of Chloe began, a wide and sparkling sea that bordered the home of Ji Mao's people the Islands of Weishua. North and east of these was an archipelago filled with mysterious monoliths, and north of this curious archipelago was the Sea of Tears. This was distinct from the Sea of Chloe, as it was overall a darker and stormier expanse of water, hence its name.

The third ocean was the Aubrnos Ocean, the great and legendary ocean that was the ultimate path of anyone trying to head for the next known landmass of significant size, Ragani Mor. It was told that the Sirens lived in these waters, a more aggressive water-succubus than their Mermaid cousins, who dwelt in the more habitable waters of the High Seas. There was no single name for the expanse of water that was identified by the words "High Seas", save for an old Weishuune name: Goroko Umanjo, "Waters of Lust and Desire". This name was, as most of the scholars in Argorro agreed, a reference to the Mermaids and Sirens, whose sensuality lured men to their death. But it was only men, most agreed, as the one Valkyrie ship that had ever gone out to sea had proven immune to their call.

"They're all meat-eaters down there, boy," Caspar heard again the words of an old and weathered sailor who claimed to have escaped from them long ago; "They sing their song, pretty as can be, with a voice that the gods would envy. Their eyes, ah, their eyes glint like jewels in that precious face; and then they rise up to tantalize you with their goods! If ye weren't hypnotized before, ye surely would be with such luminous orbs staring up at your face. They're all sorts of colors, Mermaids are, and they come in shades: the one I saw was like a pale silver; her hair was dark grey, but still luscious and wavy, and her eyes were a faded blue like the mist of the mountain heights, and her skin was purest silver, her breasts tipped with a dark grey like her hair, and her lips also, and she sang and sang, and sang... I was too absorbed, but my friend, he was all naked by then, and he jumped in to give himself to her. Ah, fool! But he saved me from death, there's the truth of it! Weren't nothing left of him but bones once she and her whoring sisters got in to him. They made their lust with him, and then ate him alive! Brr!" the man shivered, and Caspar had felt sick.

Now he remembered the story again, every word of it vivid as he stared out into those same waters. Well, close enough, at least.

"Mermaids... probably nonsense." he shrugged as he turned away from the rail to head back into the cabins.

"Any more nonsense than a Valkyrie?" Kia Re smiled as she rose up to follow.

"But I've seen Valkyries, and Elves, too." he returned with a wink.

"And you only believe in what you see?" she asked him.

"I believe that there is much I don't understand, but I more firmly believe in what I have seen. All the rest I leave to faith or fancy." Caspar said as they entered the cabins. Evelyn was combing her hair upon the bed, and Kia Re slipped up behind her to snitch the brush, only to continue using it on Evelyn herself as they giggled. Caspar headed over to a chair and sat down as he smiled.

"Do you be-lieve it, Evelyn? He only believes in women he sees." Kia Re quipped.

"Well he's seeing us for certain, and he's seen quite a lot, don't you think?" her friend laughed.

"Perhaps we should deprive him of it."

"Ah! But then we might have a third coming after him."

"I would never!" Caspar said as he turned to them.

"And what does that mean, my love?" Evelyn asked him as she kissed Kia Re's cheek.

"I mean, that she's a good friend, but a friend only." he returned with a look.

"Hmm..." Evelyn shrugged.

"She has a lovely form; though she is getting a bit plump." Kia Re remarked.

"Poor thing hadn't had a decent meal until she met us, and now she can't get enough." Evelyn shrugged again.

"And besides, you know how much time she spends with Ragya." Caspar added.

"Now that *would* be interesting." Evelyn said with a faint smile.

"But enough of that, let's be serious for a moment." Caspar returned. "Where *are* we planning to end up in all this?" he wondered, and the two of them thought upon that question for many long moments of silence. They had sailed from Argorro; all fine and good, yes--but as he had put to them, where indeed were they planning to go, once they passed through the High Seas Regions?

"Wherever our hearts lead us." Evelyn said at last.

"Now that," Kia Re remarked, "is a very unsatisfying answer."

"And yet the only one I can give without feeling as if I've lied." Evelyn returned, and the other girl nodded, sighing.

They turned, but Caspar was no longer in the room. He was back out on the deck of the ship, now climbing to the crow's nest. From this height, he gazed about at the bay; the land was receding to the north and south as they sailed steadily eastwards, and he guessed that, soon, they would see no land at all, not even this faint horizon, until they came to the Islands of Weishua. Kia Re had remained in the cabin, but Evelyn came out to find her lover, and climbed the ropes to sit with him. They sat in silence, holding hands as the moons rose up into the sky with the stars as their entourage.

"What are you thinking of? What are you feeling?" she asked him at last, her violet eyes searching his face as he gazed over the sea.

"I am thinking of how Ragya said we are never to see our homes again, and what I feel--I feel that, despite there being a solemnity in those words, that it is also... heartening. That in whatever place we end up, it will be a better world for us, one where we can truly live." he said to her. "Beyond that, all my thoughts are now numb or silent." he said, and leaned back against the mast. She snuggled next to him, and they sat there for many long minutes, until at last they came down to retire to the cabins. Kia Re was fast asleep, and they joined her in slumber moments later.

***

A day passed, and the night following it also, without much to distinguish either save the quality of light. Seabirds flew about, and they caught sight of fish and sea-creatures great and small below the waves, or jumping out to plunge back in. There was no sight or sign of land by the afternoon, and as it changed into the night they were all weary, except Ragya. They had played a game throughout the day, and hopefully this, as well as their other activities, would keep them from going completely mad, but it was still a dull day. The hours had passed slowly, and the water about them had become unending.

As the night wore on, Ragya rested as he would, ensuring that their course was straight every two hours. In this way, wind and tide soon carried them quickly across the bay, and at the end of a third evening he saw the tell-tale signs that Percy had told him to expect when entering the Sea of Chloe. Caspar came up to stand beside him before heading in to rest, and gave his friend a curious look as the Werecat's expression settled into a satisfaction.

"You looked fairly pleased; why is that, friend?" Caspar asked him.

"Look, Caspar. Tell me what you see." Ragya said to him, and Caspar looked; the water seemed to be changing. There was a stark contrast; the deep colored blues of the bay were mingling with a lighter, clearer water that was tinged with a hint of turquoise. The bottom could be seen, and it was far, far below them; diminished coral reefs meandered about the depths, and larger, more mysterious looking fish and sea-creatures swam about their depths. Caspar also felt, as if for the first time, that the air was different. He told these things to Ragya, who nodded softly.

"Indeed, my friend. And I shall tell you why: welcome, O son of kings, to the Sea of Chloe." the Werecat said, and Caspar turned to look again. They had left the bay. The *Aurora* was in the deep ocean, and Argorro was truly left behind.

Map of Eastern Argorro

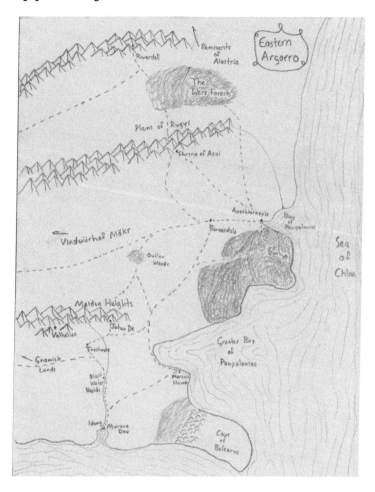

Map of Auschternople

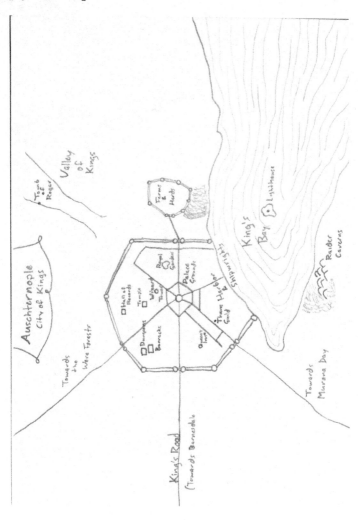

Also by the author:

The Book of Tarithia, Volumes I-V

Long ago, a man named Lucian rose up to destroy the harmony and peace of the land of Tarithia; though defeated, his goal was accomplished, and the land fell under an uneasy silence for many long years. Now, that watchful interim has ended, and the forces of darkness are rising up again. Young Lady Crysalia from the Isle of Light is sent to investigate the cause, and to seek a certain artifact that may halt the advance of evil in the land; follow along as she and those around her race across the land to thwart the machinations of evil, with each revelation they uncover worse than the last...

Fiction/Fantasy

The Locket

It was a quiet, sleepy little town, the kind you might see on a post-card; but that was only on the surface. A battle like no other was about to begin in its grounds, a battle not waged by weapons of war, but in the hearts and souls of those that lived there...

Christian Fiction/Romance

Keep an eye on the author's activity on facebook at:
https://www.facebook.com/book.of.tarithia/